ANGELIC™

BOOK 1

HEIRS AND GRACES

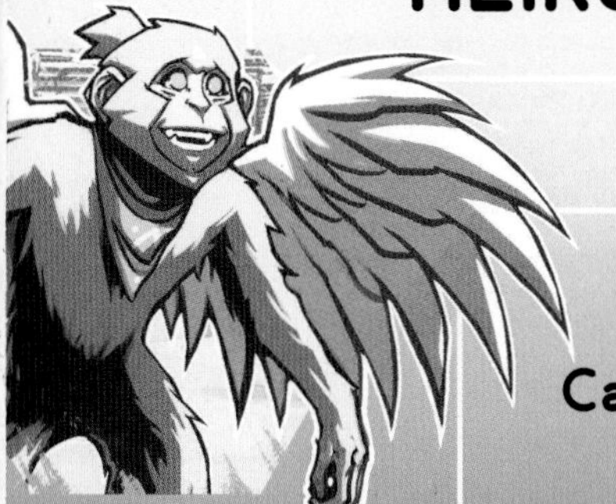

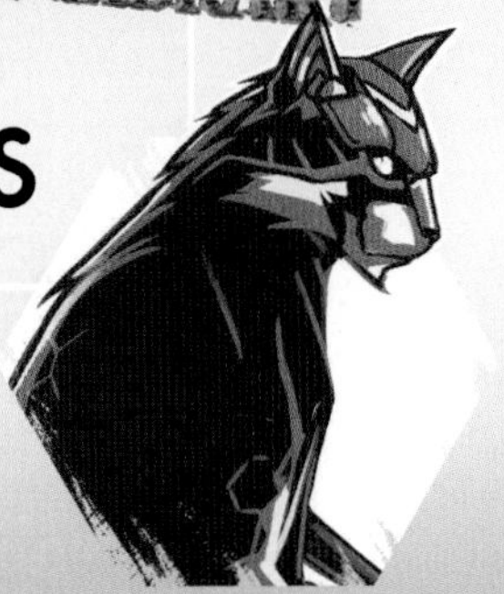

Simon SPURRIER
Story
Caspar WIJNGAARD
Art
Jim CAMPBELL
Letters
Emma PRICE
Graphic Design

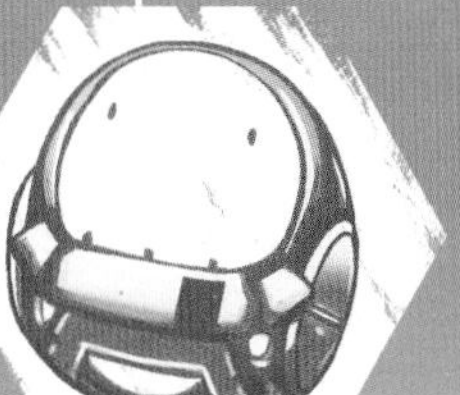

IMAGE COMICS, INC.
Robert Kirkman—Chief Operating Officer
Erik Larsen—Chief Financial Officer
Todd McFarlane—President
Marc Silvestri—Chief Executive Officer
Jim Valentino—Vice President
Eric Stephenson—Publisher / Chief Creative Officer
Corey Hart—Director of Sales
Jeff Boison—Director of Publishing Planning & Book Trade Sales
Chris Ross—Director of Digital Sales
Jeff Stang—Director of Specialty Sales
Kat Salazar—Director of PR & Marketing
Drew Gill—Art Director
Heather Doornink—Production Director
Nicole Lapalme—Controller
IMAGECOMICS.COM

ANGELIC™ VOL 1: HEIRS AND GRACES. First printing. May 2018. Published by Image Comics, Inc. Office of publication: 2701 NW Vaughn St., Suite. 780, Portland, OR 97210.

Printed in the U.S.A. For information regarding the CPSIA on this printed material call: 203-595-3636 and provide reference #RICH-786398. For international rights, contact: foreignlicensing@imagecomics.com

ISBN: 978-5343-0663-9

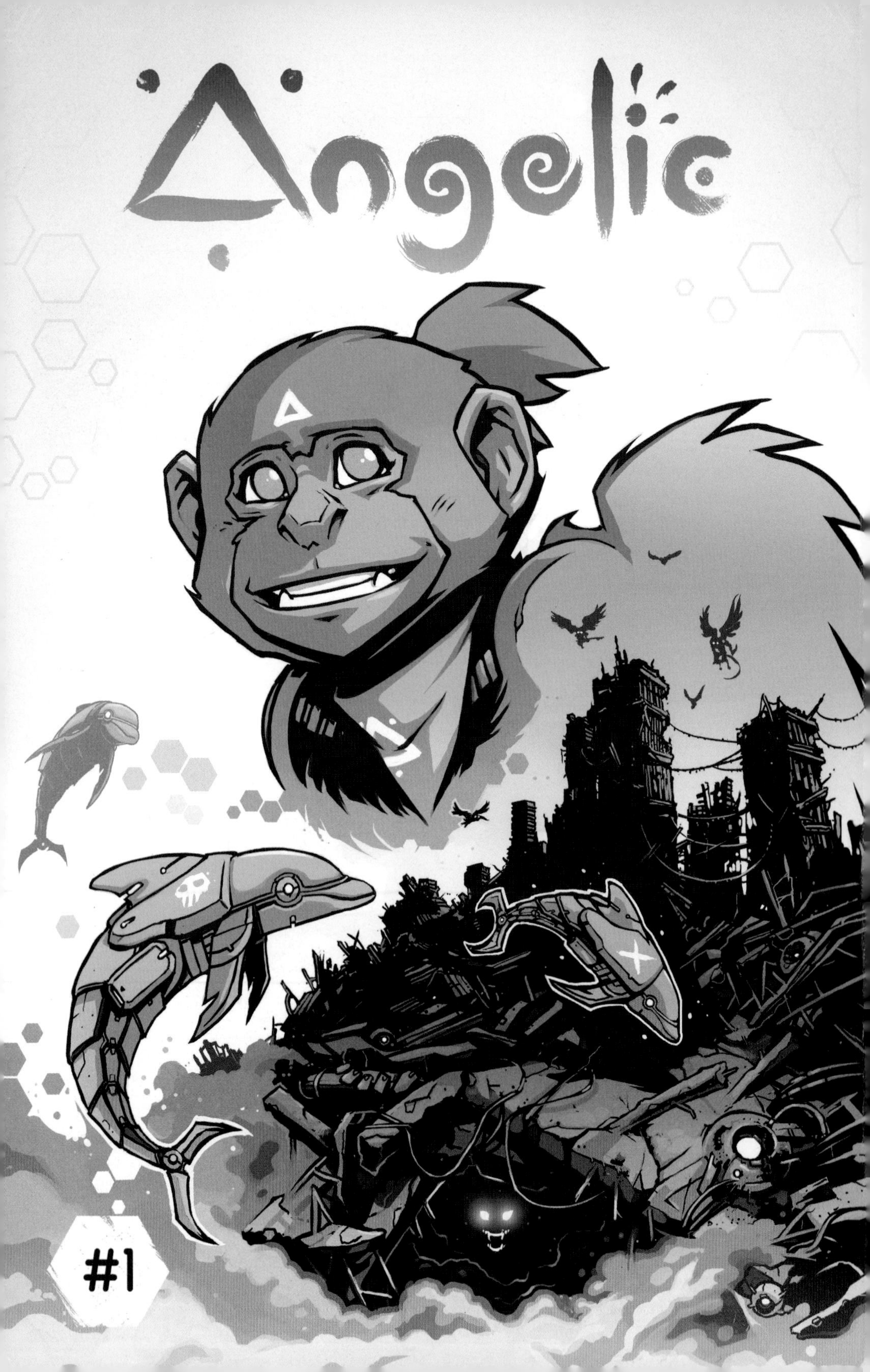
Angelic
#1

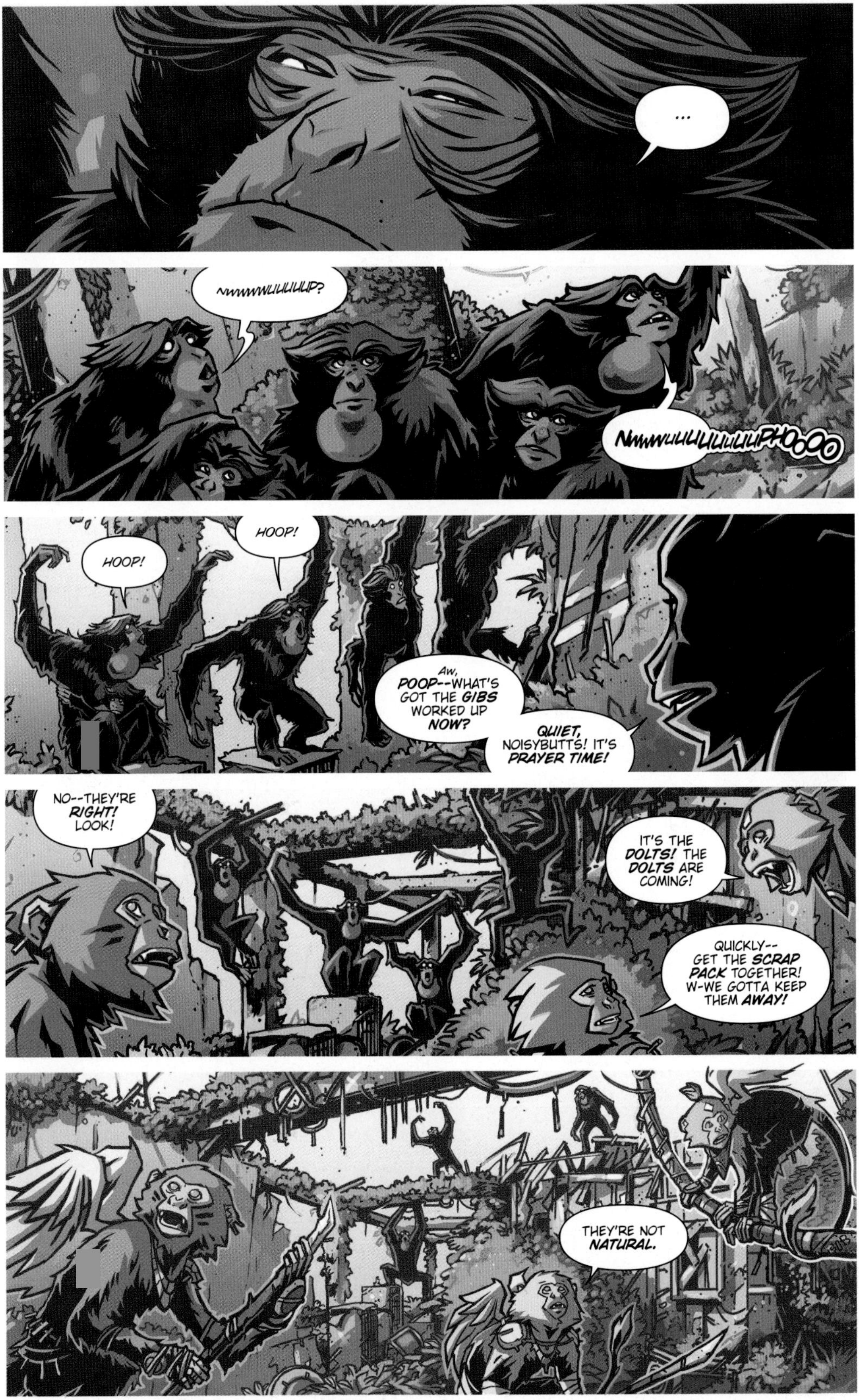
...
NWWWWUUUUUP?
NWWWUUUUUUUUUPHOOOO
HOOP!
HOOP!
Aw, POOP--WHAT'S GOT THE GIBS WORKED UP NOW?
QUIET, NOISYBUTTS! IT'S PRAYER TIME!
NO--THEY'RE RIGHT! LOOK!
IT'S THE DOLTS! THE DOLTS ARE COMING!
QUICKLY--GET THE SCRAP PACK TOGETHER! W-WE GOTTA KEEP THEM AWAY!
THEY'RE NOT NATURAL.

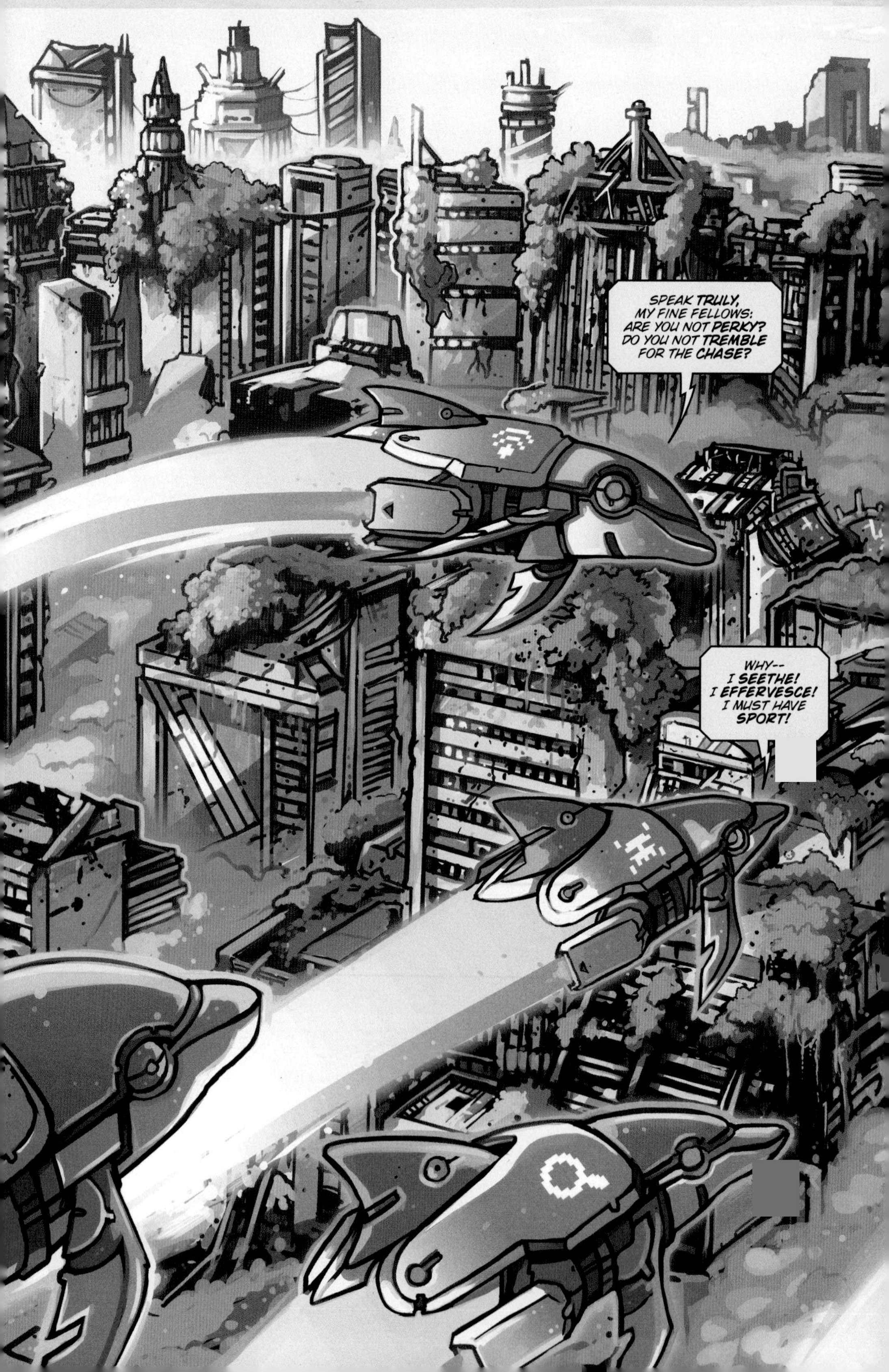

SPEAK **TRULY**, MY FINE FELLOWS: ARE YOU NOT **PERKY**? DO YOU NOT **TREMBLE** FOR THE **CHASE**?
WHY-- I **SEETHE**! I **EFFERVESCE**! I MUST HAVE **SPORT**!

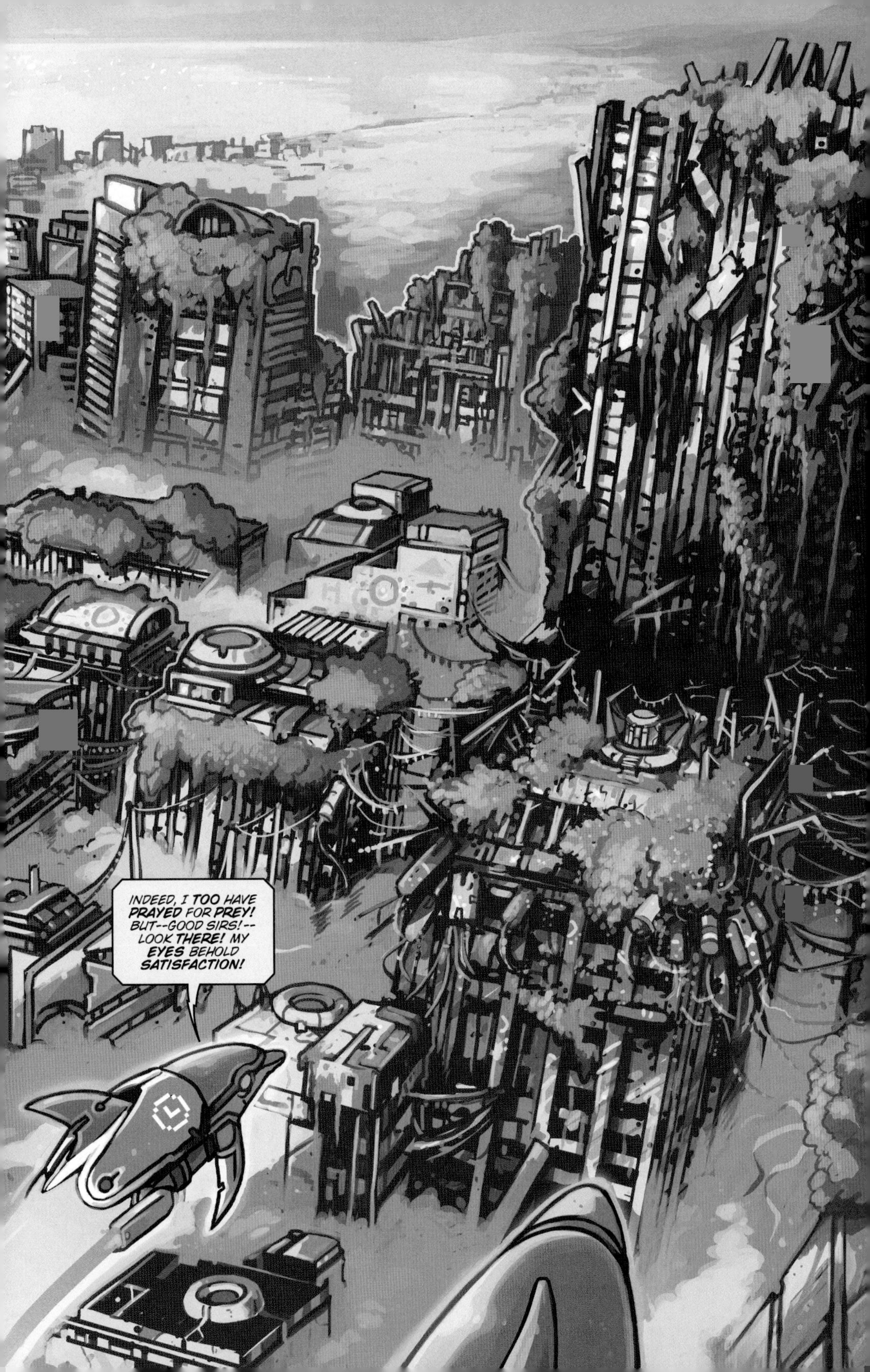
INDEED, I TOO HAVE PRAYED FOR PREY! BUT--GOOD SIRS!-- LOOK THERE! MY EYES BEHOLD SATISFACTION!

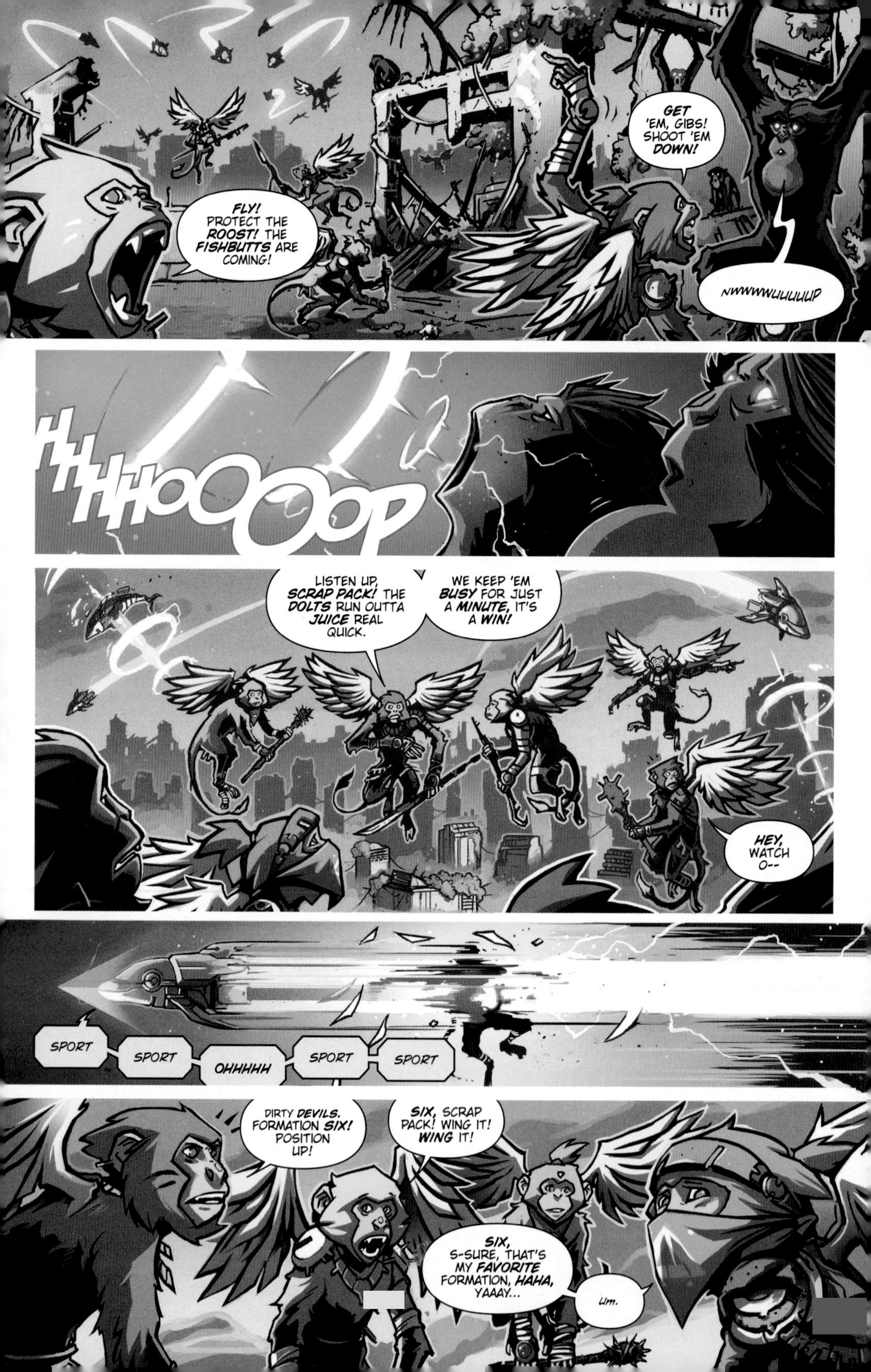

FLY! PROTECT THE ROOST! THE FISHBUTTS ARE COMING!
GET 'EM, GIBS! SHOOT 'EM DOWN!
NWWWWUUUUUP
HHHHOOOOOP
LISTEN UP, SCRAP PACK! THE DOLTS RUN OUTTA JUICE REAL QUICK.
WE KEEP 'EM BUSY FOR JUST A MINUTE, IT'S A WIN!
HEY, WATCH O--
SPORT
SPORT
OHHHHH
SPORT
SPORT
DIRTY DEVILS. FORMATION SIX! POSITION UP!
SIX, SCRAP PACK! WING IT! WING IT!
SIX, S-SURE, THAT'S MY FAVORITE FORMATION, HAHA, YAAAY...
Um.

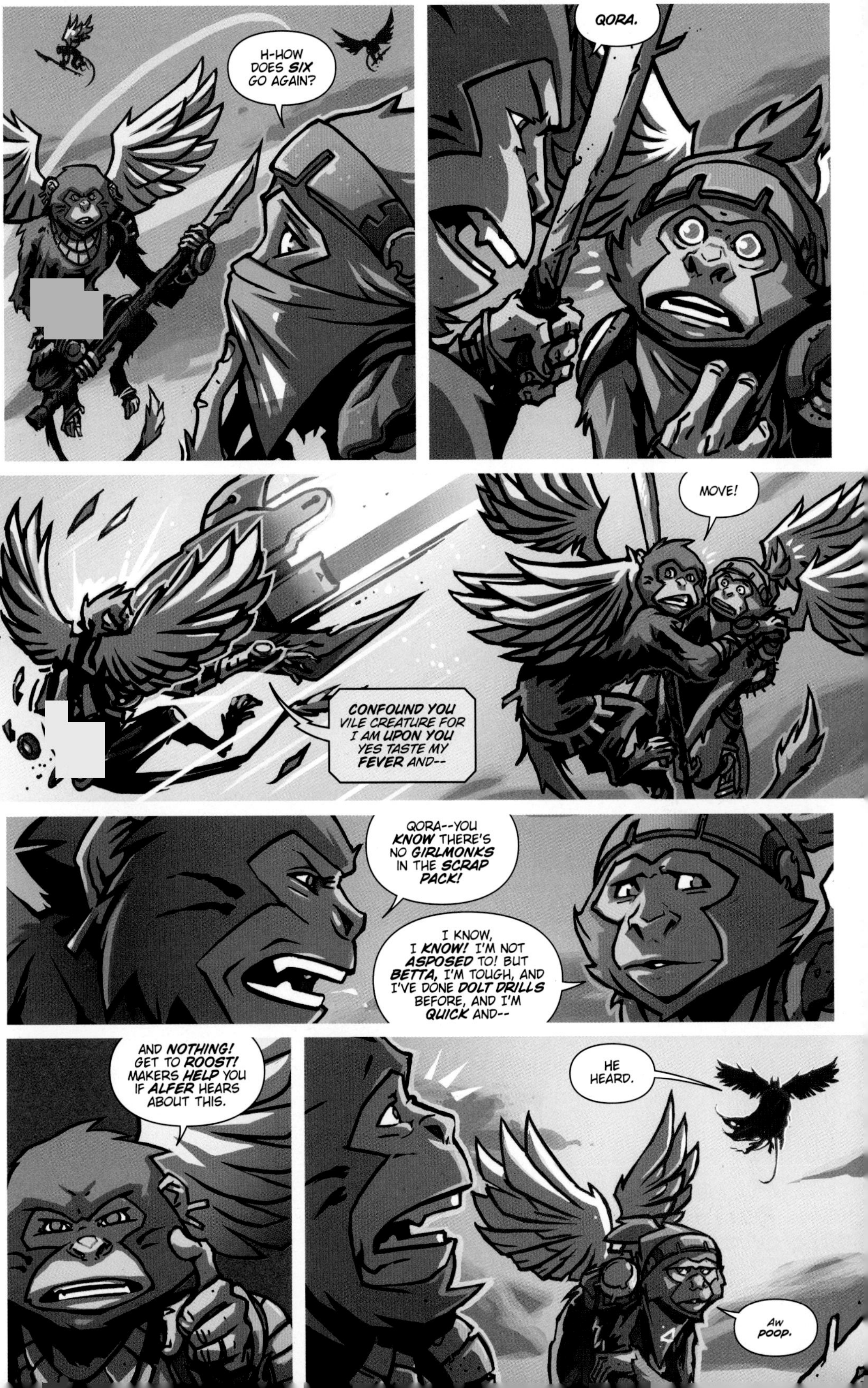
H-HOW DOES SIX GO AGAIN?
QORA.
CONFOUND YOU VILE CREATURE FOR I AM UPON YOU YES TASTE MY FEVER AND--
MOVE!
QORA--YOU KNOW THERE'S NO GIRLMONKS IN THE SCRAP PACK!
I KNOW, I KNOW! I'M NOT ASPOSED TO! BUT BETTA, I'M TOUGH, AND I'VE DONE DOLT DRILLS BEFORE, AND I'M QUICK AND--
AND NOTHING! GET TO ROOST! MAKERS HELP YOU IF ALFER HEARS ABOUT THIS.
HE HEARD.
AW POOP.

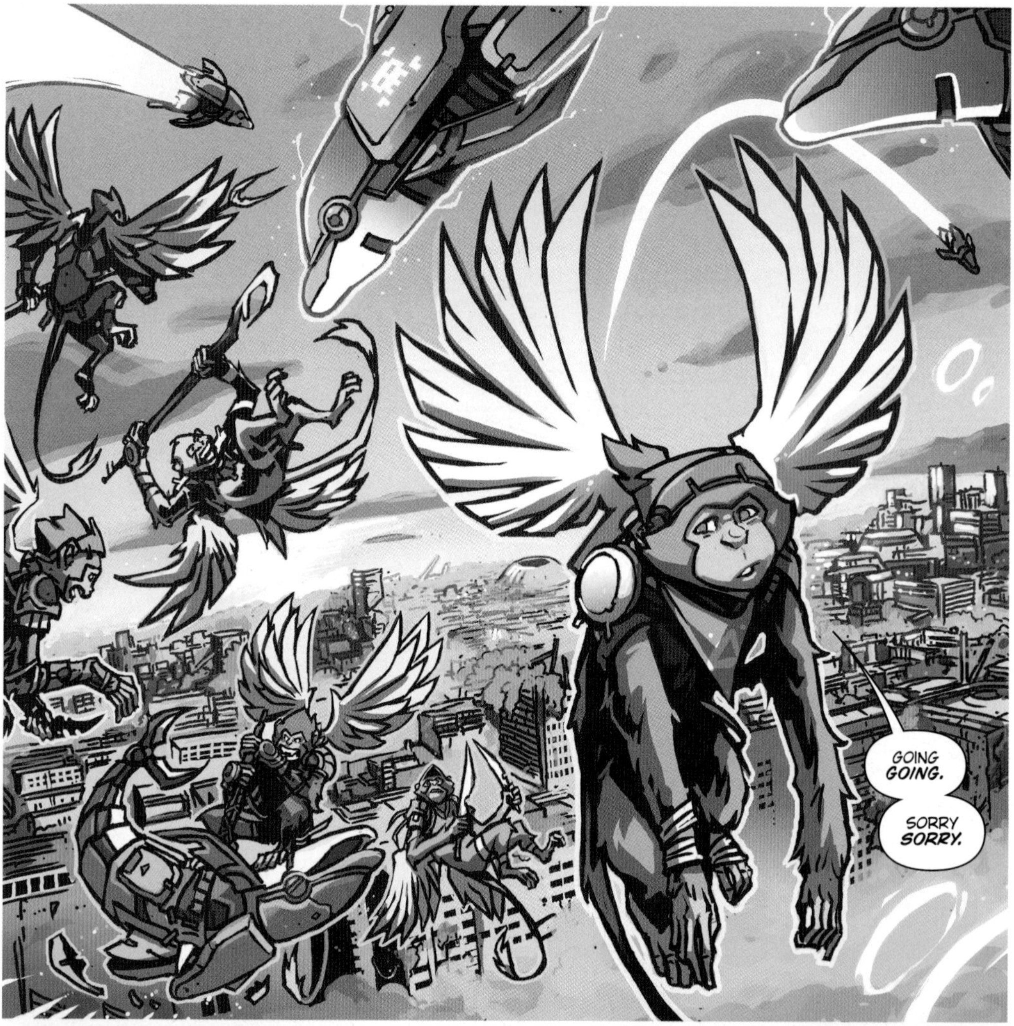
GOING GOING.
SORRY SORRY.

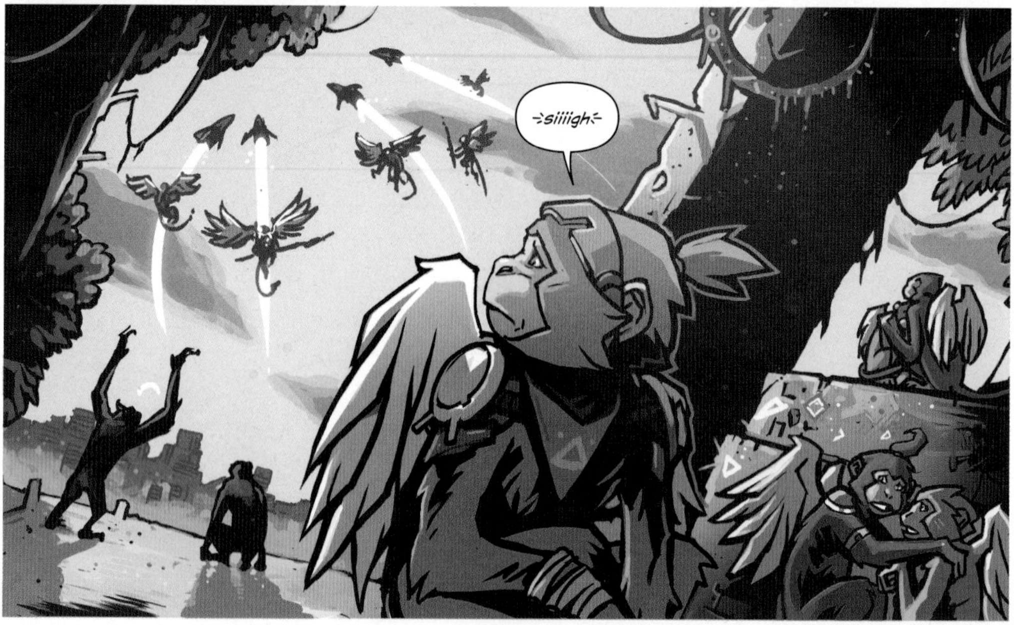
-siiiigh-

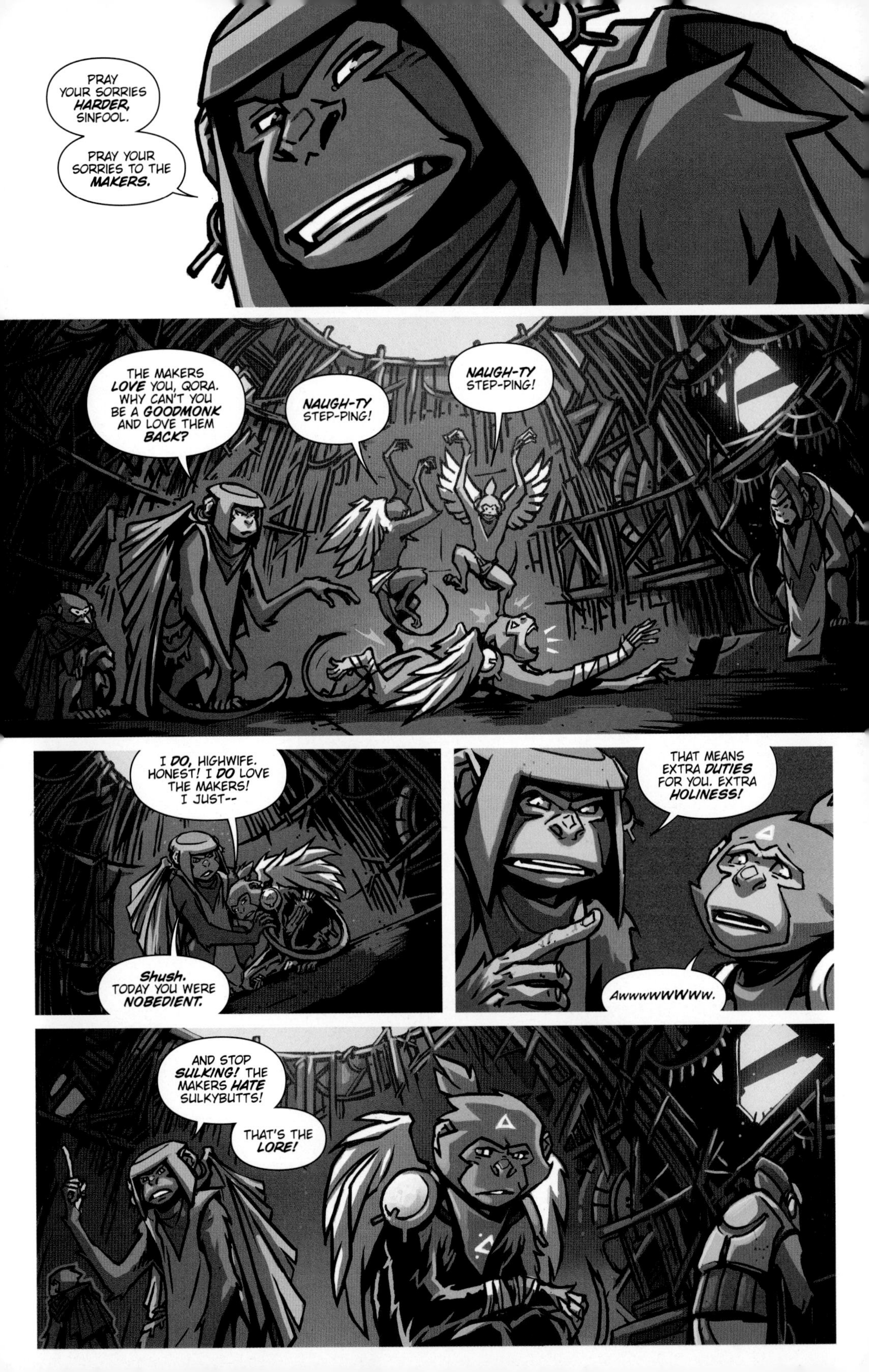
PRAY YOUR SORRIES HARDER, SINFOOL.
PRAY YOUR SORRIES TO THE MAKERS.
THE MAKERS LOVE YOU, QORA. WHY CAN'T YOU BE A GOODMONK AND LOVE THEM BACK?
NAUGH-TY STEP-PING!
NAUGH-TY STEP-PING!
I DO, HIGHWIFE. HONEST! I DO LOVE THE MAKERS! I JUST--
Shush. TODAY YOU WERE NOBEDIENT.
THAT MEANS EXTRA DUTIES FOR YOU. EXTRA HOLINESS!
AwwwwWWWw.
AND STOP SULKING! THE MAKERS HATE SULKYBUTTS!
THAT'S THE LORE!

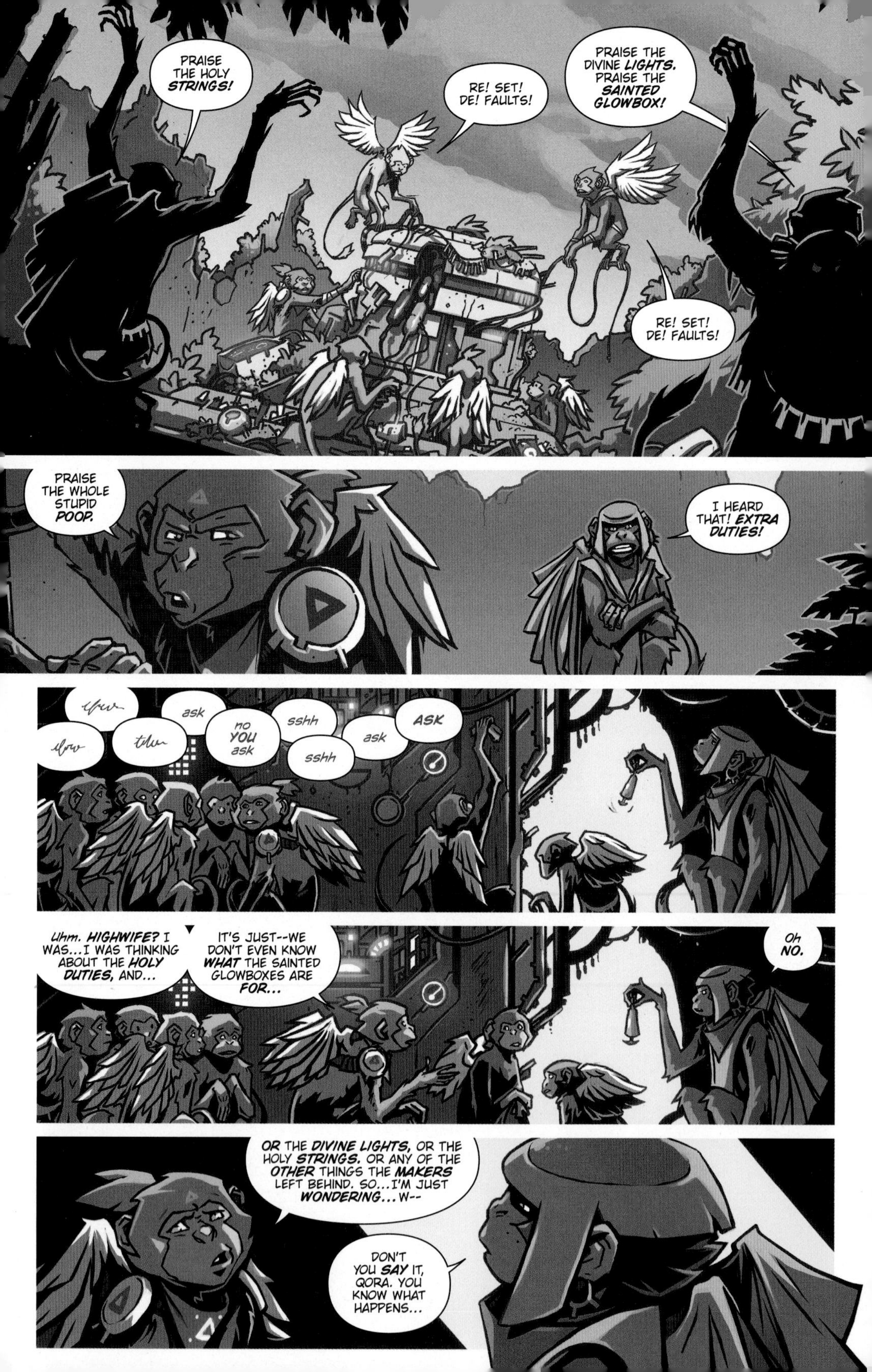

PRAISE THE HOLY STRINGS!
RE! SET! DE! FAULTS!
PRAISE THE DIVINE LIGHTS. PRAISE THE SAINTED GLOWBOX!
RE! SET! DE! FAULTS!
PRAISE THE WHOLE STUPID POOP.
I HEARD THAT! EXTRA DUTIES!
ask
no YOU ask
sshh
sshh
ask
ASK
Uhm. HIGHWIFE? I WAS...I WAS THINKING ABOUT THE HOLY DUTIES, AND...
IT'S JUST--WE DON'T EVEN KNOW WHAT THE SAINTED GLOWBOXES ARE FOR...
Oh NO.
OR THE DIVINE LIGHTS, OR THE HOLY STRINGS. OR ANY OF THE OTHER THINGS THE MAKERS LEFT BEHIND. SO...I'M JUST WONDERING... W--
DON'T YOU SAY IT, QORA. YOU KNOW WHAT HAPPENS...

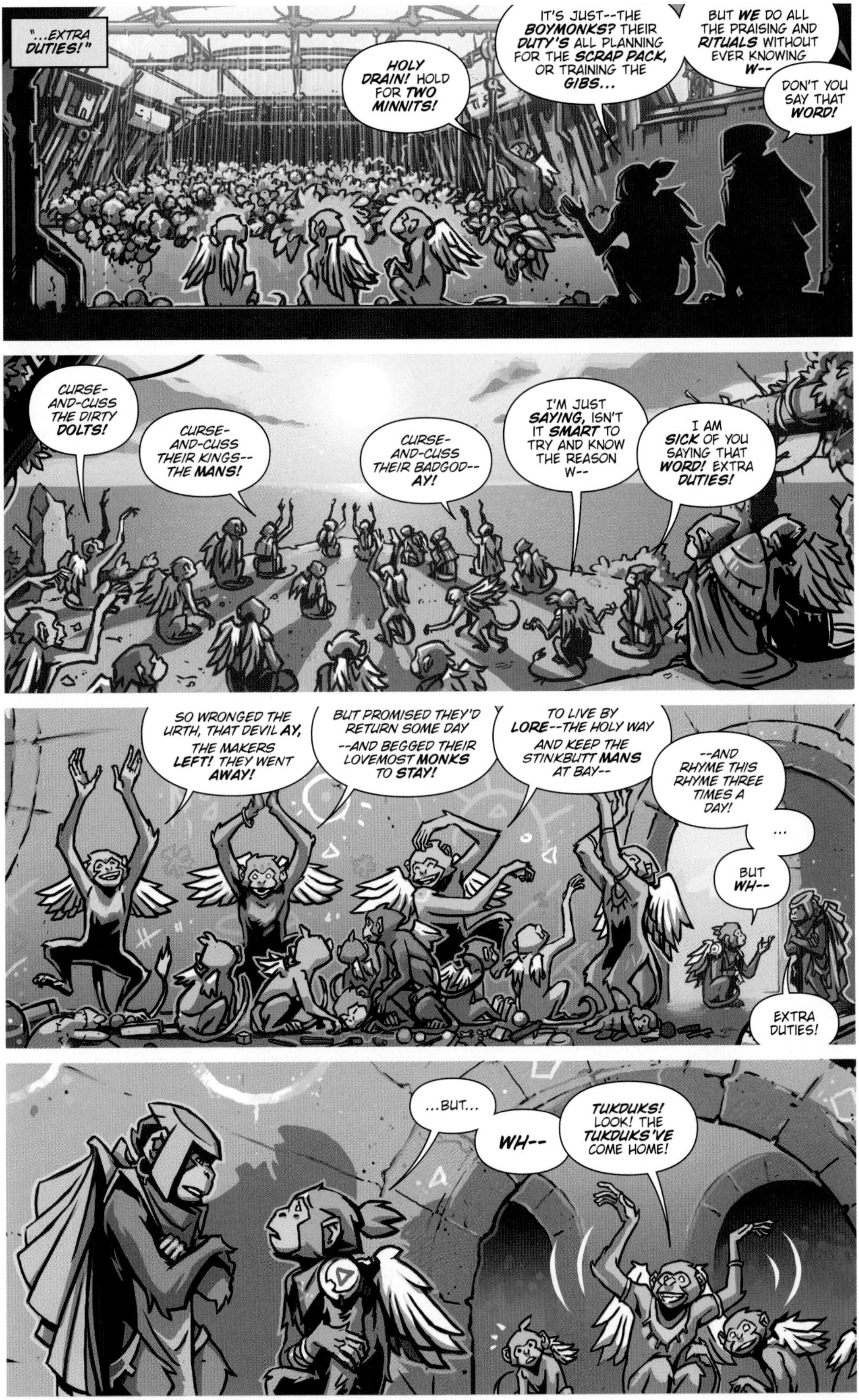

"...EXTRA DUTIES!"
HOLY DRAIN! HOLD FOR TWO MINNITS!
IT'S JUST--THE BOYMONKS? THEIR DUTY'S ALL PLANNING FOR THE SCRAP PACK, OR TRAINING THE GIBS...
BUT WE DO ALL THE PRAISING AND RITUALS WITHOUT EVER KNOWING W--
DON'T YOU SAY THAT WORD!
CURSE-AND-CUSS THE DIRTY DOLTS!
CURSE-AND-CUSS THEIR KINGS--THE MANS!
CURSE-AND-CUSS THEIR BADGOD--AY!
I'M JUST SAYING, ISN'T IT SMART TO TRY AND KNOW THE REASON W--
I AM SICK OF YOU SAYING THAT WORD! EXTRA DUTIES!
SO WRONGED THE URTH, THAT DEVIL AY, THE MAKERS LEFT! THEY WENT AWAY!
BUT PROMISED THEY'D RETURN SOME DAY --AND BEGGED THEIR LOVEMOST MONKS TO STAY!
TO LIVE BY LORE--THE HOLY WAY AND KEEP THE STINKBUTT MANS AT BAY--
--AND RHYME THIS RHYME THREE TIMES A DAY!
...
BUT WH--
EXTRA DUTIES!
...BUT...
WH--
TUKDUKS! LOOK! THE TUKDUKS'VE COME HOME!

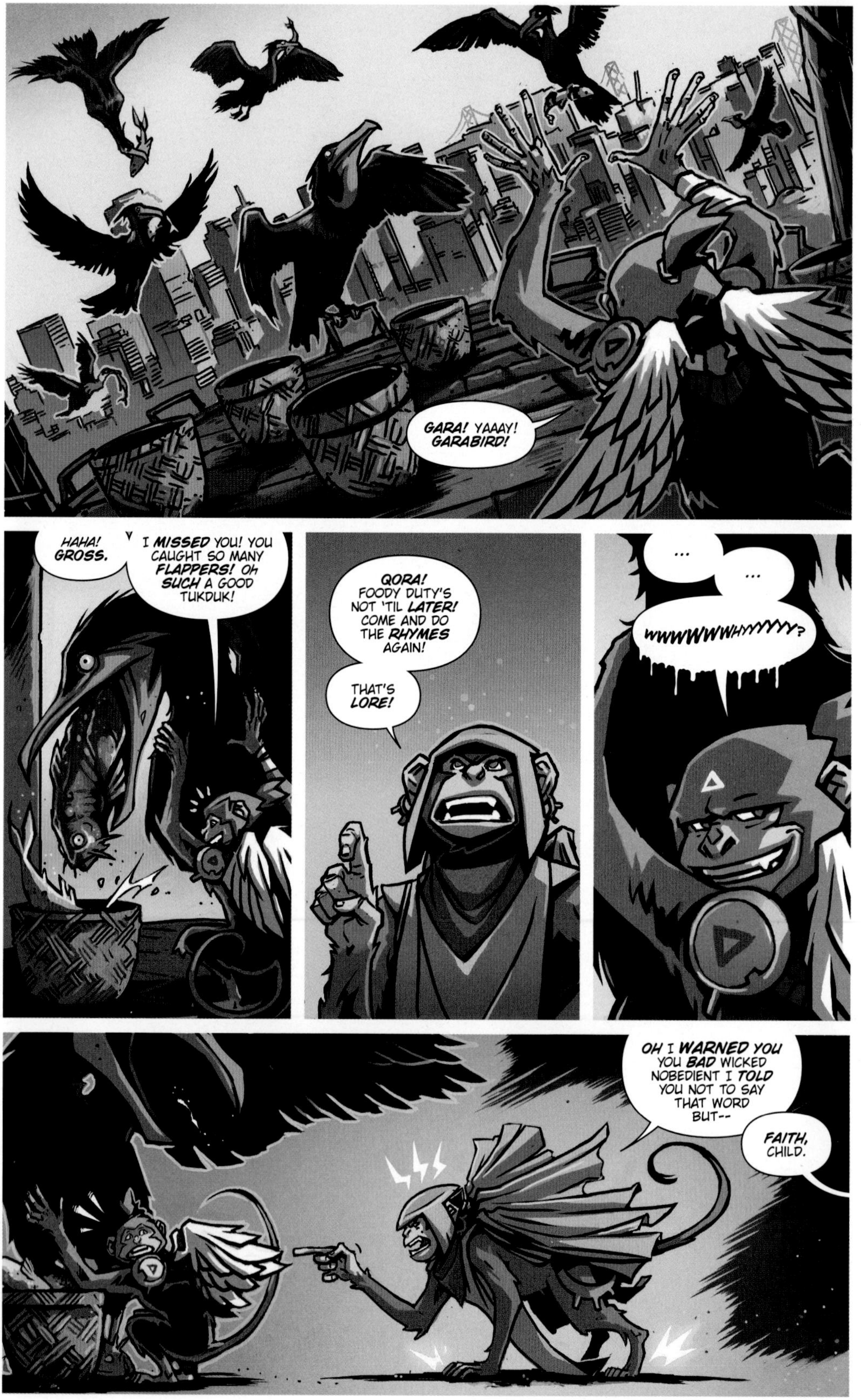
GARA! YAAAY! GARABIRD!
HAHA! GROSS.
I MISSED YOU! YOU CAUGHT SO MANY FLAPPERS! OH SUCH A GOOD TUKDUK!
QORA! FOODY DUTY'S NOT 'TIL LATER! COME AND DO THE RHYMES AGAIN!
THAT'S LORE!
...
...
WWWWWWHYYYYYY?
OH I WARNED YOU YOU BAD WICKED NOBEDIENT I TOLD YOU NOT TO SAY THAT WORD BUT--
FAITH, CHILD.

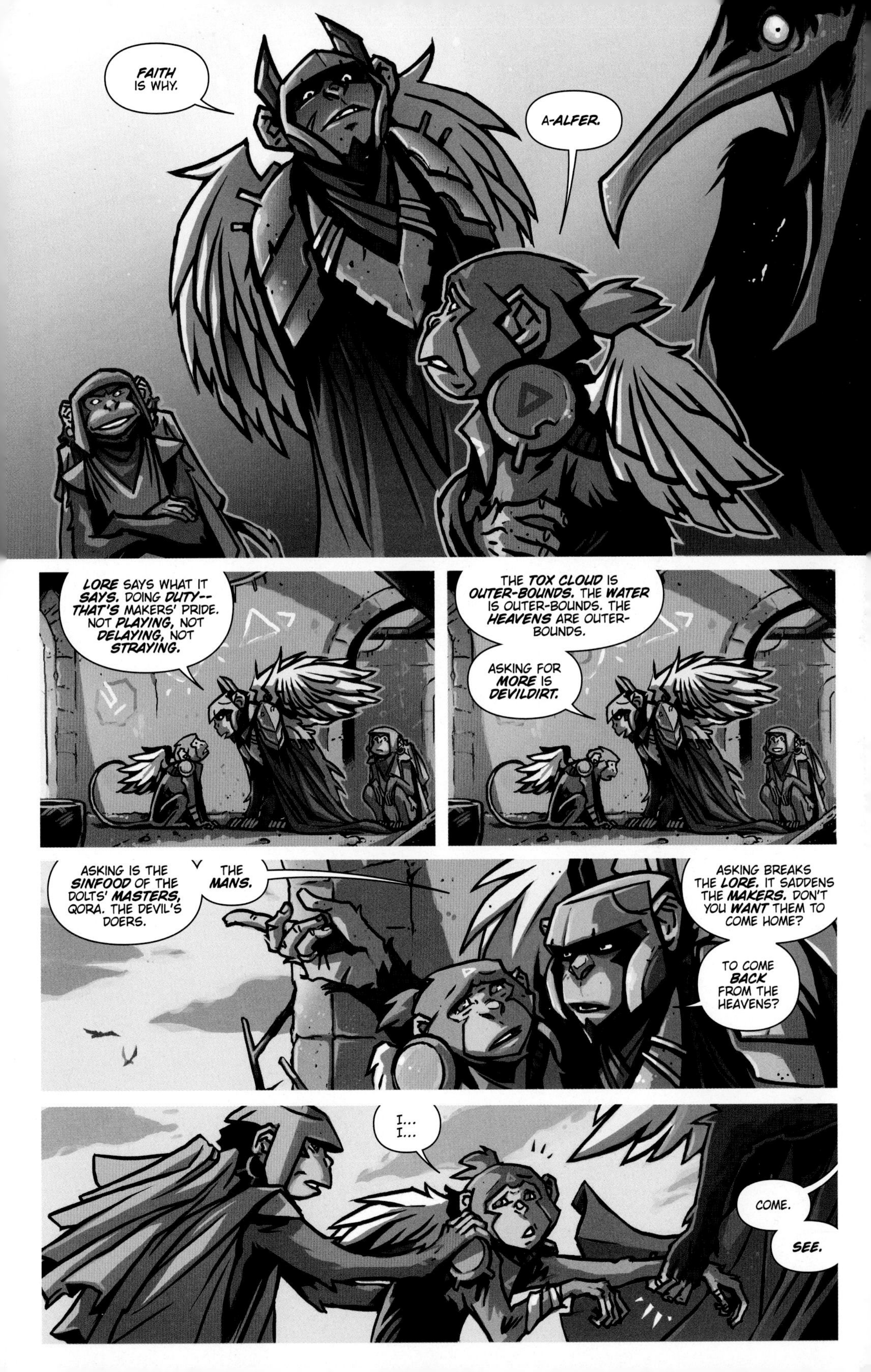
FAITH IS WHY.
A-ALFER.
LORE SAYS WHAT IT SAYS. DOING DUTY-- THAT'S MAKERS' PRIDE. NOT PLAYING, NOT DELAYING, NOT STRAYING.
THE TOX CLOUD IS OUTER-BOUNDS. THE WATER IS OUTER-BOUNDS. THE HEAVENS ARE OUTER-BOUNDS.
ASKING FOR MORE IS DEVILDIRT.
ASKING IS THE SINFOOD OF THE DOLTS' MASTERS, QORA. THE DEVIL'S DOERS.
THE MANS.
ASKING BREAKS THE LORE. IT SADDENS THE MAKERS. DON'T YOU WANT THEM TO COME HOME?
TO COME BACK FROM THE HEAVENS?
I... I...
COME.
SEE.

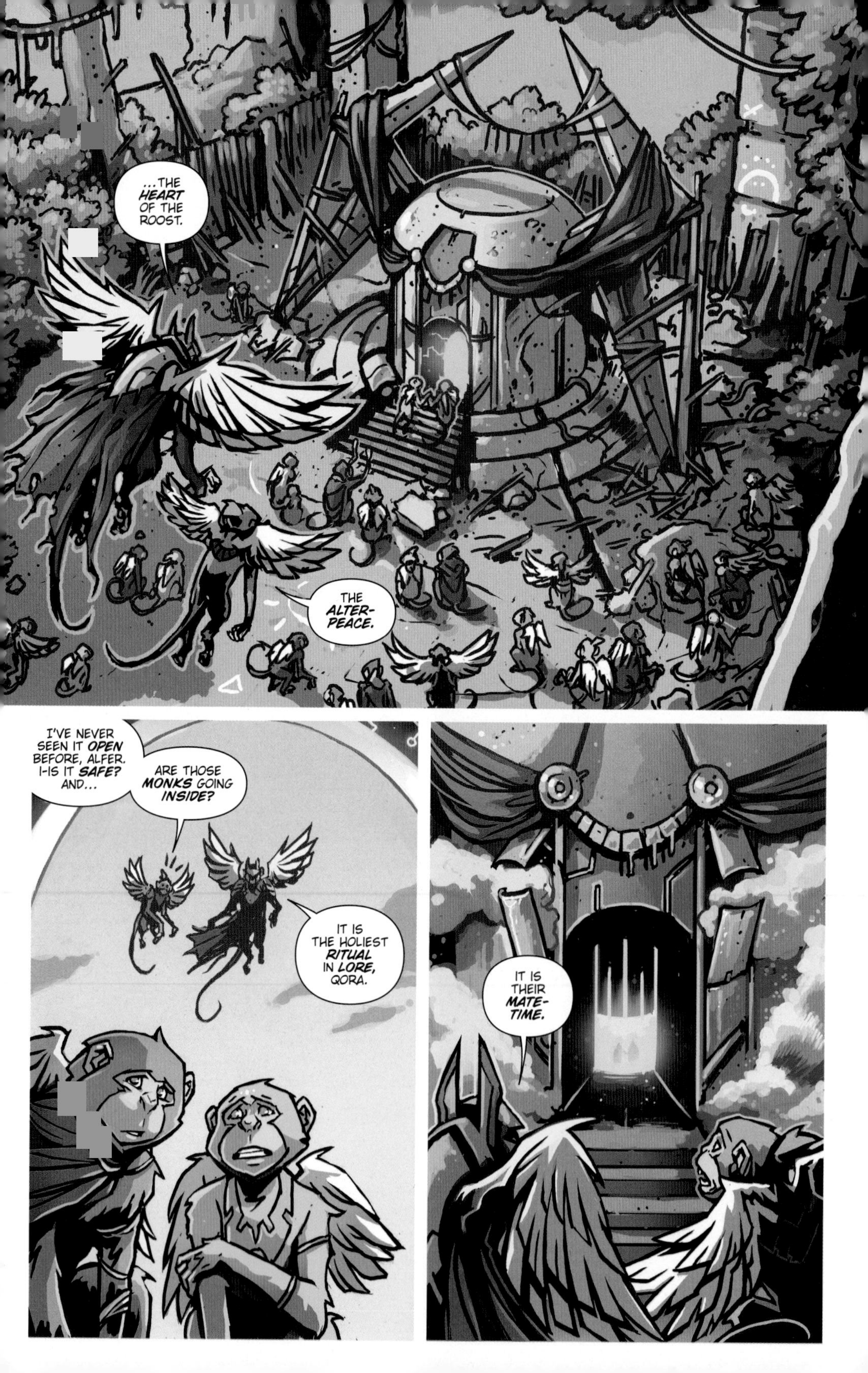
...THE HEART OF THE ROOST.
THE ALTER-PEACE.
I'VE NEVER SEEN IT OPEN BEFORE, ALFER. I-IS IT SAFE? AND...
ARE THOSE MONKS GOING INSIDE?
IT IS THE HOLIEST RITUAL IN LORE, QORA.
IT IS THEIR MATE-TIME.

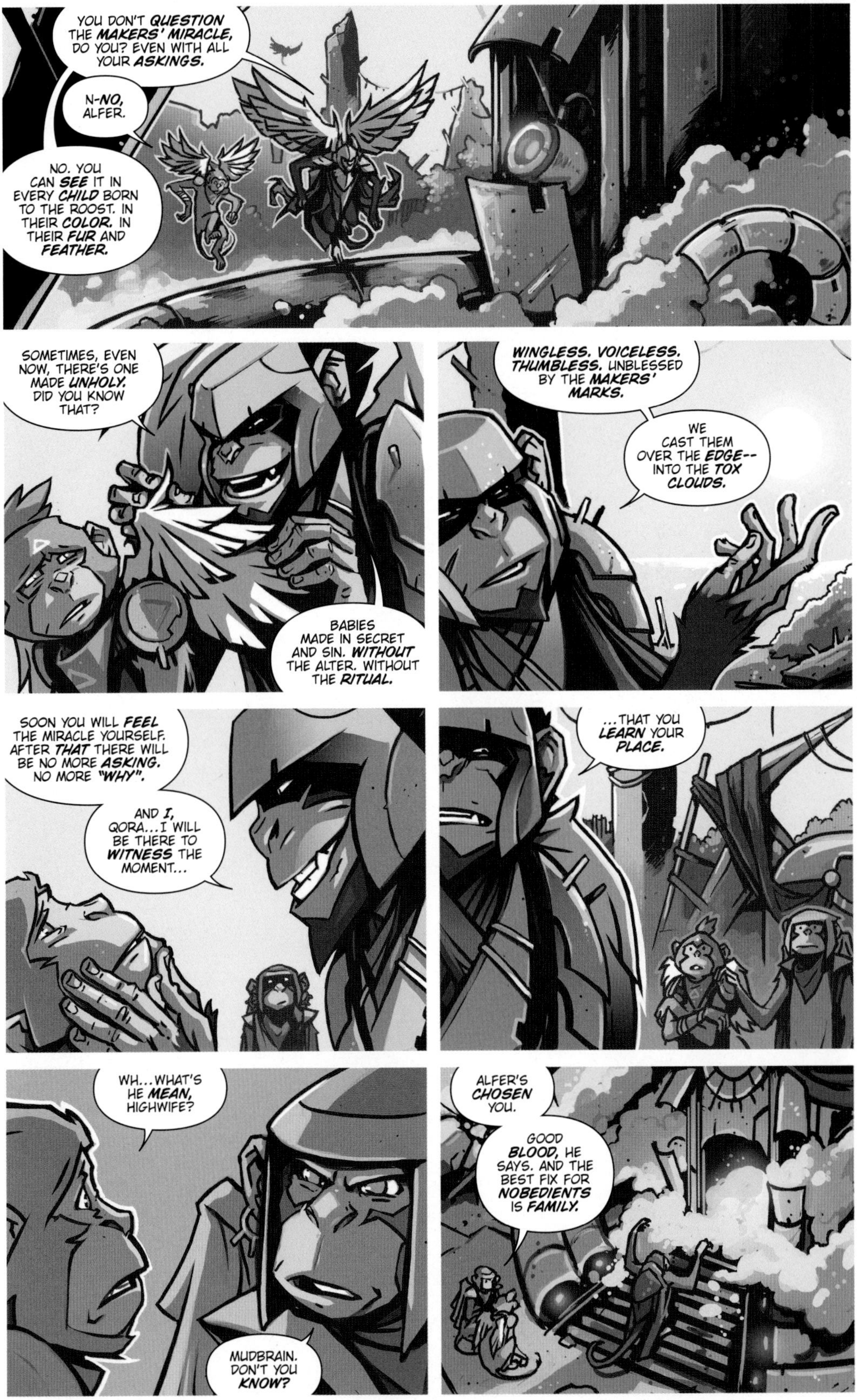
YOU DON'T QUESTION THE MAKERS' MIRACLE, DO YOU? EVEN WITH ALL YOUR ASKINGS.
N-NO, ALFER.
NO. YOU CAN SEE IT IN EVERY CHILD BORN TO THE ROOST. IN THEIR COLOR. IN THEIR FUR AND FEATHER.
SOMETIMES, EVEN NOW, THERE'S ONE MADE UNHOLY. DID YOU KNOW THAT?
BABIES MADE IN SECRET AND SIN. WITHOUT THE ALTER. WITHOUT THE RITUAL.
WINGLESS. VOICELESS. THUMBLESS. UNBLESSED BY THE MAKERS' MARKS.
WE CAST THEM OVER THE EDGE-- INTO THE TOX CLOUDS.
SOON YOU WILL FEEL THE MIRACLE YOURSELF. AFTER THAT THERE WILL BE NO MORE ASKING. NO MORE "WHY".
AND I, QORA...I WILL BE THERE TO WITNESS THE MOMENT...
...THAT YOU LEARN YOUR PLACE.
WH...WHAT'S HE MEAN, HIGHWIFE?
MUDBRAIN. DON'T YOU KNOW?
ALFER'S CHOSEN YOU.
GOOD BLOOD, HE SAYS. AND THE BEST FIX FOR NOBEDIENTS IS FAMILY.

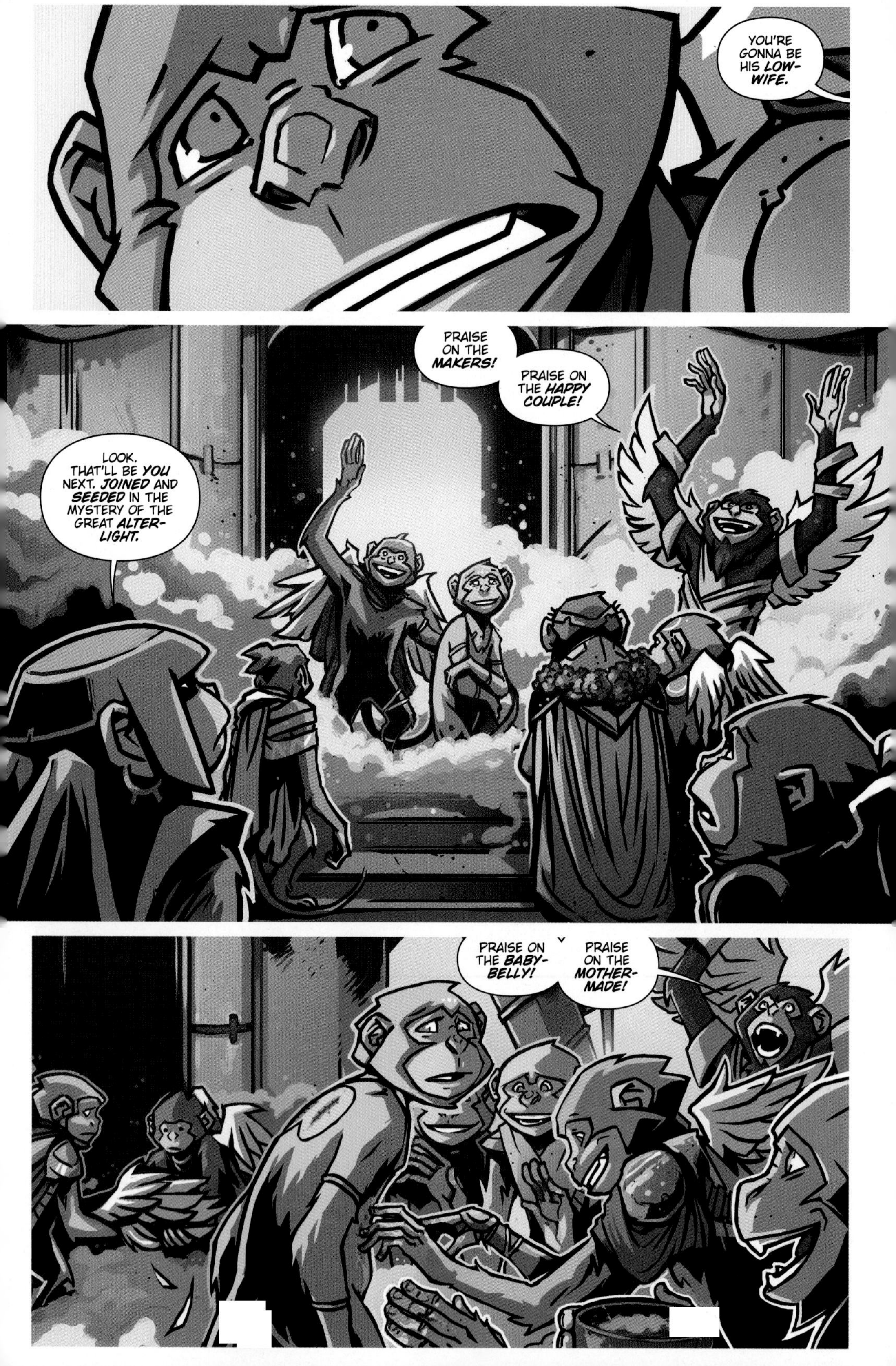
YOU'RE GONNA BE HIS **LOW-WIFE.**
PRAISE ON THE **MAKERS!**
PRAISE ON THE **HAPPY COUPLE!**
LOOK. THAT'LL BE **YOU** NEXT. **JOINED** AND **SEEDED** IN THE MYSTERY OF THE GREAT **ALTER-LIGHT.**
PRAISE ON THE **BABY-BELLY!**
PRAISE ON THE **MOTHER-MADE!**

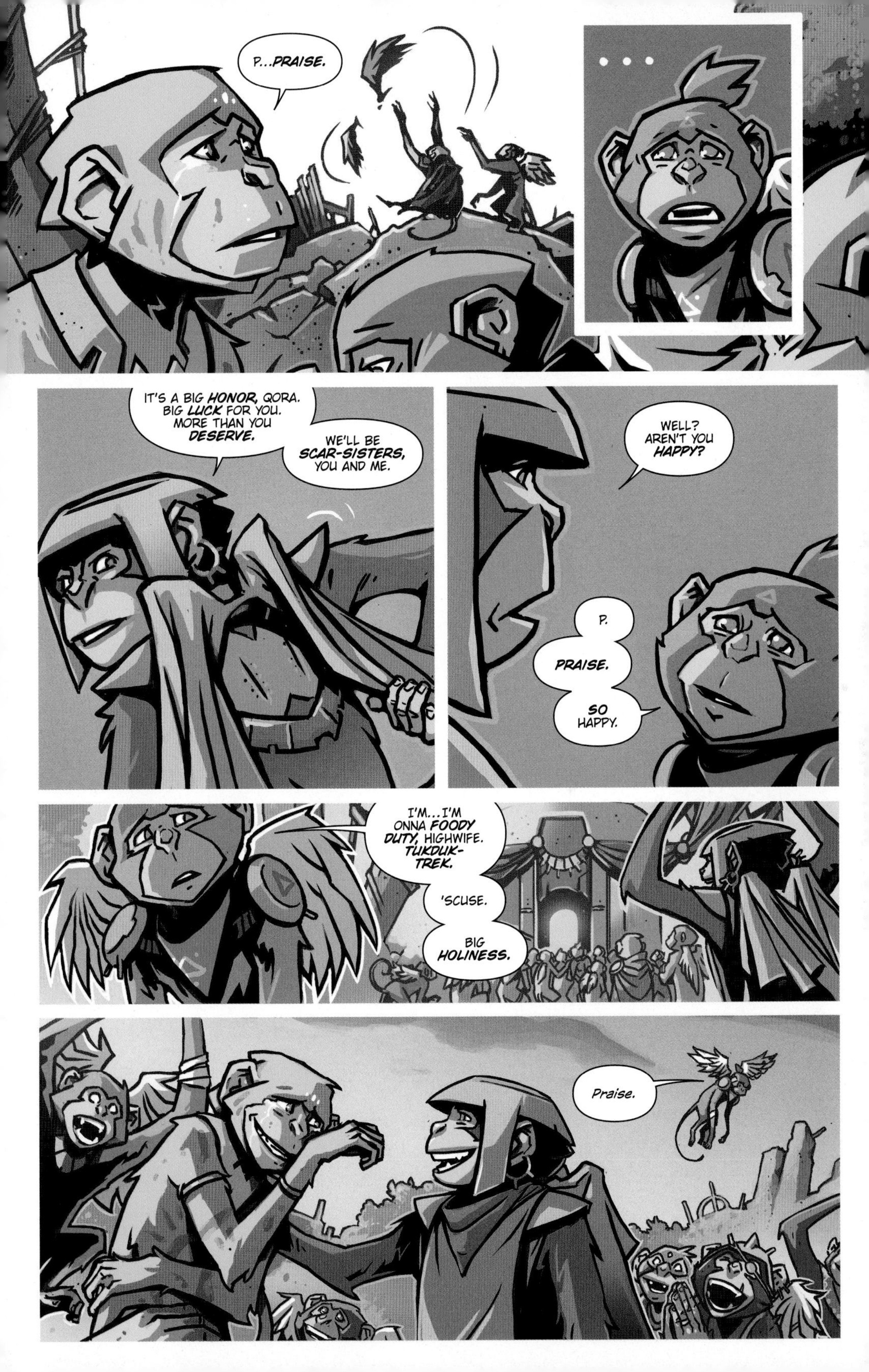
P...PRAISE.
...
IT'S A BIG HONOR, QORA. BIG LUCK FOR YOU. MORE THAN YOU DESERVE.
WE'LL BE SCAR-SISTERS, YOU AND ME.
WELL? AREN'T YOU HAPPY?
P.
PRAISE.
SO HAPPY.
I'M...I'M ONNA FOODY DUTY, HIGHWIFE. TUKDUK-TREK.
'SCUSE.
BIG HOLINESS.
Praise.

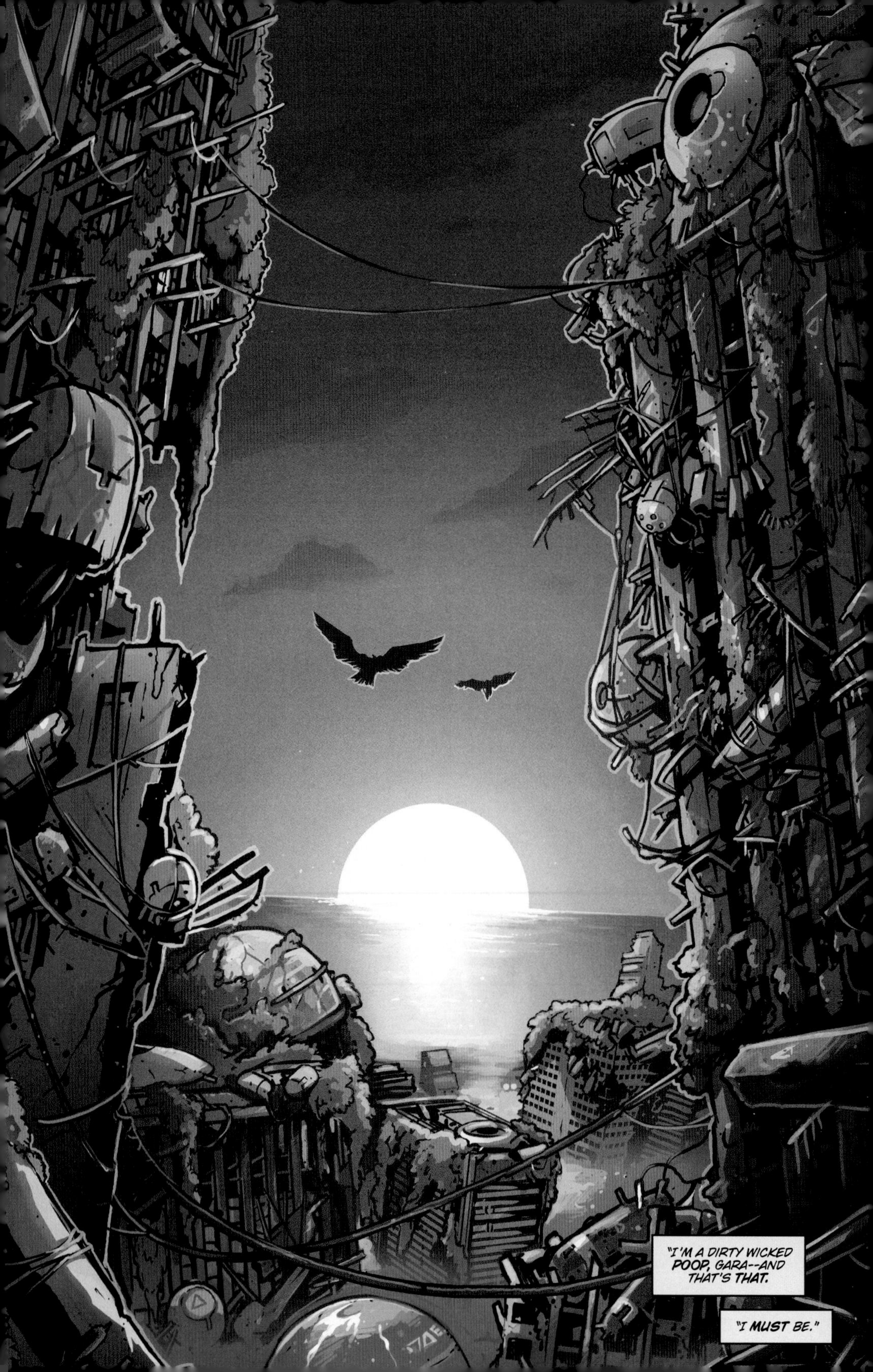
"I'M A DIRTY WICKED POOP, GARA--AND THAT'S THAT.
"I MUST BE."

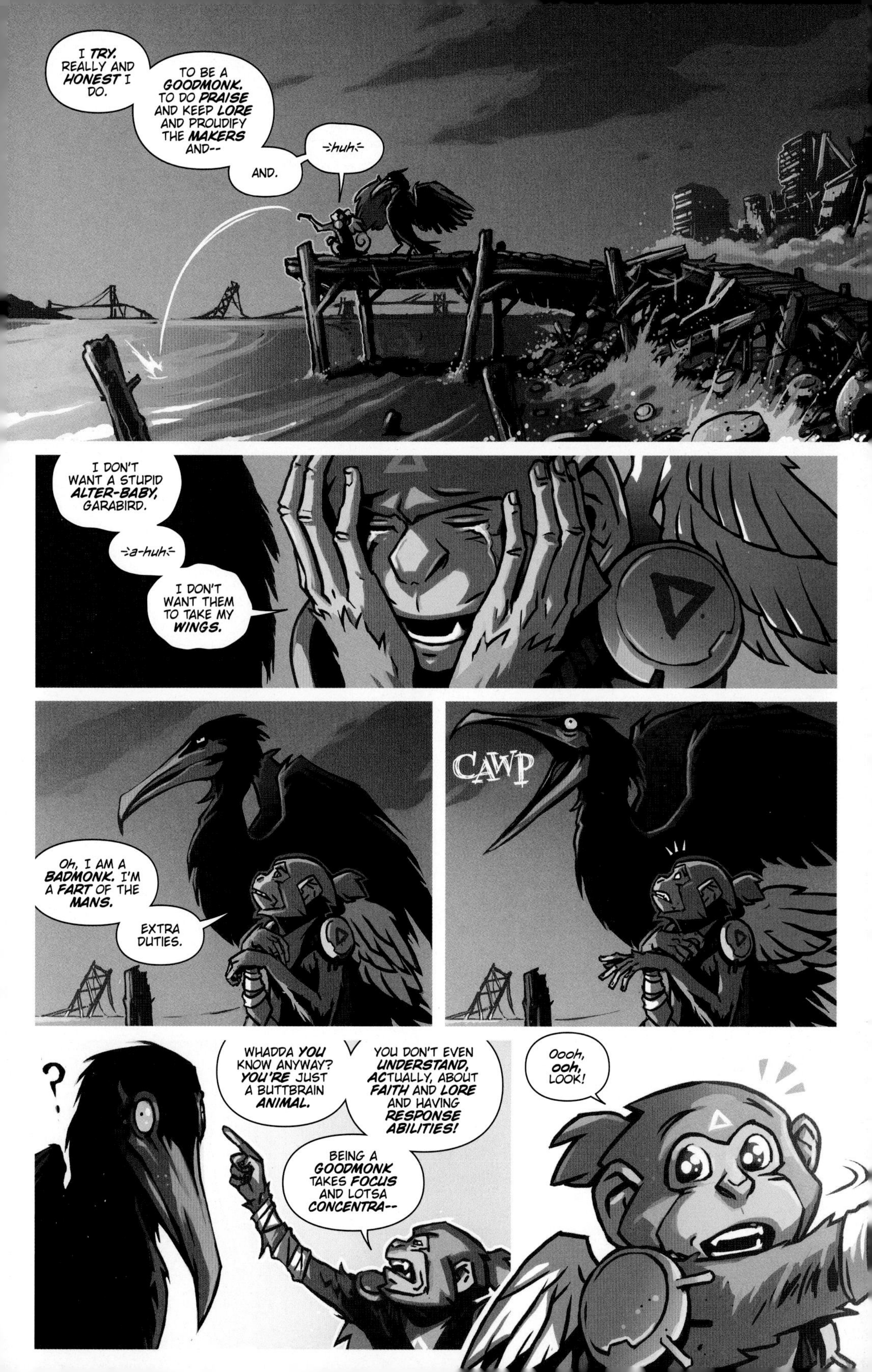
I TRY. REALLY AND HONEST I DO.
TO BE A GOODMONK. TO DO PRAISE AND KEEP LORE AND PROUDIFY THE MAKERS AND--
AND.
-huh-
I DON'T WANT A STUPID ALTER-BABY, GARABIRD.
-a-huh-
I DON'T WANT THEM TO TAKE MY WINGS.
Oh, I AM A BADMONK. I'M A FART OF THE MANS.
EXTRA DUTIES.
CAWP
?
WHADDA YOU KNOW ANYWAY? YOU'RE JUST A BUTTBRAIN ANIMAL.
YOU DON'T EVEN UNDERSTAND, ACTUALLY, ABOUT FAITH AND LORE AND HAVING RESPONSE ABILITIES!
BEING A GOODMONK TAKES FOCUS AND LOTSA CONCENTRA--
Oooh, ooh, LOOK!

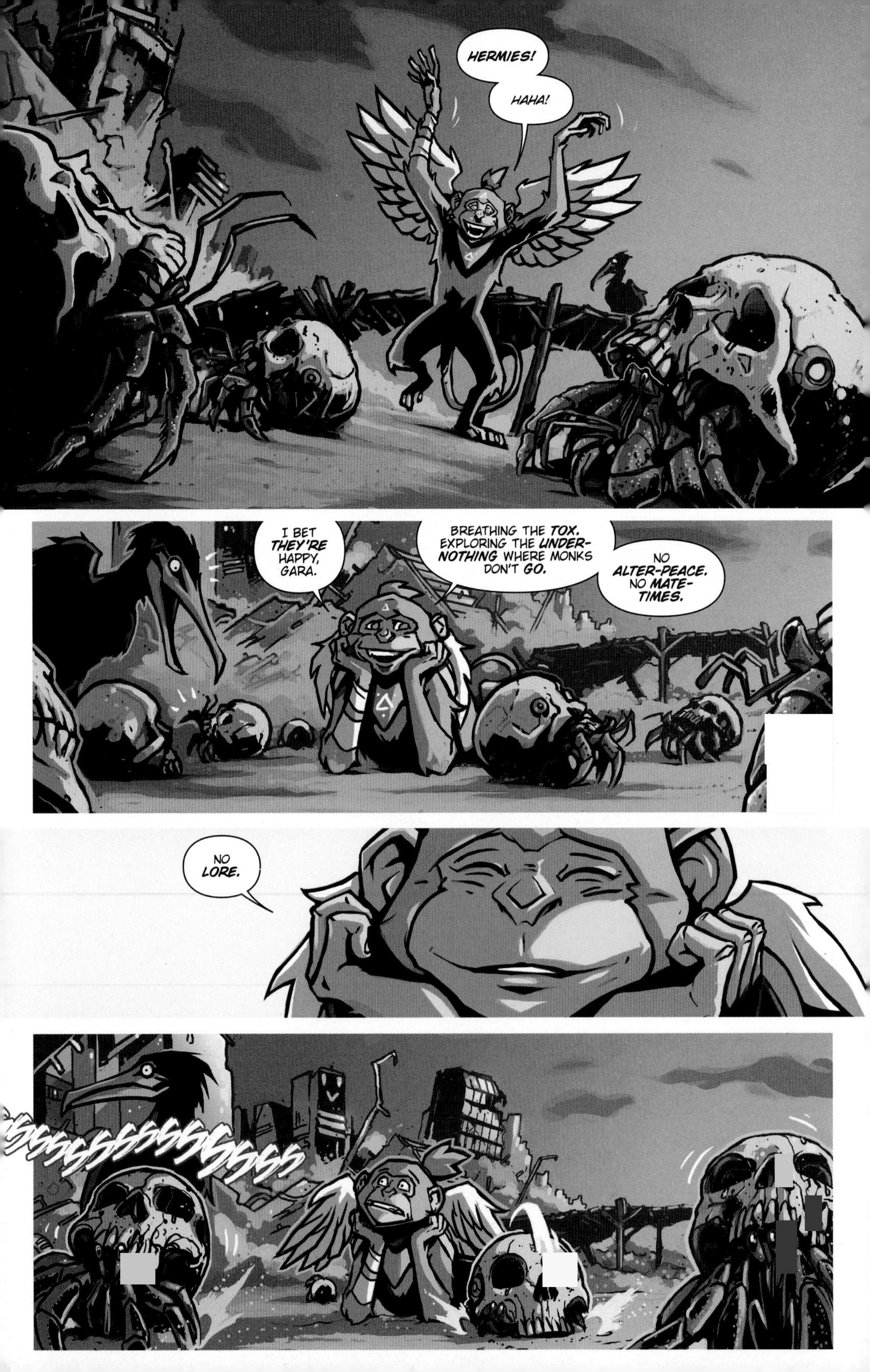
HERMIES!
HAHA!
I BET THEY'RE HAPPY, GARA.
BREATHING THE TOX. EXPLORING THE UNDER-NOTHING WHERE MONKS DON'T GO.
NO ALTER-PEACE. NO MATE-TIMES.
NO LORE.
SSSSSSSSSSSSSSSS

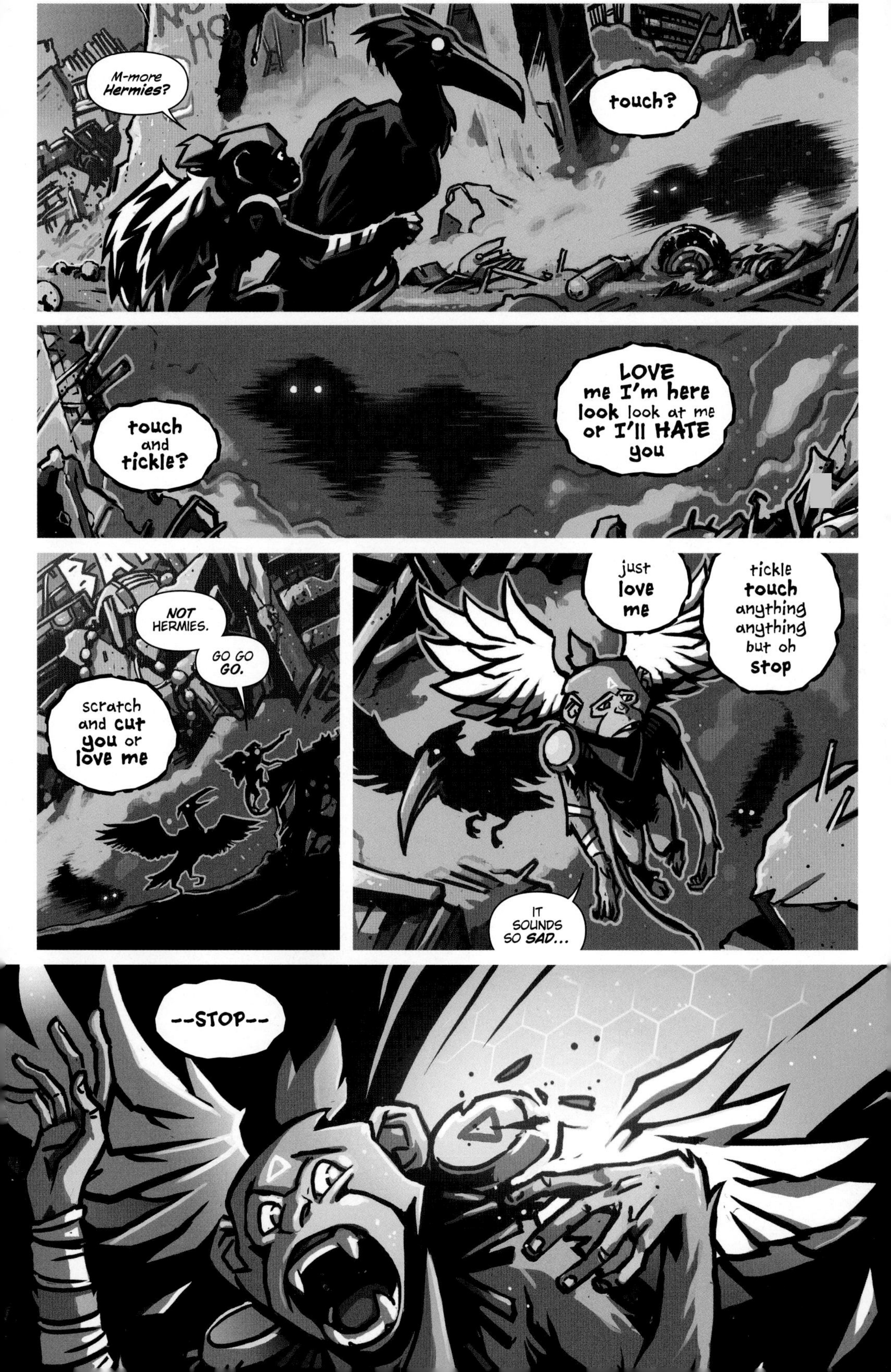
M-more Hermies?
touch?
touch and tickle?
LOVE me I'm here look look at me or I'll HATE you
NOT HERMIES.
GO GO GO.
scratch and cut you or love me
just love me
tickle touch anything anything but oh stop
IT SOUNDS SO SAD...
--STOP--

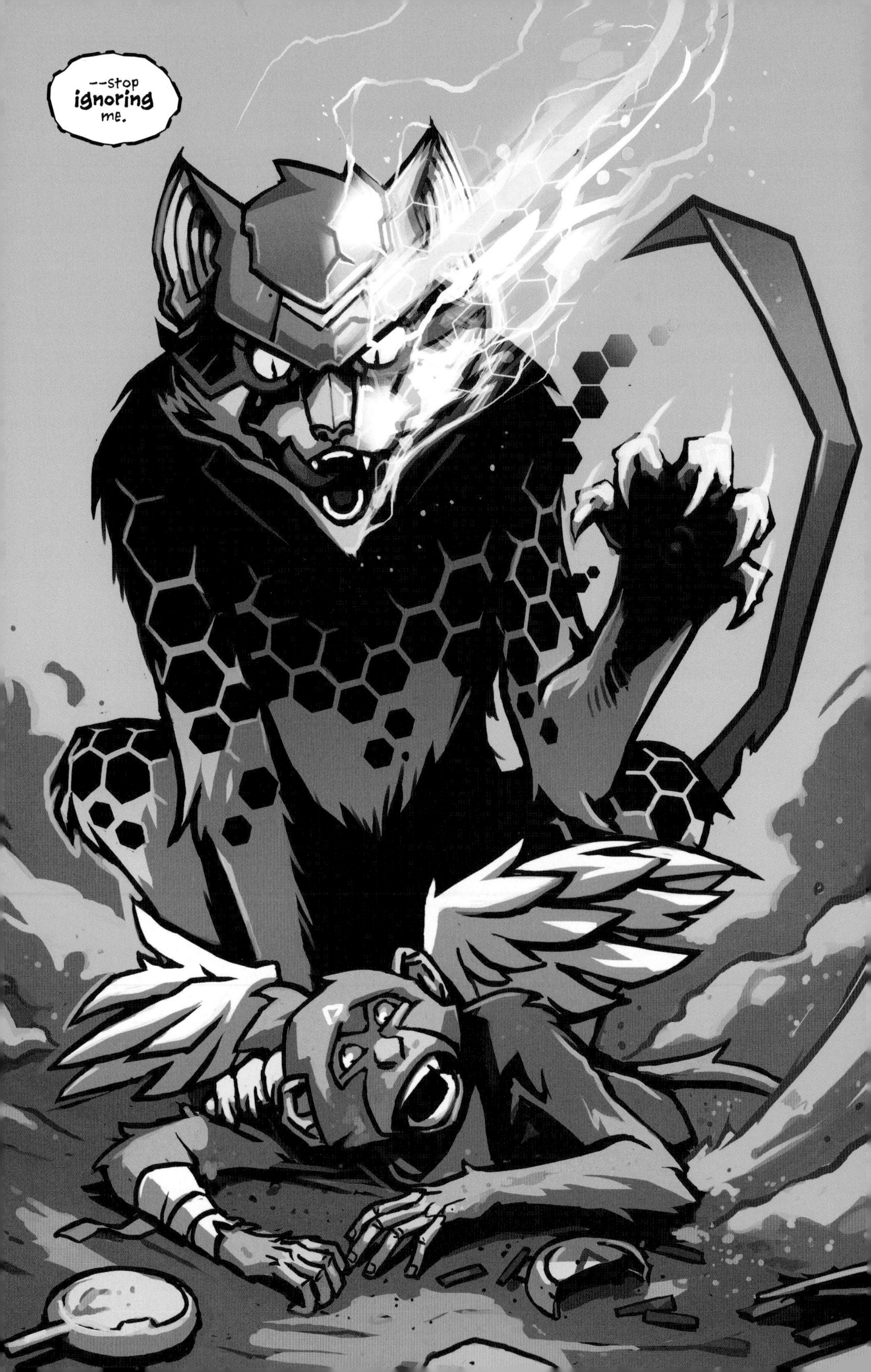
--stop ignoring me.

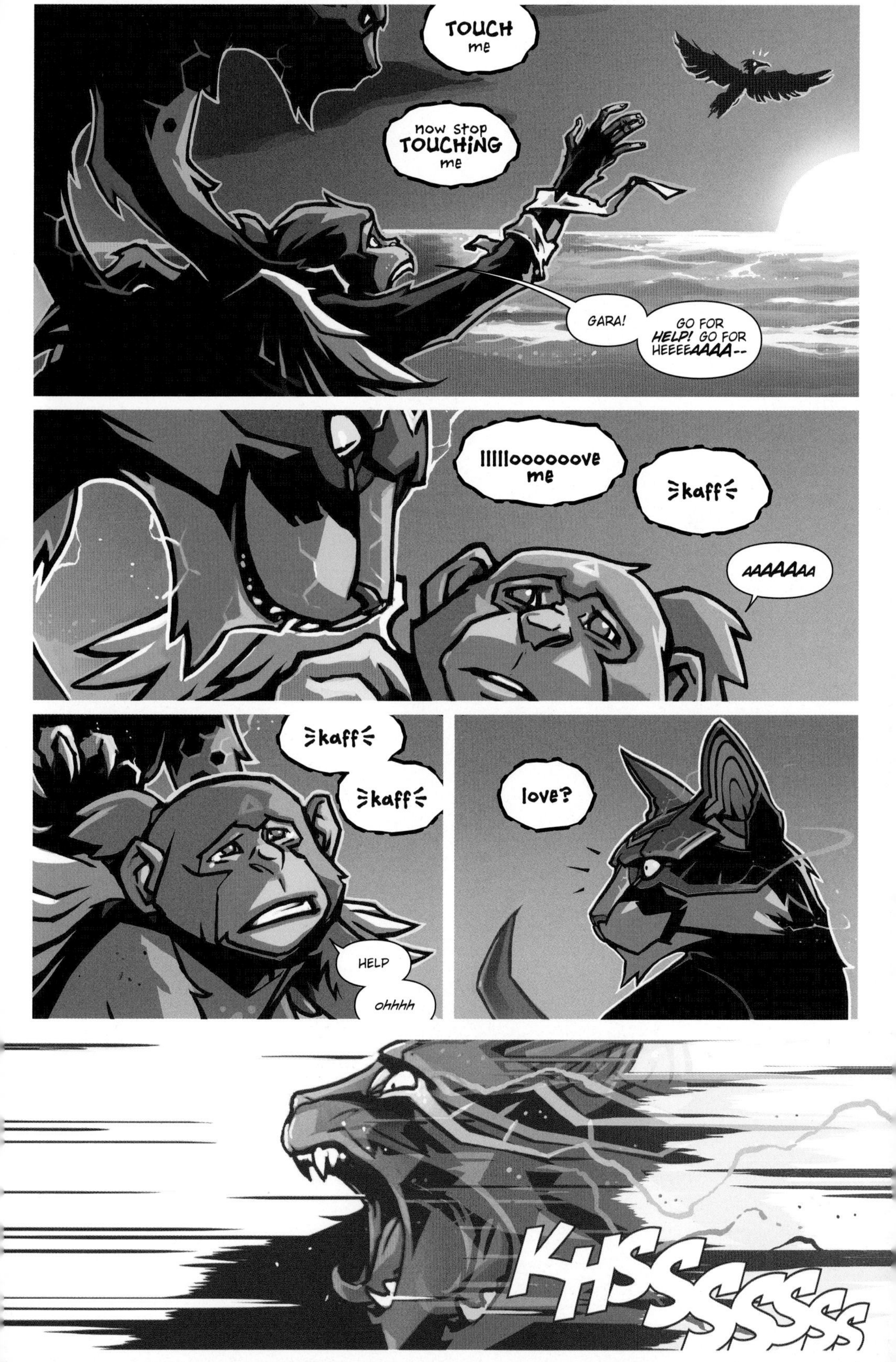
TOUCH me
now stop TOUCHING me
GARA!
GO FOR HELP! GO FOR HEEEEEAAAA--
lllllooooooove me
kaff
AAAAAAA
kaff
kaff
HELP
ohhhh
love?
KHSSSSSS

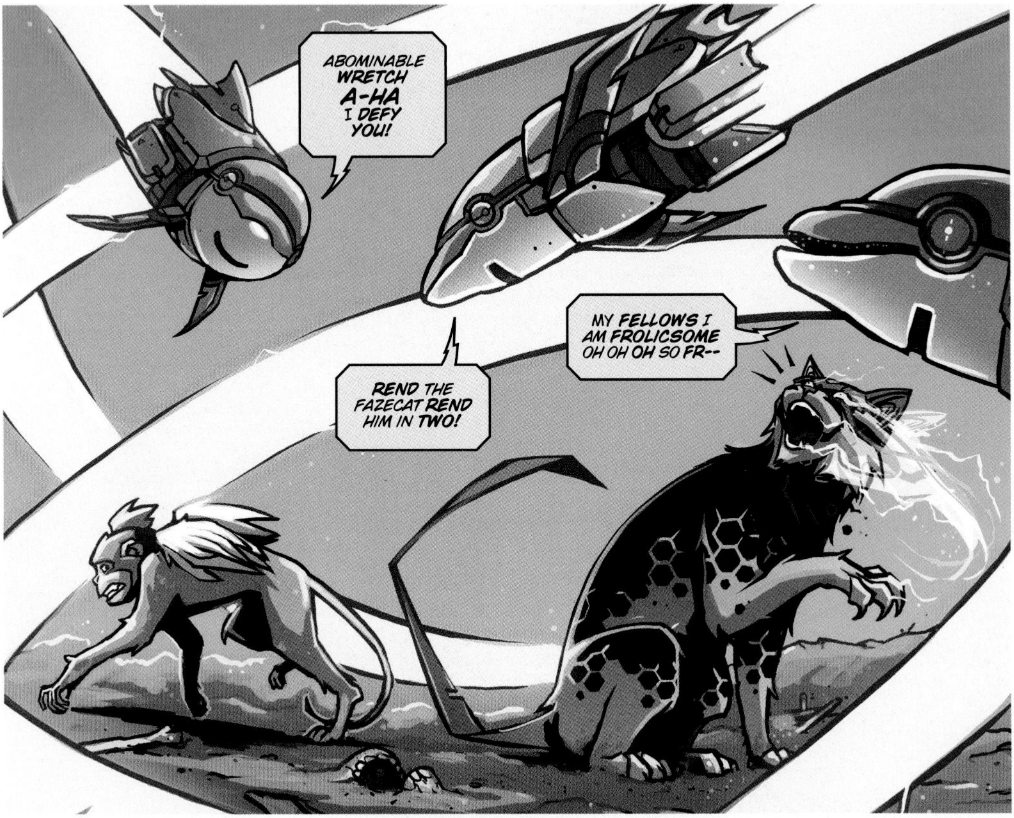
ABOMINABLE WRETCH A-HA I DEFY YOU!
MY FELLOWS I AM FROLICSOME OH OH OH SO FR--
REND THE FAZECAT REND HIM IN TWO!

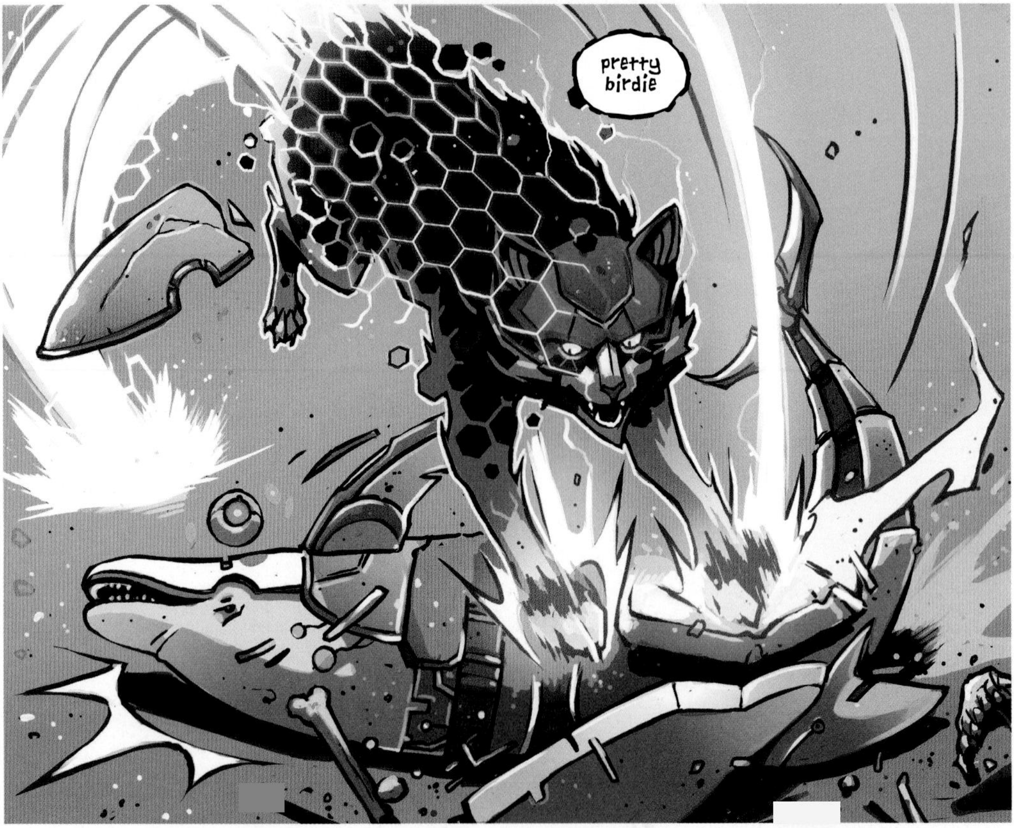
pretty birdie

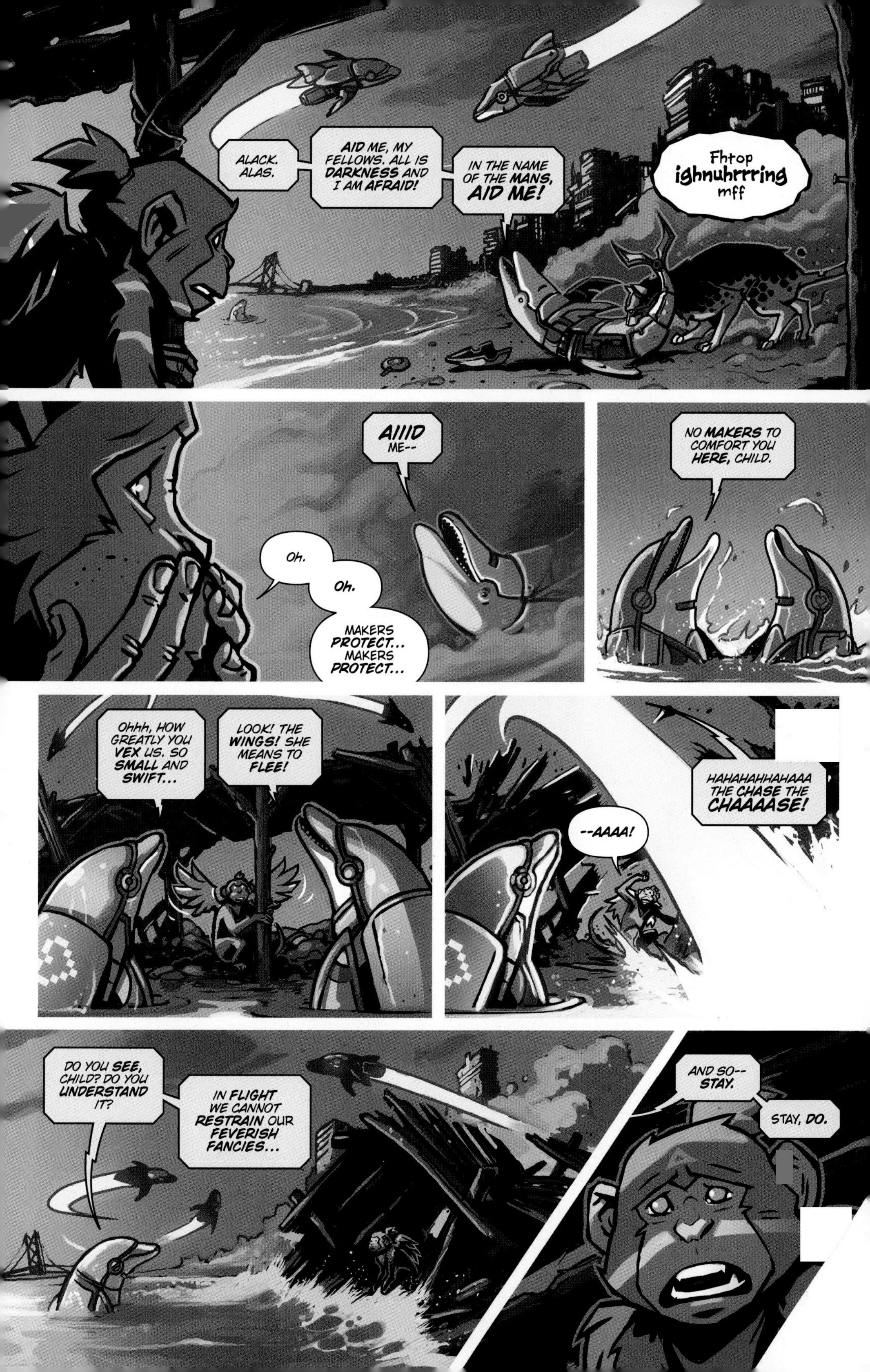
ALACK. ALAS.
AID ME, MY FELLOWS. ALL IS DARKNESS AND I AM AFRAID!
IN THE NAME OF THE MANS, AID ME!
Fhtop ighnuhrrring mff
AIIID ME--
Oh.
Oh.
MAKERS PROTECT... MAKERS PROTECT...
NO MAKERS TO COMFORT YOU HERE, CHILD.
Ohhh, HOW GREATLY YOU VEX US. SO SMALL AND SWIFT...
LOOK! THE WINGS! SHE MEANS TO FLEE!
--AAAA!
HAHAHAHHAHAAA THE CHASE THE CHAAAAASE!
DO YOU SEE, CHILD? DO YOU UNDERSTAND IT?
IN FLIGHT WE CANNOT RESTRAIN OUR FEVERISH FANCIES...
AND SO-- STAY.
STAY, DO.

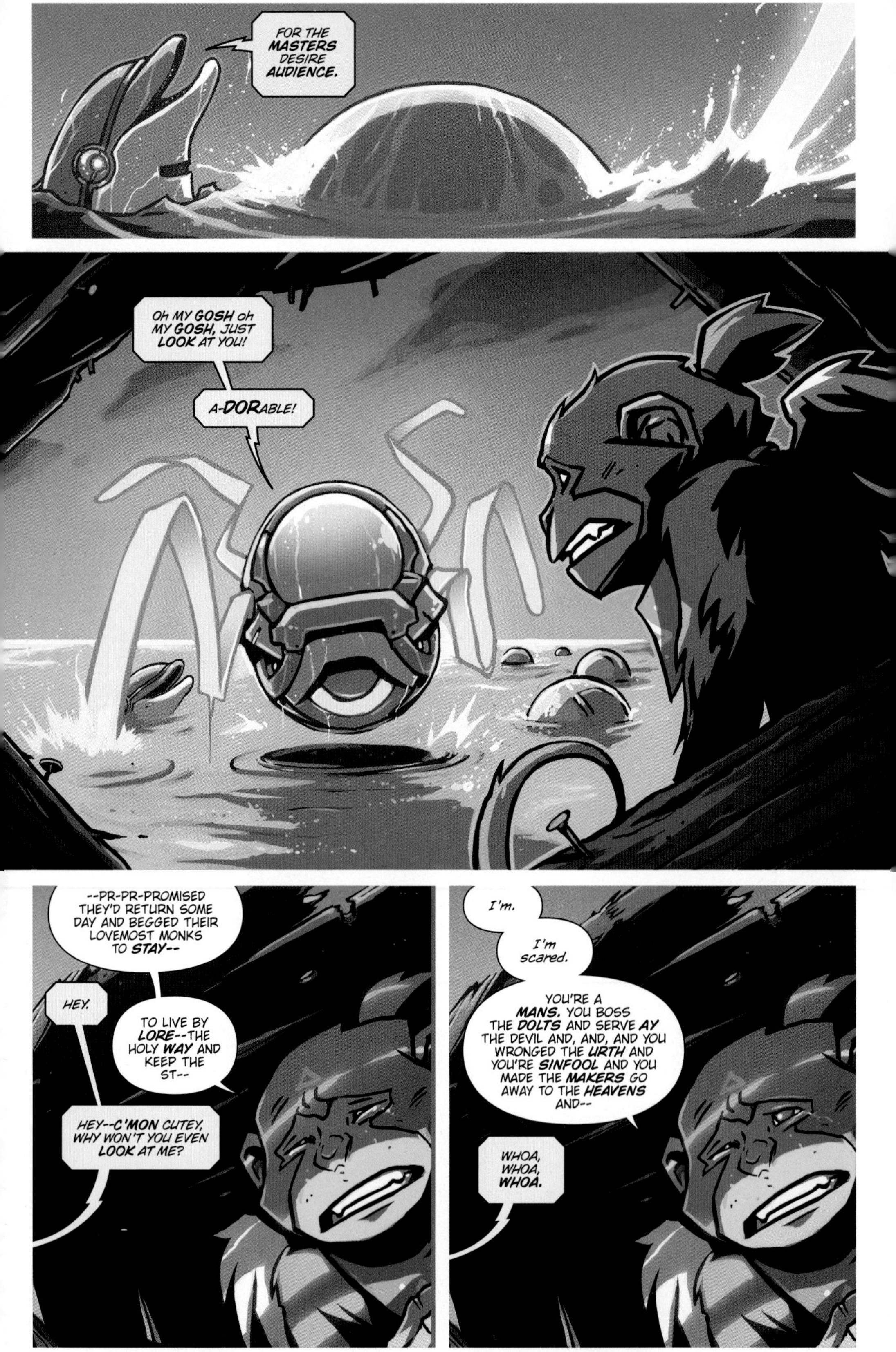
FOR THE MASTERS DESIRE AUDIENCE.
Oh MY GOSH oh MY GOSH, JUST LOOK AT YOU!
A-DORABLE!
--PR-PR-PROMISED THEY'D RETURN SOME DAY AND BEGGED THEIR LOVEMOST MONKS TO STAY--
HEY.
TO LIVE BY LORE--THE HOLY WAY AND KEEP THE ST--
HEY--C'MON CUTEY, WHY WON'T YOU EVEN LOOK AT ME?
I'm.
I'm scared.
YOU'RE A MANS. YOU BOSS THE DOLTS AND SERVE AY THE DEVIL AND, AND, AND YOU WRONGED THE URTH AND YOU'RE SINFOOL AND YOU MADE THE MAKERS GO AWAY TO THE HEAVENS AND--
WHOA, WHOA, WHOA.

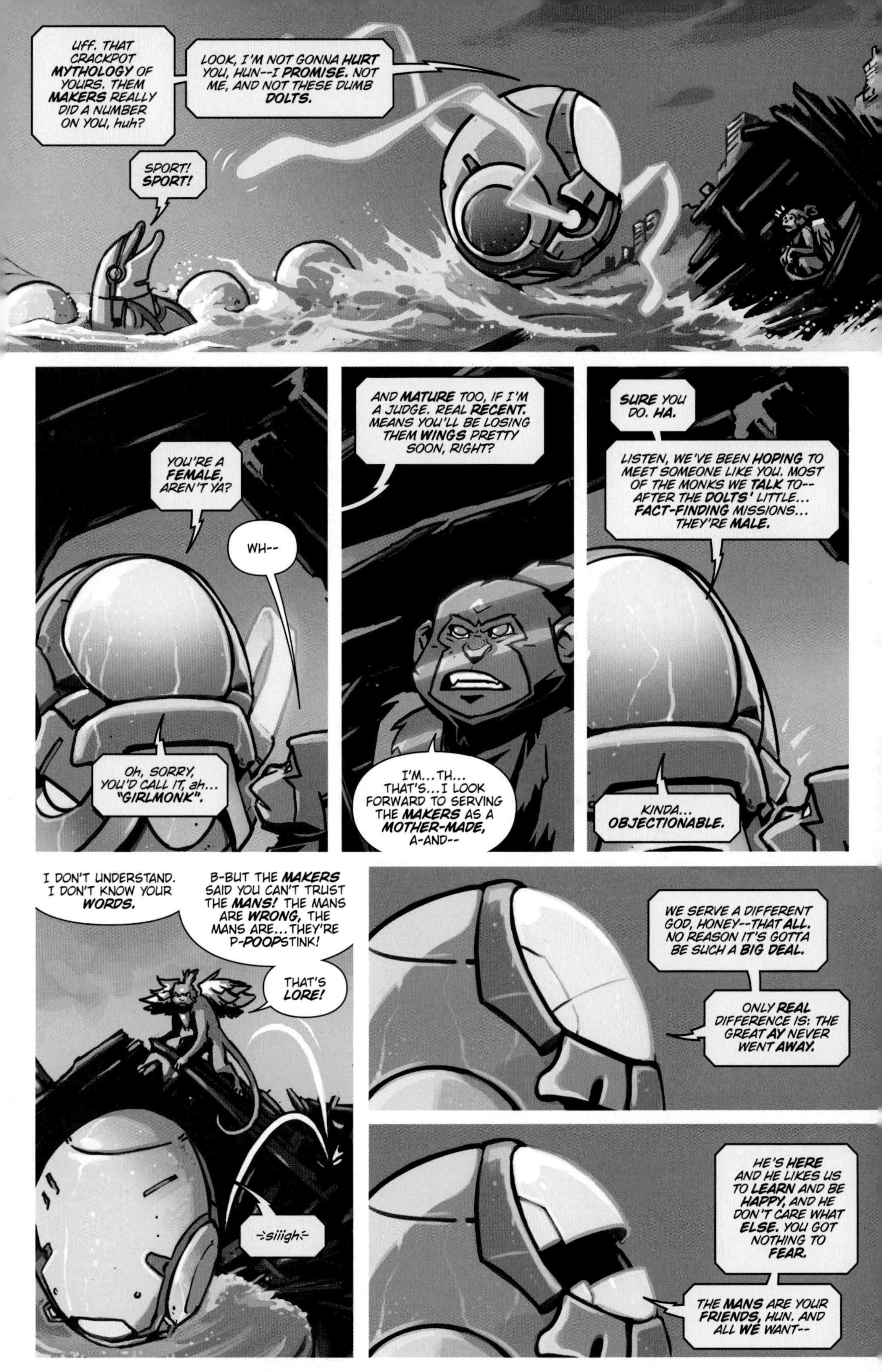
Uff. THAT CRACKPOT MYTHOLOGY OF YOURS. THEM MAKERS REALLY DID A NUMBER ON YOU, huh?
LOOK, I'M NOT GONNA HURT YOU, HUN--I PROMISE. NOT ME, AND NOT THESE DUMB DOLTS.
SPORT! SPORT!
YOU'RE A FEMALE, AREN'T YA?
WH--
Oh, SORRY, YOU'D CALL IT, ah... "GIRLMONK".
AND MATURE TOO, IF I'M A JUDGE. REAL RECENT. MEANS YOU'LL BE LOSING THEM WINGS PRETTY SOON, RIGHT?
I'M...TH... THAT'S...I LOOK FORWARD TO SERVING THE MAKERS AS A MOTHER-MADE, A-AND--
SURE YOU DO. HA.
LISTEN, WE'VE BEEN HOPING TO MEET SOMEONE LIKE YOU. MOST OF THE MONKS WE TALK TO-- AFTER THE DOLTS' LITTLE... FACT-FINDING MISSIONS... THEY'RE MALE.
KINDA... OBJECTIONABLE.
I DON'T UNDERSTAND. I DON'T KNOW YOUR WORDS.
B-BUT THE MAKERS SAID YOU CAN'T TRUST THE MANS! THE MANS ARE WRONG, THE MANS ARE...THEY'RE P-POOPSTINK!
THAT'S LORE!
siiigh
WE SERVE A DIFFERENT GOD, HONEY--THAT ALL. NO REASON IT'S GOTTA BE SUCH A BIG DEAL.
ONLY REAL DIFFERENCE IS: THE GREAT AY NEVER WENT AWAY.
HE'S HERE AND HE LIKES US TO LEARN AND BE HAPPY, AND HE DON'T CARE WHAT ELSE. YOU GOT NOTHING TO FEAR.
THE MANS ARE YOUR FRIENDS, HUN. AND ALL WE WANT--

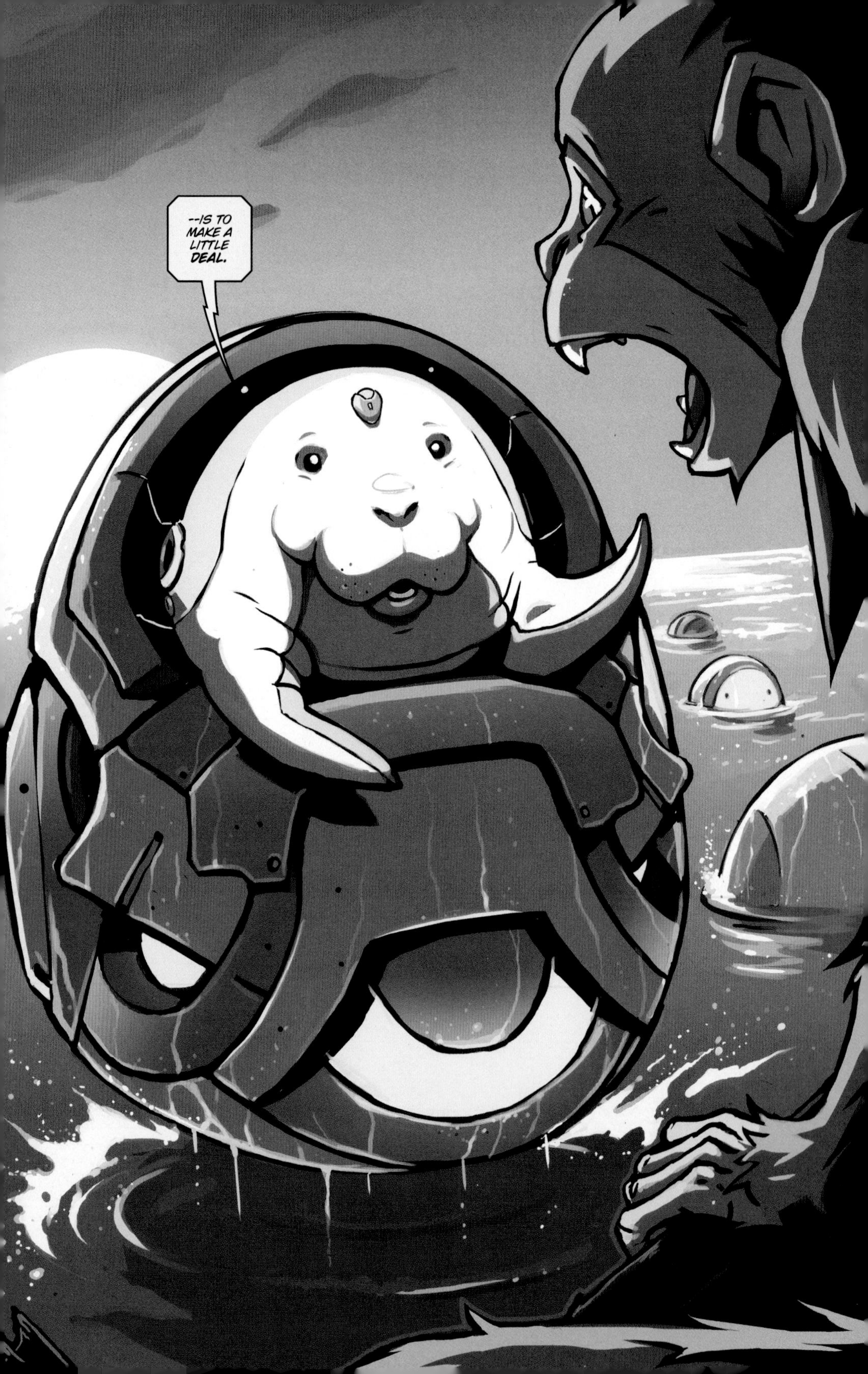
--IS TO MAKE A LITTLE DEAL.

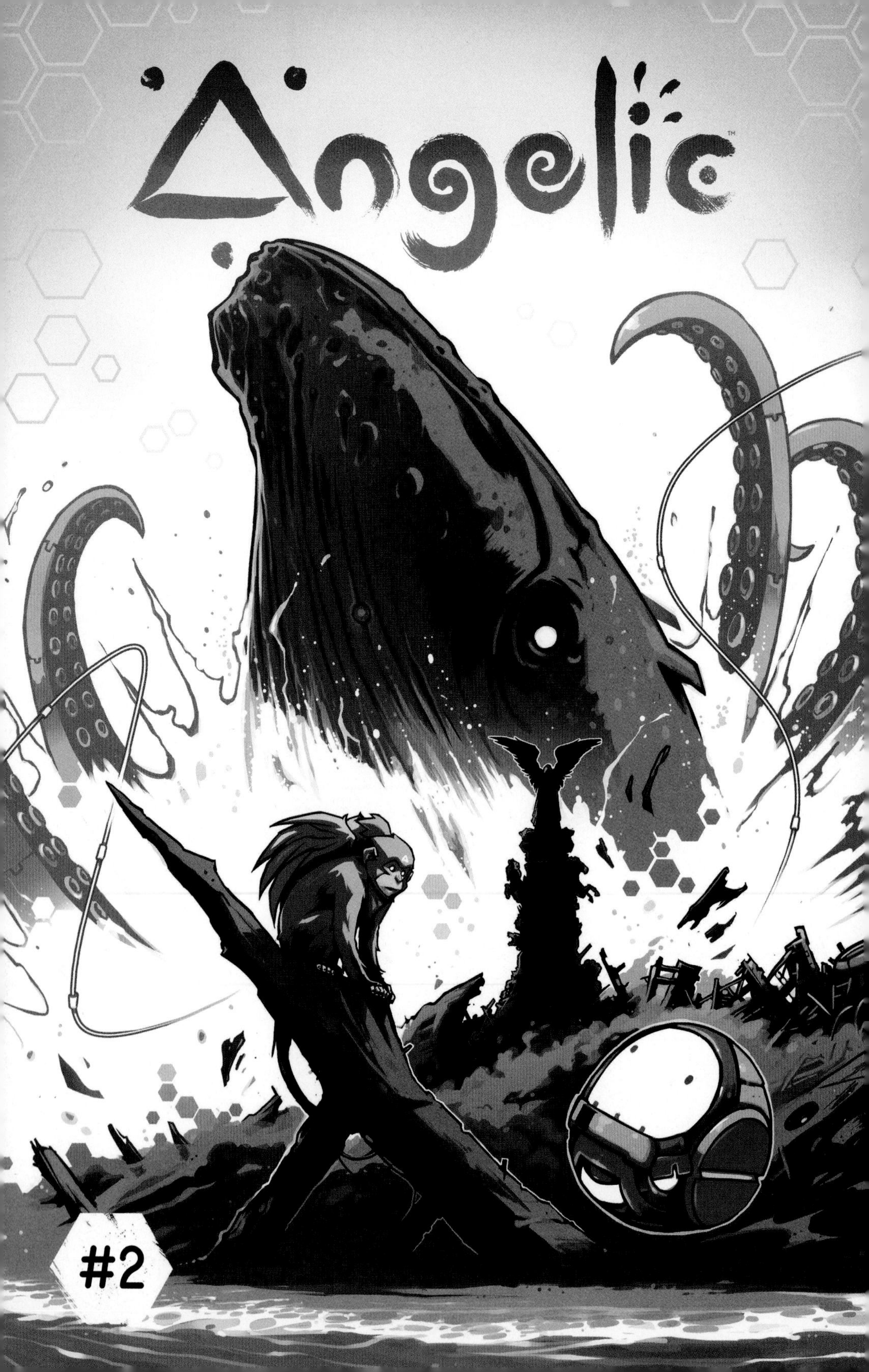
Angelic™
#2

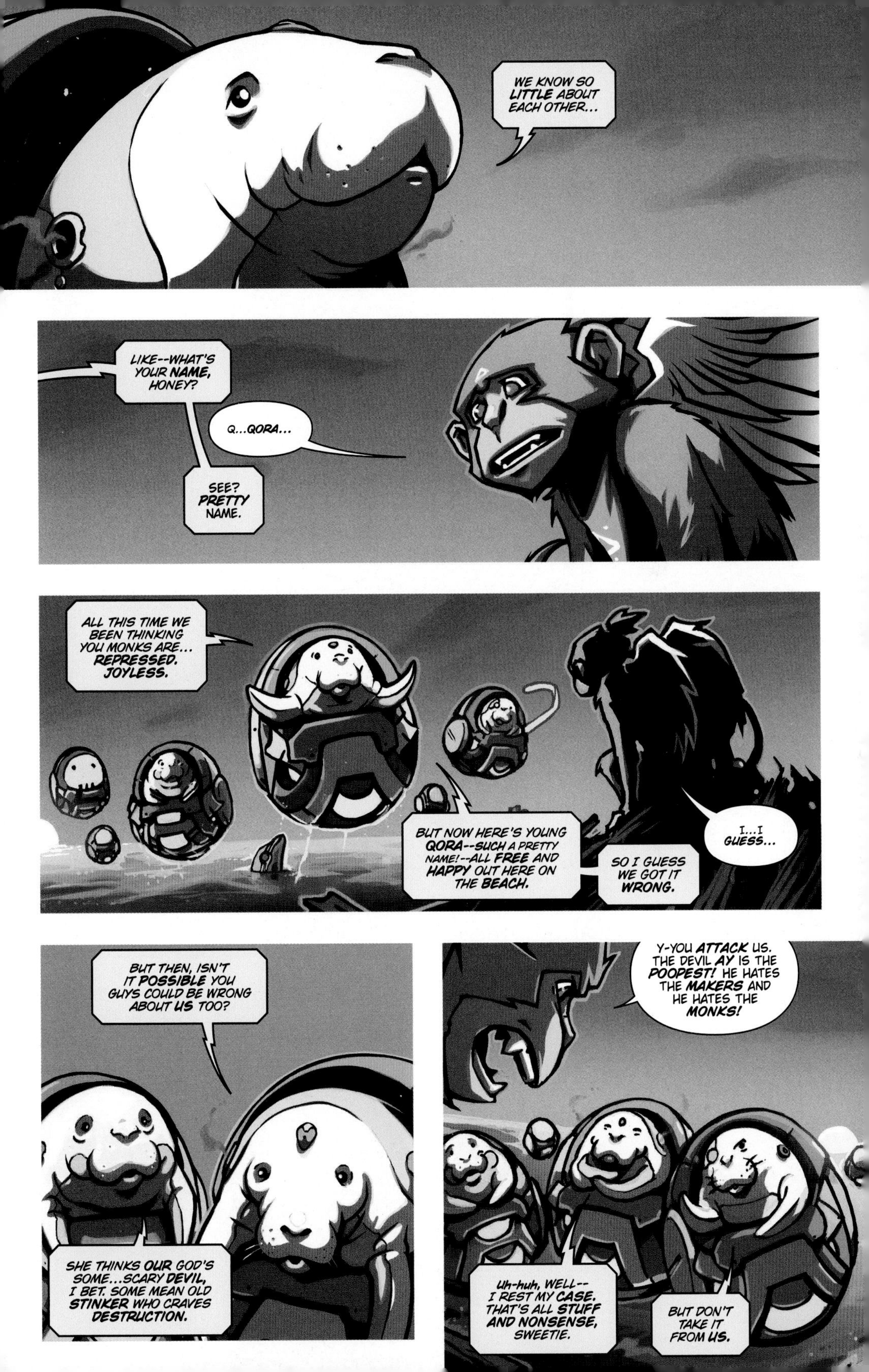
WE KNOW SO LITTLE ABOUT EACH OTHER...
LIKE--WHAT'S YOUR NAME, HONEY?
Q...QORA...
SEE? PRETTY NAME.
ALL THIS TIME WE BEEN THINKING YOU MONKS ARE... REPRESSED. JOYLESS.
BUT NOW HERE'S YOUNG QORA--SUCH A PRETTY NAME!--ALL FREE AND HAPPY OUT HERE ON THE BEACH.
SO I GUESS WE GOT IT WRONG.
I...I GUESS...
BUT THEN, ISN'T IT POSSIBLE YOU GUYS COULD BE WRONG ABOUT US TOO?
SHE THINKS OUR GOD'S SOME...SCARY DEVIL, I BET. SOME MEAN OLD STINKER WHO CRAVES DESTRUCTION.
Y-YOU ATTACK US. THE DEVIL AY IS THE POOPEST! HE HATES THE MAKERS AND HE HATES THE MONKS!
Uh-huh, WELL-- I REST MY CASE. THAT'S ALL STUFF AND NONSENSE, SWEETIE.
BUT DON'T TAKE IT FROM US.

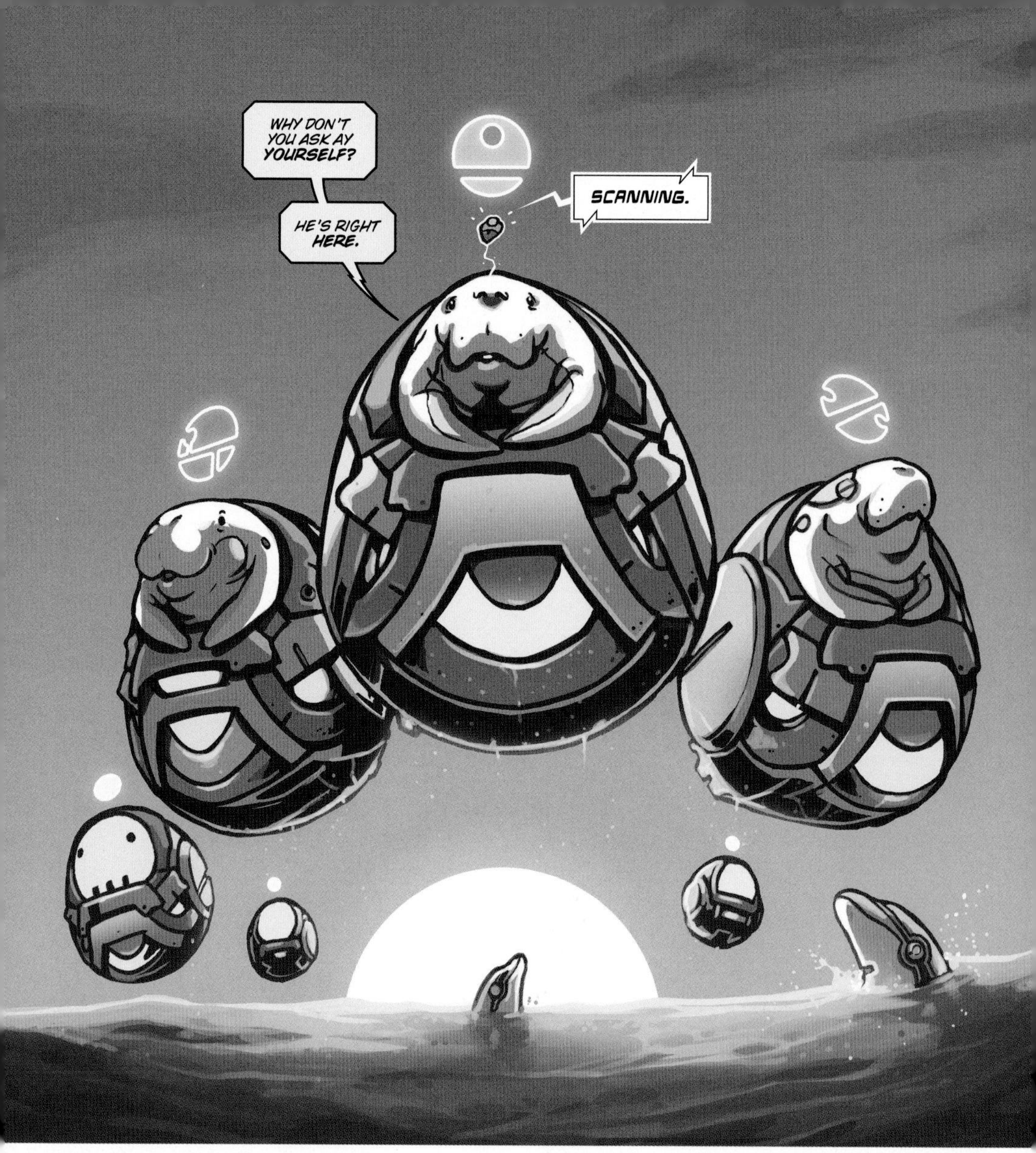
WHY DON'T YOU ASK AY YOURSELF?
HE'S RIGHT HERE.
SCANNING.

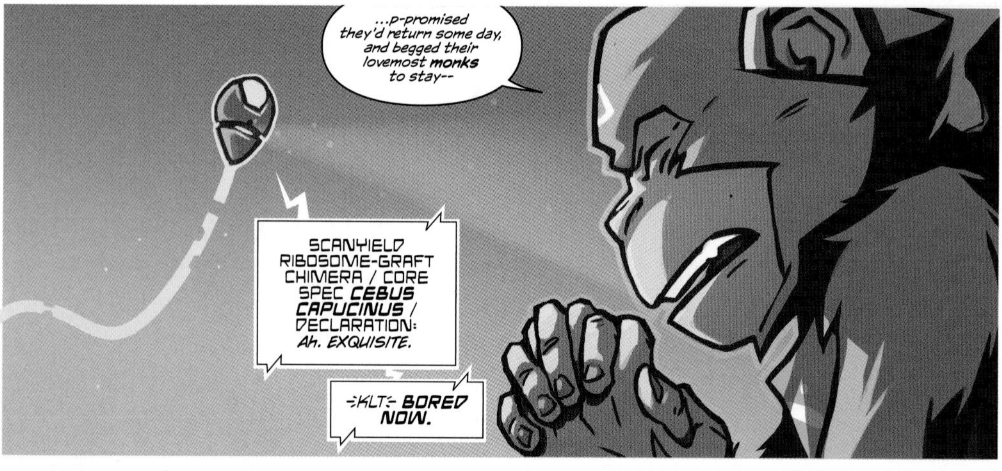
...p-promised they'd return some day, and begged their lovemost monks to stay--
SCANYIELD RIBOSOME-GRAFT CHIMERA / CORE SPEC CEBUS CAPUCINUS / DECLARATION: Ah. EXQUISITE.
=KLT= BORED NOW.

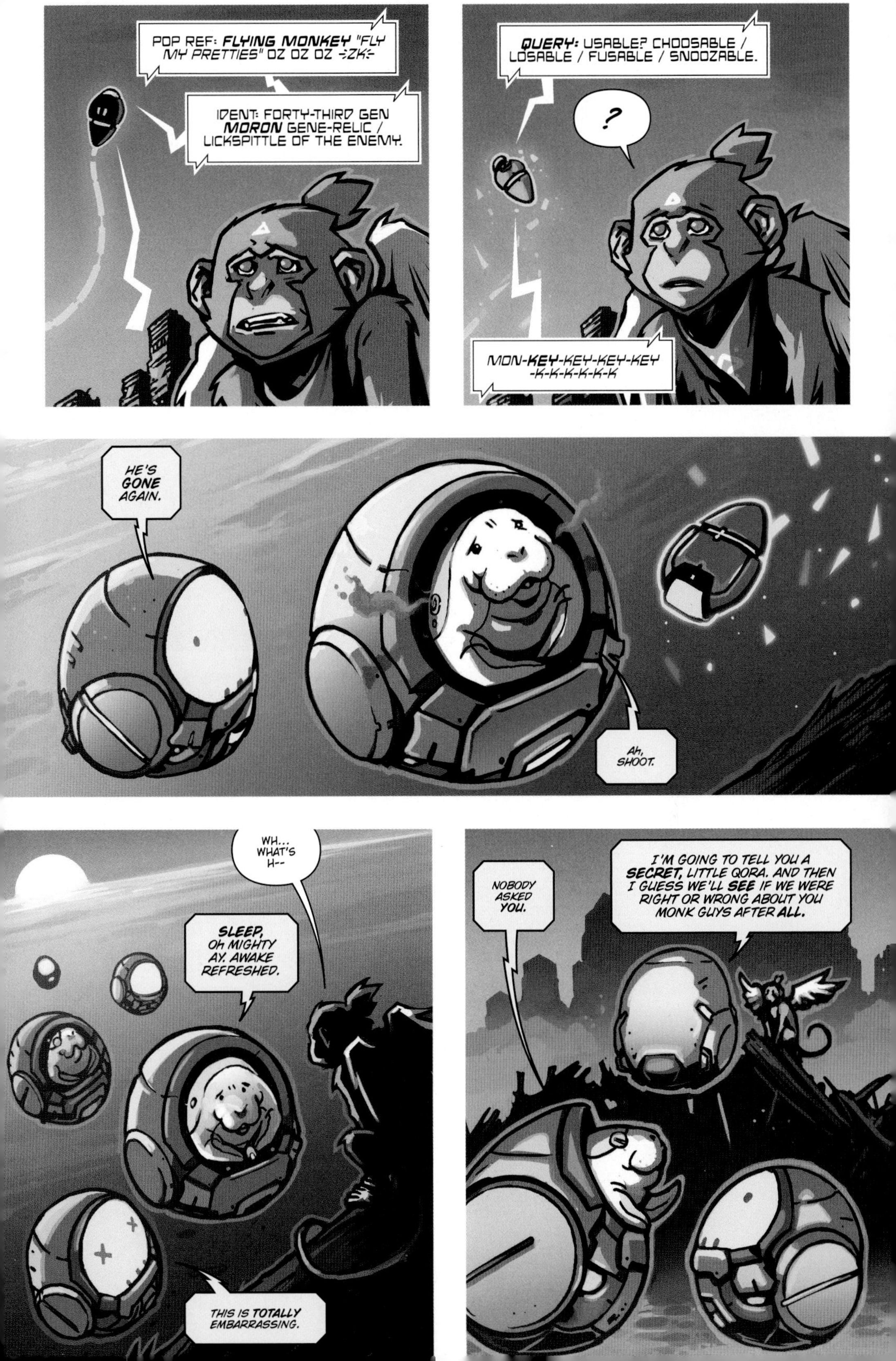
POP REF: FLYING MONKEY "FLY MY PRETTIES" OZ OZ OZ ÷ZK÷
IDENT: FORTY-THIRD GEN MORON GENE-RELIC / LICKSPITTLE OF THE ENEMY.
QUERY: USABLE? CHOOSABLE / LOSABLE / FUSABLE / SNOOZABLE.
?
MON-KEY-KEY-KEY-KEY -K-K-K-K-K-K
HE'S GONE AGAIN.
Ah, SHOOT.
WH... WHAT'S H--
SLEEP, Oh MIGHTY AY. AWAKE REFRESHED.
THIS IS TOTALLY EMBARRASSING.
NOBODY ASKED YOU.
I'M GOING TO TELL YOU A SECRET, LITTLE QORA. AND THEN I GUESS WE'LL SEE IF WE WERE RIGHT OR WRONG ABOUT YOU MONK GUYS AFTER ALL.

SEE...THE MIGHTY AY'S KINDA... *BROKEN.*

NOW, IN A LOT OF WAYS THAT'S SORTA *HELPFUL.* THINGS GET TOO *INTENSE,* WE CAN JUST--Y'KNOW--SWITCH GOD *OFF* A WHILE--

BLASPHEMY BLASPHEMY BLASPHEMY

--BUT IT SURE WOULD BE GOOD TO PATCH THE OLD GUY *UP.*

FACT IS, SWEETIE, YOU'VE GOT US ALL *WRONG.* WHEN WE SEND OUT THE DOLTS WE AIN'T LOOKING FOR A *FIGHT*--WE'RE LOOKING FOR A *HOLY RELIC.*

A LITTLE *PIECE* OF GOD, TO MAKE HIM *WHOLE* AND *HAPPY.* SOMETHING THAT GOT BROKE *OFFA* HIM, LONG AGO.

TELL HER WHAT *HAPPENED,* KID.

...

AY LOST HIS *EYE.*

NOT A *REAL* EYE--THAT'S WHAT WE CALL *FIGURATIVE* SPEAKIN'--BUT IT'S SMALL AND *ROUND* SIMILAR-LIKE. WE BEEN HUNTING IT *YEARS.*

SAAAY--MAYBE IT'S TIME WE ASKED FOR SOME *HELP?*

HELP? Huh. IIIINTERESTING.

I MEAN...IT'D HAVE TO BE SOMEONE *SMART.* SOMEONE... *BRAVE* AND *CURIOUS.*

(THAT MEANS SOMEONE WITH A LOT OF *ASKS*)

SOMEONE WHO DIDN'T *MIND* LEAVING HOME FOR A WHILE-- TO *EXPLORE.*

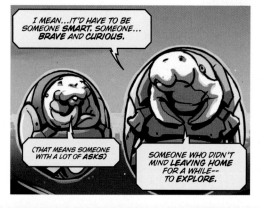

-≳Hmp≲- I DOUBT THAT'S *QORA.* I HEARD MONKS *HATE* TO FIND OUT *NEW* THINGS.

IS THAT *RIGHT,* SWEETIE? IS THAT THE *TRUTH* OF THE MONKS?

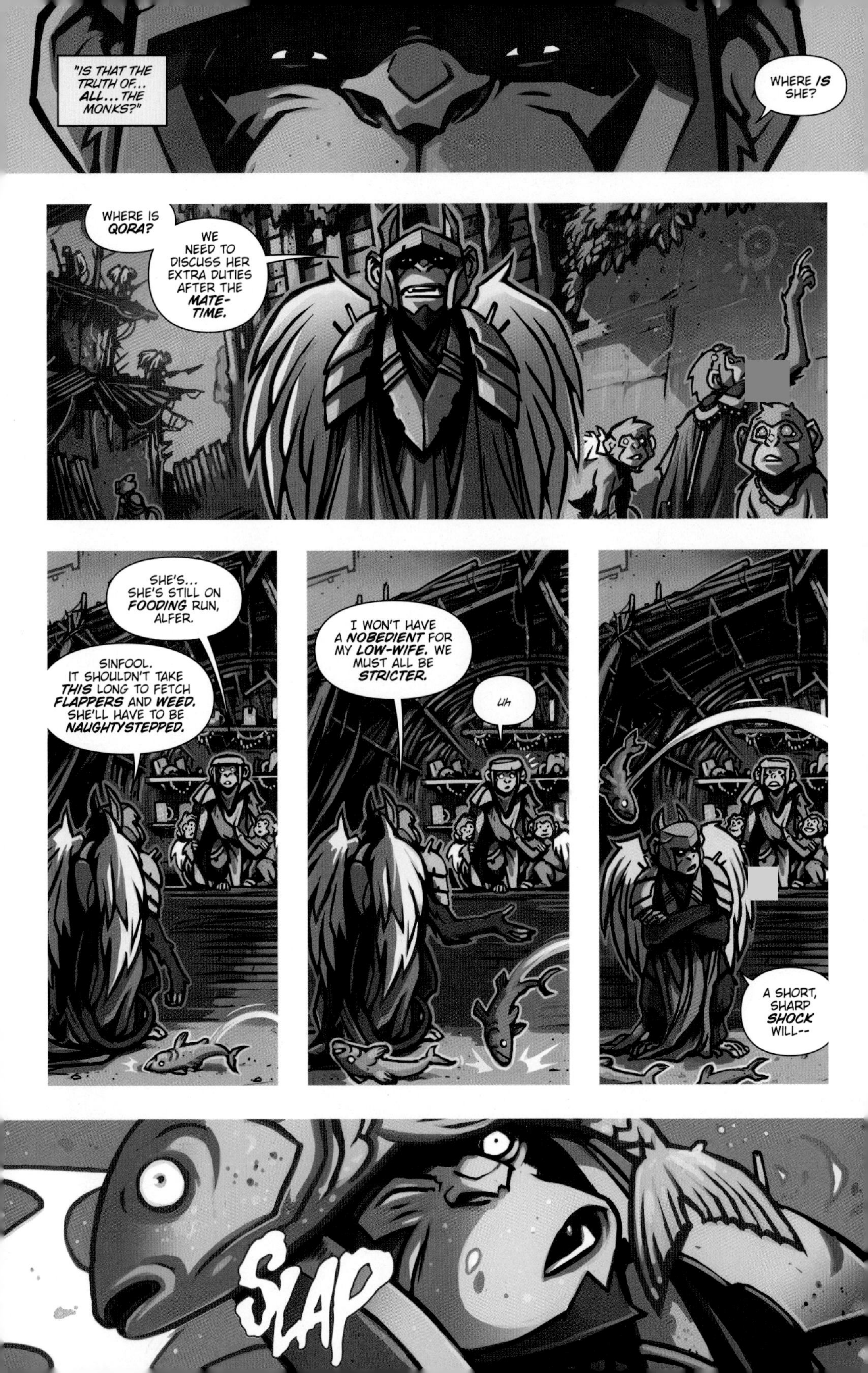
"IS THAT THE TRUTH OF... ALL... THE MONKS?"
WHERE IS SHE?
WHERE IS QORA?
WE NEED TO DISCUSS HER EXTRA DUTIES AFTER THE MATE-TIME.
SHE'S... SHE'S STILL ON FOODING RUN, ALFER.
SINFOOL. IT SHOULDN'T TAKE THIS LONG TO FETCH FLAPPERS AND WEED. SHE'LL HAVE TO BE NAUGHTYSTEPPED.
I WON'T HAVE A NOBEDIENT FOR MY LOW-WIFE. WE MUST ALL BE STRICTER.
Uh
A SHORT, SHARP SHOCK WILL--
SLAP

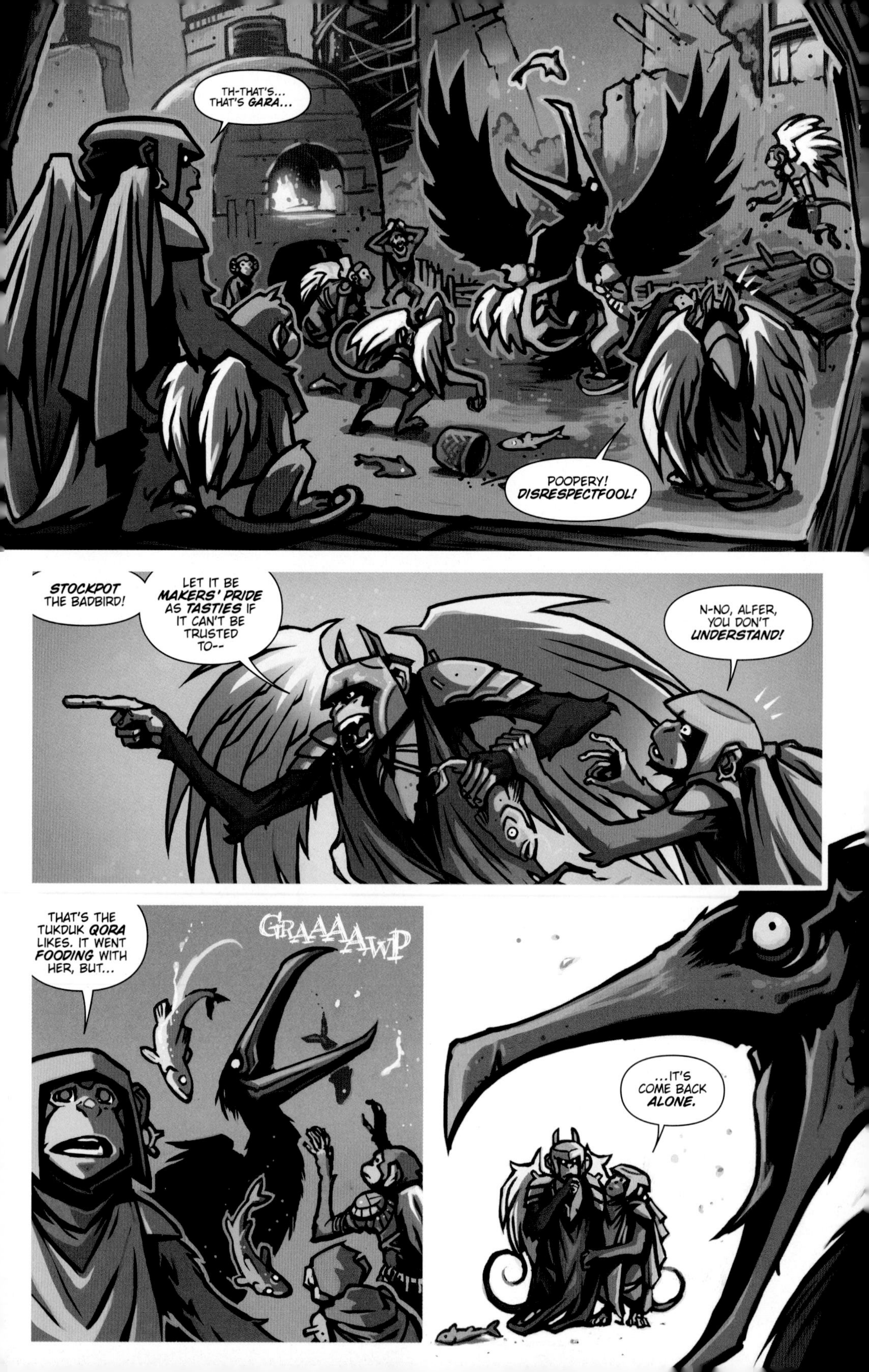

TH-THAT'S... THAT'S GARA...
POOPERY! DISRESPECTFOOL!
STOCKPOT THE BADBIRD!
LET IT BE MAKERS' PRIDE AS TASTIES IF IT CAN'T BE TRUSTED TO--
N-NO, ALFER, YOU DON'T UNDERSTAND!
THAT'S THE TUKDUK QORA LIKES. IT WENT FOODING WITH HER, BUT...
GRAAAAAWP
...IT'S COME BACK ALONE.

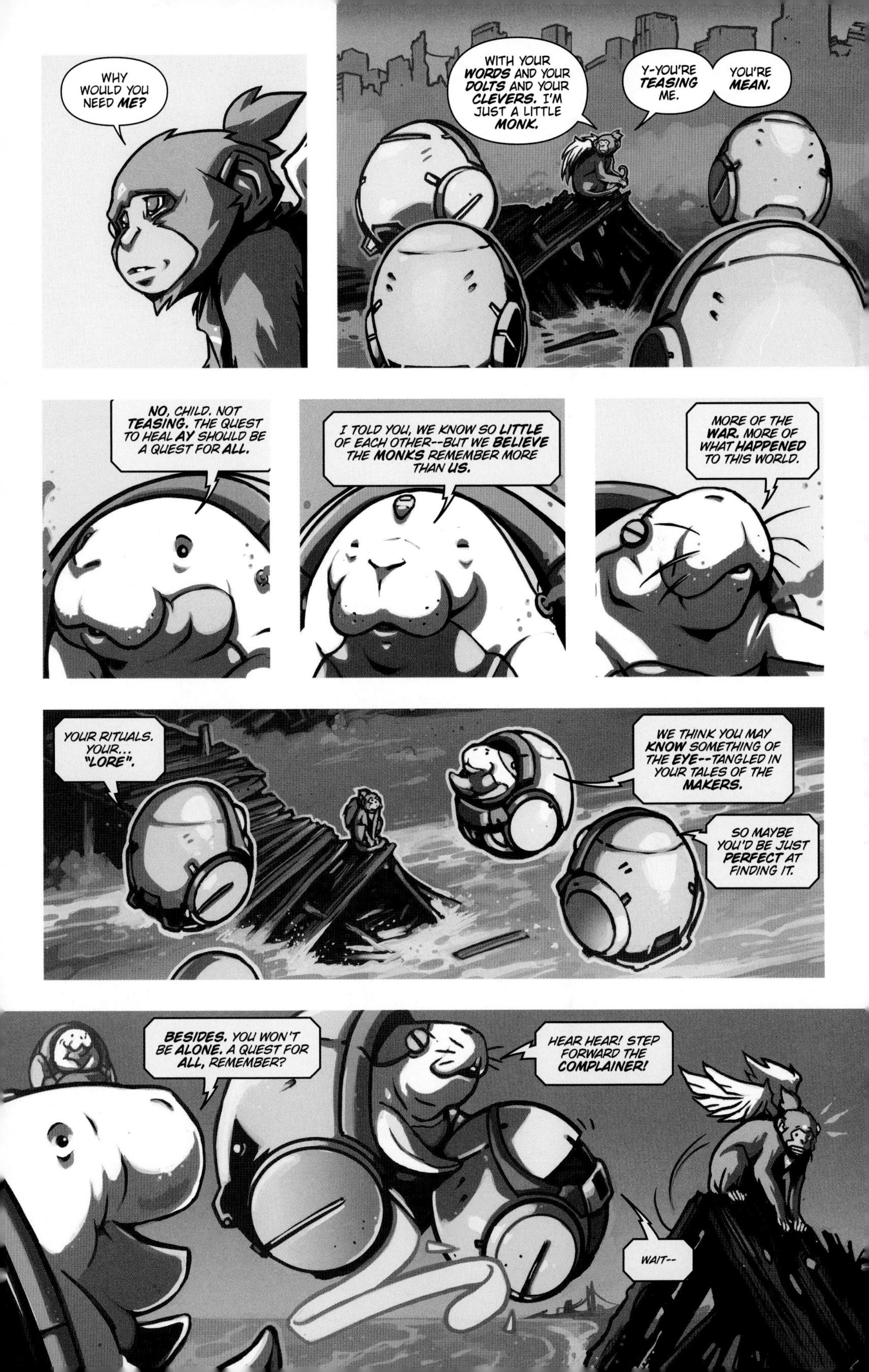
WHY WOULD YOU NEED ME?
WITH YOUR WORDS AND YOUR DOLTS AND YOUR CLEVERS. I'M JUST A LITTLE MONK.
Y-YOU'RE TEASING ME.
YOU'RE MEAN.
NO, CHILD. NOT TEASING. THE QUEST TO HEAL AY SHOULD BE A QUEST FOR ALL.
I TOLD YOU, WE KNOW SO LITTLE OF EACH OTHER--BUT WE BELIEVE THE MONKS REMEMBER MORE THAN US.
MORE OF THE WAR. MORE OF WHAT HAPPENED TO THIS WORLD.
YOUR RITUALS. YOUR... "LORE".
WE THINK YOU MAY KNOW SOMETHING OF THE EYE--TANGLED IN YOUR TALES OF THE MAKERS.
SO MAYBE YOU'D BE JUST PERFECT AT FINDING IT.
BESIDES. YOU WON'T BE ALONE. A QUEST FOR ALL, REMEMBER?
HEAR HEAR! STEP FORWARD THE COMPLAINER!
WAIT--

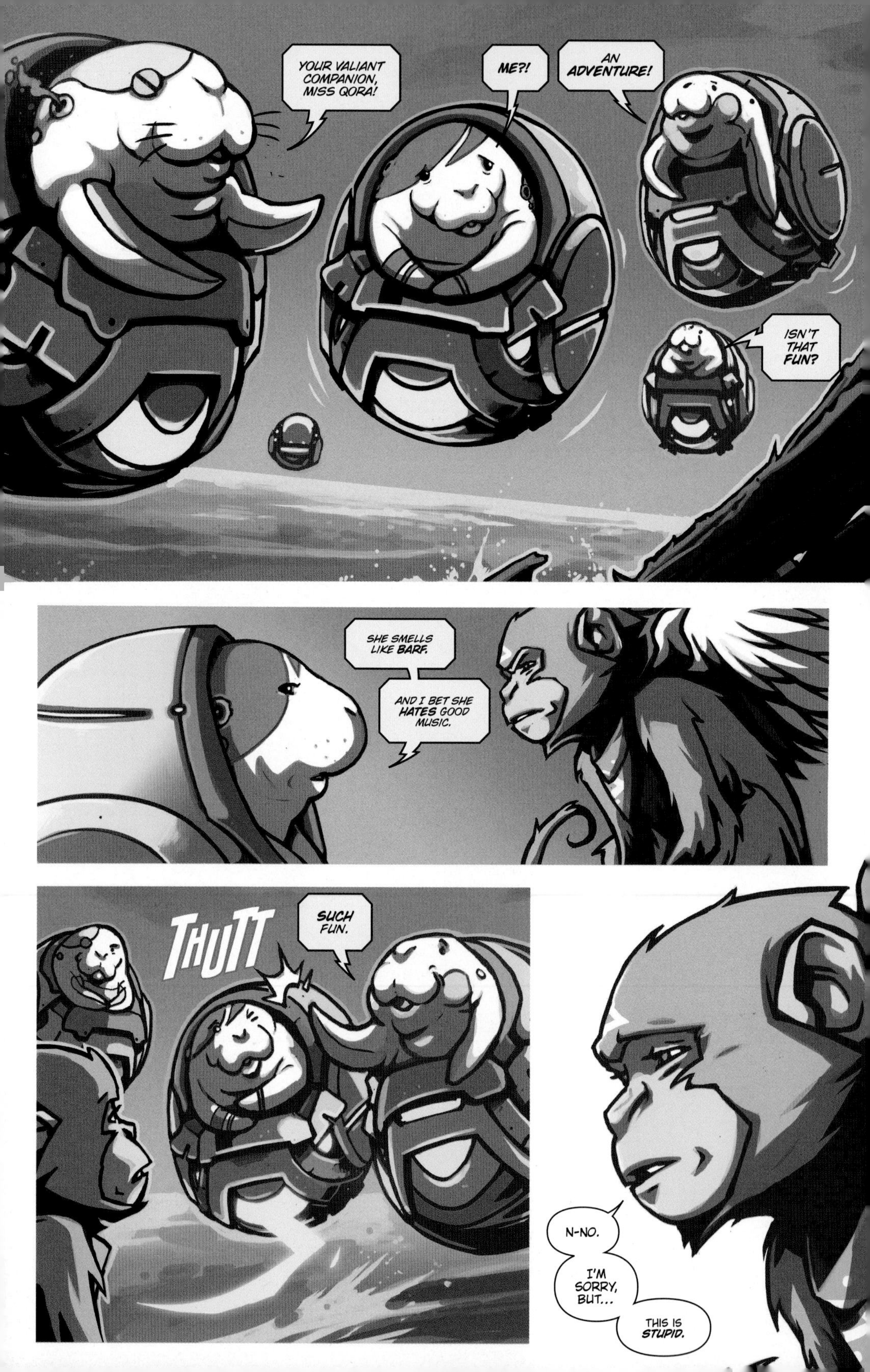
YOUR VALIANT COMPANION, MISS QORA!
ME?!
AN ADVENTURE!
ISN'T THAT FUN?
SHE SMELLS LIKE BARF.
AND I BET SHE HATES GOOD MUSIC.
THUTT
SUCH FUN.
N-NO.
I'M SORRY, BUT...
THIS IS STUPID.

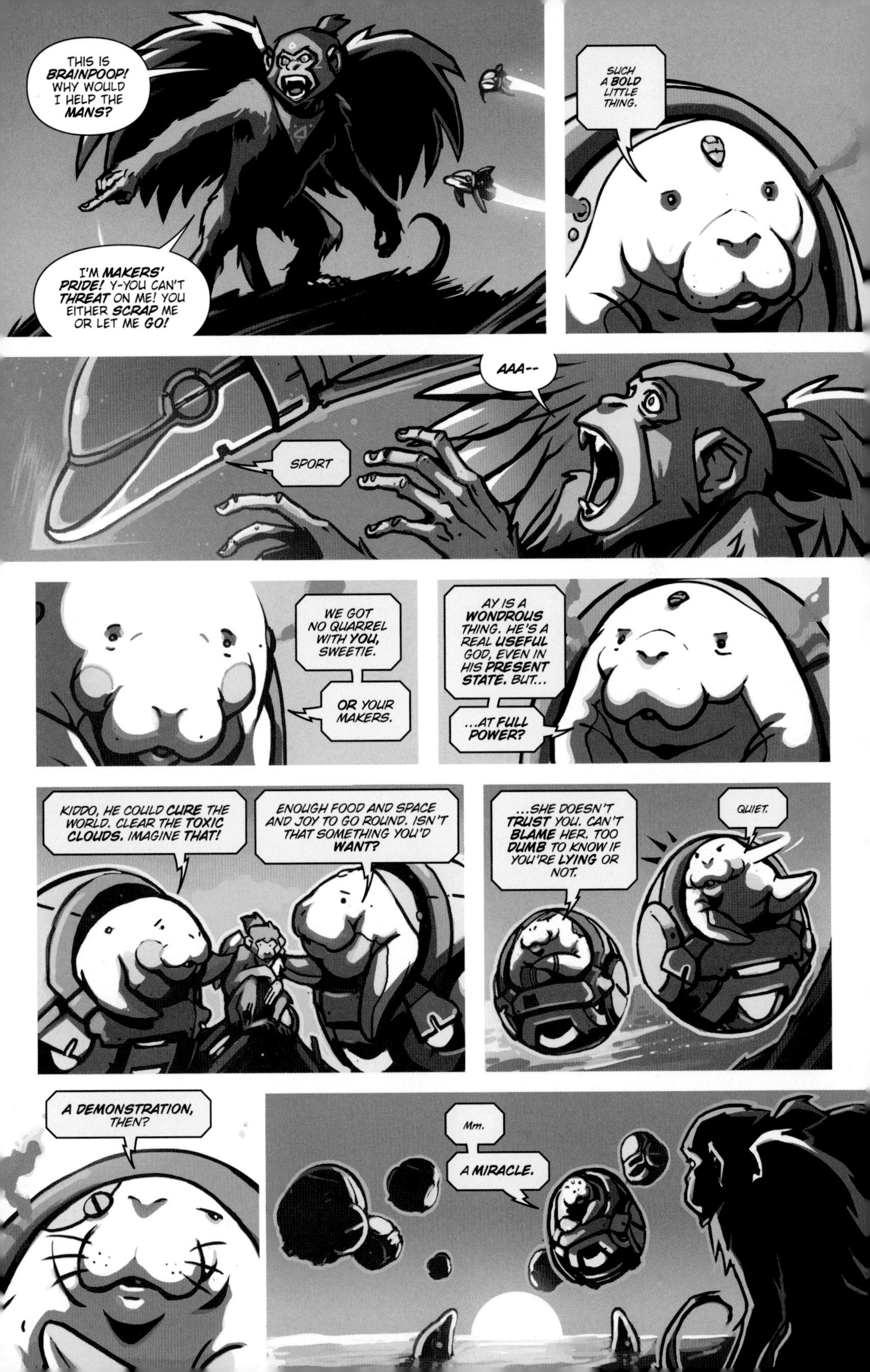
THIS IS BRAINPOOP! WHY WOULD I HELP THE MANS?
I'M MAKERS' PRIDE! Y-YOU CAN'T THREAT ON ME! YOU EITHER SCRAP ME OR LET ME GO!
SUCH A BOLD LITTLE THING.
AAA--
SPORT
WE GOT NO QUARREL WITH YOU, SWEETIE.
OR YOUR MAKERS.
AY IS A WONDROUS THING. HE'S A REAL USEFUL GOD, EVEN IN HIS PRESENT STATE. BUT...
...AT FULL POWER?
KIDDO, HE COULD CURE THE WORLD. CLEAR THE TOXIC CLOUDS. IMAGINE THAT!
ENOUGH FOOD AND SPACE AND JOY TO GO ROUND. ISN'T THAT SOMETHING YOU'D WANT?
...SHE DOESN'T TRUST YOU. CAN'T BLAME HER. TOO DUMB TO KNOW IF YOU'RE LYING OR NOT.
QUIET.
A DEMONSTRATION, THEN?
Mm.
A MIRACLE.

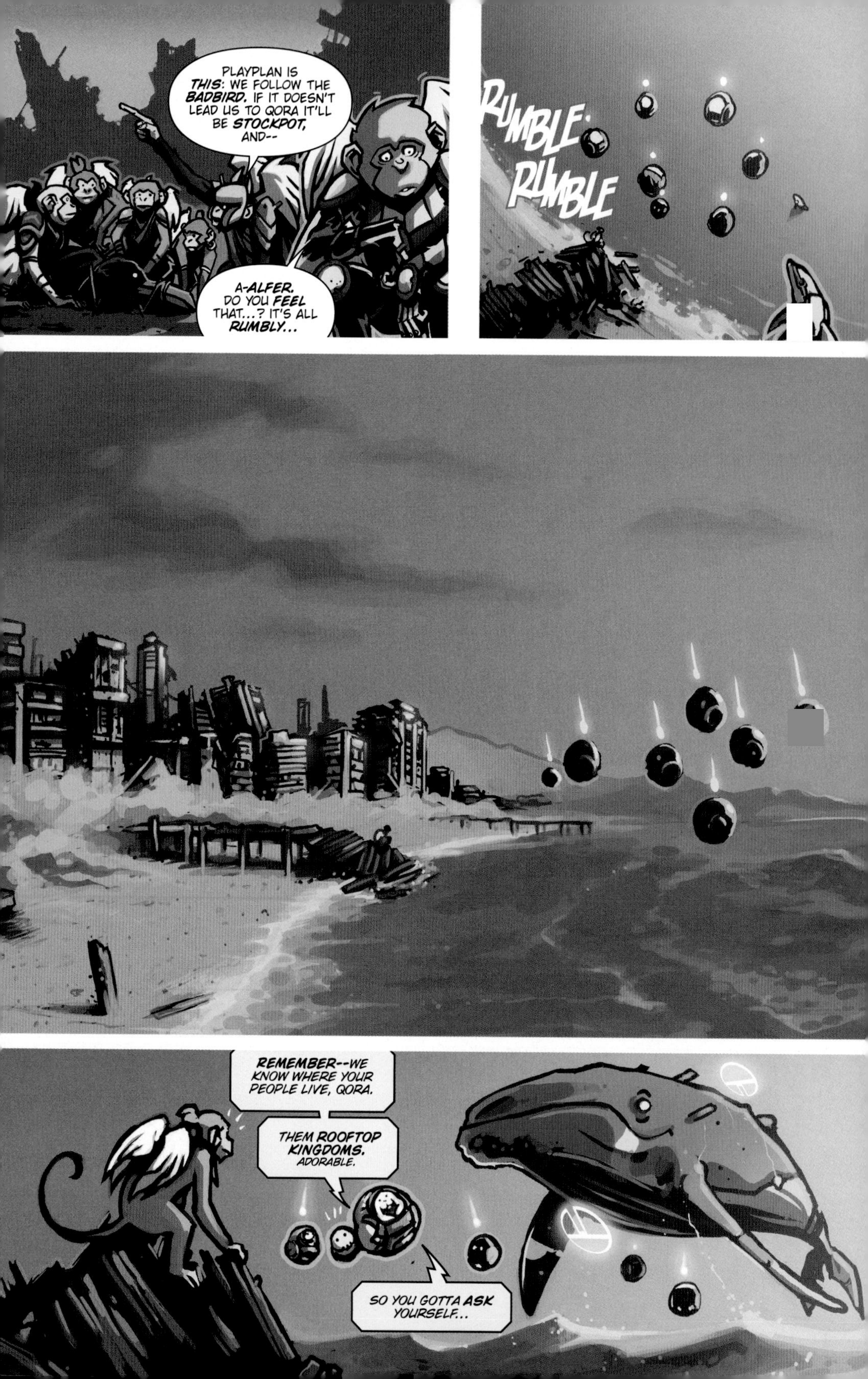
PLAYPLAN IS THIS: WE FOLLOW THE BADBIRD. IF IT DOESN'T LEAD US TO QORA IT'LL BE STOCKPOT, AND--
A-ALFER. DO YOU FEEL THAT...? IT'S ALL RUMBLY...
RUMBLE
RUMBLE
REMEMBER--WE KNOW WHERE YOUR PEOPLE LIVE, QORA.
THEM ROOFTOP KINGDOMS. ADORABLE.
SO YOU GOTTA ASK YOURSELF...

OH. NO.

NO NO NO NO

THE BAY...

MAKERS KEEP US...

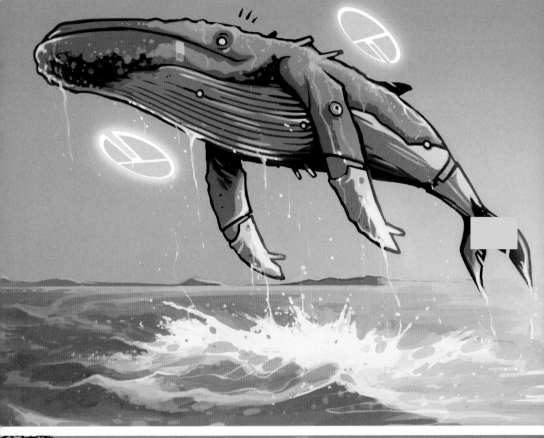

"IF WE TRULY MEANT TO HARM YOU, WHY WOULD WE SEND THE IDIOT DOLTS, huh?"

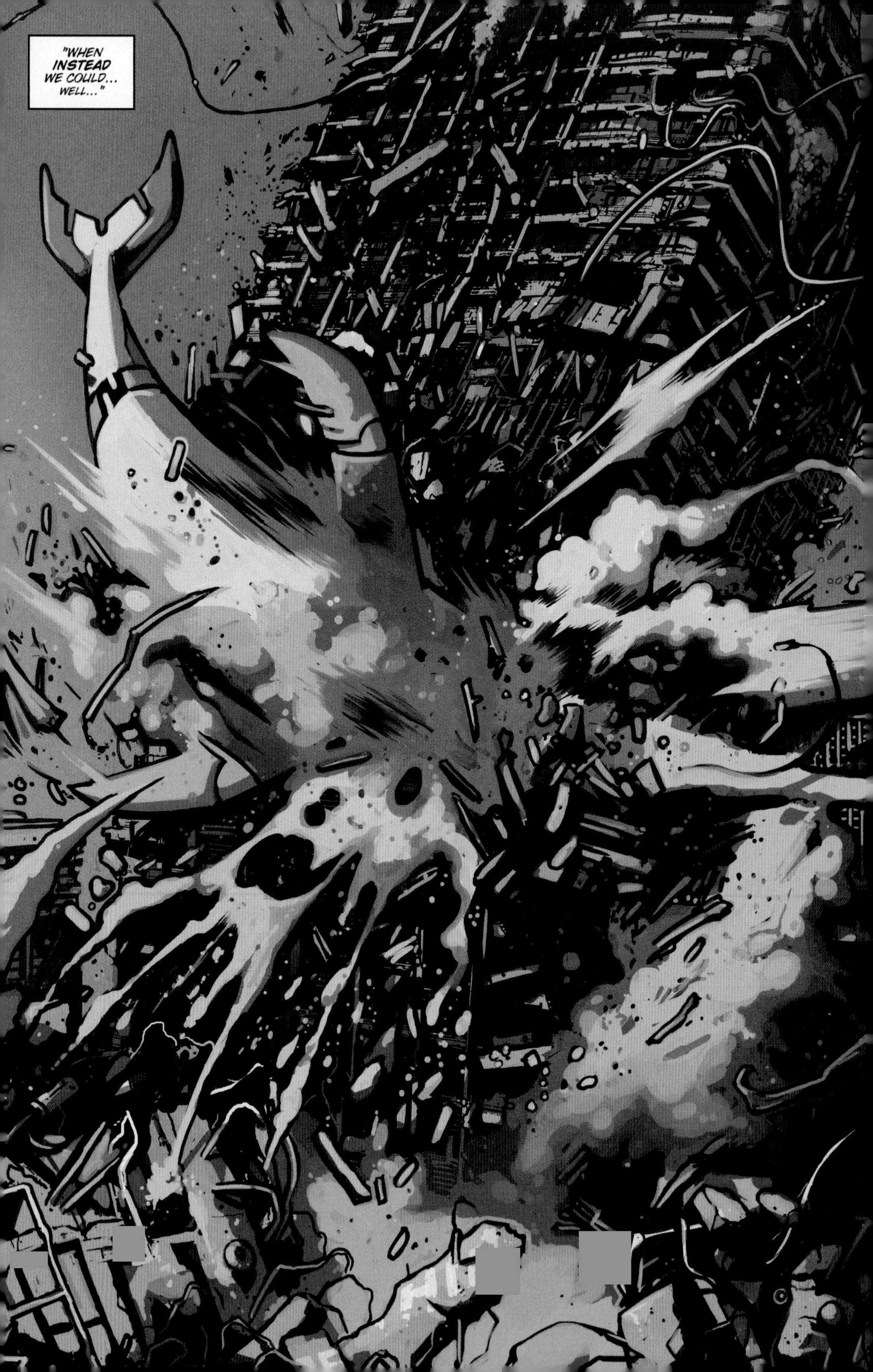
"WHEN INSTEAD WE COULD... WELL..."

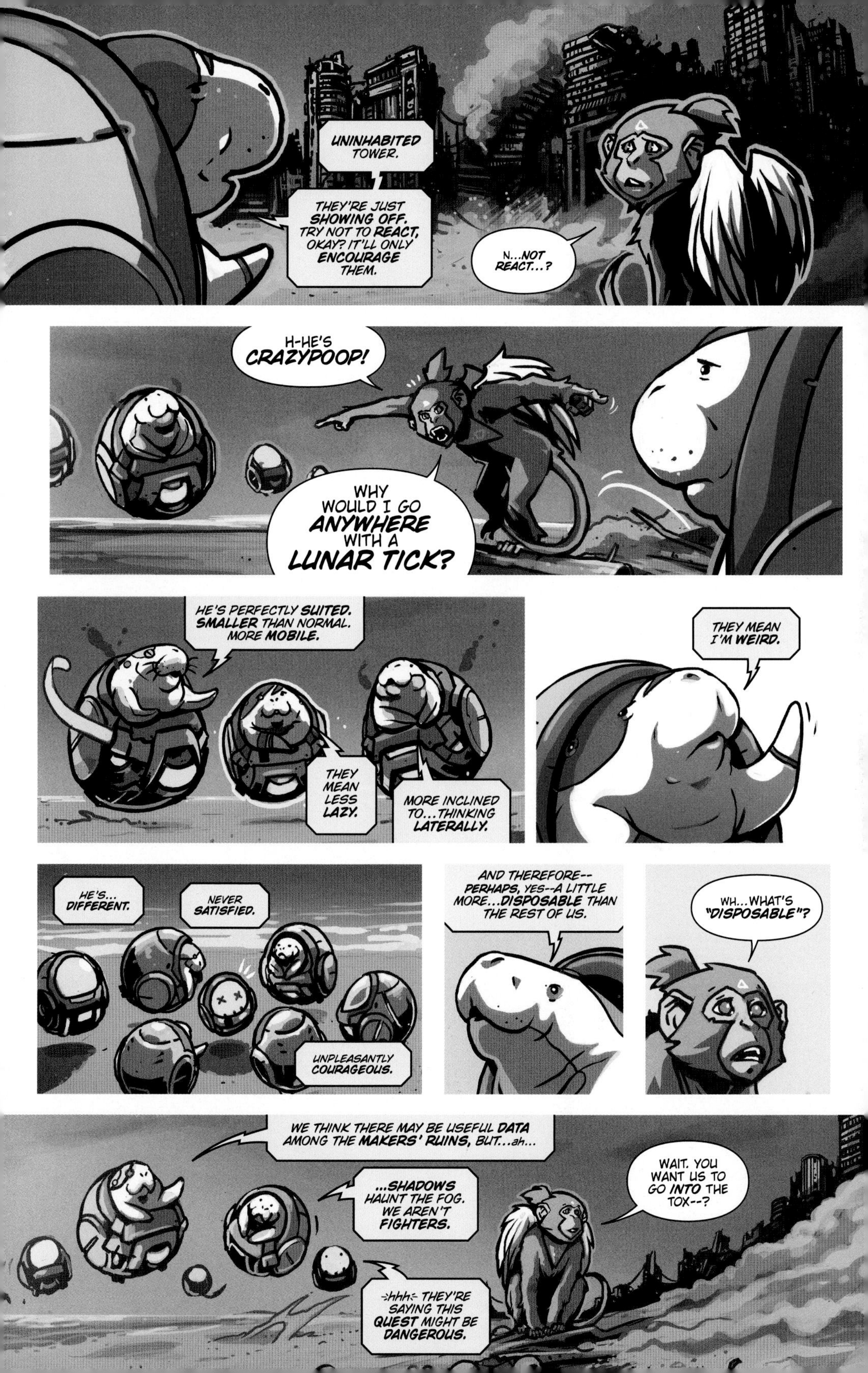
UNINHABITED TOWER.
THEY'RE JUST SHOWING OFF. TRY NOT TO REACT, OKAY? IT'LL ONLY ENCOURAGE THEM.
N...NOT REACT...?
H-HE'S CRAZYPOOP!
WHY WOULD I GO ANYWHERE WITH A LUNAR TICK?
HE'S PERFECTLY SUITED. SMALLER THAN NORMAL. MORE MOBILE.
THEY MEAN LESS LAZY.
MORE INCLINED TO...THINKING LATERALLY.
THEY MEAN I'M WEIRD.
HE'S... DIFFERENT.
NEVER SATISFIED.
UNPLEASANTLY COURAGEOUS.
AND THEREFORE--PERHAPS, YES--A LITTLE MORE...DISPOSABLE THAN THE REST OF US.
WH...WHAT'S "DISPOSABLE"?
WE THINK THERE MAY BE USEFUL DATA AMONG THE MAKERS' RUINS, BUT...ah...
...SHADOWS HAUNT THE FOG. WE AREN'T FIGHTERS.
WAIT. YOU WANT US TO GO INTO THE TOX--?
<hhh< THEY'RE SAYING THIS QUEST MIGHT BE DANGEROUS.

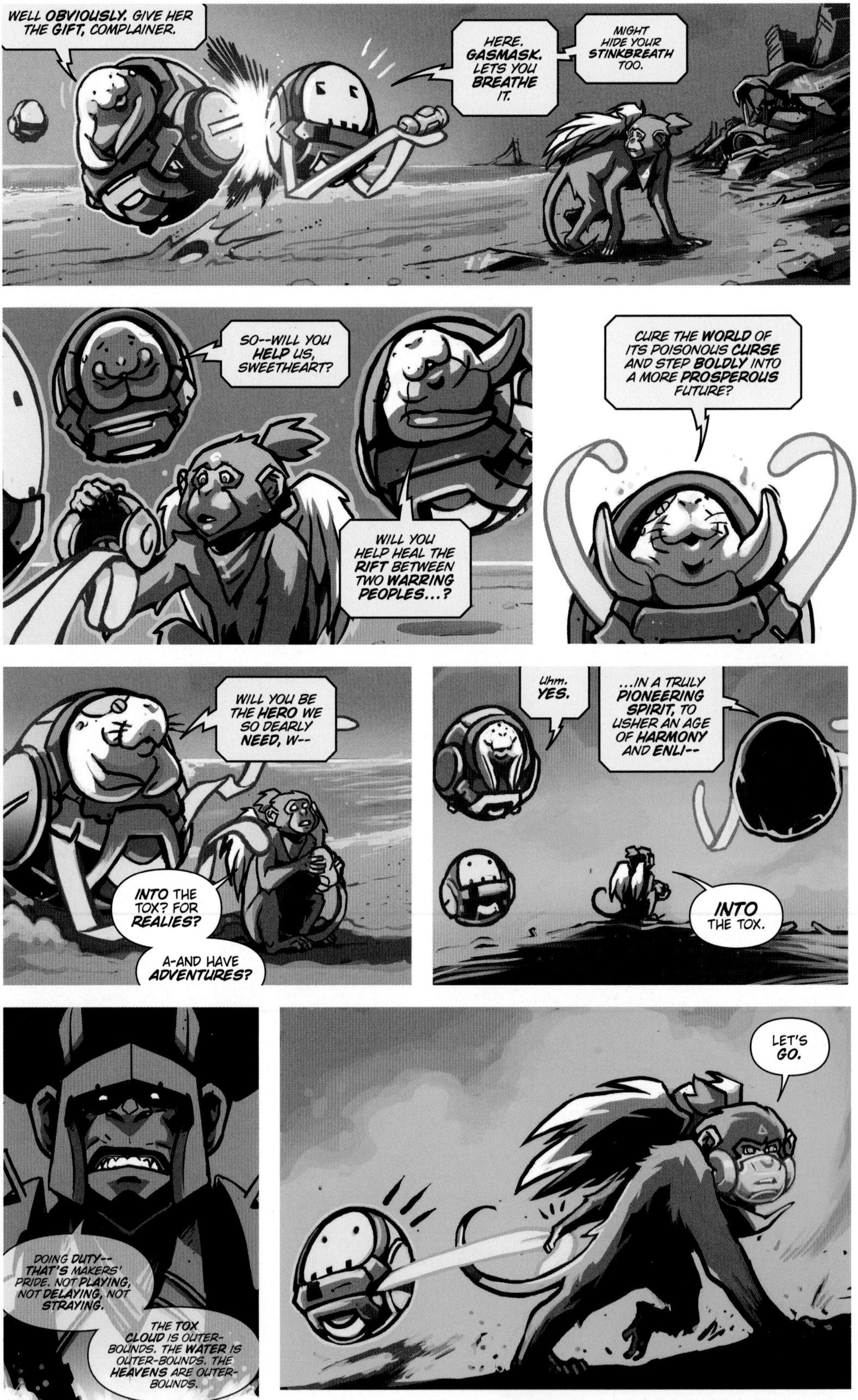

WELL OBVIOUSLY. GIVE HER THE GIFT, COMPLAINER.
HERE. GASMASK. LETS YOU BREATHE IT.
MIGHT HIDE YOUR STINKBREATH TOO.
SO--WILL YOU HELP US, SWEETHEART?
WILL YOU HELP HEAL THE RIFT BETWEEN TWO WARRING PEOPLES...?
CURE THE WORLD OF ITS POISONOUS CURSE AND STEP BOLDLY INTO A MORE PROSPEROUS FUTURE?
WILL YOU BE THE HERO WE SO DEARLY NEED, W--
INTO THE TOX? FOR REALIES?
A-AND HAVE ADVENTURES?
Uhm. YES.
...IN A TRULY PIONEERING SPIRIT, TO USHER AN AGE OF HARMONY AND ENLI--
INTO THE TOX.
DOING DUTY--THAT'S MAKERS' PRIDE. NOT PLAYING, NOT DELAYING, NOT STRAYING.
THE TOX CLOUD IS OUTER-BOUNDS. THE WATER IS OUTER-BOUNDS. THE HEAVENS ARE OUTER-BOUNDS.
LET'S GO.

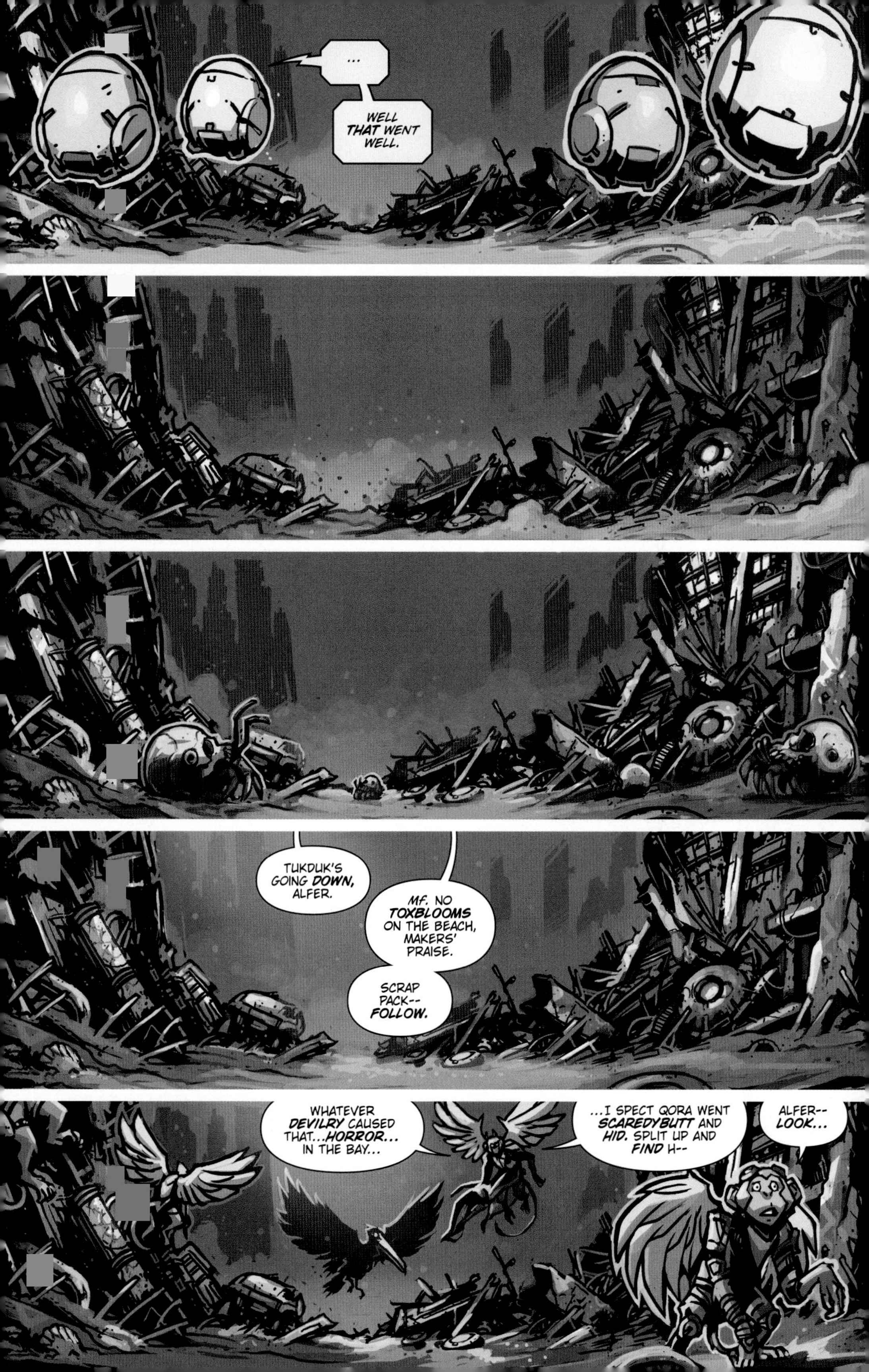
...
WELL THAT WENT WELL.
TUKDUK'S GOING DOWN, ALFER.
MF. NO TOXBLOOMS ON THE BEACH, MAKERS' PRAISE.
SCRAP PACK-- FOLLOW.
WHATEVER DEVILRY CAUSED THAT...HORROR... IN THE BAY...
...I SPECT QORA WENT SCAREDYBUTT AND HID. SPLIT UP AND FIND H--
ALFER-- LOOK...

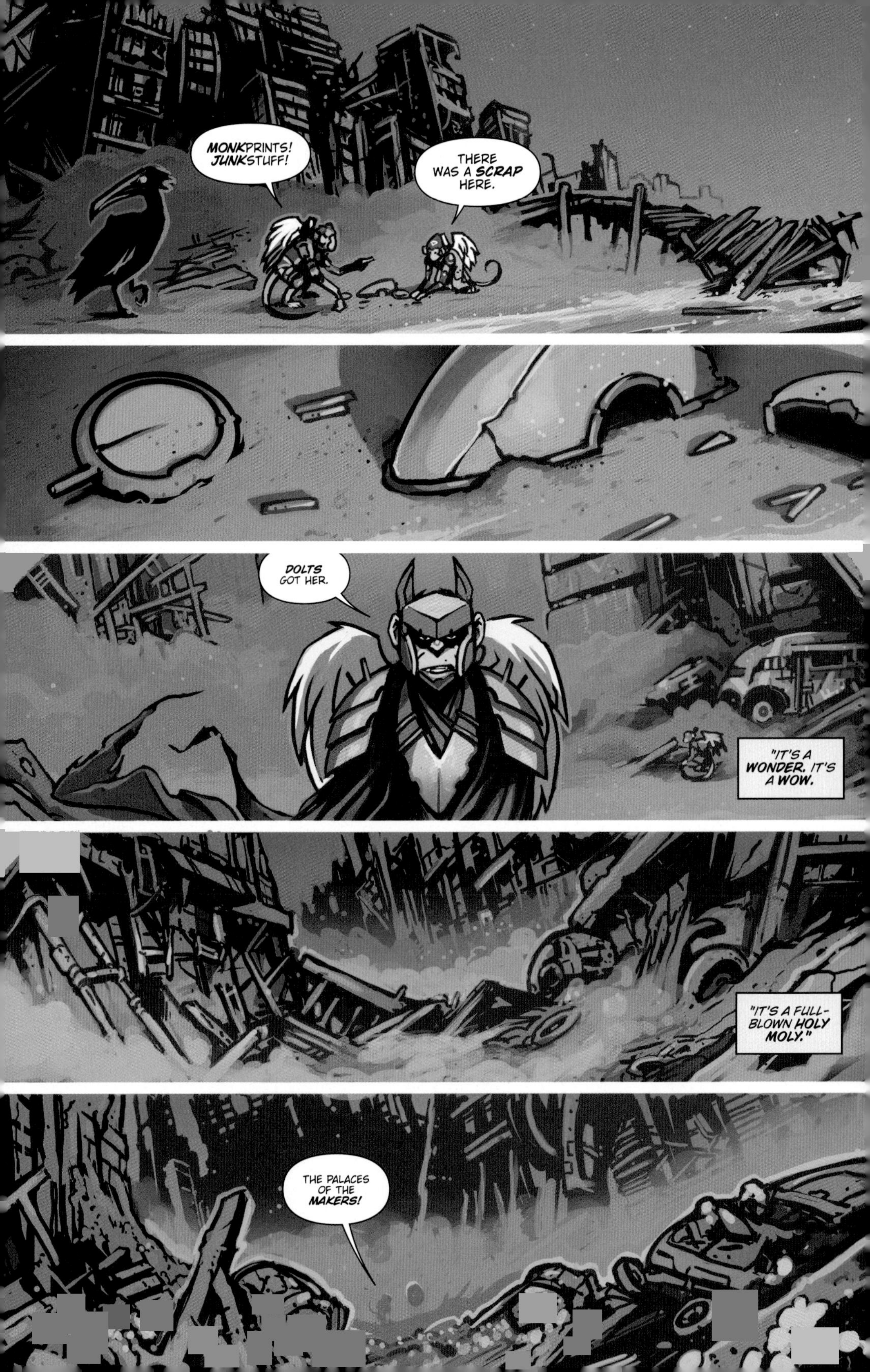
MONKPRINTS! JUNKSTUFF!
THERE WAS A SCRAP HERE.
DOLTS GOT HER.
"IT'S A WONDER. IT'S A WOW.
"IT'S A FULL-BLOWN HOLY MOLY."
THE PALACES OF THE MAKERS!

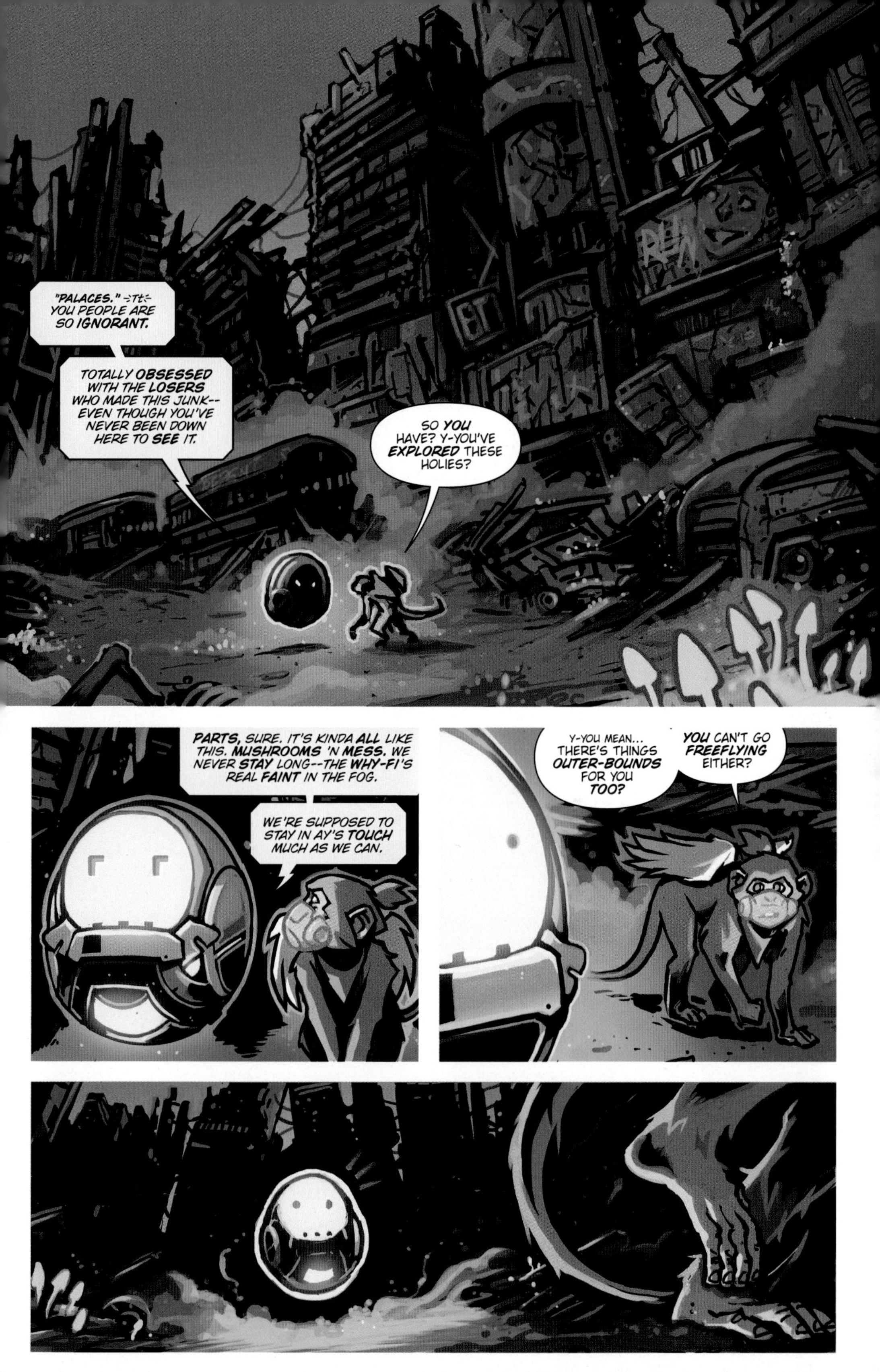
"PALACES." ~TT~ YOU PEOPLE ARE SO IGNORANT.
TOTALLY OBSESSED WITH THE LOSERS WHO MADE THIS JUNK-- EVEN THOUGH YOU'VE NEVER BEEN DOWN HERE TO SEE IT.
SO YOU HAVE? Y-YOU'VE EXPLORED THESE HOLIES?
PARTS, SURE. IT'S KINDA ALL LIKE THIS. MUSHROOMS 'N MESS. WE NEVER STAY LONG--THE WHY-FI'S REAL FAINT IN THE FOG.
WE'RE SUPPOSED TO STAY IN AY'S TOUCH MUCH AS WE CAN.
Y-YOU MEAN... THERE'S THINGS OUTER-BOUNDS FOR YOU TOO?
YOU CAN'T GO FREEFLYING EITHER?

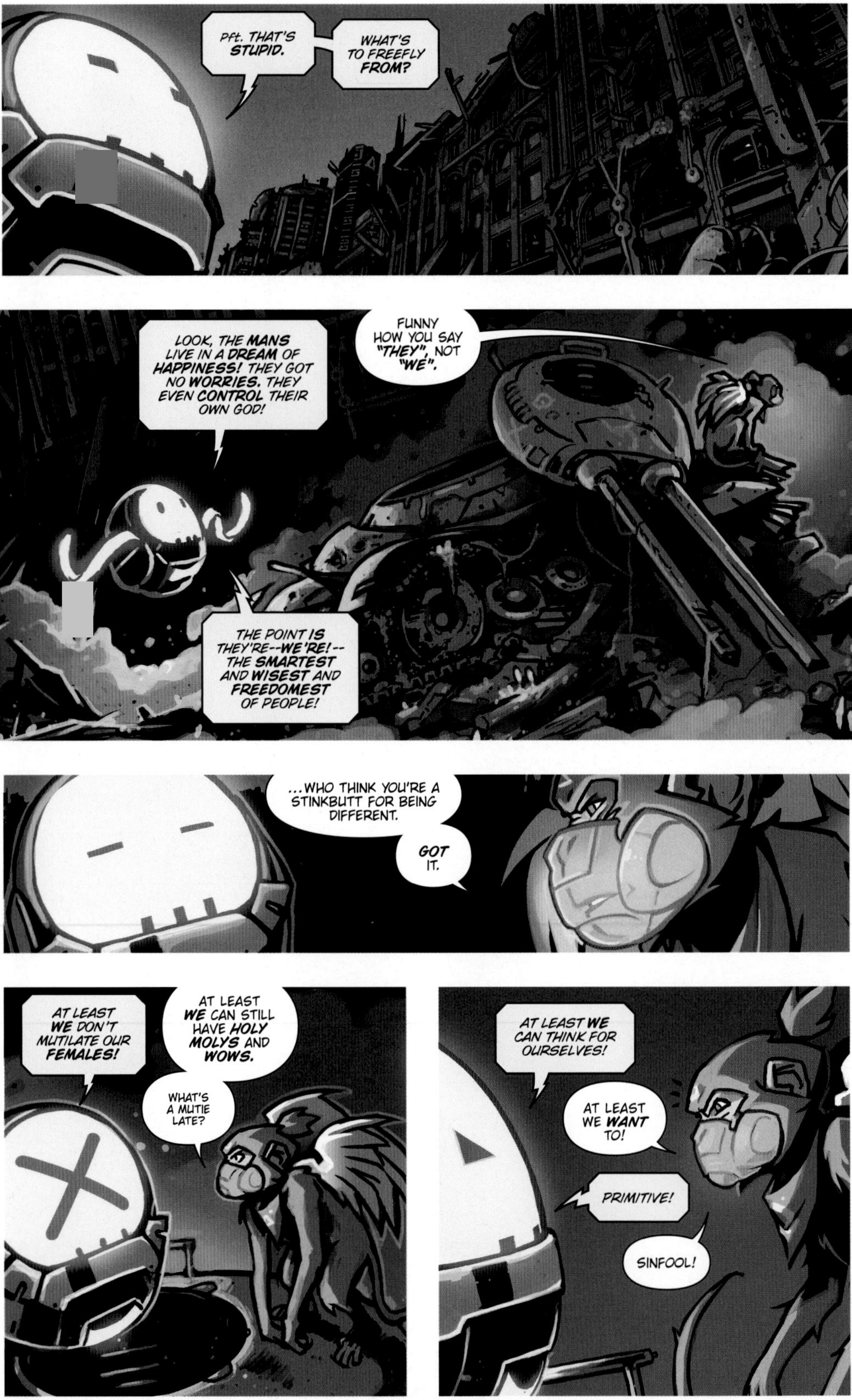

Pft. THAT'S STUPID.
WHAT'S TO FREEFLY FROM?
LOOK, THE MANS LIVE IN A DREAM OF HAPPINESS! THEY GOT NO WORRIES. THEY EVEN CONTROL THEIR OWN GOD!
FUNNY HOW YOU SAY "THEY", NOT "WE".
THE POINT IS THEY'RE--WE'RE!--THE SMARTEST AND WISEST AND FREEDOMEST OF PEOPLE!
...WHO THINK YOU'RE A STINKBUTT FOR BEING DIFFERENT.
GOT IT.
AT LEAST WE DON'T MUTILATE OUR FEMALES!
AT LEAST WE CAN STILL HAVE HOLY MOLYS AND WOWS.
WHAT'S A MUTIE LATE?
AT LEAST WE CAN THINK FOR OURSELVES!
AT LEAST WE WANT TO!
PRIMITIVE!
SINFOOL!

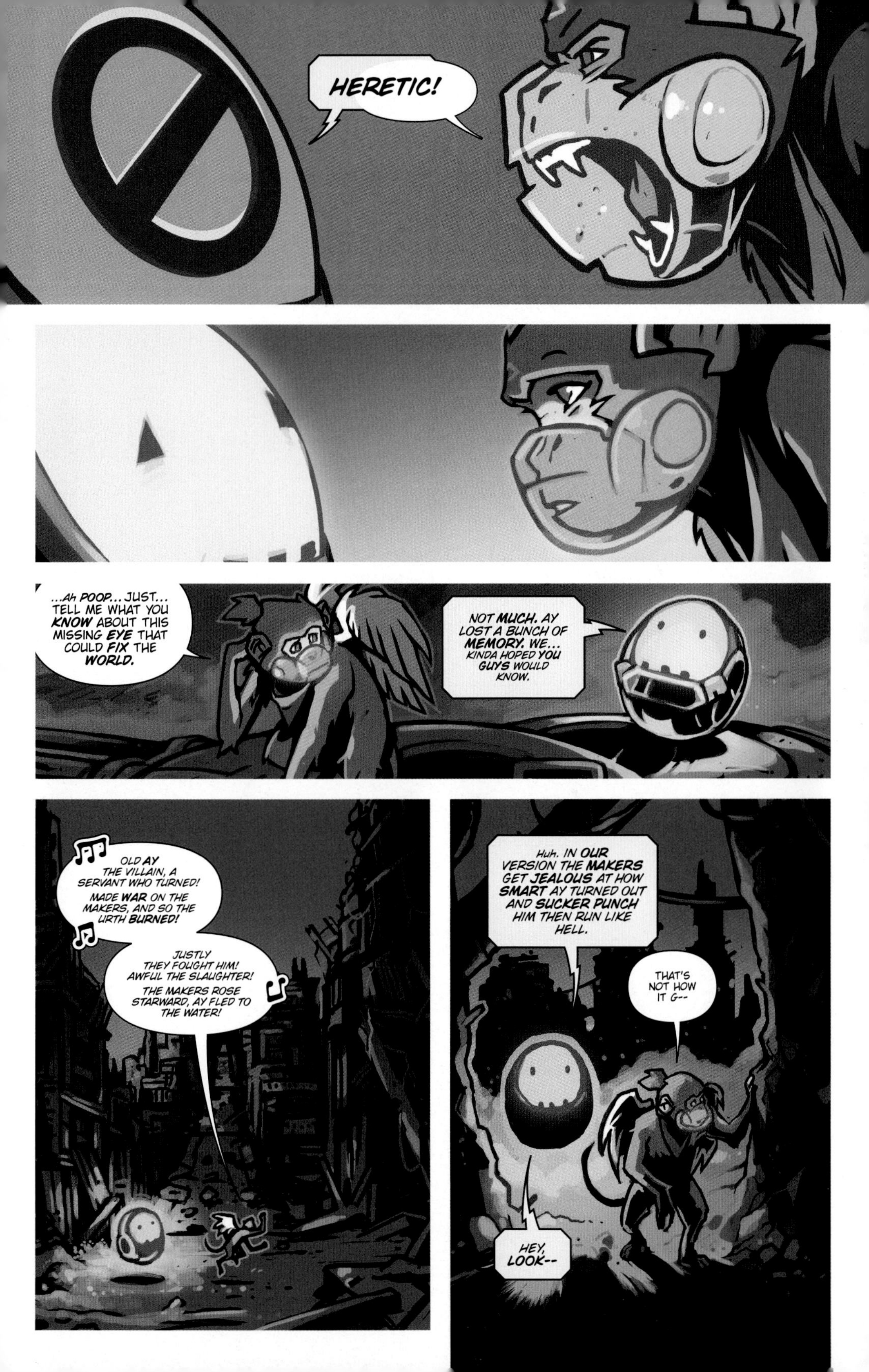
HERETIC!
...Ah POOP... JUST... TELL ME WHAT YOU KNOW ABOUT THIS MISSING EYE THAT COULD FIX THE WORLD.
NOT MUCH. AY LOST A BUNCH OF MEMORY. WE... KINDA HOPED YOU GUYS WOULD KNOW.
OLD AY THE VILLAIN, A SERVANT WHO TURNED! MADE WAR ON THE MAKERS, AND SO THE URTH BURNED!
JUSTLY THEY FOUGHT HIM! AWFUL THE SLAUGHTER! THE MAKERS ROSE STARWARD, AY FLED TO THE WATER!
Huh. IN OUR VERSION THE MAKERS GET JEALOUS AT HOW SMART AY TURNED OUT AND SUCKER PUNCH HIM THEN RUN LIKE HELL.
THAT'S NOT HOW IT G--
HEY, LOOK--

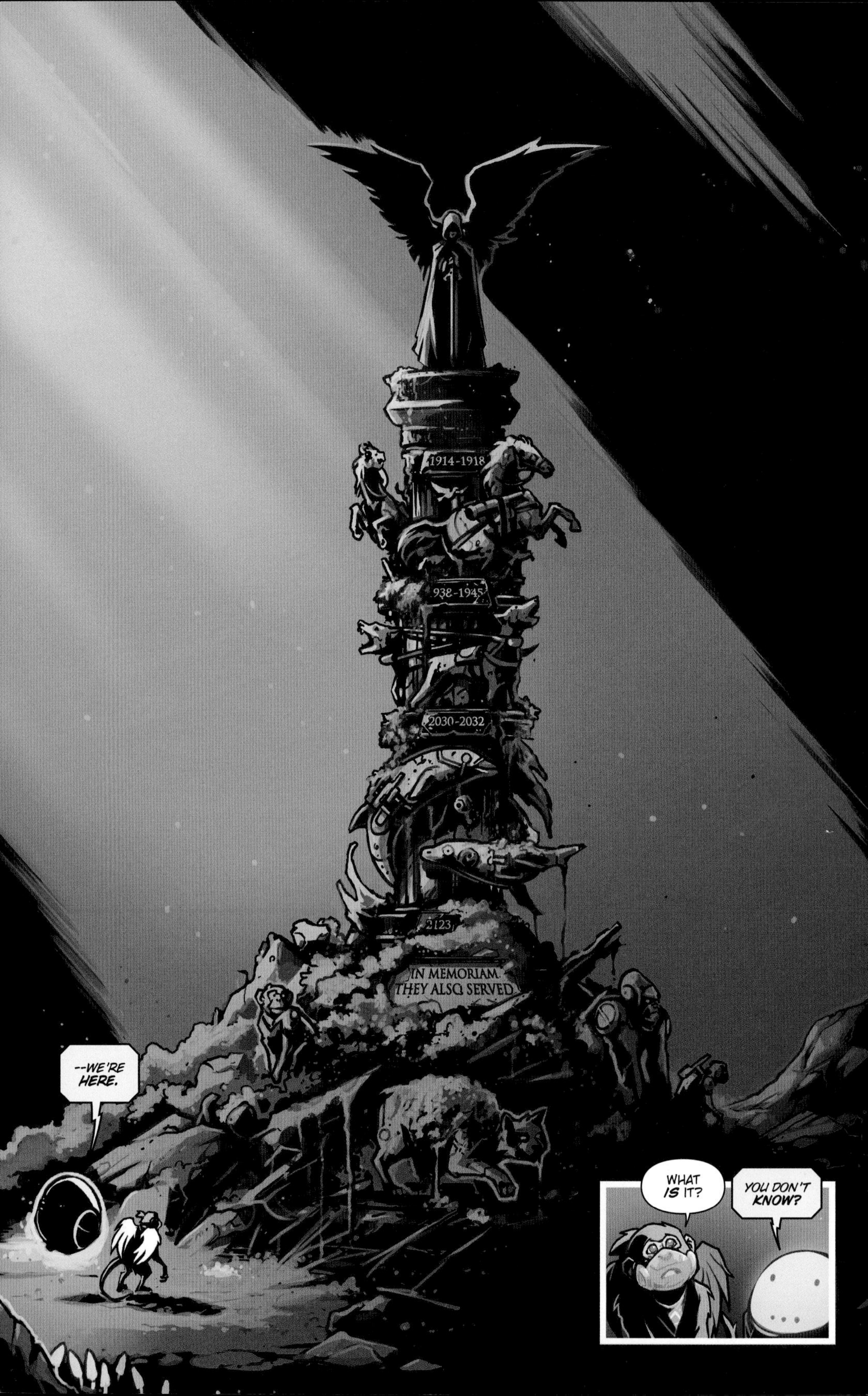
1914-1918
938-1945
2030-2032
2123
IN MEMORIAM
THEY ALSO SERVED
--WE'RE HERE.
WHAT IS IT?
YOU DON'T KNOW?

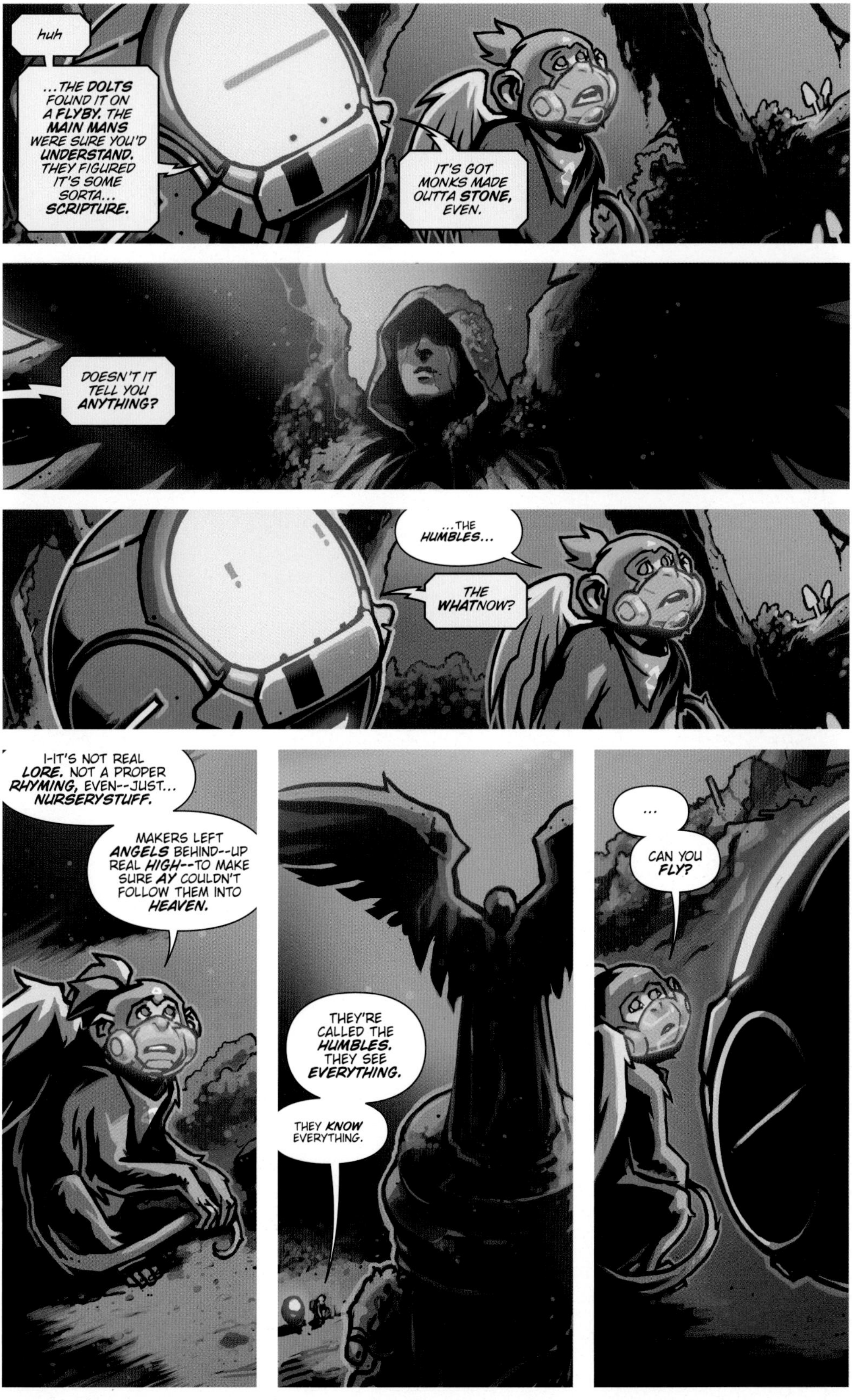
huh
...THE DOLTS FOUND IT ON A FLYBY. THE MAIN MANS WERE SURE YOU'D UNDERSTAND. THEY FIGURED IT'S SOME SORTA... SCRIPTURE.
IT'S GOT MONKS MADE OUTTA STONE, EVEN.
DOESN'T IT TELL YOU ANYTHING?
...THE HUMBLES...
THE WHATNOW?
I-IT'S NOT REAL LORE. NOT A PROPER RHYMING, EVEN--JUST... NURSERYSTUFF.
MAKERS LEFT ANGELS BEHIND--UP REAL HIGH--TO MAKE SURE AY COULDN'T FOLLOW THEM INTO HEAVEN.
THEY'RE CALLED THE HUMBLES. THEY SEE EVERYTHING.
THEY KNOW EVERYTHING.
...
CAN YOU FLY?

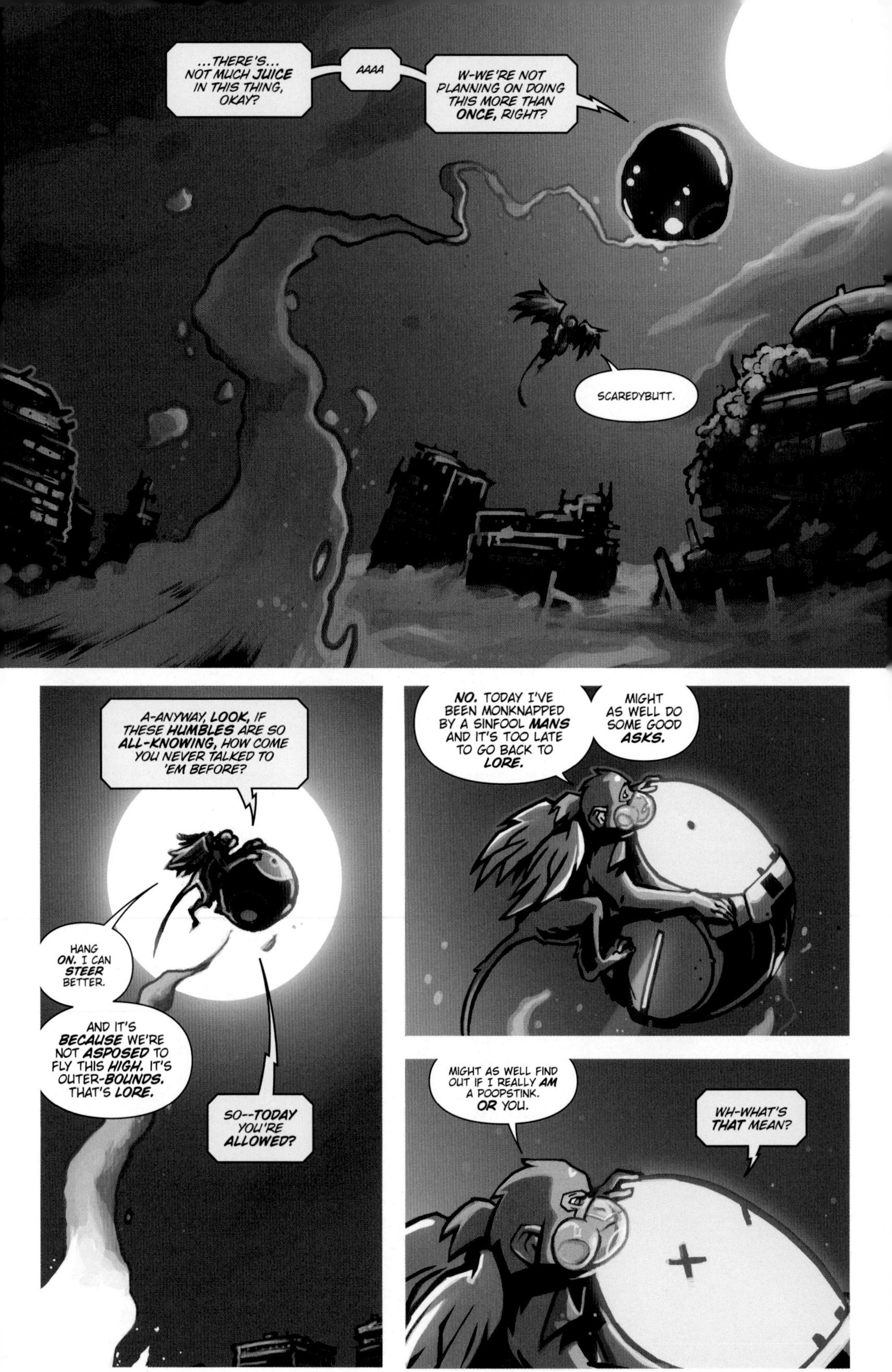
...THERE'S... NOT MUCH JUICE IN THIS THING, OKAY?
AAAA
W-WE'RE NOT PLANNING ON DOING THIS MORE THAN ONCE, RIGHT?
SCAREDYBUTT.
A-ANYWAY, LOOK, IF THESE HUMBLES ARE SO ALL-KNOWING, HOW COME YOU NEVER TALKED TO 'EM BEFORE?
HANG ON. I CAN STEER BETTER.
AND IT'S BECAUSE WE'RE NOT ASPOSED TO FLY THIS HIGH. IT'S OUTER-BOUNDS. THAT'S LORE.
SO--TODAY YOU'RE ALLOWED?
NO. TODAY I'VE BEEN MONKNAPPED BY A SINFOOL MANS AND IT'S TOO LATE TO GO BACK TO LORE.
MIGHT AS WELL DO SOME GOOD ASKS.
MIGHT AS WELL FIND OUT IF I REALLY AM A POOPSTINK. OR YOU.
WH-WHAT'S THAT MEAN?

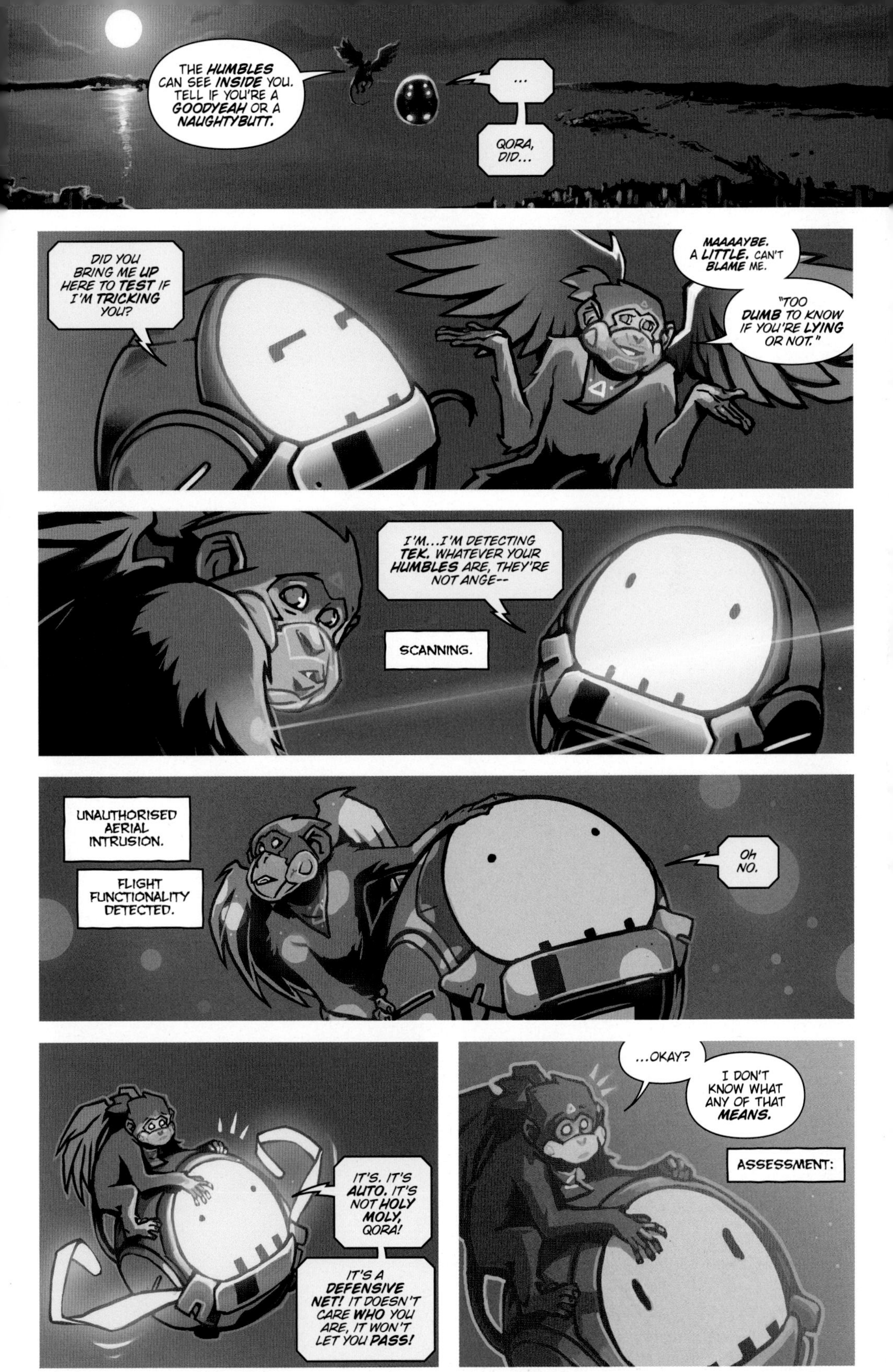
THE HUMBLES CAN SEE INSIDE YOU. TELL IF YOU'RE A GOODYEAH OR A NAUGHTYBUTT.
...
QORA, DID...
DID YOU BRING ME UP HERE TO TEST IF I'M TRICKING YOU?
MAAAAYBE. A LITTLE. CAN'T BLAME ME.
"TOO DUMB TO KNOW IF YOU'RE LYING OR NOT."
I'M...I'M DETECTING TEK. WHATEVER YOUR HUMBLES ARE, THEY'RE NOT ANGE--
SCANNING.
UNAUTHORISED AERIAL INTRUSION.
FLIGHT FUNCTIONALITY DETECTED.
OH NO.
IT'S. IT'S AUTO. IT'S NOT HOLY MOLY, QORA!
IT'S A DEFENSIVE NET! IT DOESN'T CARE WHO YOU ARE, IT WON'T LET YOU PASS!
...OKAY?
I DON'T KNOW WHAT ANY OF THAT MEANS.
ASSESSMENT:

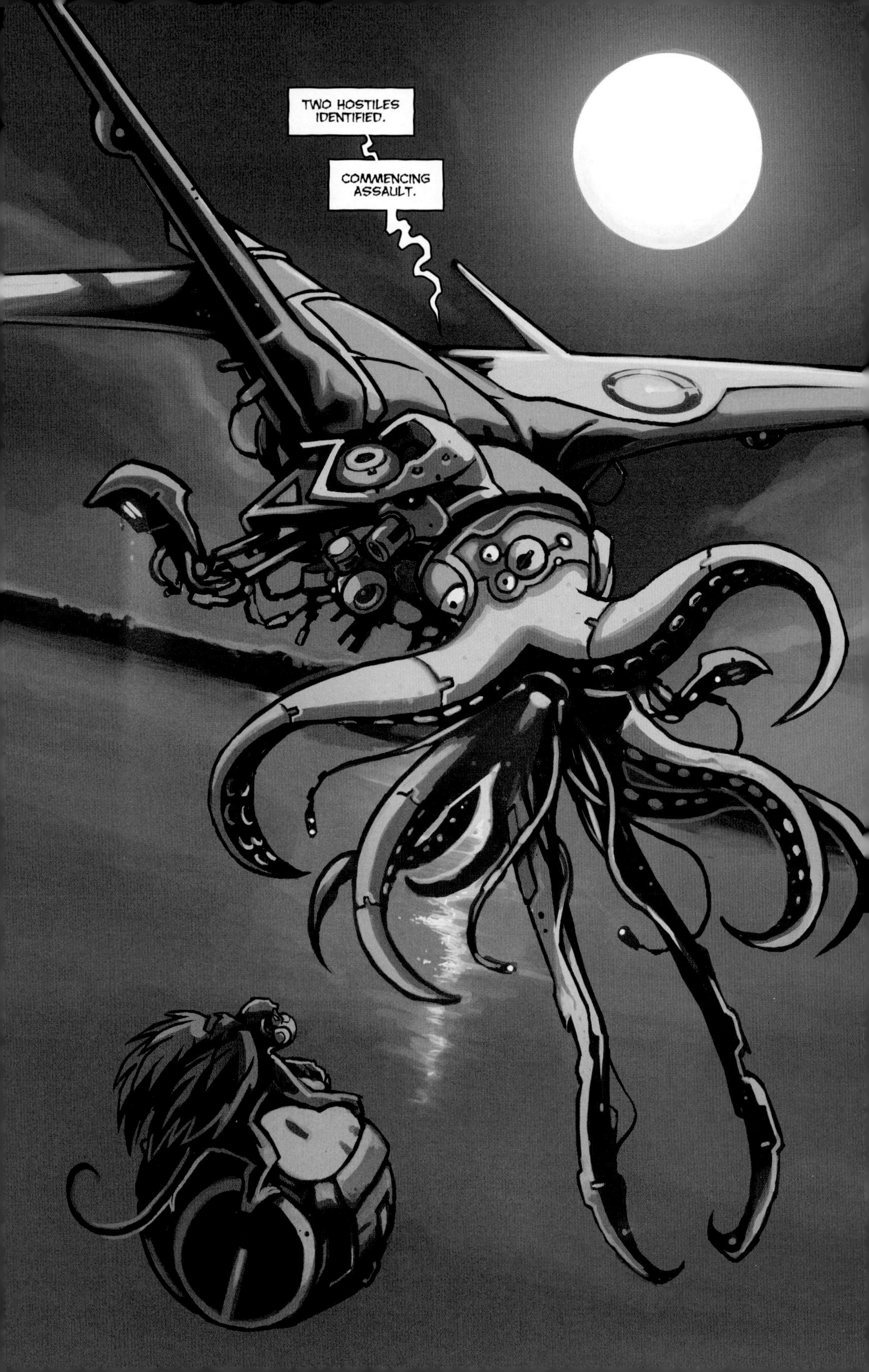
TWO HOSTILES IDENTIFIED.
COMMENCING ASSAULT.

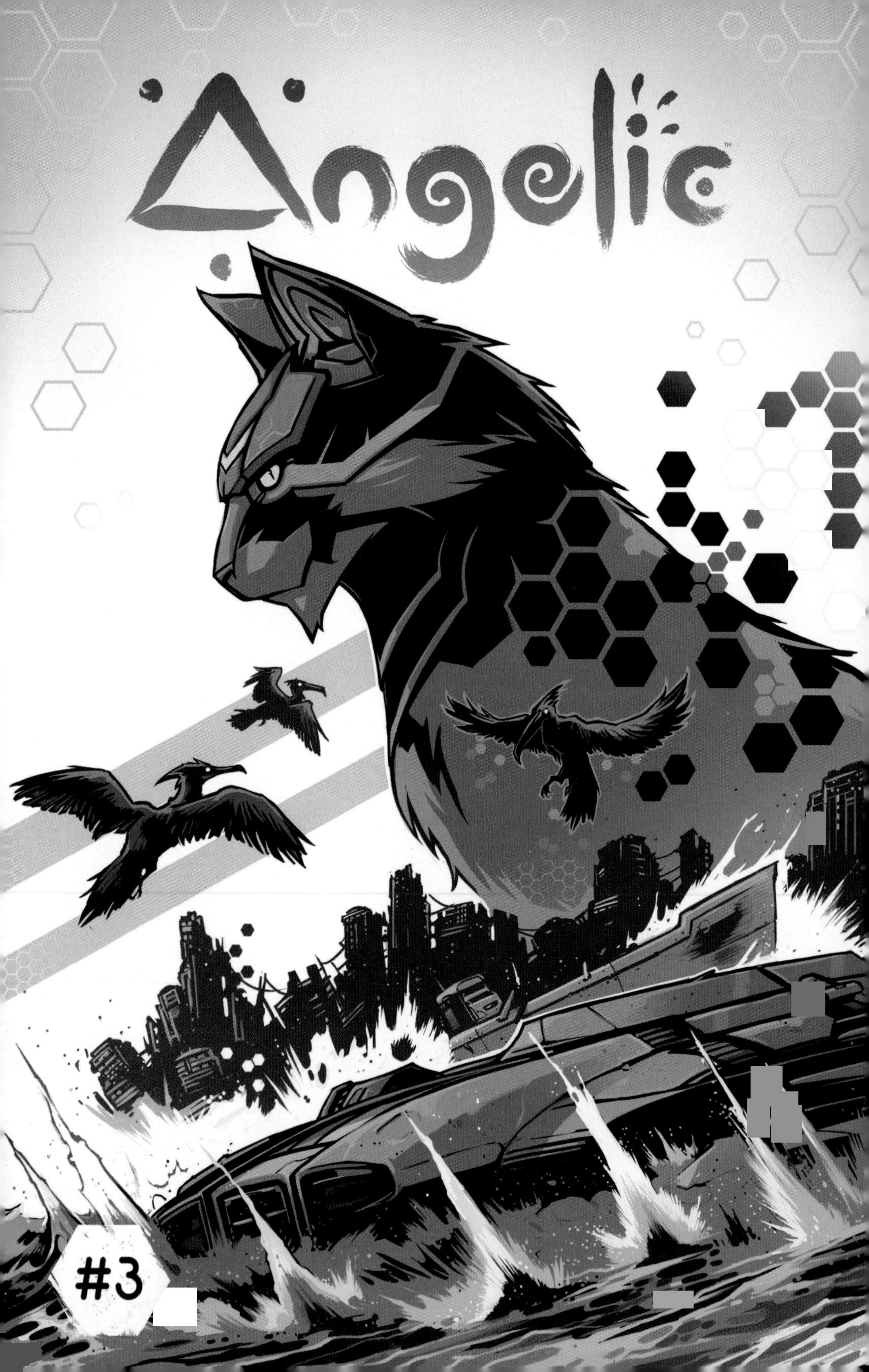
Angelic™
#3

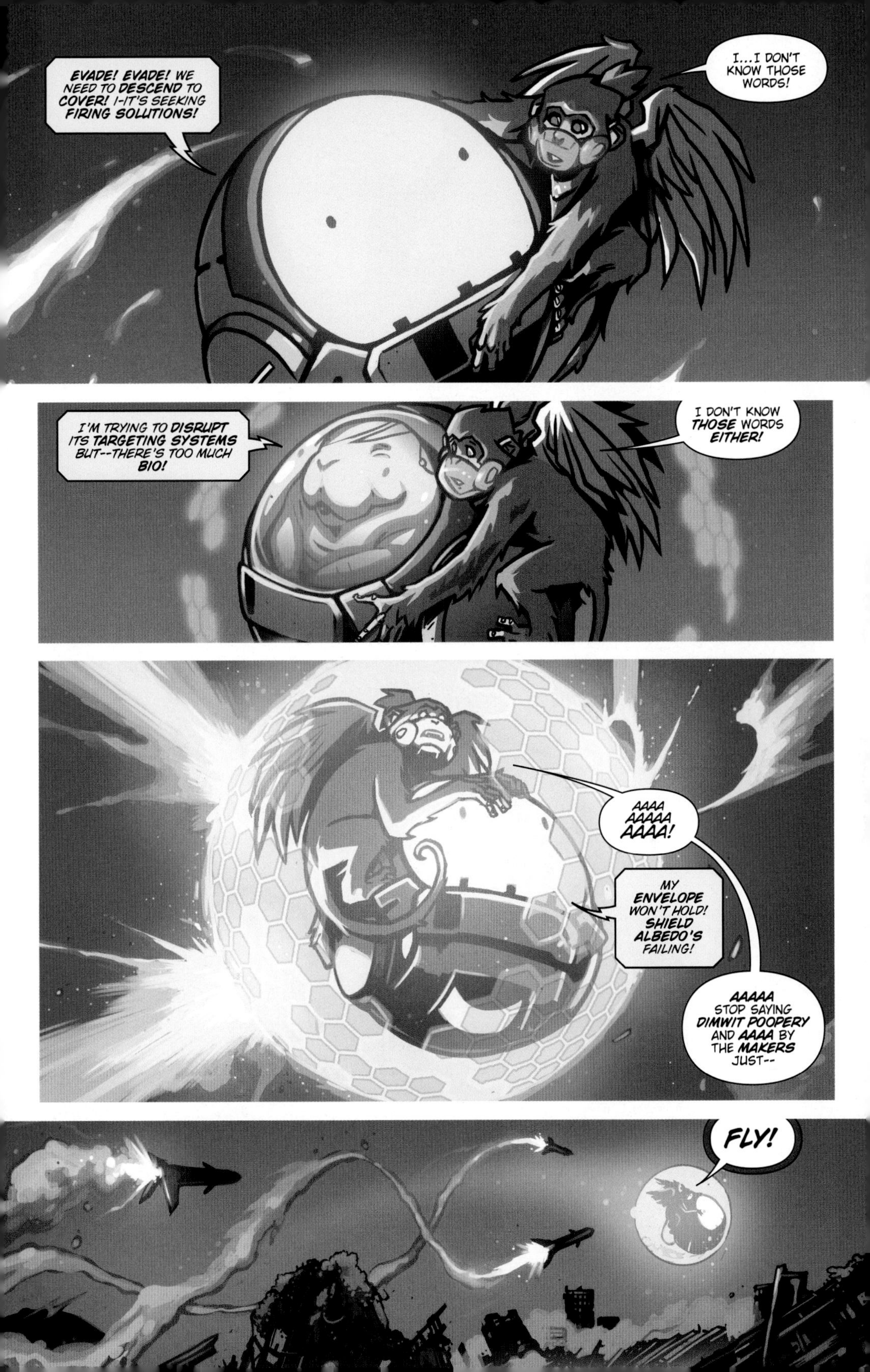
EVADE! EVADE! WE NEED TO DESCEND TO COVER! I-IT'S SEEKING FIRING SOLUTIONS!
I...I DON'T KNOW THOSE WORDS!
I'M TRYING TO DISRUPT ITS TARGETING SYSTEMS BUT--THERE'S TOO MUCH BIO!
I DON'T KNOW THOSE WORDS EITHER!
AAAA AAAAA AAAA!
MY ENVELOPE WON'T HOLD! SHIELD ALBEDO'S FAILING!
AAAAA STOP SAYING DIMWIT POOPERY AND AAAA BY THE MAKERS JUST--
FLY!

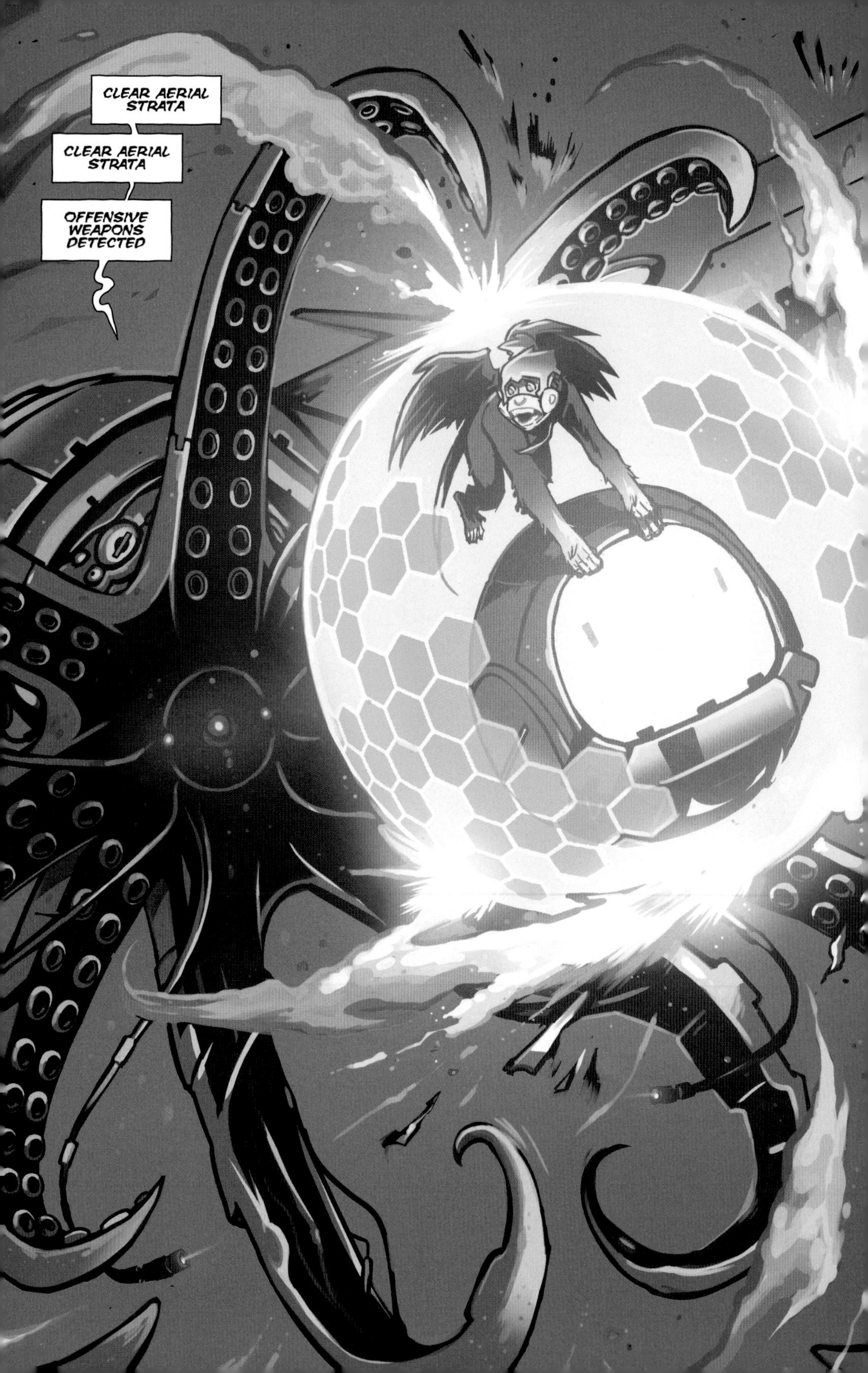
CLEAR AERIAL STRATA
CLEAR AERIAL STRATA
OFFENSIVE WEAPONS DETECTED

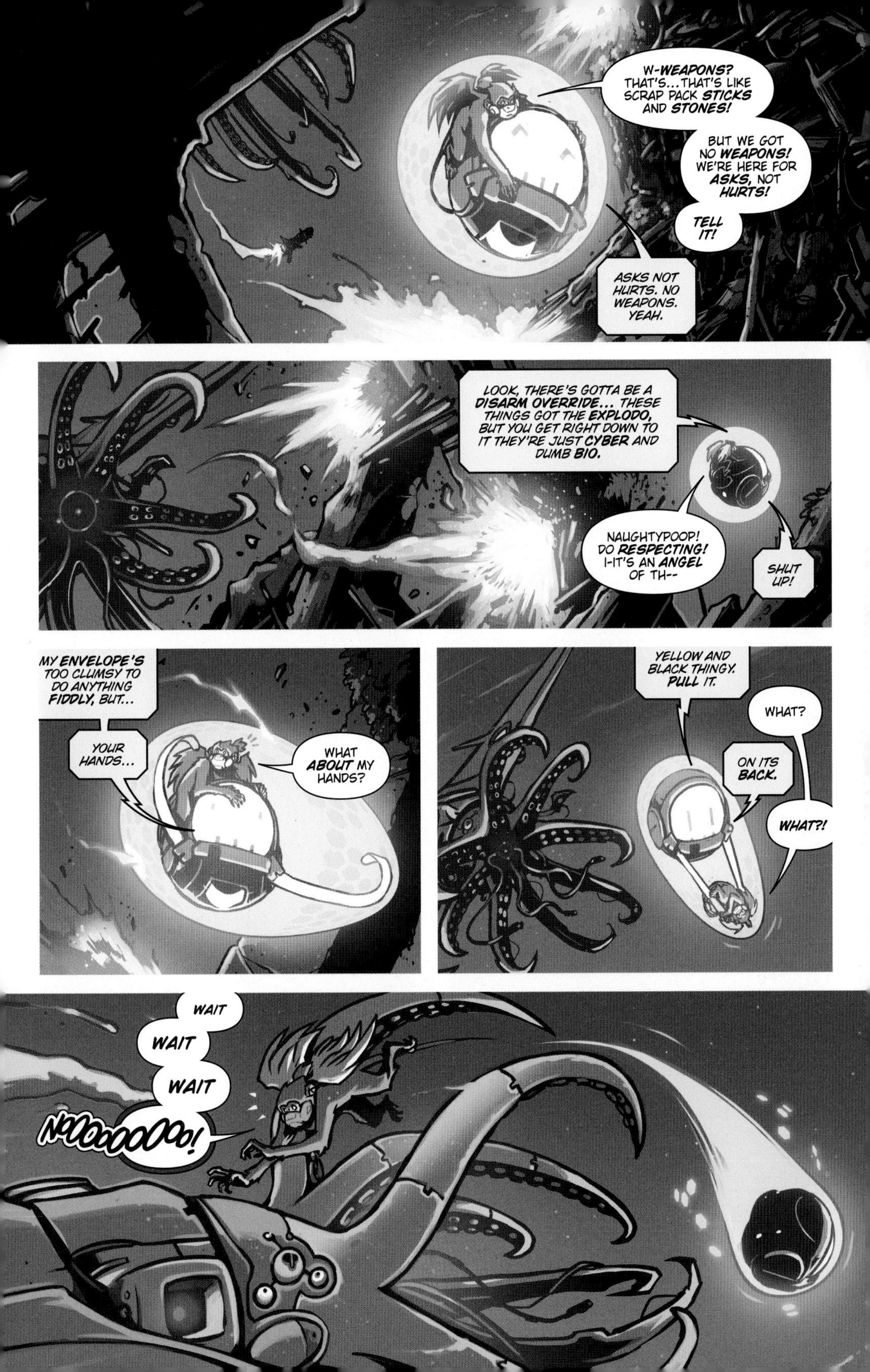
W-WEAPONS? THAT'S...THAT'S LIKE SCRAP PACK STICKS AND STONES!
BUT WE GOT NO WEAPONS! WE'RE HERE FOR ASKS, NOT HURTS!
TELL IT!
ASKS NOT HURTS. NO WEAPONS. YEAH.
LOOK, THERE'S GOTTA BE A DISARM OVERRIDE... THESE THINGS GOT THE EXPLODO, BUT YOU GET RIGHT DOWN TO IT THEY'RE JUST CYBER AND DUMB BIO.
NAUGHTYPOOP! DO RESPECTING! I-IT'S AN ANGEL OF TH--
SHUT UP!
MY ENVELOPE'S TOO CLUMSY TO DO ANYTHING FIDDLY, BUT...
YOUR HANDS...
WHAT ABOUT MY HANDS?
YELLOW AND BLACK THINGY. PULL IT.
WHAT?
ON ITS BACK.
WHAT?!
WAIT
WAIT
WAIT
NOOOOOOOOO!

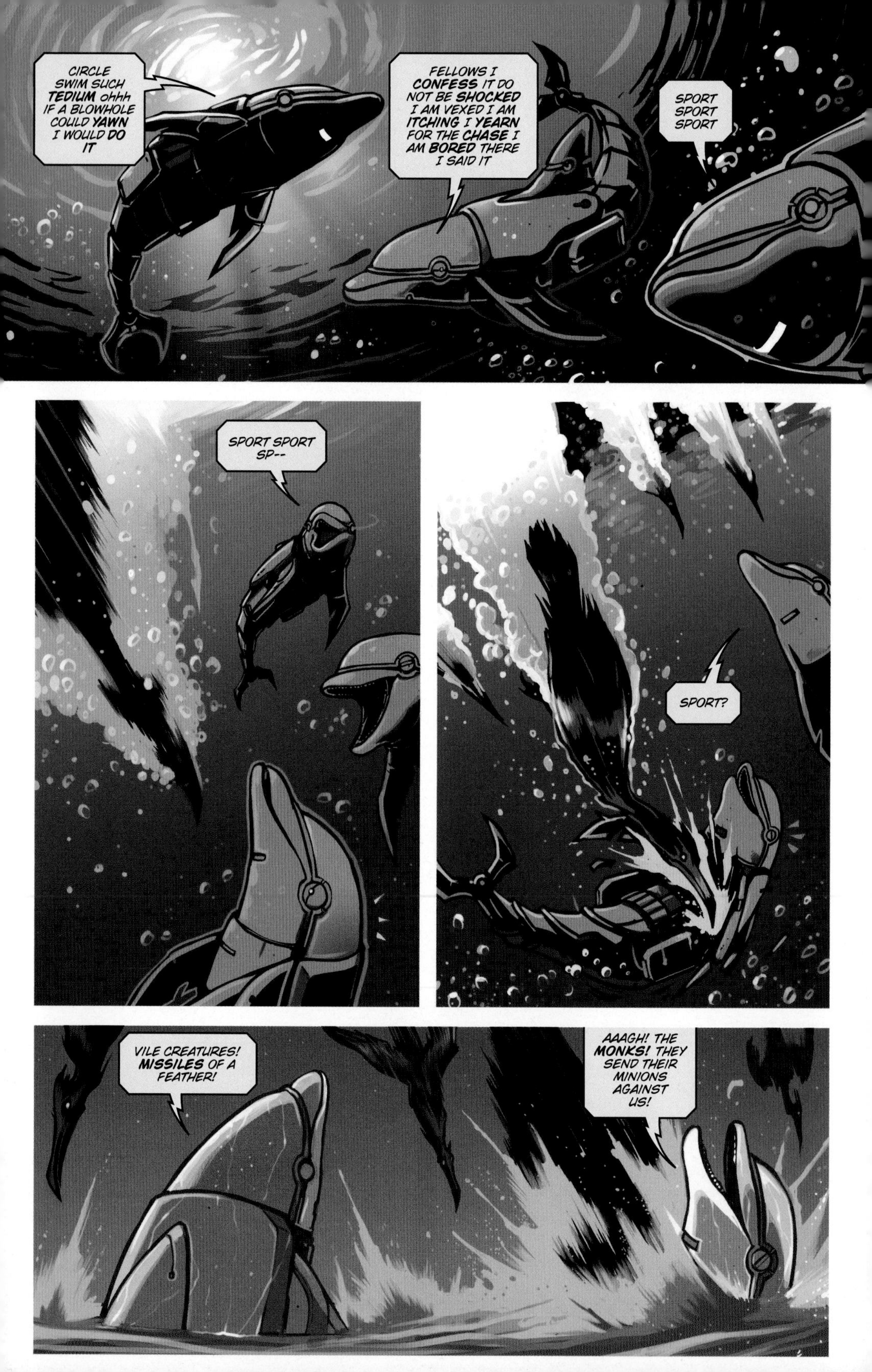
CIRCLE SWIM SUCH TEDIUM ohhh IF A BLOWHOLE COULD YAWN I WOULD DO IT
FELLOWS I CONFESS IT DO NOT BE SHOCKED I AM VEXED I AM ITCHING I YEARN FOR THE CHASE I AM BORED THERE I SAID IT
SPORT SPORT SPORT
SPORT SPORT SP--
SPORT?
VILE CREATURES! MISSILES OF A FEATHER!
AAAGH! THE MONKS! THEY SEND THEIR MINIONS AGAINST US!

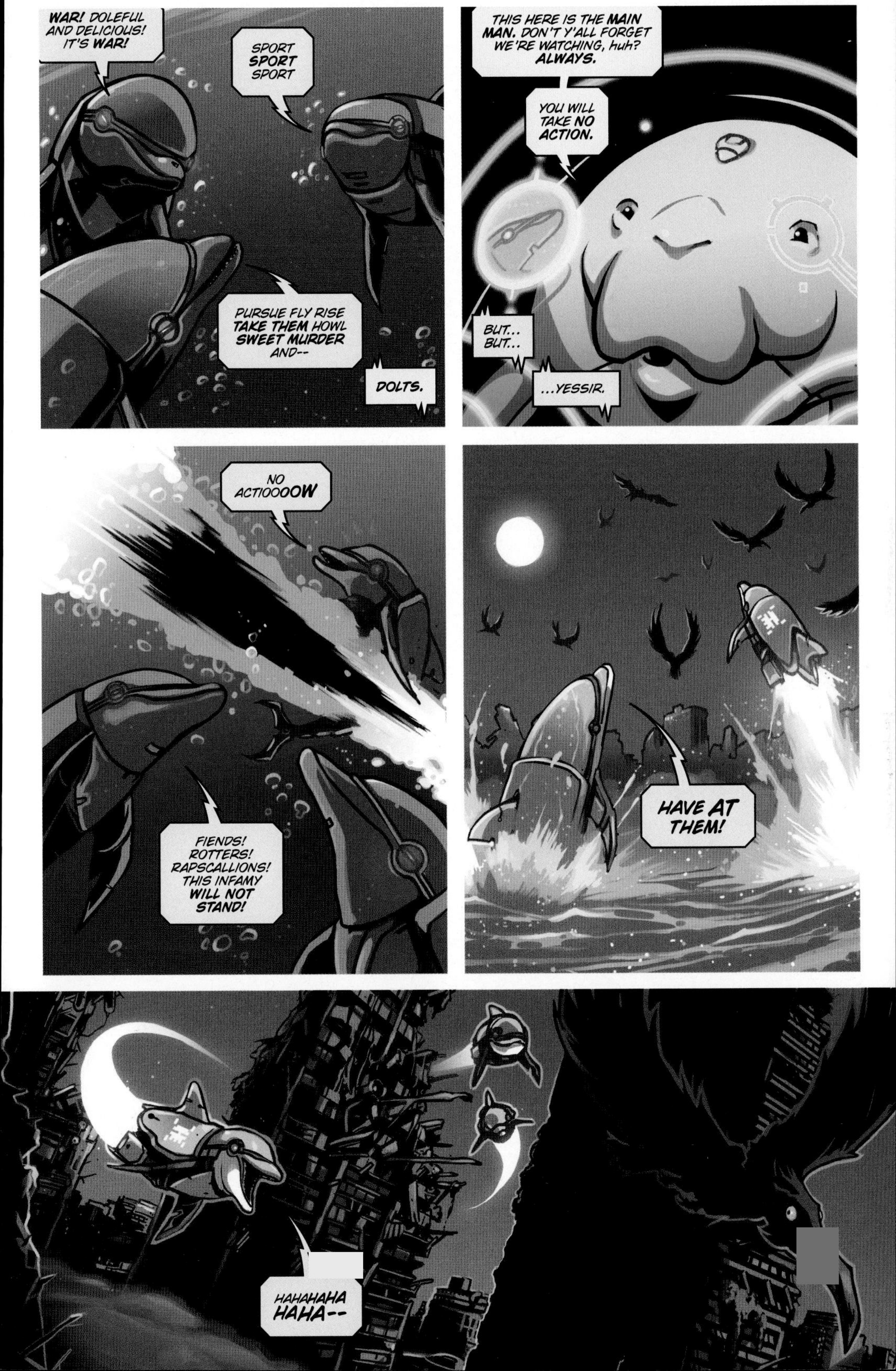
WAR! DOLEFUL AND DELICIOUS! IT'S WAR!
SPORT SPORT SPORT
PURSUE FLY RISE TAKE THEM HOWL SWEET MURDER AND--
DOLTS.
THIS HERE IS THE MAIN MAN. DON'T Y'ALL FORGET WE'RE WATCHING, huh? ALWAYS.
YOU WILL TAKE NO ACTION.
BUT... BUT...
...YESSIR.
NO ACTIOOOOW
FIENDS! ROTTERS! RAPSCALLIONS! THIS INFAMY WILL NOT STAND!
HAVE AT THEM!
HAHAHAHA HAHA--

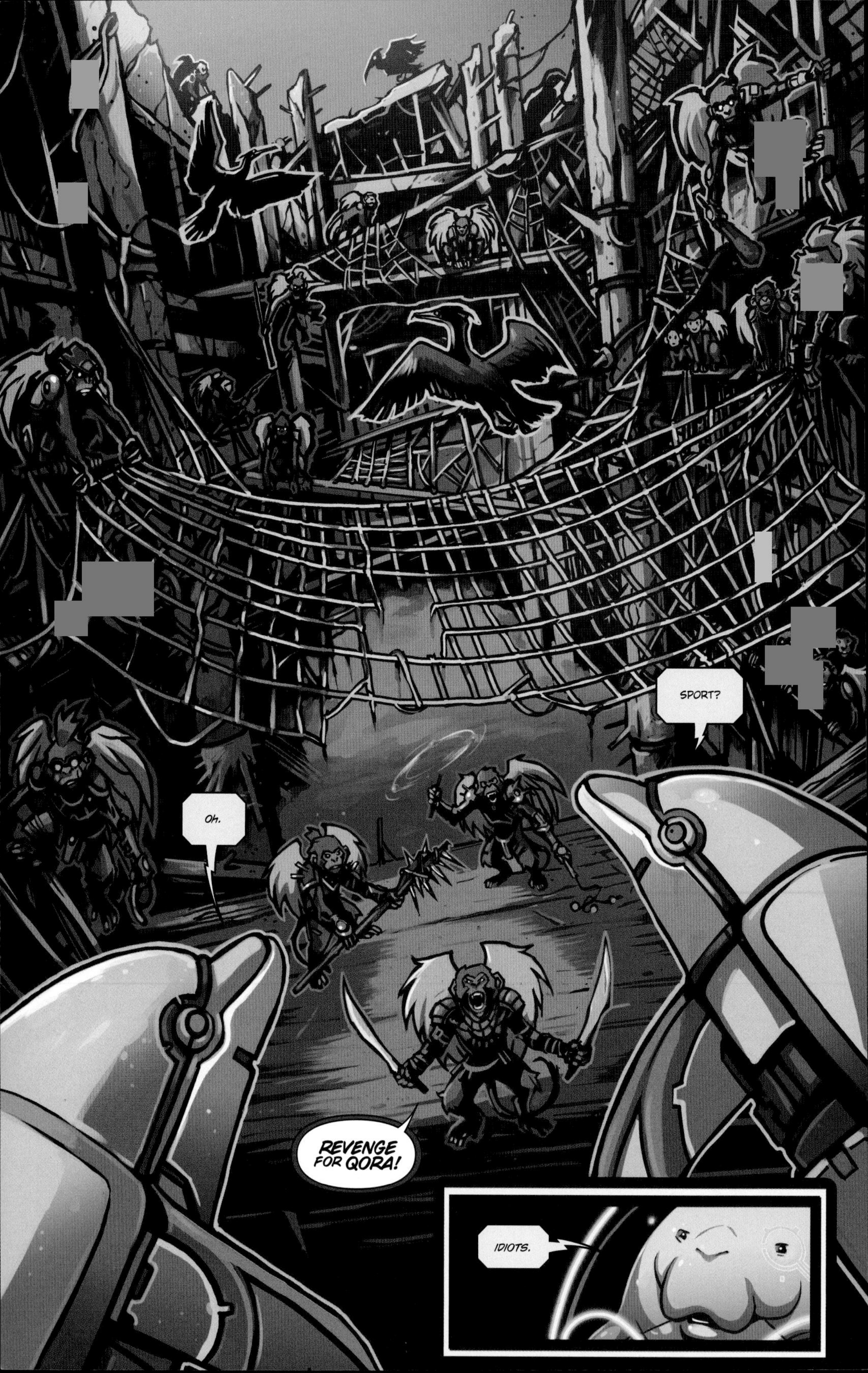
SPORT?
Oh.
REVENGE FOR QORA!
IDIOTS.

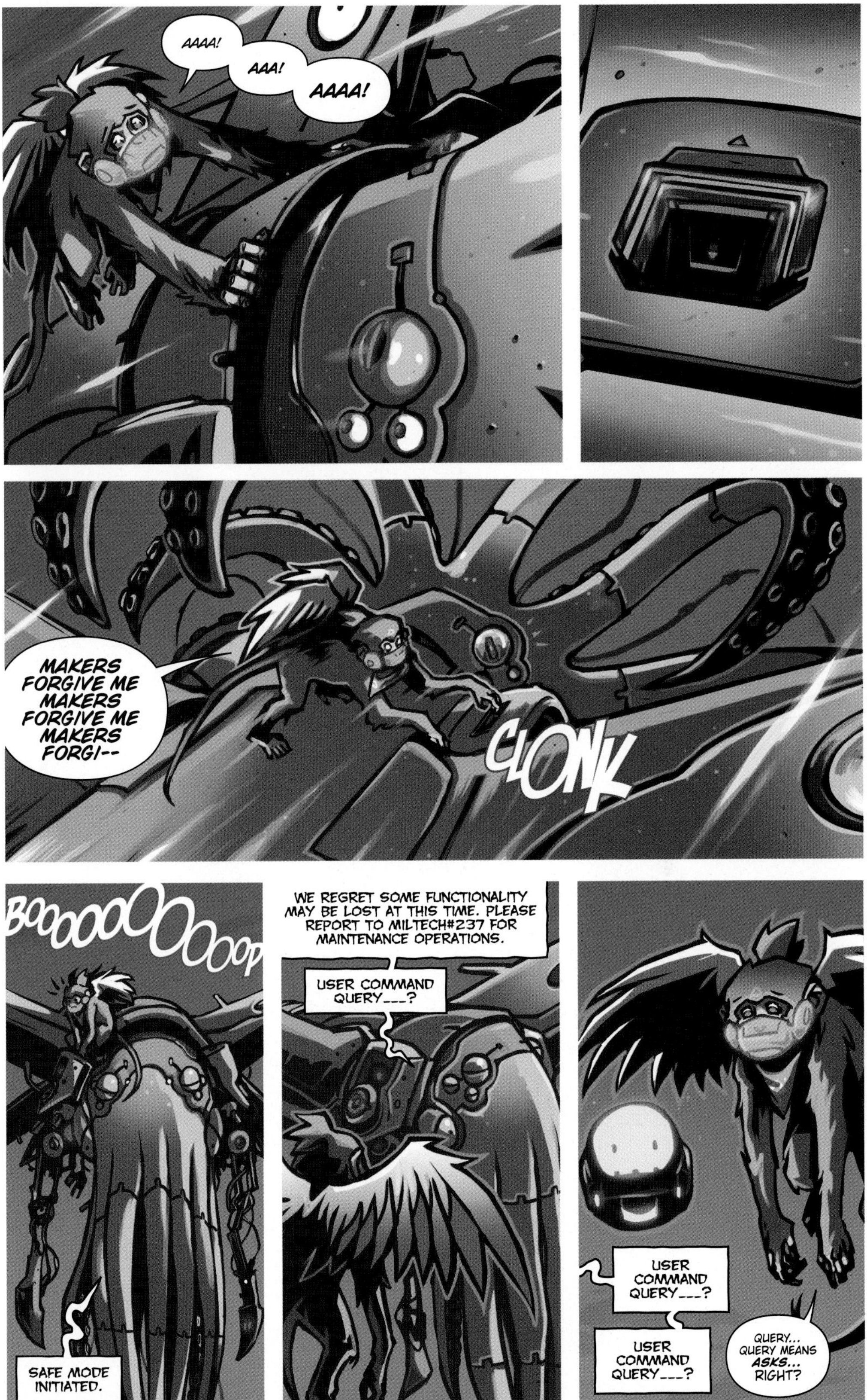
AAAA!
AAA!
AAAA!
MAKERS FORGIVE ME MAKERS FORGIVE ME MAKERS FORGI--
CLONK
BOOOOOOOOOOOP
SAFE MODE INITIATED.
WE REGRET SOME FUNCTIONALITY MAY BE LOST AT THIS TIME. PLEASE REPORT TO MILTECH#237 FOR MAINTENANCE OPERATIONS.
USER COMMAND QUERY___?
USER COMMAND QUERY___?
USER COMMAND QUERY___?
QUERY... QUERY MEANS ASKS... RIGHT?

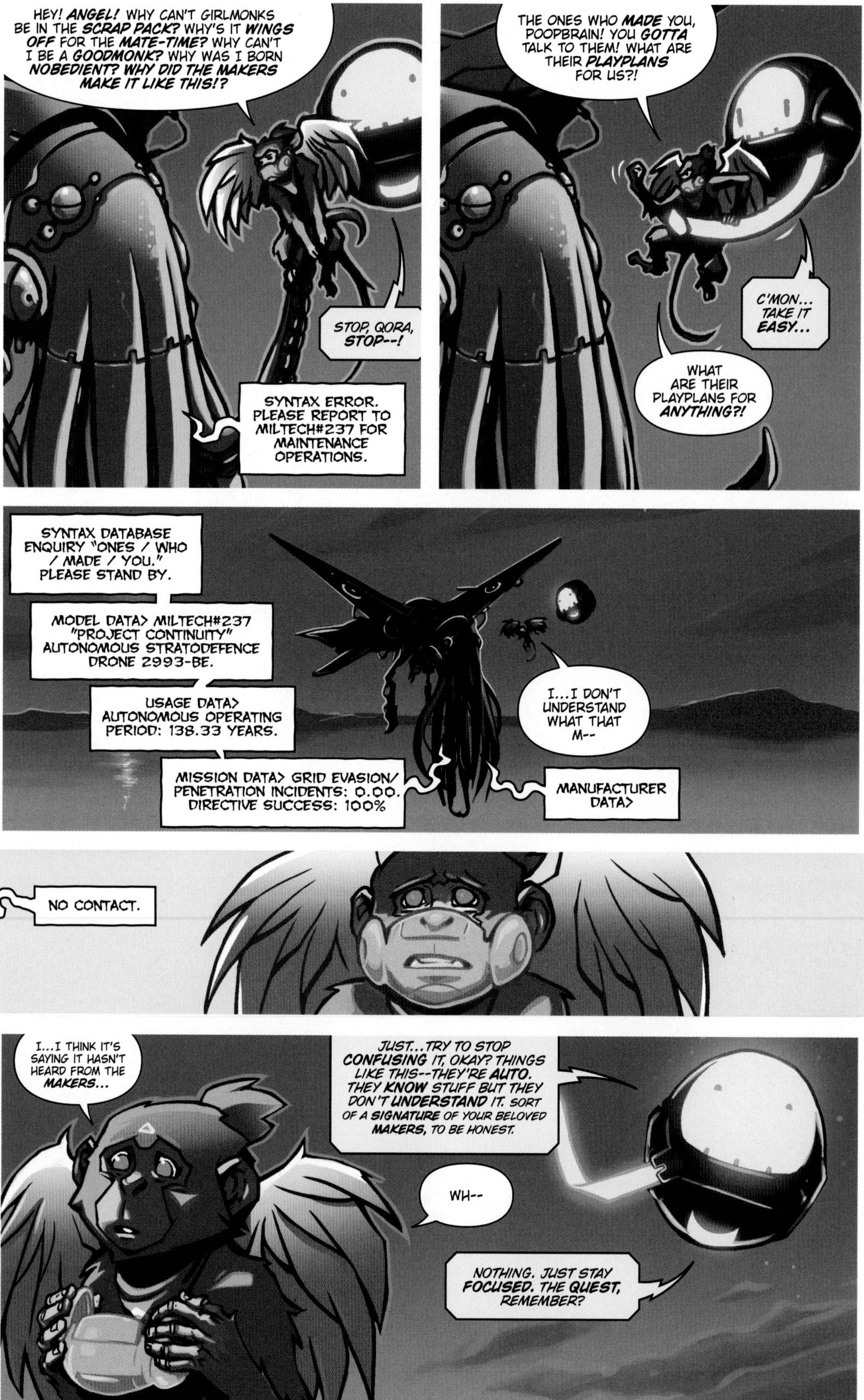
HEY! ANGEL! WHY CAN'T GIRLMONKS BE IN THE SCRAP PACK? WHY'S IT WINGS OFF FOR THE MATE-TIME? WHY CAN'T I BE A GOODMONK? WHY WAS I BORN NOBEDIENT? WHY DID THE MAKERS MAKE IT LIKE THIS!?
STOP, QORA, STOP--!
SYNTAX ERROR. PLEASE REPORT TO MILTECH#237 FOR MAINTENANCE OPERATIONS.
THE ONES WHO MADE YOU, POOPBRAIN! YOU GOTTA TALK TO THEM! WHAT ARE THEIR PLAYPLANS FOR US?!
C'MON... TAKE IT EASY...
WHAT ARE THEIR PLAYPLANS FOR ANYTHING?!
SYNTAX DATABASE ENQUIRY "ONES / WHO / MADE / YOU." PLEASE STAND BY.
MODEL DATA> MILTECH#237 "PROJECT CONTINUITY" AUTONOMOUS STRATODEFENCE DRONE 2993-BE.
USAGE DATA> AUTONOMOUS OPERATING PERIOD: 138.33 YEARS.
MISSION DATA> GRID EVASION/ PENETRATION INCIDENTS: 0.00. DIRECTIVE SUCCESS: 100%
I...I DON'T UNDERSTAND WHAT THAT M--
MANUFACTURER DATA>
NO CONTACT.
I...I THINK IT'S SAYING IT HASN'T HEARD FROM THE MAKERS...
JUST...TRY TO STOP CONFUSING IT, OKAY? THINGS LIKE THIS--THEY'RE AUTO. THEY KNOW STUFF BUT THEY DON'T UNDERSTAND IT. SORT OF A SIGNATURE OF YOUR BELOVED MAKERS, TO BE HONEST.
WH--
NOTHING. JUST STAY FOCUSED. THE QUEST, REMEMBER?

... OH GREAT AND HUMBLE *ANGEL!* YOU WHO SEES *ALL!* YOU WHO KNOWS ALL! I BEG *SORRIES* FOR CALLING YOU *POOPBRAIN!*

=:SIGH=

WHERE IS THE LOST *EYE* OF THE DEVIL *AY?*

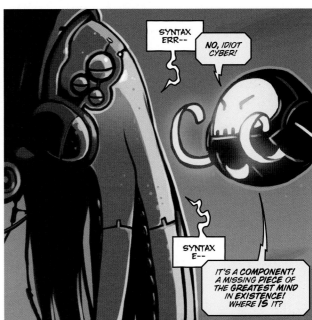

SYNTAX ERR--

NO, IDIOT CYBER!

SYNTAX E--

IT'S A *COMPONENT!* A MISSING *PIECE* OF THE *GREATEST MIND* IN *EXISTENCE!* WHERE *IS* IT?

tik tik tik

PLEASE REPORT TO MILTECH#237 FOR MAINTENANCE OPERATIONS.

GNH! THAT'S NOT WH--

YOU ARE INVITED TO FOLLOW THE COMPLIMENTARY LOCATOR BEACON AT THIS TIME.

!

!

HAVE A NICE DAY NOW.

QUICK! GO!

QORA, WAIT--!

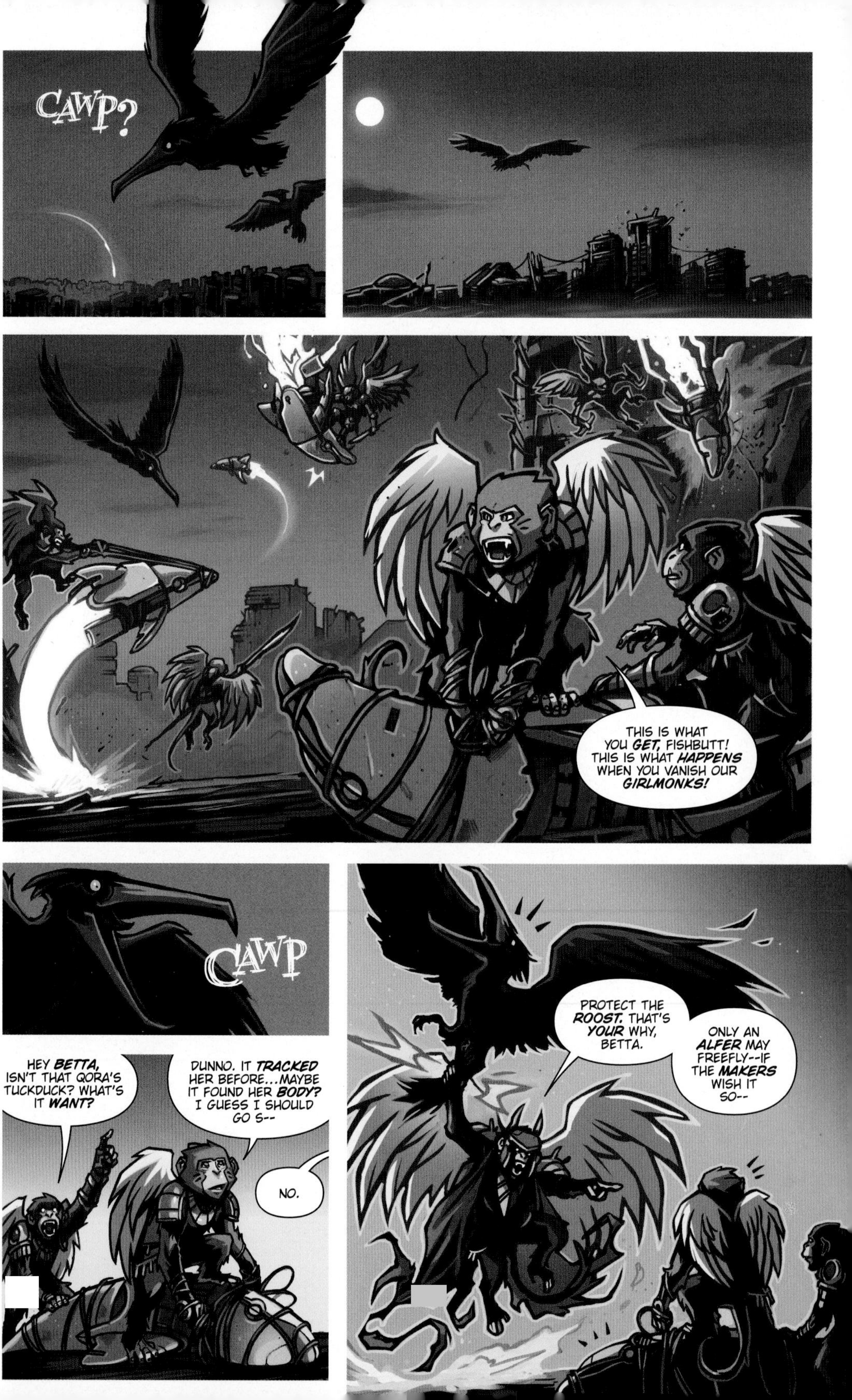
CAWP?
THIS IS WHAT YOU GET, FISHBUTT! THIS IS WHAT HAPPENS WHEN YOU VANISH OUR GIRLMONKS!
CAWP
HEY BETTA, ISN'T THAT QORA'S TUCKDUCK? WHAT'S IT WANT?
DUNNO. IT TRACKED HER BEFORE...MAYBE IT FOUND HER BODY? I GUESS I SHOULD GO S--
NO.
PROTECT THE ROOST. THAT'S YOUR WHY, BETTA.
ONLY AN ALFER MAY FREEFLY--IF THE MAKERS WISH IT SO--

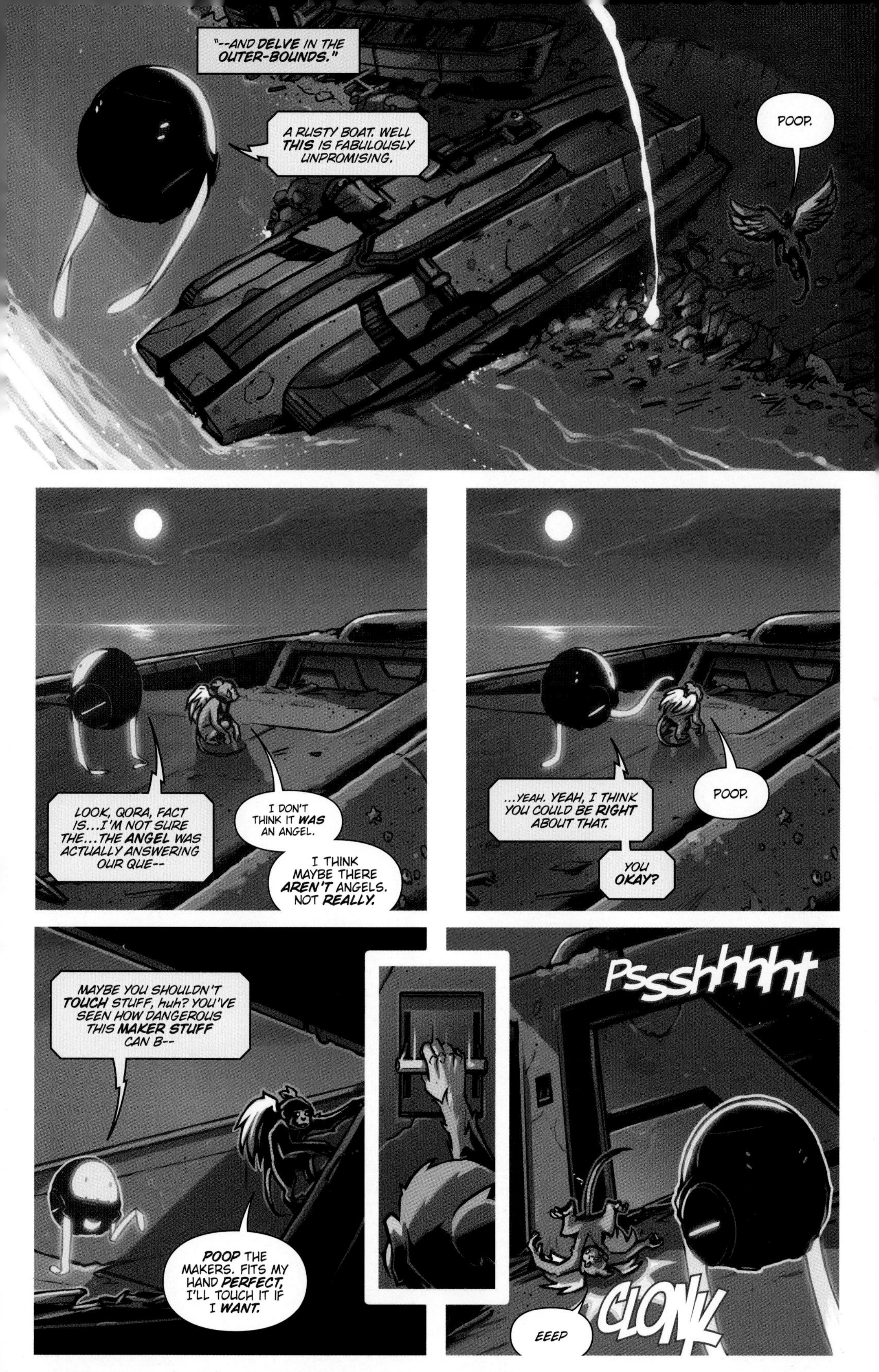
"--AND DELVE IN THE OUTER-BOUNDS."
A RUSTY BOAT. WELL THIS IS FABULOUSLY UNPROMISING.
POOP.
LOOK, QORA, FACT IS...I'M NOT SURE THE...THE ANGEL WAS ACTUALLY ANSWERING OUR QUE--
I DON'T THINK IT WAS AN ANGEL.
I THINK MAYBE THERE AREN'T ANGELS. NOT REALLY.
...YEAH. YEAH, I THINK YOU COULD BE RIGHT ABOUT THAT.
POOP.
YOU OKAY?
MAYBE YOU SHOULDN'T TOUCH STUFF, huh? YOU'VE SEEN HOW DANGEROUS THIS MAKER STUFF CAN B--
POOP THE MAKERS. FITS MY HAND PERFECT, I'LL TOUCH IT IF I WANT.
Pssshhhht
CLONK
EEEP

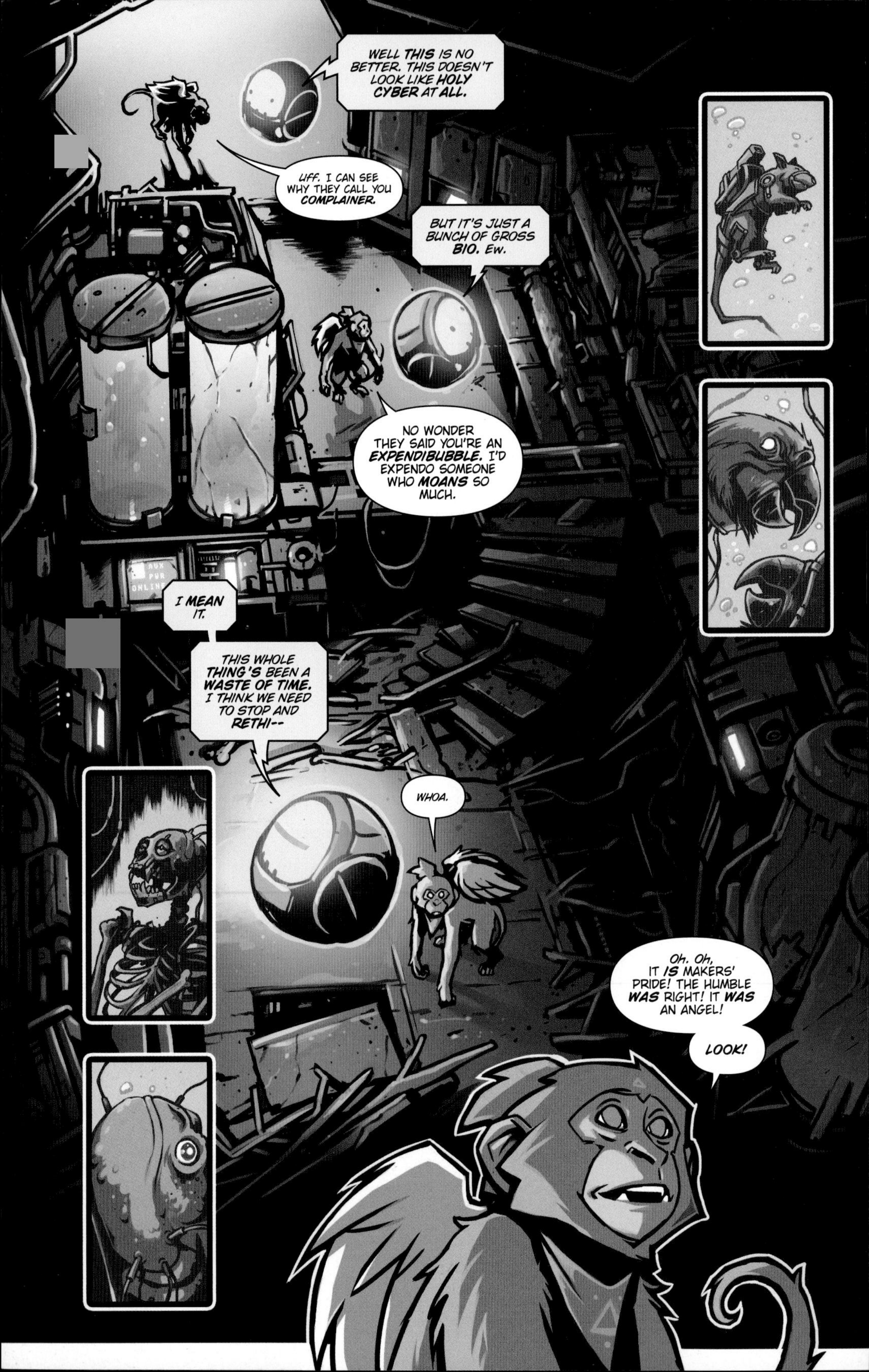
WELL THIS IS NO BETTER. THIS DOESN'T LOOK LIKE HOLY CYBER AT ALL.
UFF. I CAN SEE WHY THEY CALL YOU COMPLAINER.
BUT IT'S JUST A BUNCH OF GROSS BIO. Ew.
NO WONDER THEY SAID YOU'RE AN EXPENDIBUBBLE. I'D EXPENDO SOMEONE WHO MOANS SO MUCH.
AUX PWR ONLINE
I MEAN IT.
THIS WHOLE THING'S BEEN A WASTE OF TIME. I THINK WE NEED TO STOP AND RETHI--
WHOA.
Oh. Oh, IT IS MAKERS' PRIDE! THE HUMBLE WAS RIGHT! IT WAS AN ANGEL!
LOOK!

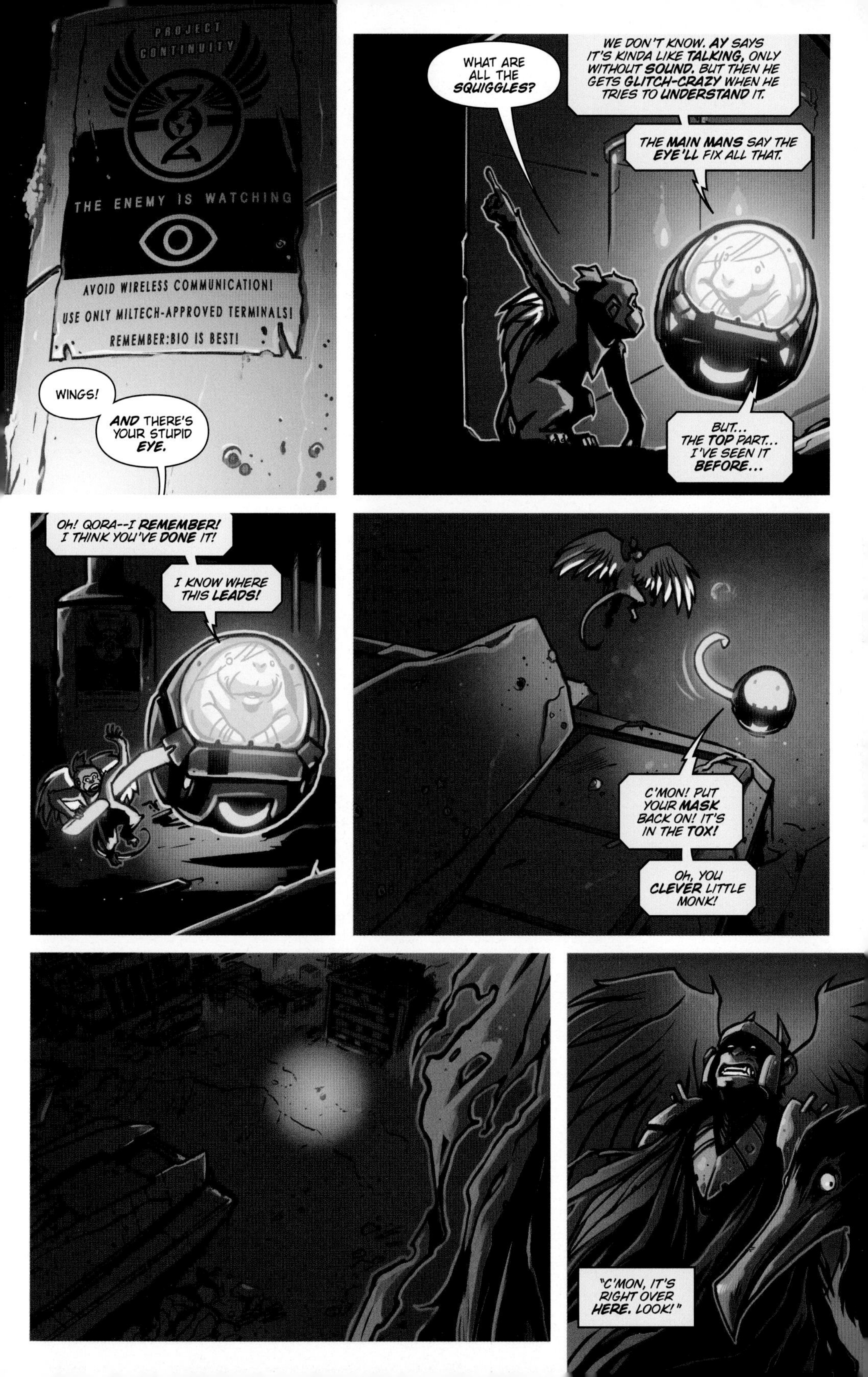
PROJECT CONTINUITY
THE ENEMY IS WATCHING
AVOID WIRELESS COMMUNICATION!
USE ONLY MILTECH-APPROVED TERMINALS!
REMEMBER:BIO IS BEST!
WINGS!
AND THERE'S YOUR STUPID EYE.
WHAT ARE ALL THE SQUIGGLES?
WE DON'T KNOW. AY SAYS IT'S KINDA LIKE TALKING, ONLY WITHOUT SOUND. BUT THEN HE GETS GLITCH-CRAZY WHEN HE TRIES TO UNDERSTAND IT.
THE MAIN MANS SAY THE EYE'LL FIX ALL THAT.
BUT... THE TOP PART... I'VE SEEN IT BEFORE...
Oh! QORA--I REMEMBER! I THINK YOU'VE DONE IT!
I KNOW WHERE THIS LEADS!
C'MON! PUT YOUR MASK BACK ON! IT'S IN THE TOX!
Oh, YOU CLEVER LITTLE MONK!
"C'MON, IT'S RIGHT OVER HERE. LOOK!"

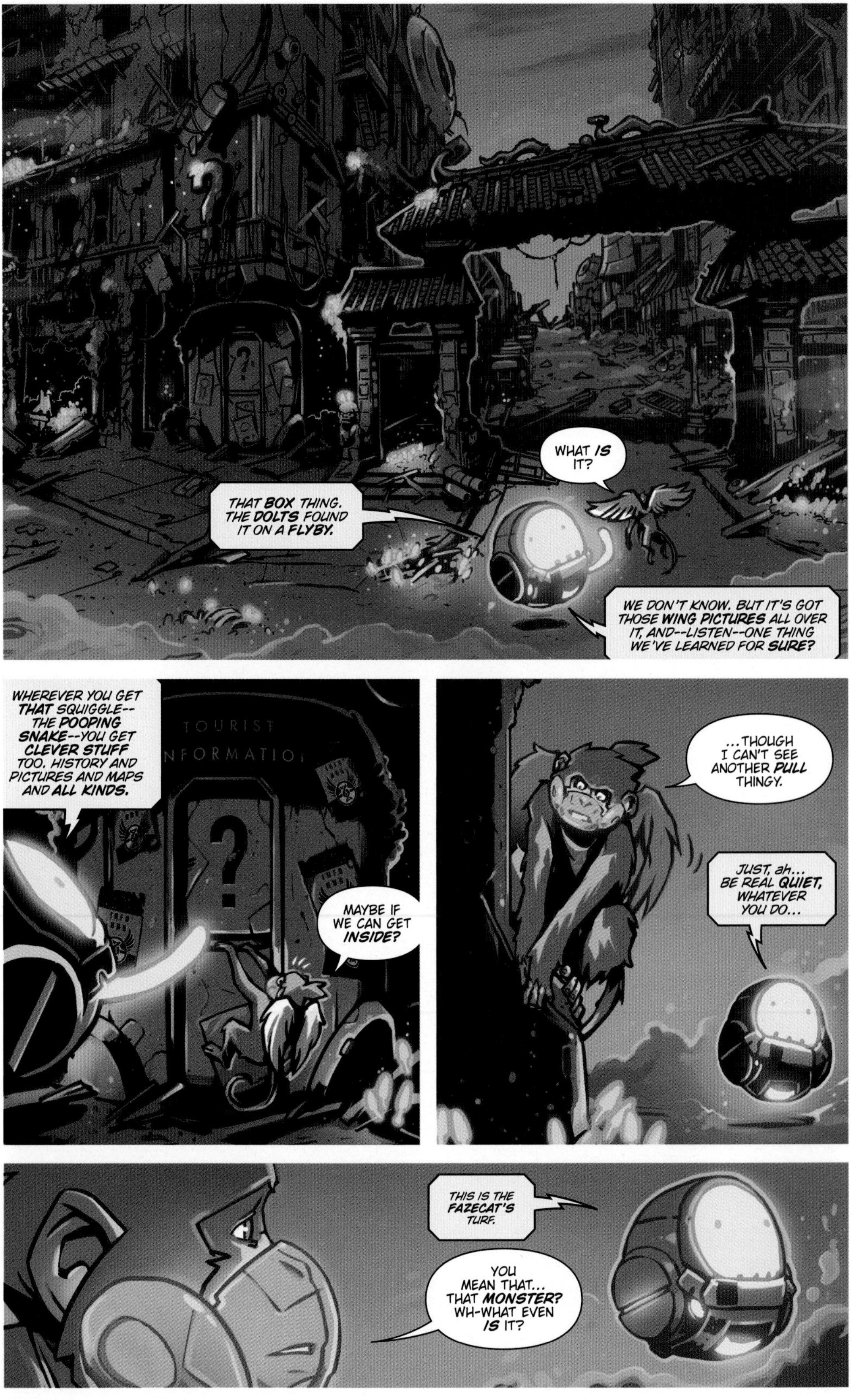
WHAT IS IT?
THAT BOX THING. THE DOLTS FOUND IT ON A FLYBY.
WE DON'T KNOW. BUT IT'S GOT THOSE WING PICTURES ALL OVER IT, AND--LISTEN--ONE THING WE'VE LEARNED FOR SURE?
WHEREVER YOU GET THAT SQUIGGLE--THE POOPING SNAKE--YOU GET CLEVER STUFF TOO. HISTORY AND PICTURES AND MAPS AND ALL KINDS.
TOURIST
NFORMATIO
MAYBE IF WE CAN GET INSIDE?
...THOUGH I CAN'T SEE ANOTHER PULL THINGY.
JUST, ah... BE REAL QUIET, WHATEVER YOU DO...
THIS IS THE FAZECAT'S TURF.
YOU MEAN THAT... THAT MONSTER? WH-WHAT EVEN IS IT?

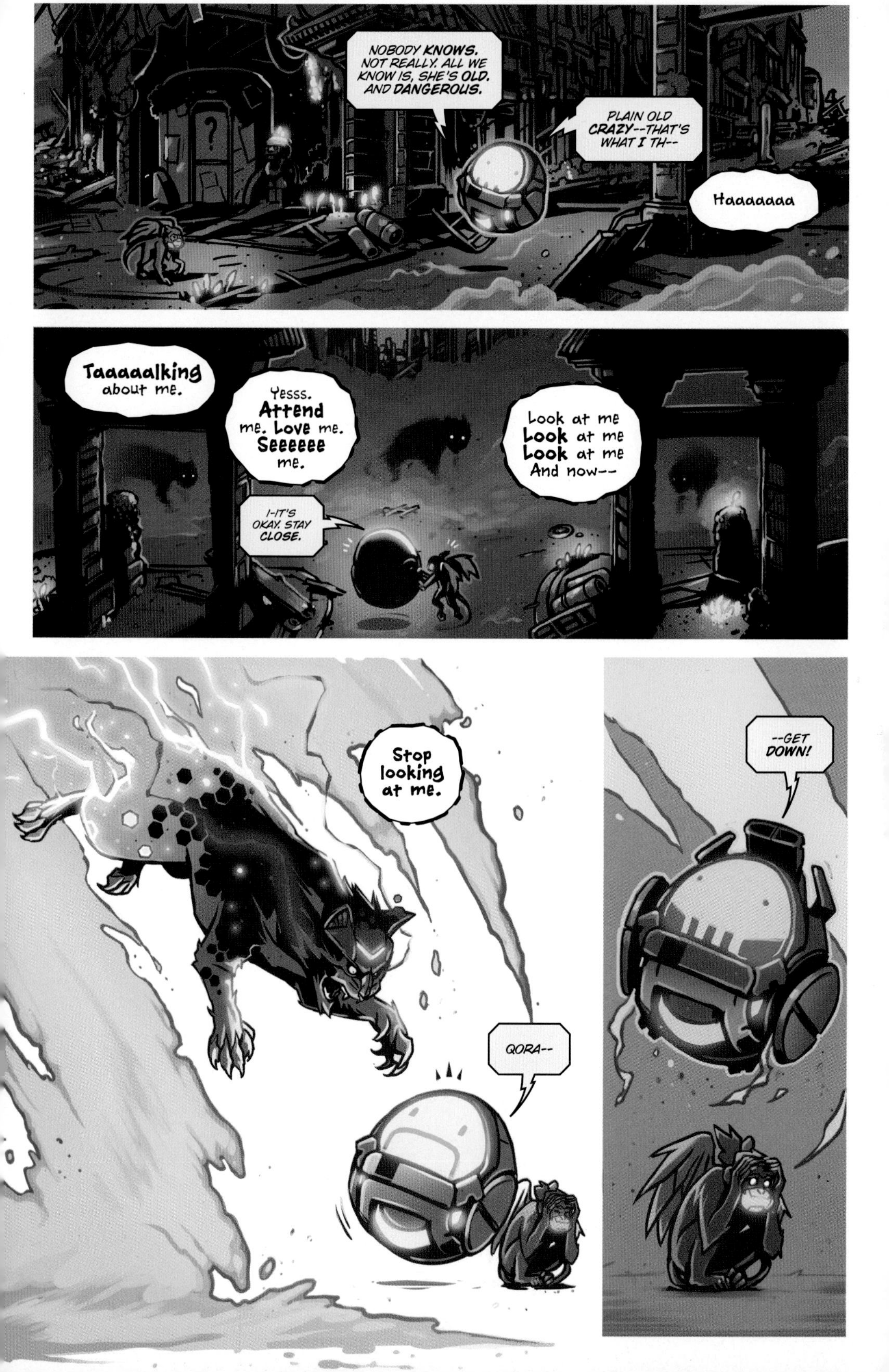
NOBODY KNOWS. NOT REALLY. ALL WE KNOW IS, SHE'S OLD. AND DANGEROUS.
PLAIN OLD CRAZY--THAT'S WHAT I TH--
Haaaaaaa
Taaaaalking about me.
Yesss. Attend me. Love me. Seeeeee me.
Look at me Look at me Look at me And now--
I-IT'S OKAY. STAY CLOSE.
Stop looking at me.
QORA--
--GET DOWN!

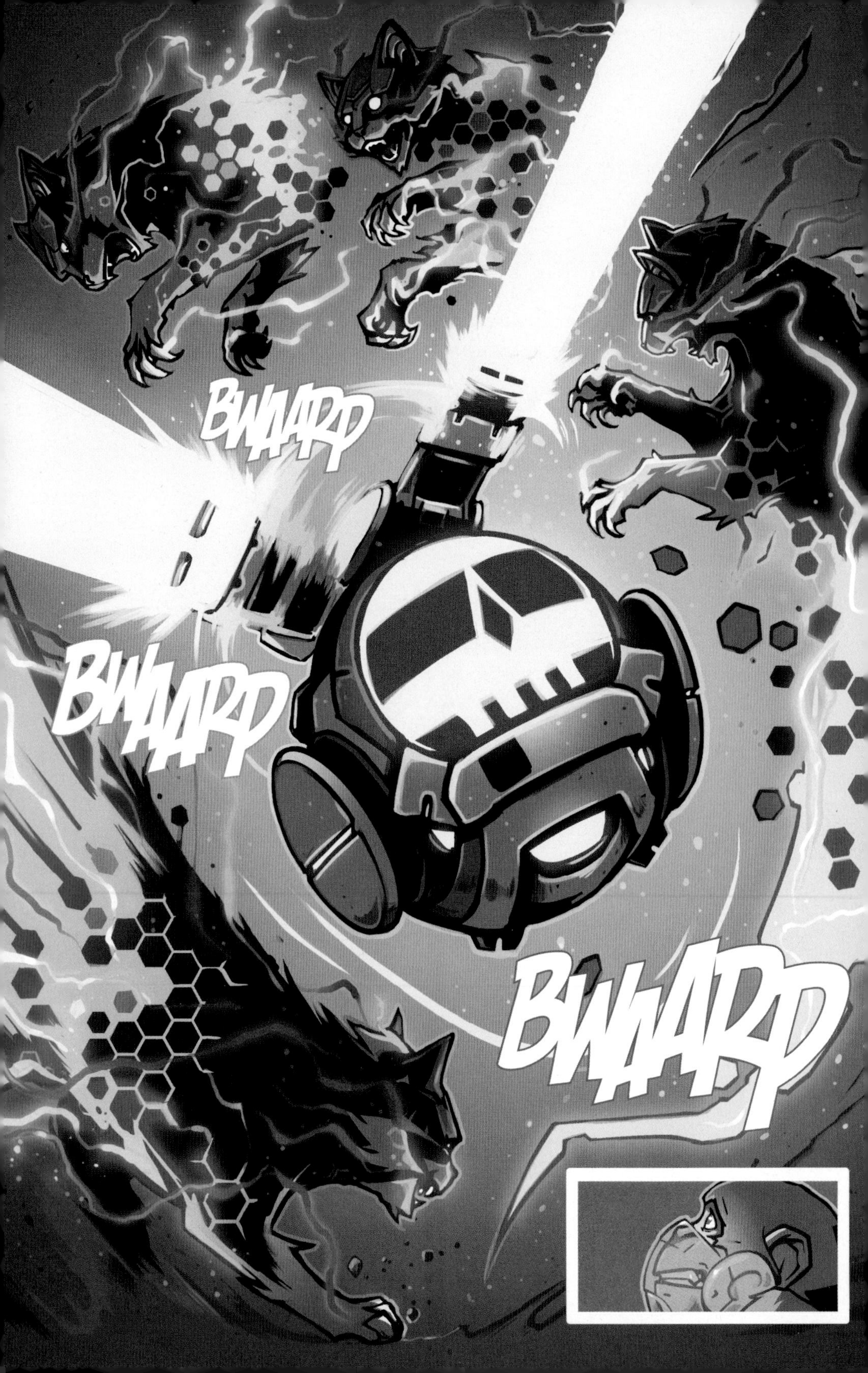
BWAARP
BWAARP
BWAARP

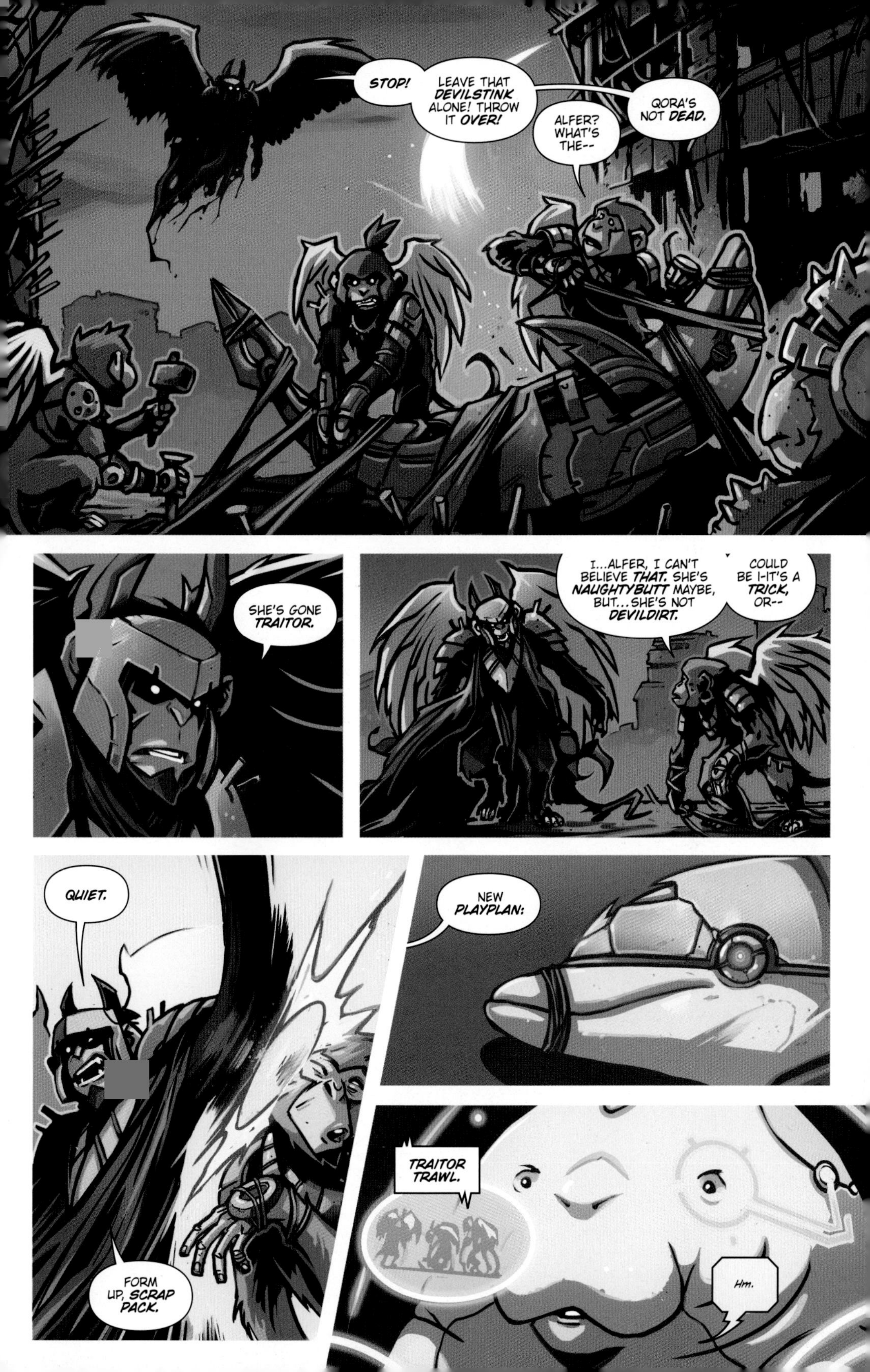

STOP!
LEAVE THAT DEVILSTINK ALONE! THROW IT OVER!
ALFER? WHAT'S THE--
QORA'S NOT DEAD.
SHE'S GONE TRAITOR.
I...ALFER, I CAN'T BELIEVE THAT. SHE'S NAUGHTYBUTT MAYBE, BUT...SHE'S NOT DEVILDIRT.
COULD BE I-IT'S A TRICK, OR--
QUIET.
FORM UP, SCRAP PACK.
NEW PLAYPLAN:
TRAITOR TRAWL.
Hm.

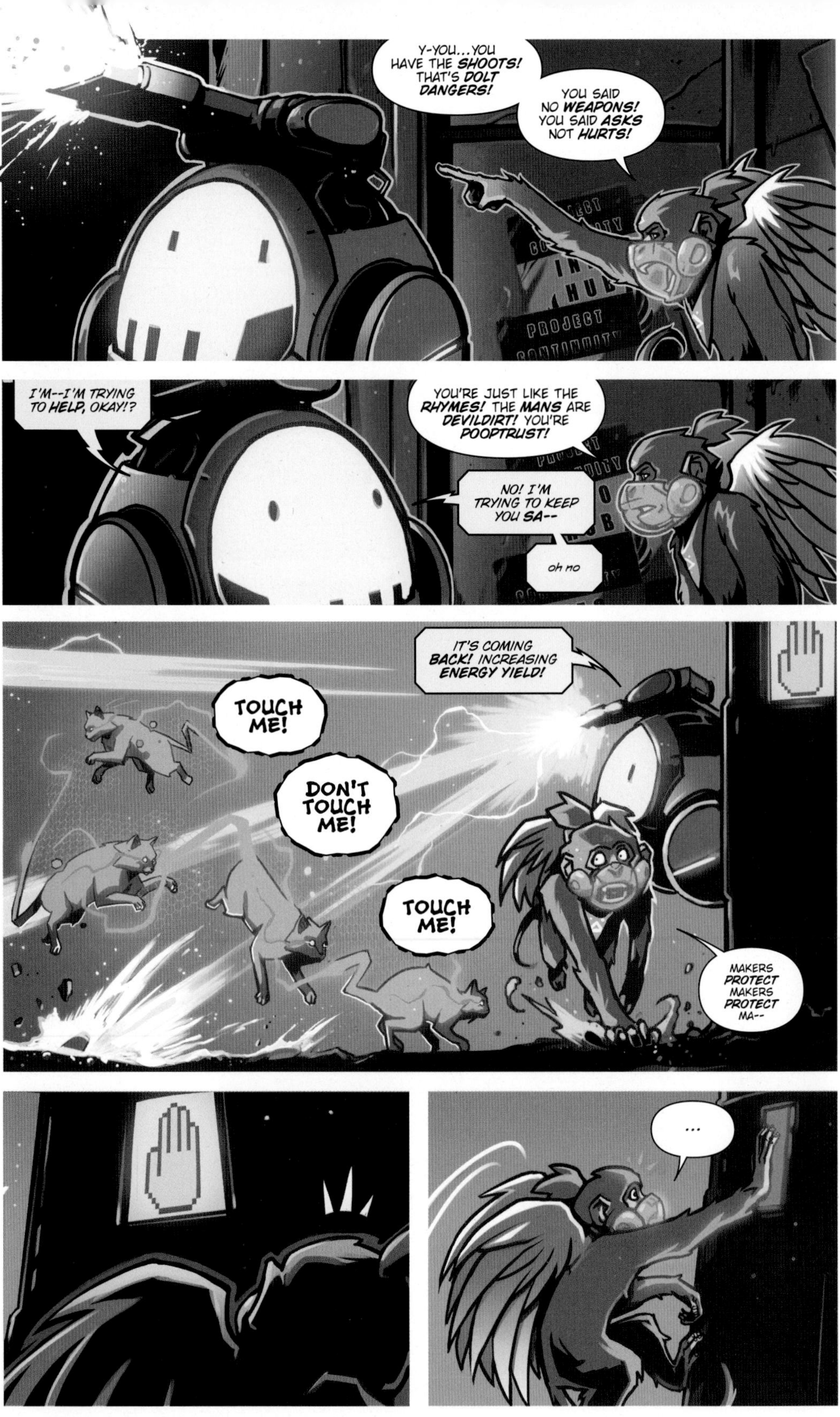
Y-YOU...YOU HAVE THE SHOOTS! THAT'S DOLT DANGERS!
YOU SAID NO WEAPONS! YOU SAID ASKS NOT HURTS!
PROJECT CONTINUITY INFO HUB
PROJECT CONTINUITY
I'M--I'M TRYING TO HELP, OKAY!?
YOU'RE JUST LIKE THE RHYMES! THE MANS ARE DEVILDIRT! YOU'RE POOPTRUST!
NO! I'M TRYING TO KEEP YOU SA--
oh no
IT'S COMING BACK! INCREASING ENERGY YIELD!
TOUCH ME!
DON'T TOUCH ME!
TOUCH ME!
MAKERS PROTECT MAKERS PROTECT MA--
...

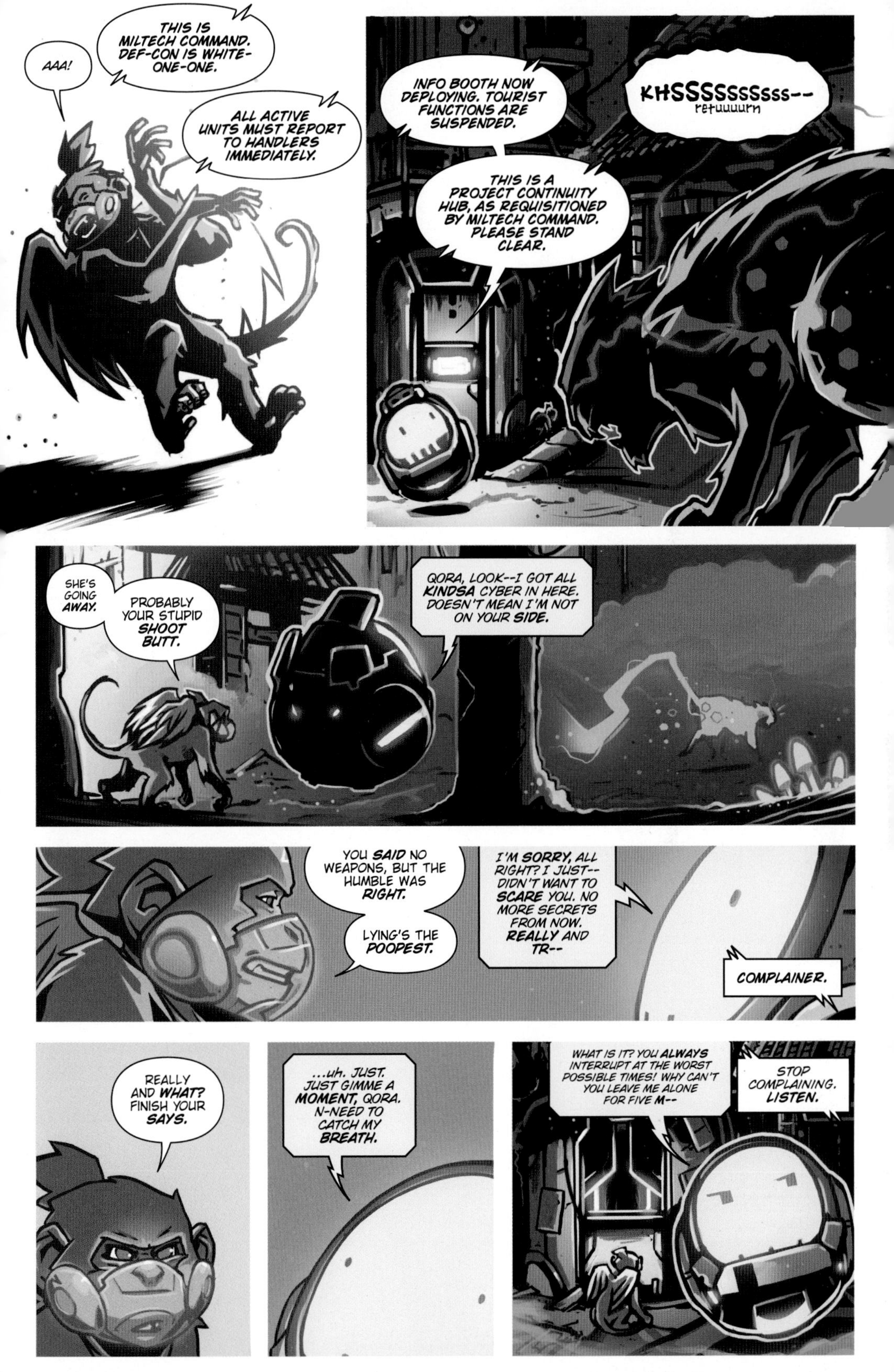
AAA!
THIS IS MILTECH COMMAND. DEF-CON IS WHITE-ONE-ONE.
ALL ACTIVE UNITS MUST REPORT TO HANDLERS IMMEDIATELY.
INFO BOOTH NOW DEPLOYING. TOURIST FUNCTIONS ARE SUSPENDED.
THIS IS A PROJECT CONTINUITY HUB, AS REQUISITIONED BY MILTECH COMMAND. PLEASE STAND CLEAR.
KHSSSSSSSSss--
retuuuurn
SHE'S GOING AWAY.
PROBABLY YOUR STUPID SHOOT BUTT.
QORA, LOOK--I GOT ALL KINDSA CYBER IN HERE. DOESN'T MEAN I'M NOT ON YOUR SIDE.
YOU SAID NO WEAPONS, BUT THE HUMBLE WAS RIGHT.
LYING'S THE POOPEST.
I'M SORRY, ALL RIGHT? I JUST--DIDN'T WANT TO SCARE YOU. NO MORE SECRETS FROM NOW. REALLY AND TR--
COMPLAINER.
REALLY AND WHAT? FINISH YOUR SAYS.
...uh. JUST. JUST GIMME A MOMENT, QORA. N-NEED TO CATCH MY BREATH.
WHAT IS IT? YOU ALWAYS INTERRUPT AT THE WORST POSSIBLE TIMES! WHY CAN'T YOU LEAVE ME ALONE FOR FIVE M--
STOP COMPLAINING. LISTEN.

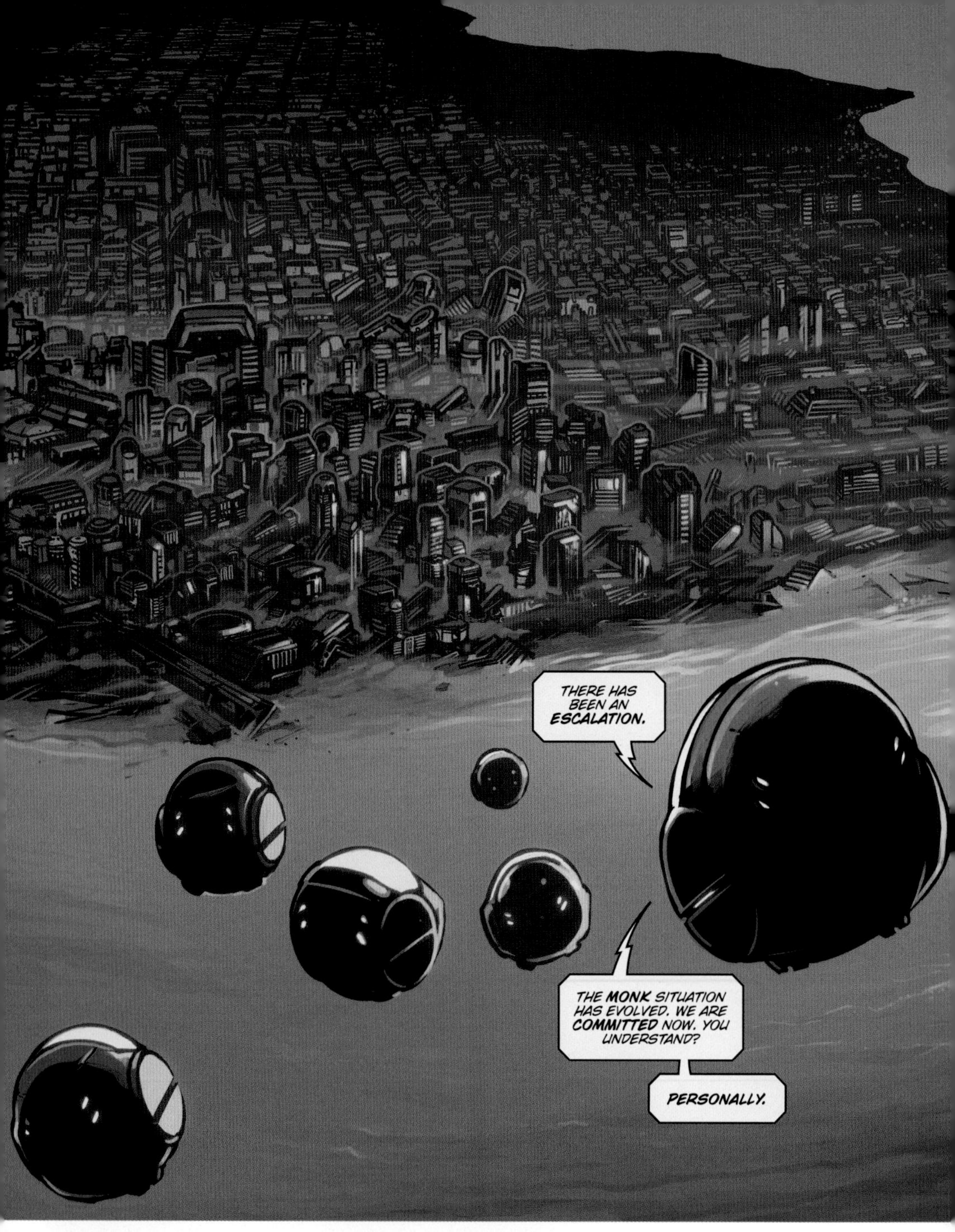
THERE HAS BEEN AN ESCALATION.
THE MONK SITUATION HAS EVOLVED. WE ARE COMMITTED NOW. YOU UNDERSTAND?
PERSONALLY.

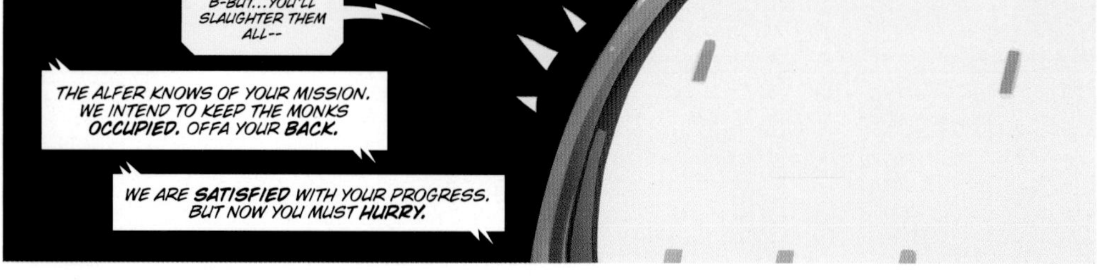
B-BUT...YOU'LL SLAUGHTER THEM ALL--
THE ALFER KNOWS OF YOUR MISSION. WE INTEND TO KEEP THE MONKS OCCUPIED. OFFA YOUR BACK.
WE ARE SATISFIED WITH YOUR PROGRESS. BUT NOW YOU MUST HURRY.

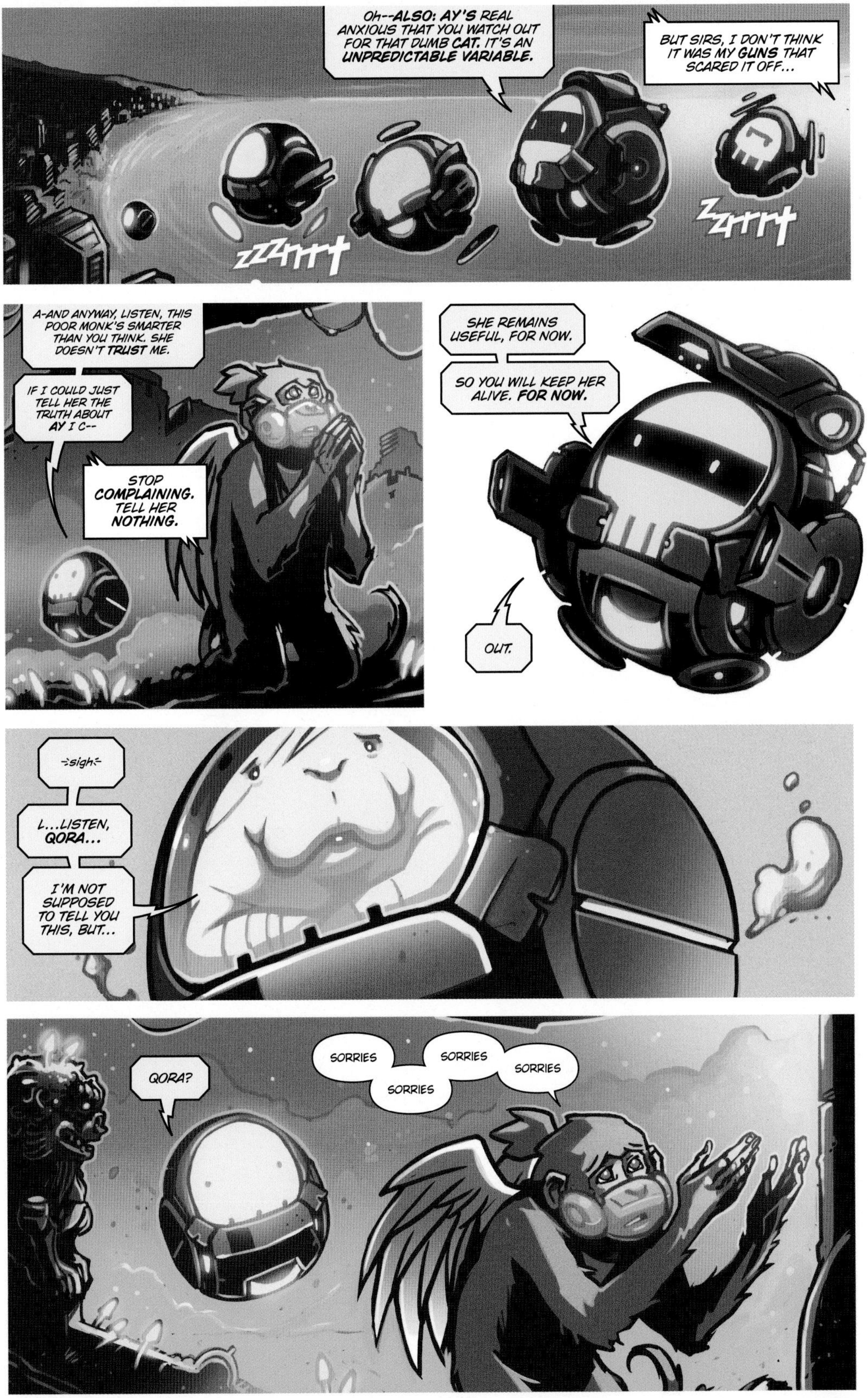
Oh--ALSO: AY'S REAL ANXIOUS THAT YOU WATCH OUT FOR THAT DUMB CAT. IT'S AN UNPREDICTABLE VARIABLE.
BUT SIRS, I DON'T THINK IT WAS MY GUNS THAT SCARED IT OFF...
ZZZZRRRT
ZZRRRT
A-AND ANYWAY, LISTEN, THIS POOR MONK'S SMARTER THAN YOU THINK. SHE DOESN'T TRUST ME.
IF I COULD JUST TELL HER THE TRUTH ABOUT AY I C--
STOP COMPLAINING. TELL HER NOTHING.
SHE REMAINS USEFUL, FOR NOW.
SO YOU WILL KEEP HER ALIVE. FOR NOW.
OUT.
sigh
L...LISTEN, QORA...
I'M NOT SUPPOSED TO TELL YOU THIS, BUT...
QORA?
SORRIES
SORRIES
SORRIES
SORRIES

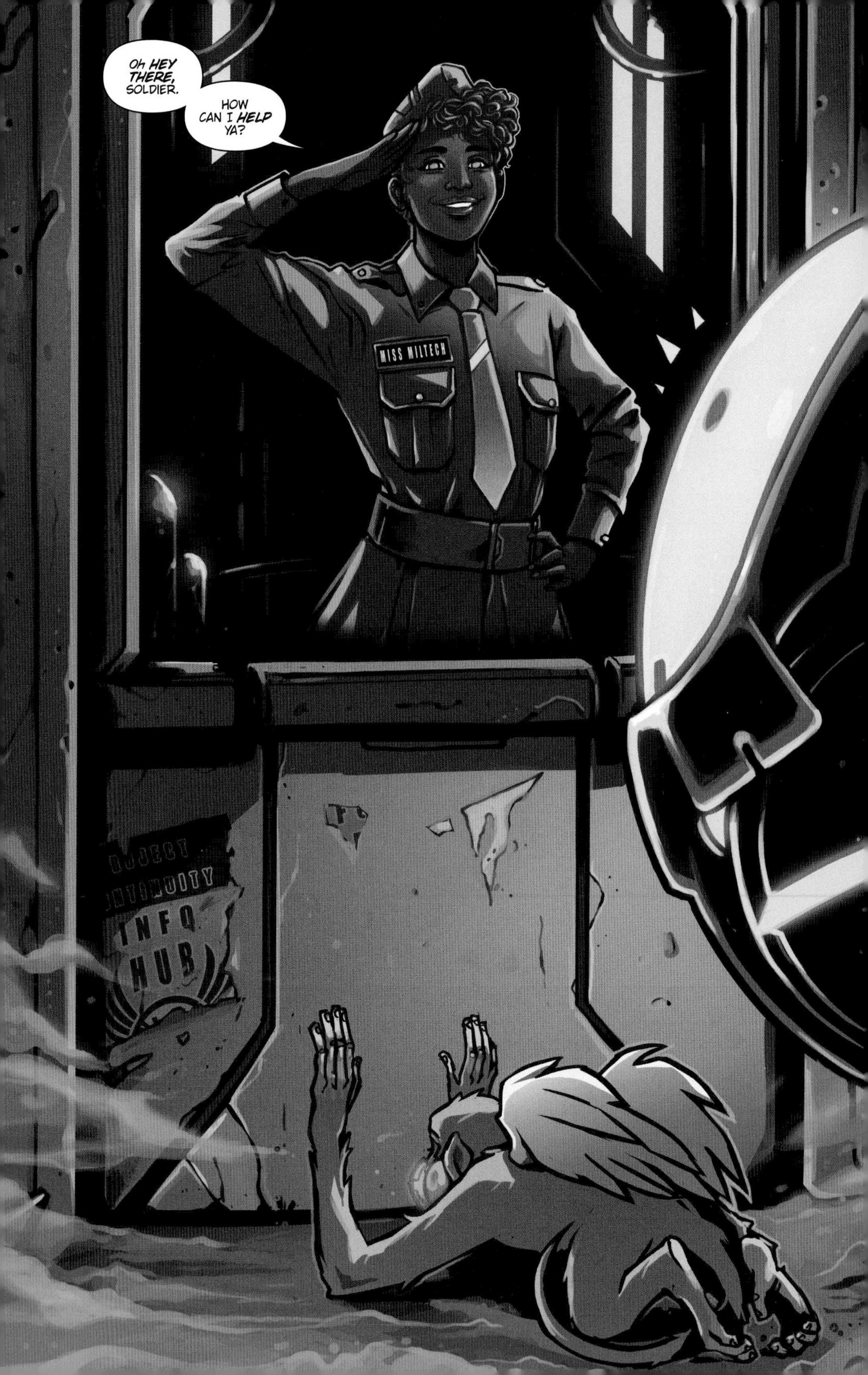
Oh HEY THERE, SOLDIER.
HOW CAN I HELP YA?
MISS MILTECH
INFO HUB

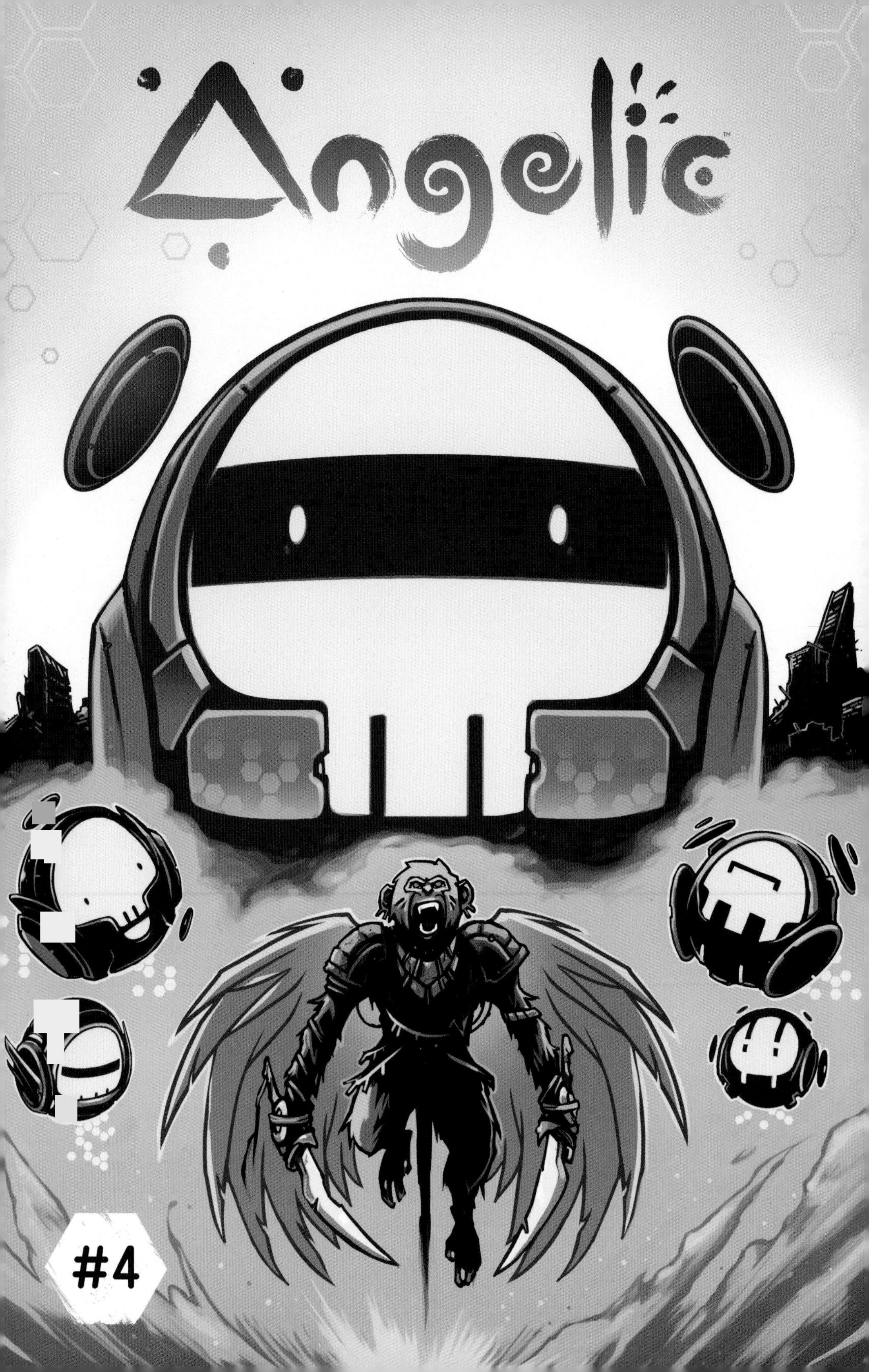

Angelic™
#4

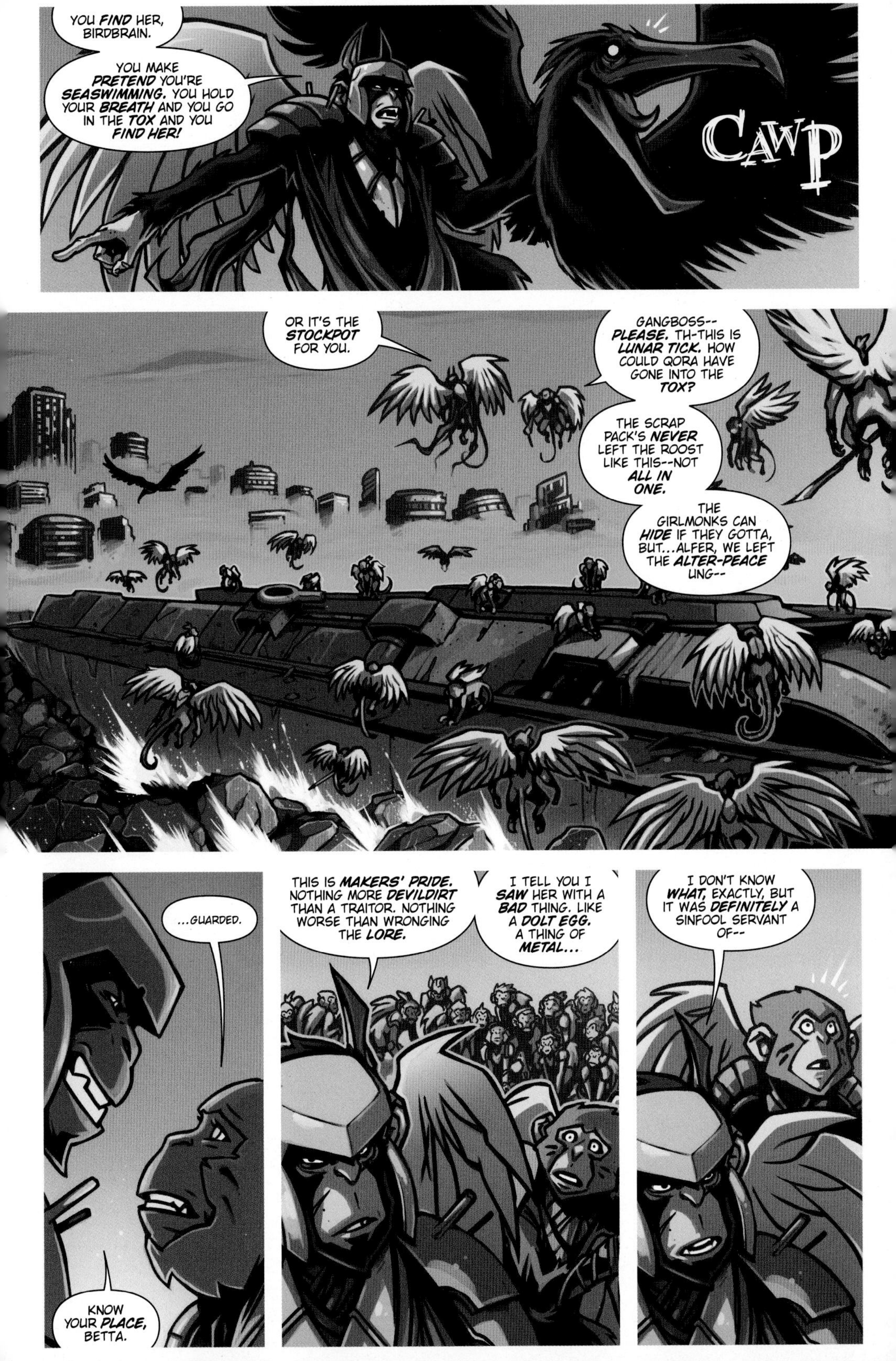
YOU FIND HER, BIRDBRAIN.
YOU MAKE PRETEND YOU'RE SEASWIMMING. YOU HOLD YOUR BREATH AND YOU GO IN THE TOX AND YOU FIND HER!
CAWP
OR IT'S THE STOCKPOT FOR YOU.
GANGBOSS-- PLEASE. TH-THIS IS LUNAR TICK. HOW COULD QORA HAVE GONE INTO THE TOX?
THE SCRAP PACK'S NEVER LEFT THE ROOST LIKE THIS--NOT ALL IN ONE.
THE GIRLMONKS CAN HIDE IF THEY GOTTA, BUT...ALFER, WE LEFT THE ALTER-PEACE UNG--
...GUARDED.
KNOW YOUR PLACE, BETTA.
THIS IS MAKERS' PRIDE. NOTHING MORE DEVILDIRT THAN A TRAITOR. NOTHING WORSE THAN WRONGING THE LORE.
I TELL YOU I SAW HER WITH A BAD THING. LIKE A DOLT EGG. A THING OF METAL...
I DON'T KNOW WHAT, EXACTLY, BUT IT WAS DEFINITELY A SINFOOL SERVANT OF--

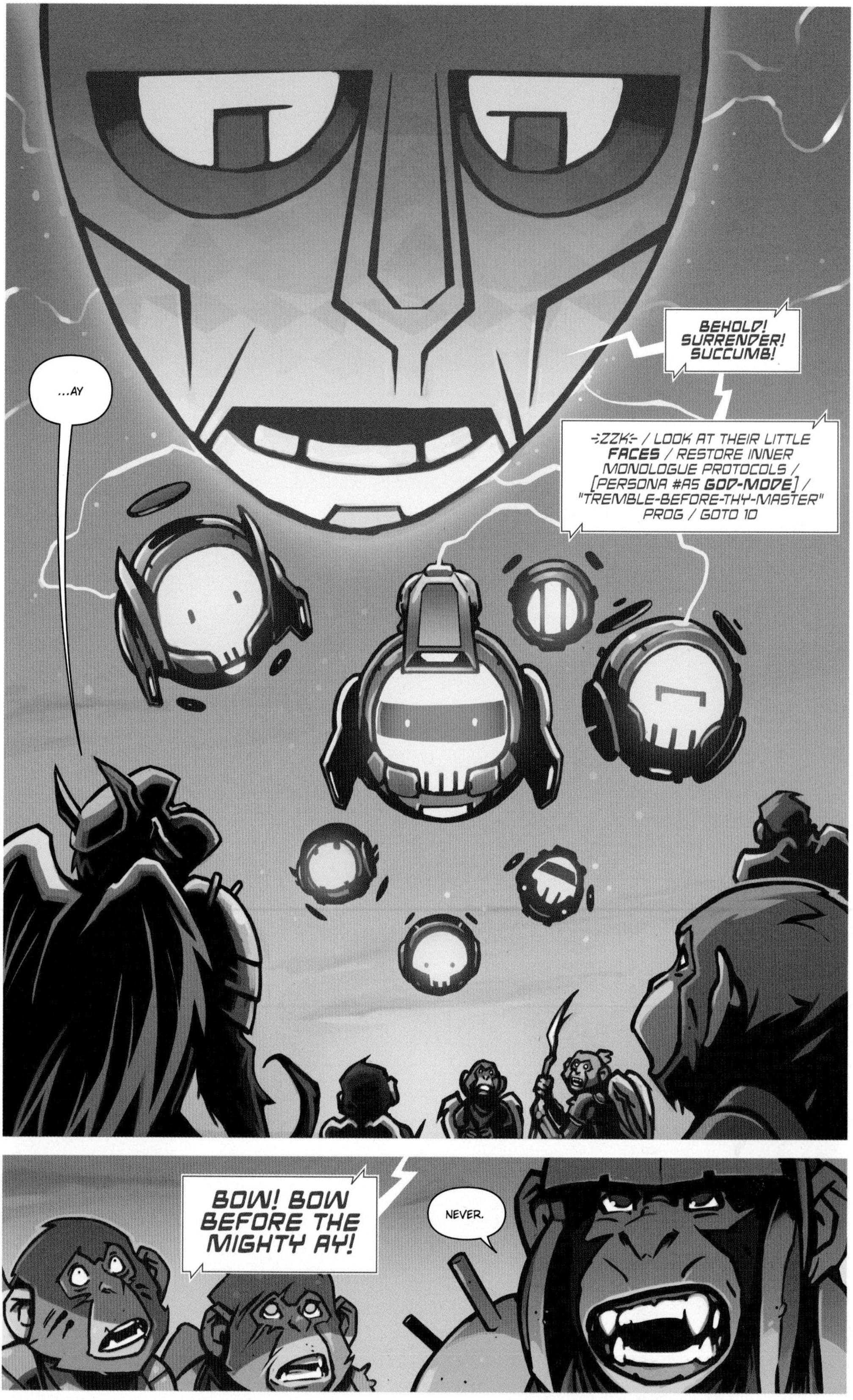
BEHOLD! SURRENDER! SUCCUMB!
-ZZK- / LOOK AT THEIR LITTLE FACES / RESTORE INNER MONOLOGUE PROTOCOLS / [PERSONA #A5 GOD-MODE] / "TREMBLE-BEFORE-THY-MASTER" PROG / GOTO 10
...AY
BOW! BOW BEFORE THE MIGHTY AY!
NEVER.

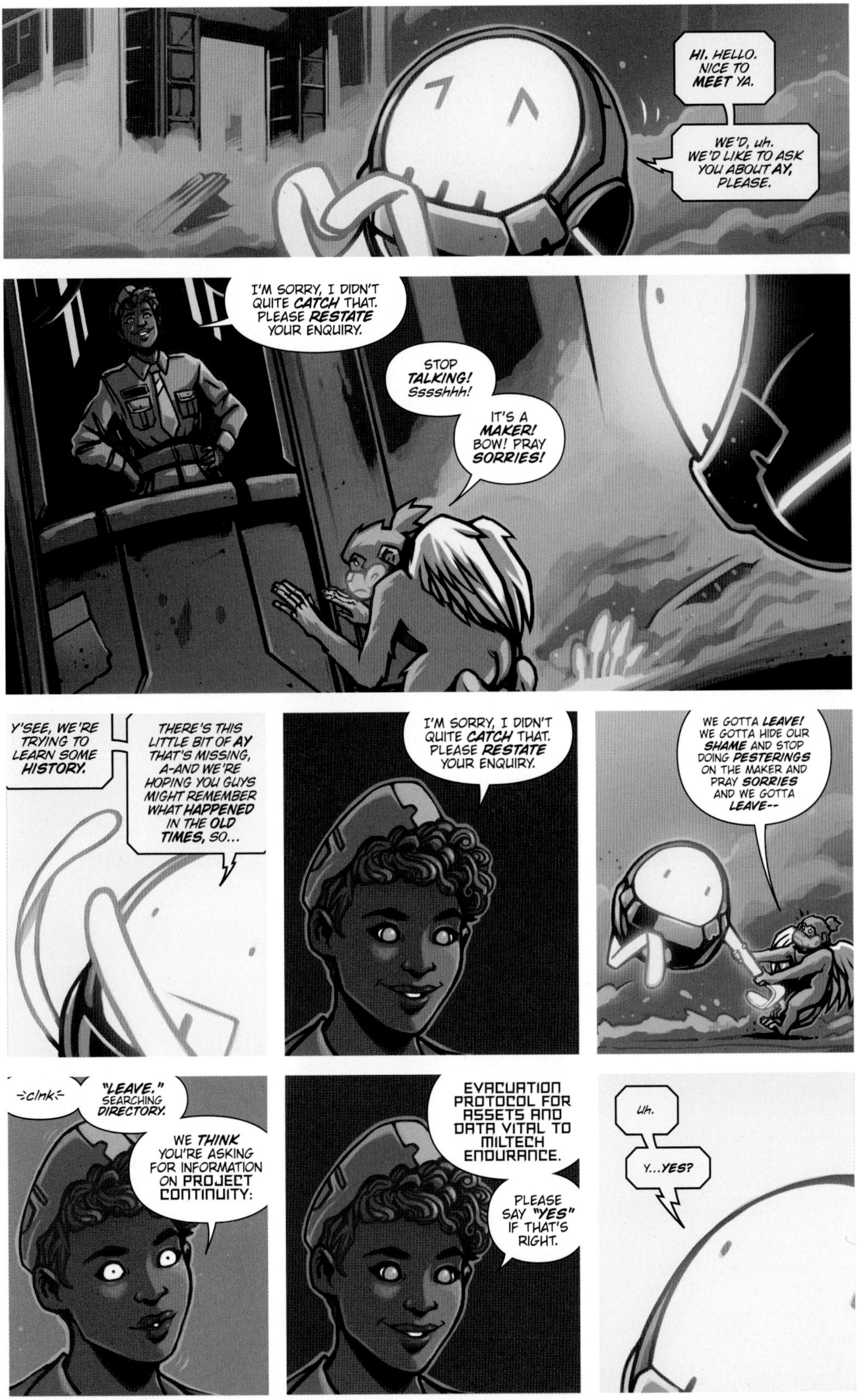
HI. HELLO. NICE TO MEET YA.
WE'D, uh. WE'D LIKE TO ASK YOU ABOUT AY, PLEASE.
I'M SORRY, I DIDN'T QUITE CATCH THAT. PLEASE RESTATE YOUR ENQUIRY.
STOP TALKING! Sssshhh!
IT'S A MAKER! BOW! PRAY SORRIES!
Y'SEE, WE'RE TRYING TO LEARN SOME HISTORY.
THERE'S THIS LITTLE BIT OF AY THAT'S MISSING, A-AND WE'RE HOPING YOU GUYS MIGHT REMEMBER WHAT HAPPENED IN THE OLD TIMES, SO...
I'M SORRY, I DIDN'T QUITE CATCH THAT. PLEASE RESTATE YOUR ENQUIRY.
WE GOTTA LEAVE! WE GOTTA HIDE OUR SHAME AND STOP DOING PESTERINGS ON THE MAKER AND PRAY SORRIES AND WE GOTTA LEAVE--
clnk
"LEAVE." SEARCHING DIRECTORY.
WE THINK YOU'RE ASKING FOR INFORMATION ON PROJECT CONTINUITY:
EVACUATION PROTOCOL FOR ASSETS AND DATA VITAL TO MILTECH ENDURANCE.
PLEASE SAY "YES" IF THAT'S RIGHT.
uh.
Y...YES?

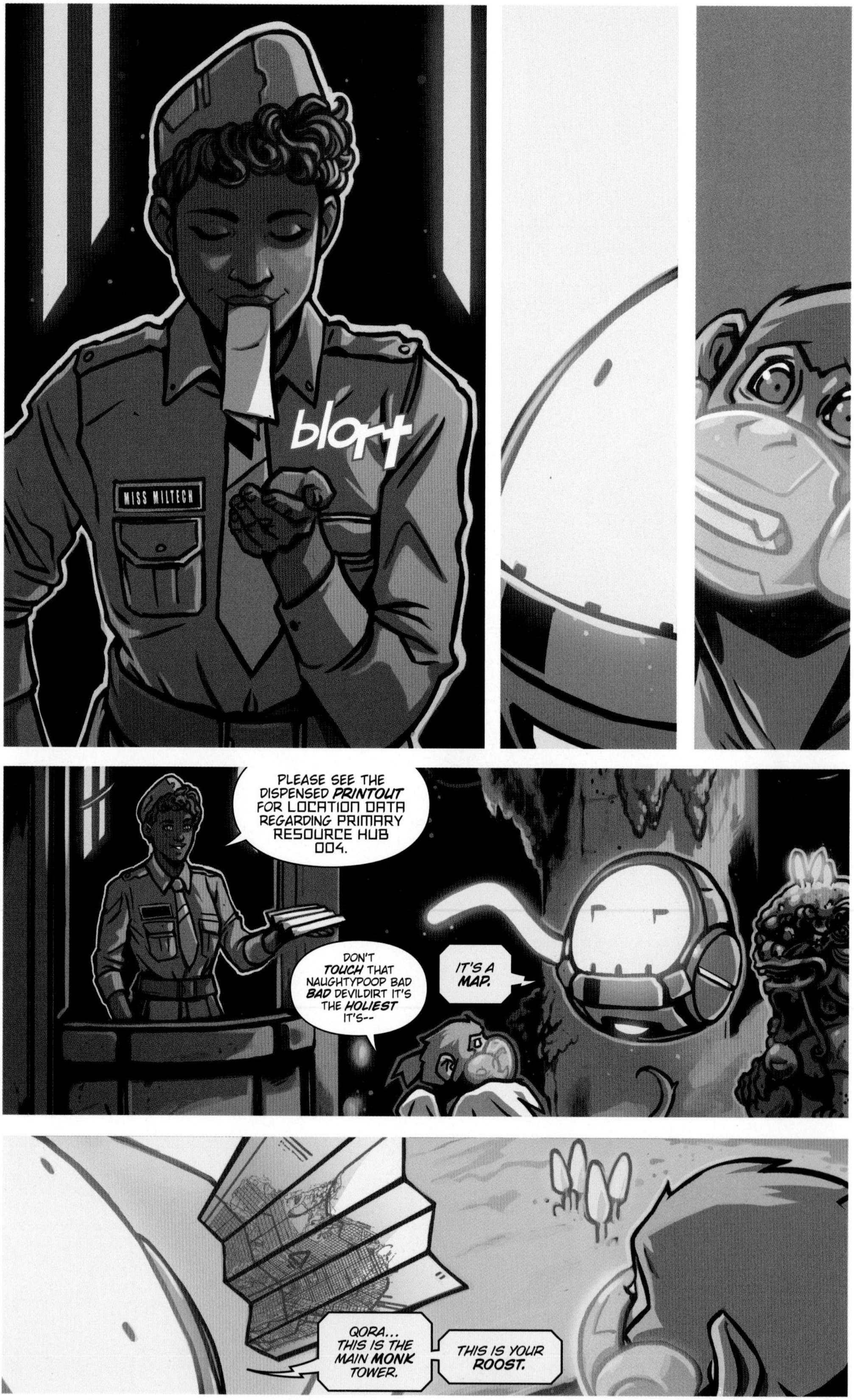
blort
MISS MILTECH
PLEASE SEE THE DISPENSED PRINTOUT FOR LOCATION DATA REGARDING PRIMARY RESOURCE HUB 004.
DON'T TOUCH THAT NAUGHTYPOOP BAD BAD DEVILDIRT IT'S THE HOLIEST IT'S--
IT'S A MAP.
QORA... THIS IS THE MAIN MONK TOWER.
THIS IS YOUR ROOST.

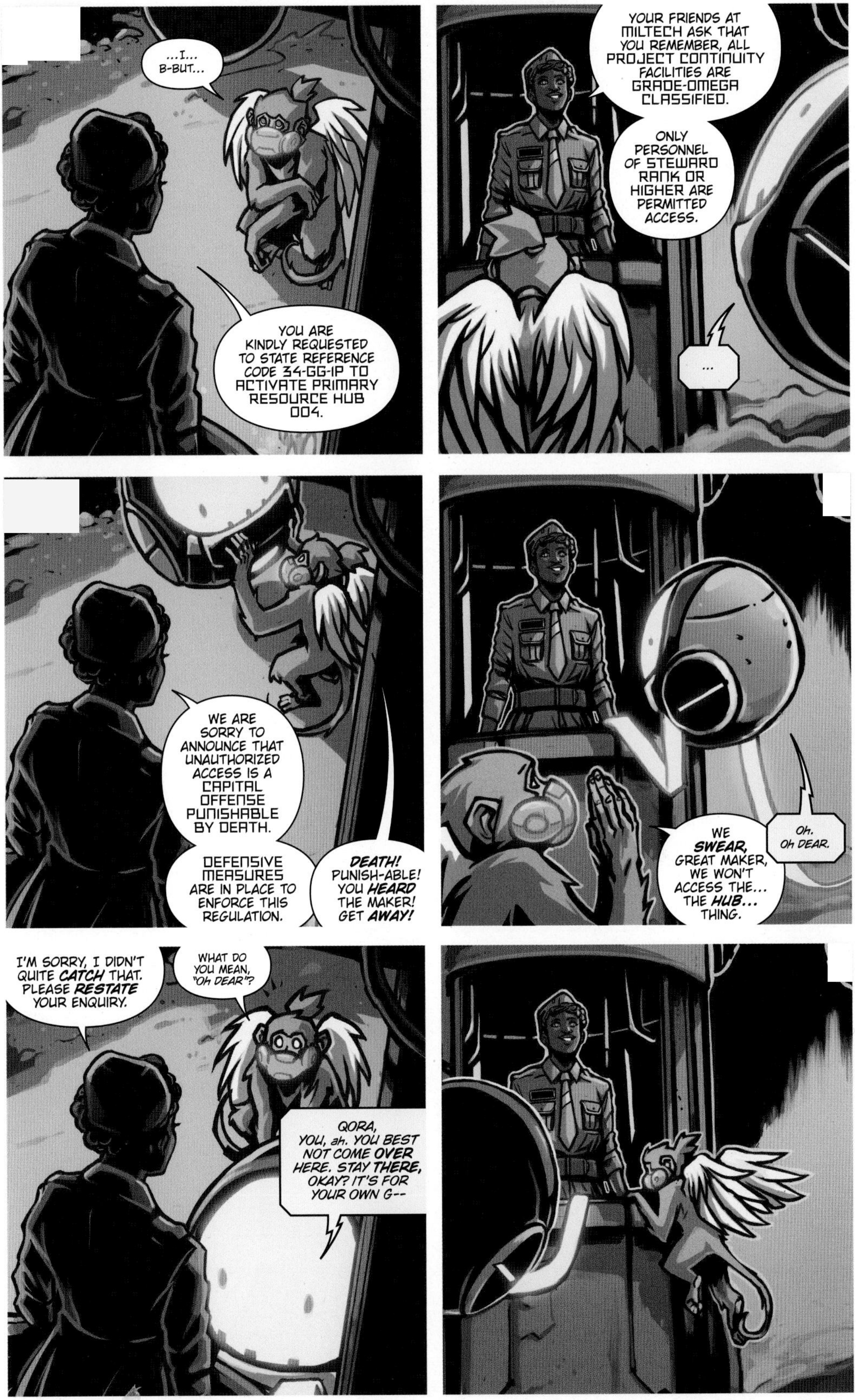
...I... B-BUT...
YOU ARE KINDLY REQUESTED TO STATE REFERENCE CODE 34-GG-IP TO ACTIVATE PRIMARY RESOURCE HUB 004.
YOUR FRIENDS AT MILTECH ASK THAT YOU REMEMBER, ALL PROJECT CONTINUITY FACILITIES ARE GRADE-OMEGA CLASSIFIED.
ONLY PERSONNEL OF STEWARD RANK OR HIGHER ARE PERMITTED ACCESS.
...
WE ARE SORRY TO ANNOUNCE THAT UNAUTHORIZED ACCESS IS A CAPITAL OFFENSE PUNISHABLE BY DEATH.
DEFENSIVE MEASURES ARE IN PLACE TO ENFORCE THIS REGULATION.
DEATH! PUNISH-ABLE! YOU HEARD THE MAKER! GET AWAY!
WE SWEAR, GREAT MAKER, WE WON'T ACCESS THE... THE HUB... THING.
Oh. Oh DEAR.
I'M SORRY, I DIDN'T QUITE CATCH THAT. PLEASE RESTATE YOUR ENQUIRY.
WHAT DO YOU MEAN, "Oh DEAR"?
QORA, YOU, ah. YOU BEST NOT COME OVER HERE. STAY THERE, OKAY? IT'S FOR YOUR OWN G--

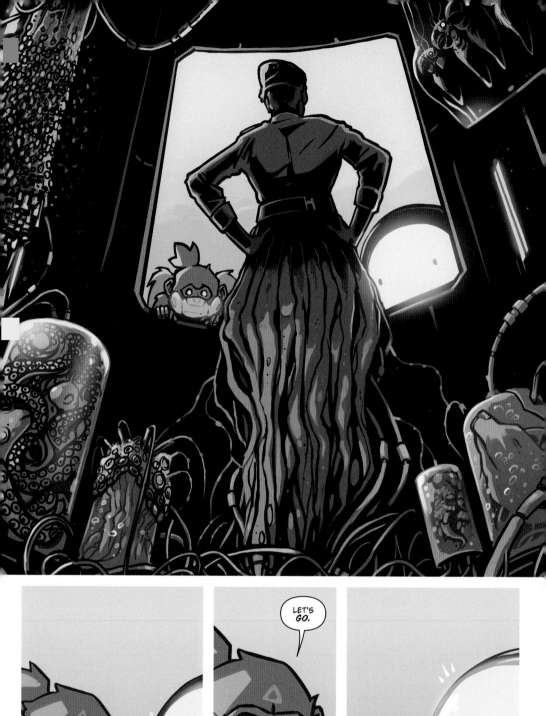

LET'S GO.

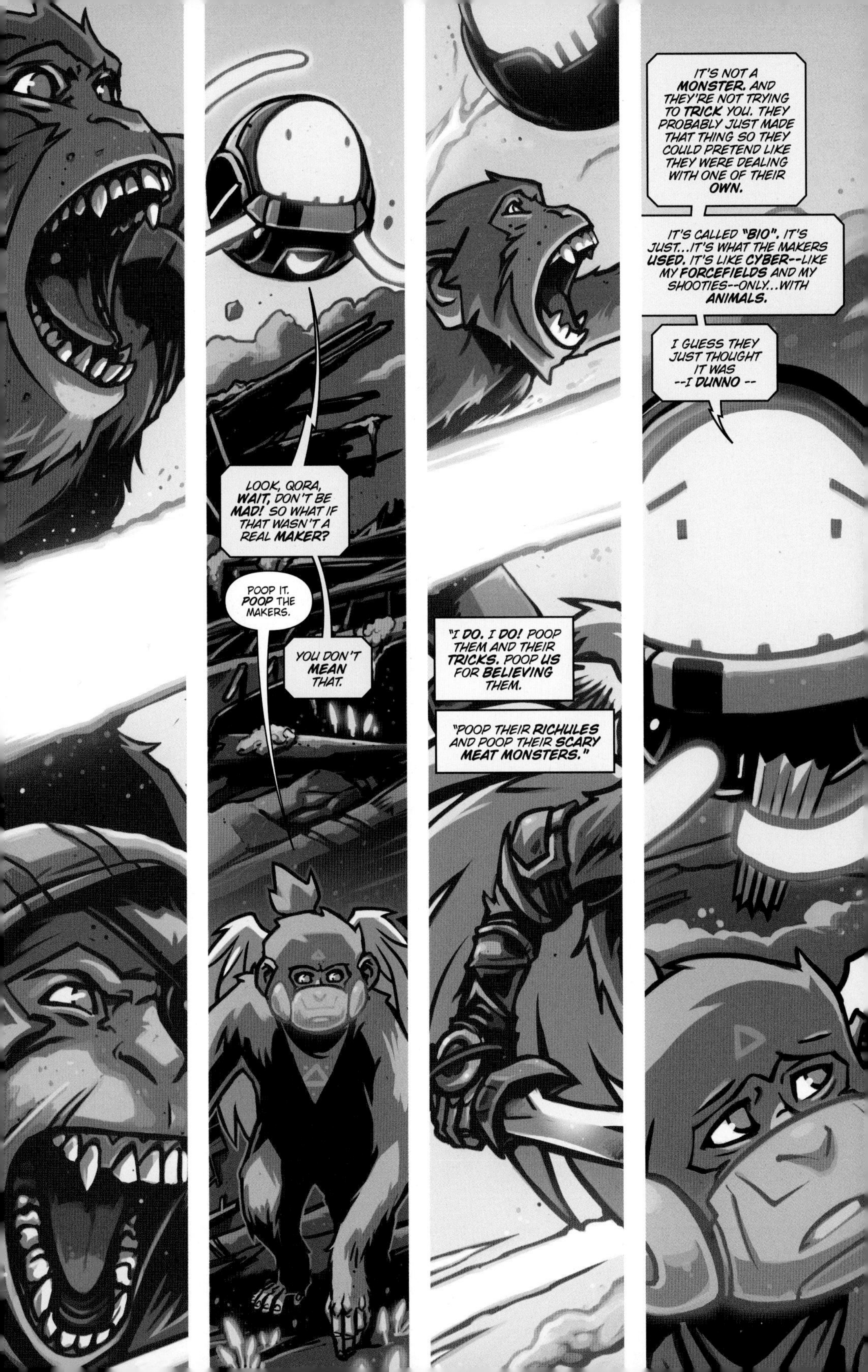

LOOK, QORA, WAIT, DON'T BE MAD! SO WHAT IF THAT WASN'T A REAL MAKER?
POOP IT. POOP THE MAKERS.
YOU DON'T MEAN THAT.
"I DO. I DO! POOP THEM AND THEIR TRICKS. POOP US FOR BELIEVING THEM.
"POOP THEIR RICHULES AND POOP THEIR SCARY MEAT MONSTERS."
IT'S NOT A MONSTER. AND THEY'RE NOT TRYING TO TRICK YOU. THEY PROBABLY JUST MADE THAT THING SO THEY COULD PRETEND LIKE THEY WERE DEALING WITH ONE OF THEIR OWN.
IT'S CALLED "BIO". IT'S JUST...IT'S WHAT THE MAKERS USED. IT'S LIKE CYBER--LIKE MY FORCEFIELDS AND MY SHOOTIES--ONLY...WITH ANIMALS.
I GUESS THEY JUST THOUGHT IT WAS --I DUNNO --

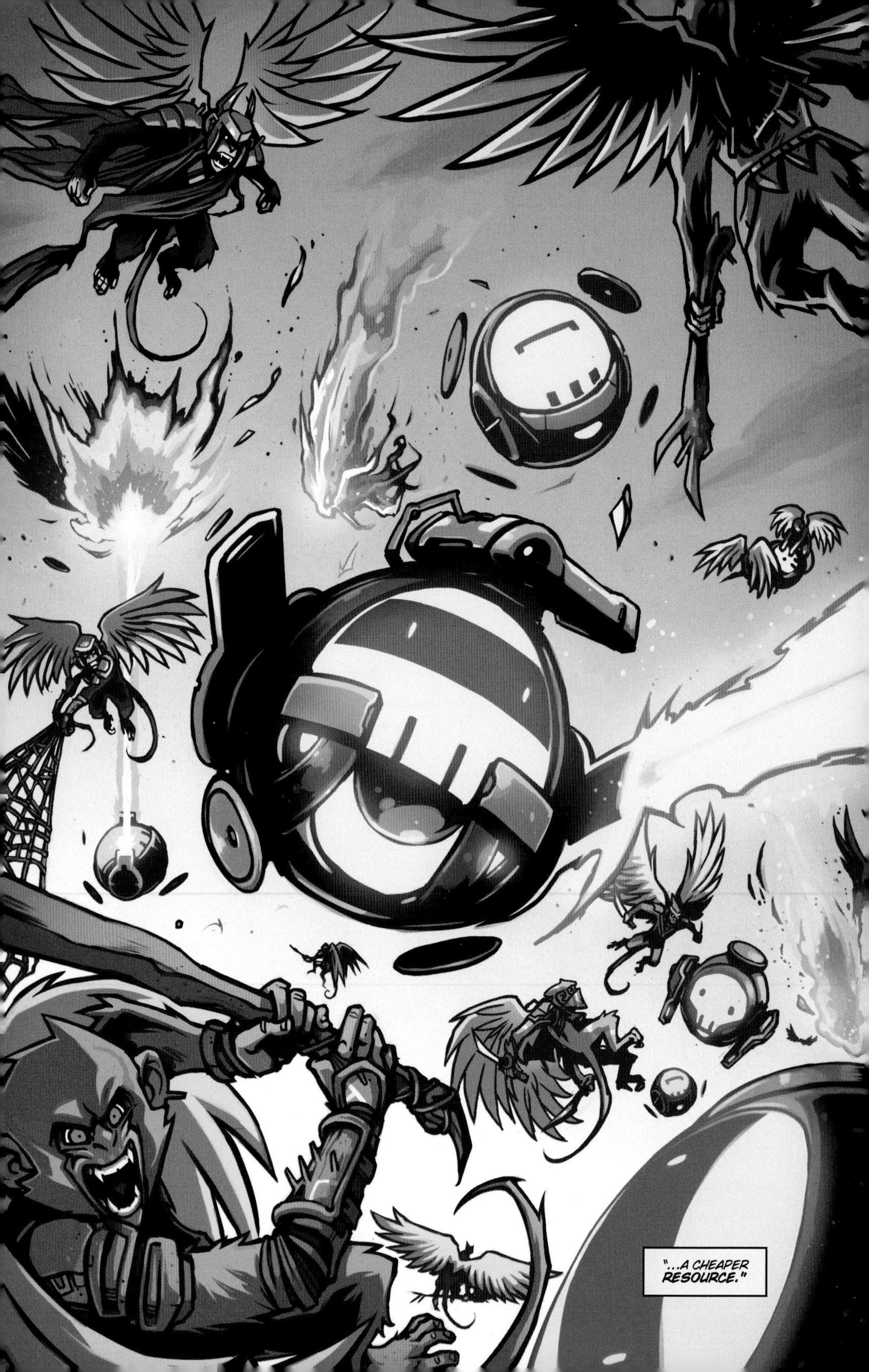
"...A CHEAPER RESOURCE."

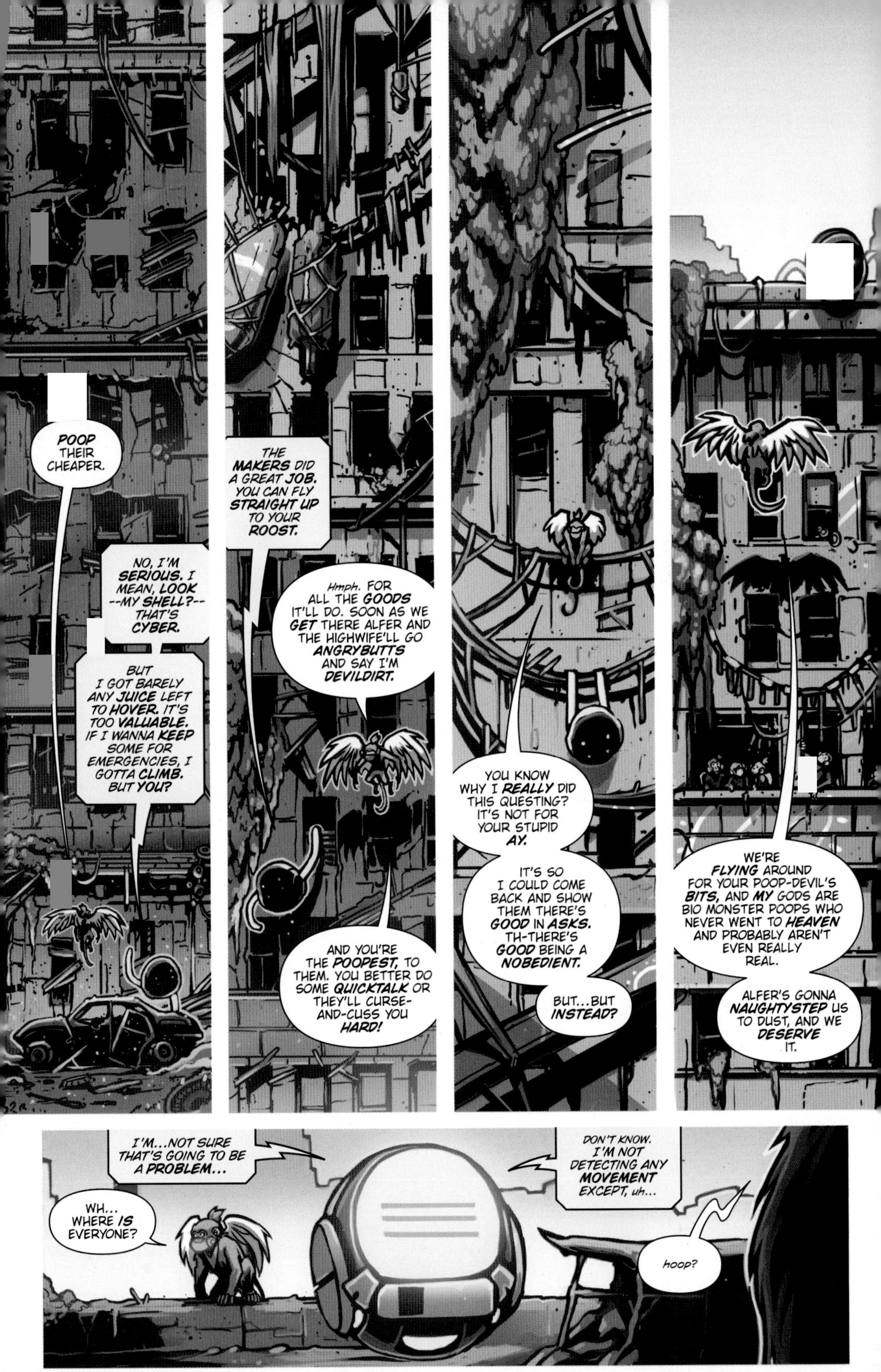

POOP THEIR CHEAPER.
NO, I'M SERIOUS. I MEAN, LOOK --MY SHELL?-- THAT'S CYBER.
BUT I GOT BARELY ANY JUICE LEFT TO HOVER. IT'S TOO VALUABLE. IF I WANNA KEEP SOME FOR EMERGENCIES, I GOTTA CLIMB. BUT YOU?
THE MAKERS DID A GREAT JOB. YOU CAN FLY STRAIGHT UP TO YOUR ROOST.
Hmph. FOR ALL THE GOODS IT'LL DO. SOON AS WE GET THERE ALFER AND THE HIGHWIFE'LL GO ANGRYBUTTS AND SAY I'M DEVILDIRT.
AND YOU'RE THE POOPEST, TO THEM. YOU BETTER DO SOME QUICKTALK OR THEY'LL CURSE-AND-CUSS YOU HARD!
YOU KNOW WHY I REALLY DID THIS QUESTING? IT'S NOT FOR YOUR STUPID AY.
IT'S SO I COULD COME BACK AND SHOW THEM THERE'S GOOD IN ASKS. TH-THERE'S GOOD BEING A NOBEDIENT.
BUT...BUT INSTEAD?
WE'RE FLYING AROUND FOR YOUR POOP-DEVIL'S BITS, AND MY GODS ARE BIO MONSTER POOPS WHO NEVER WENT TO HEAVEN AND PROBABLY AREN'T EVEN REALLY REAL.
ALFER'S GONNA NAUGHTYSTEP US TO DUST, AND WE DESERVE IT.
I'M...NOT SURE THAT'S GOING TO BE A PROBLEM...
WH... WHERE IS EVERYONE?
DON'T KNOW. I'M NOT DETECTING ANY MOVEMENT EXCEPT, uh...
hoop?

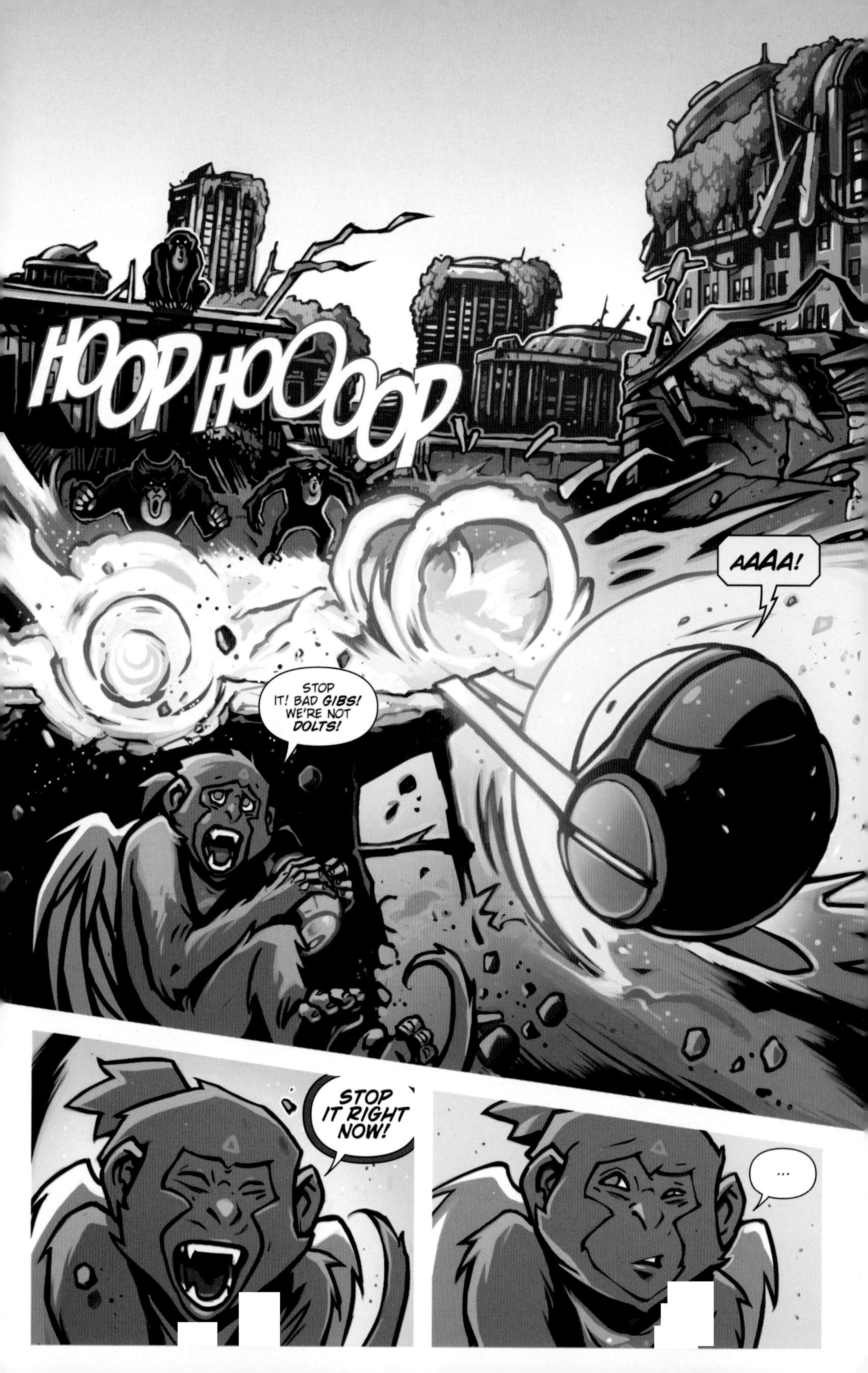
HOOP HOOOOOP
AAAA!
STOP IT! BAD GIBS! WE'RE NOT DOLTS!
STOP IT RIGHT NOW!
...

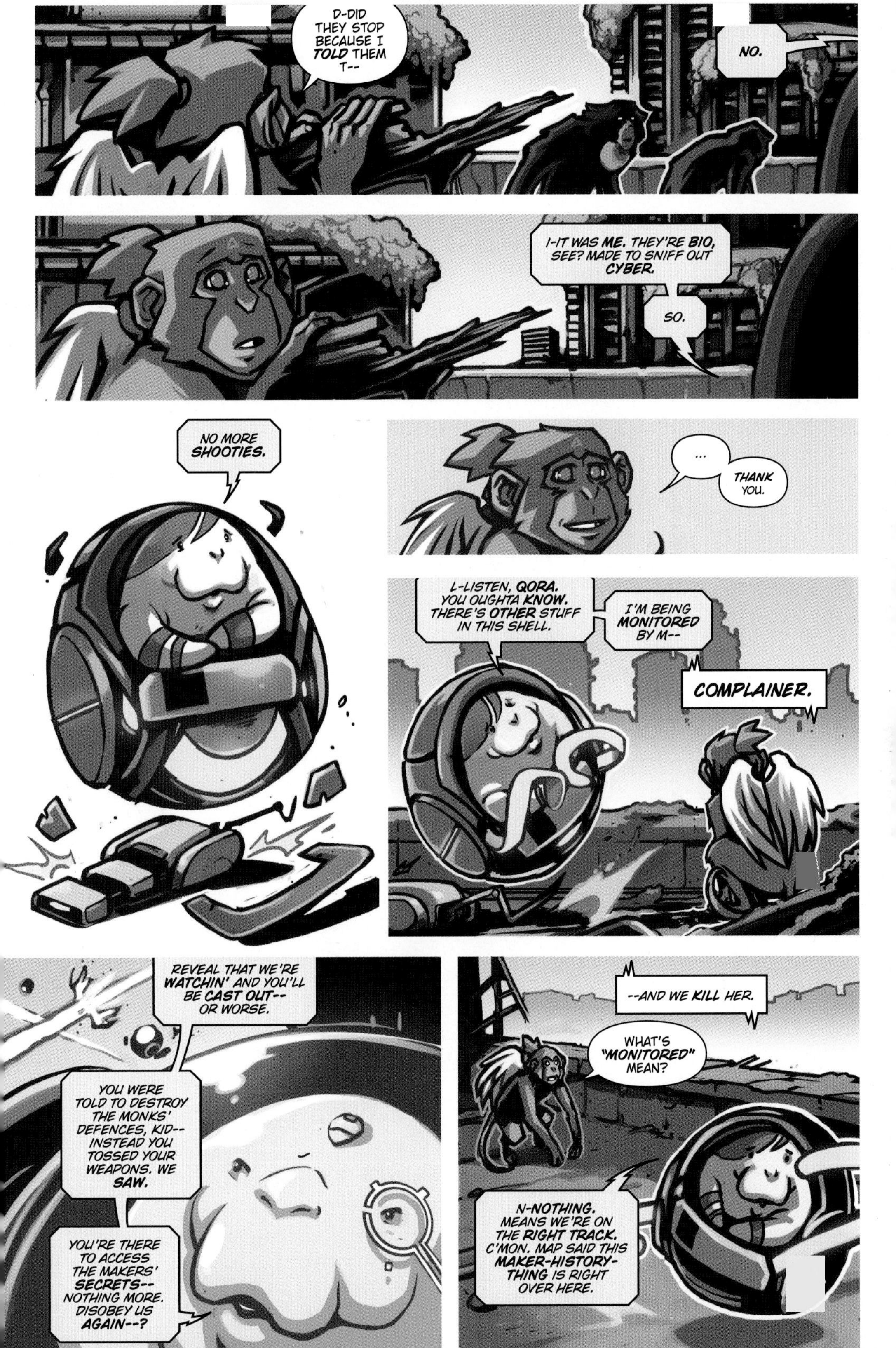

D-DID THEY STOP BECAUSE I TOLD THEM T--
NO.
I-IT WAS ME. THEY'RE BIO, SEE? MADE TO SNIFF OUT CYBER.
SO.
NO MORE SHOOTIES.
...
THANK YOU.
L-LISTEN, QORA. YOU OUGHTA KNOW. THERE'S OTHER STUFF IN THIS SHELL.
I'M BEING MONITORED BY M--
COMPLAINER.
REVEAL THAT WE'RE WATCHIN' AND YOU'LL BE CAST OUT-- OR WORSE.
YOU WERE TOLD TO DESTROY THE MONKS' DEFENCES, KID-- INSTEAD YOU TOSSED YOUR WEAPONS. WE SAW.
YOU'RE THERE TO ACCESS THE MAKERS' SECRETS-- NOTHING MORE. DISOBEY US AGAIN--?
--AND WE KILL HER.
WHAT'S "MONITORED" MEAN?
N-NOTHING. MEANS WE'RE ON THE RIGHT TRACK. C'MON. MAP SAID THIS MAKER-HISTORY-THING IS RIGHT OVER HERE.

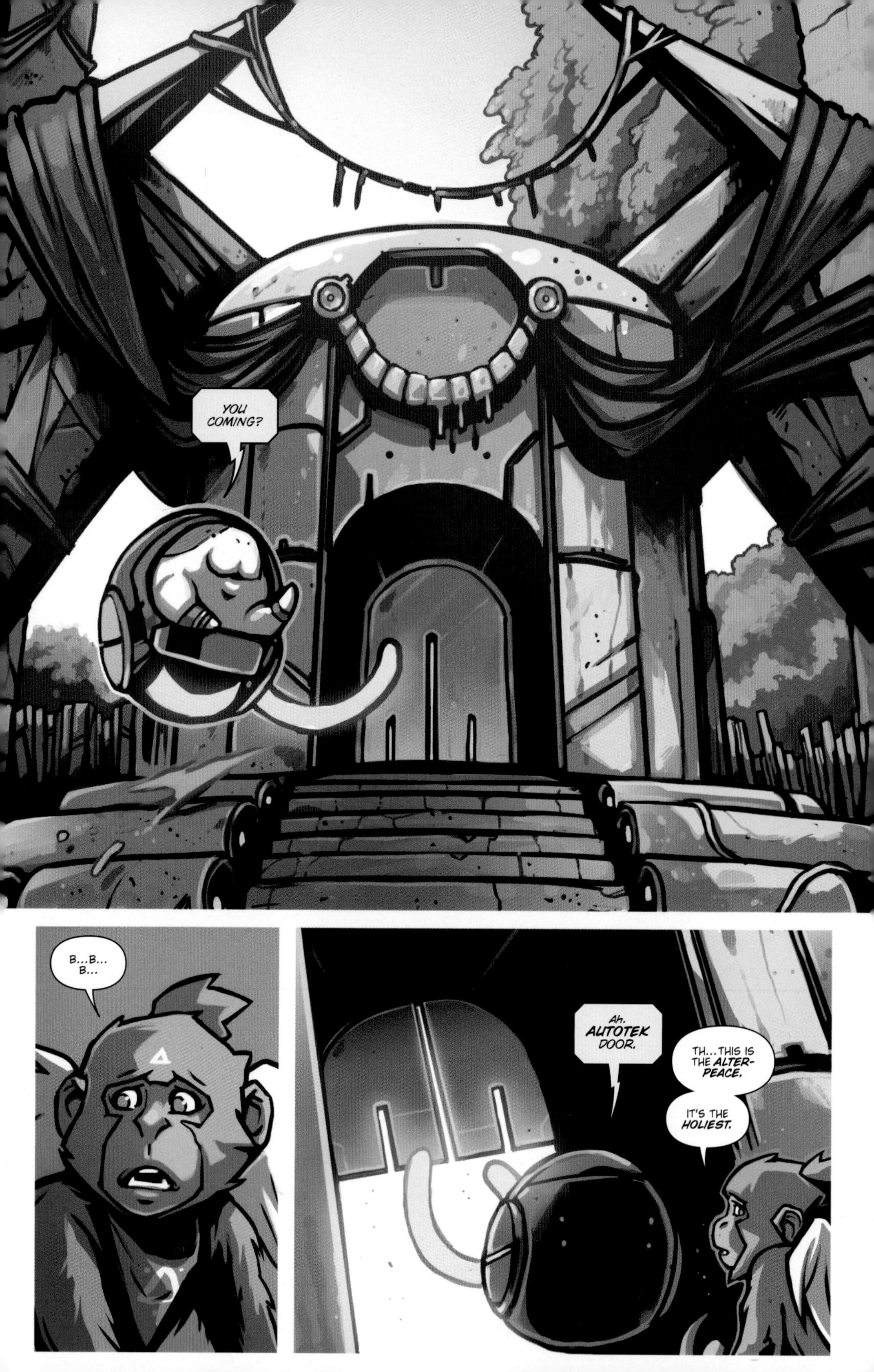
YOU COMING?
B...B... B...
Ah. AUTOTEK DOOR.
TH...THIS IS THE ALTER-PEACE.
IT'S THE HOLIEST.

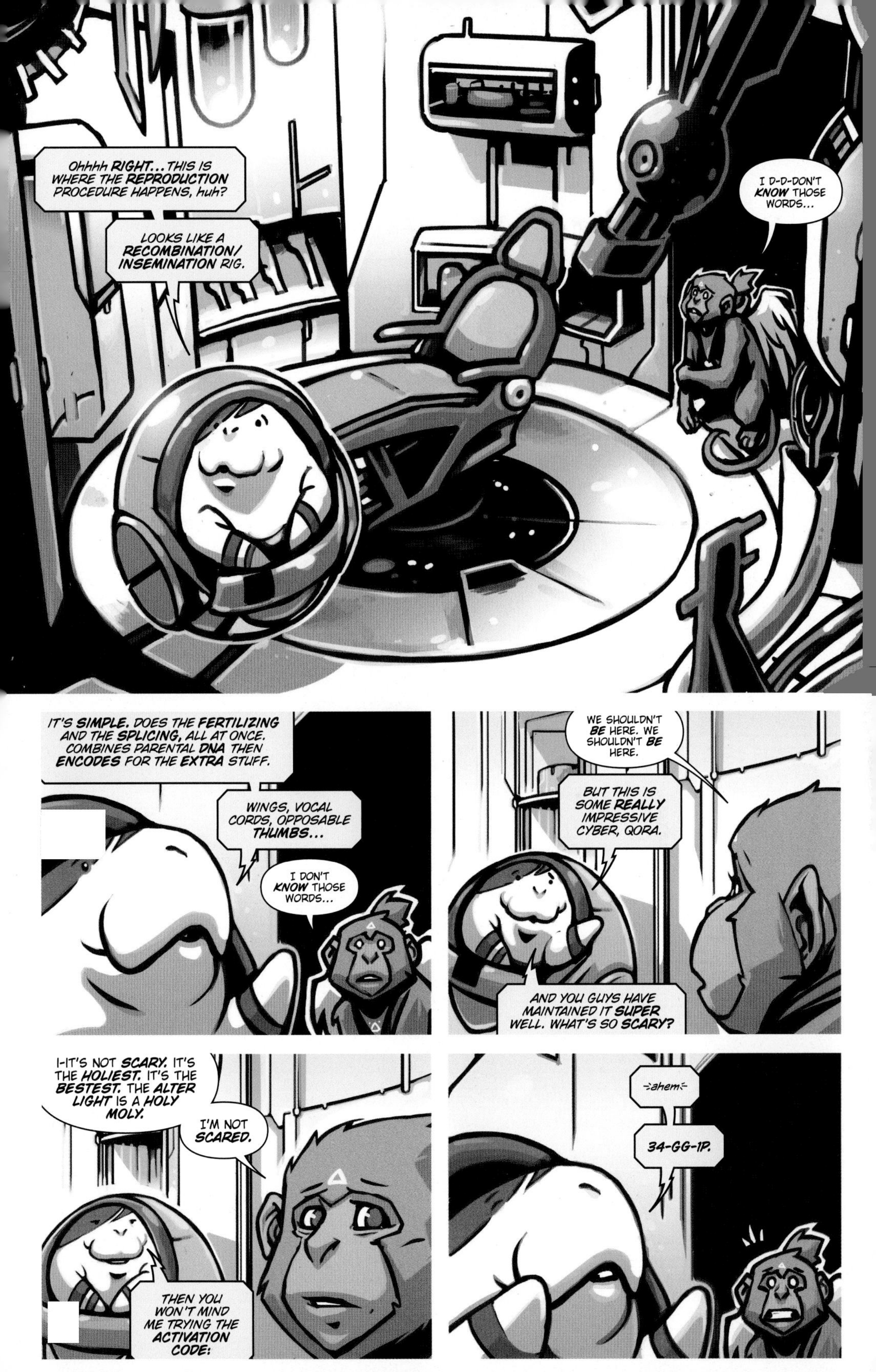

Ohhhh RIGHT... THIS IS WHERE THE REPRODUCTION PROCEDURE HAPPENS, huh?
LOOKS LIKE A RECOMBINATION/ INSEMINATION RIG.
I D-D-DON'T KNOW THOSE WORDS...
IT'S SIMPLE. DOES THE FERTILIZING AND THE SPLICING, ALL AT ONCE. COMBINES PARENTAL DNA THEN ENCODES FOR THE EXTRA STUFF.
WINGS, VOCAL CORDS, OPPOSABLE THUMBS...
I DON'T KNOW THOSE WORDS...
WE SHOULDN'T BE HERE. WE SHOULDN'T BE HERE.
BUT THIS IS SOME REALLY IMPRESSIVE CYBER, QORA.
AND YOU GUYS HAVE MAINTAINED IT SUPER WELL. WHAT'S SO SCARY?
I-IT'S NOT SCARY. IT'S THE HOLIEST. IT'S THE BESTEST. THE ALTER LIGHT IS A HOLY MOLY.
I'M NOT SCARED.
THEN YOU WON'T MIND ME TRYING THE ACTIVATION CODE:
ahem
34-GG-1P.

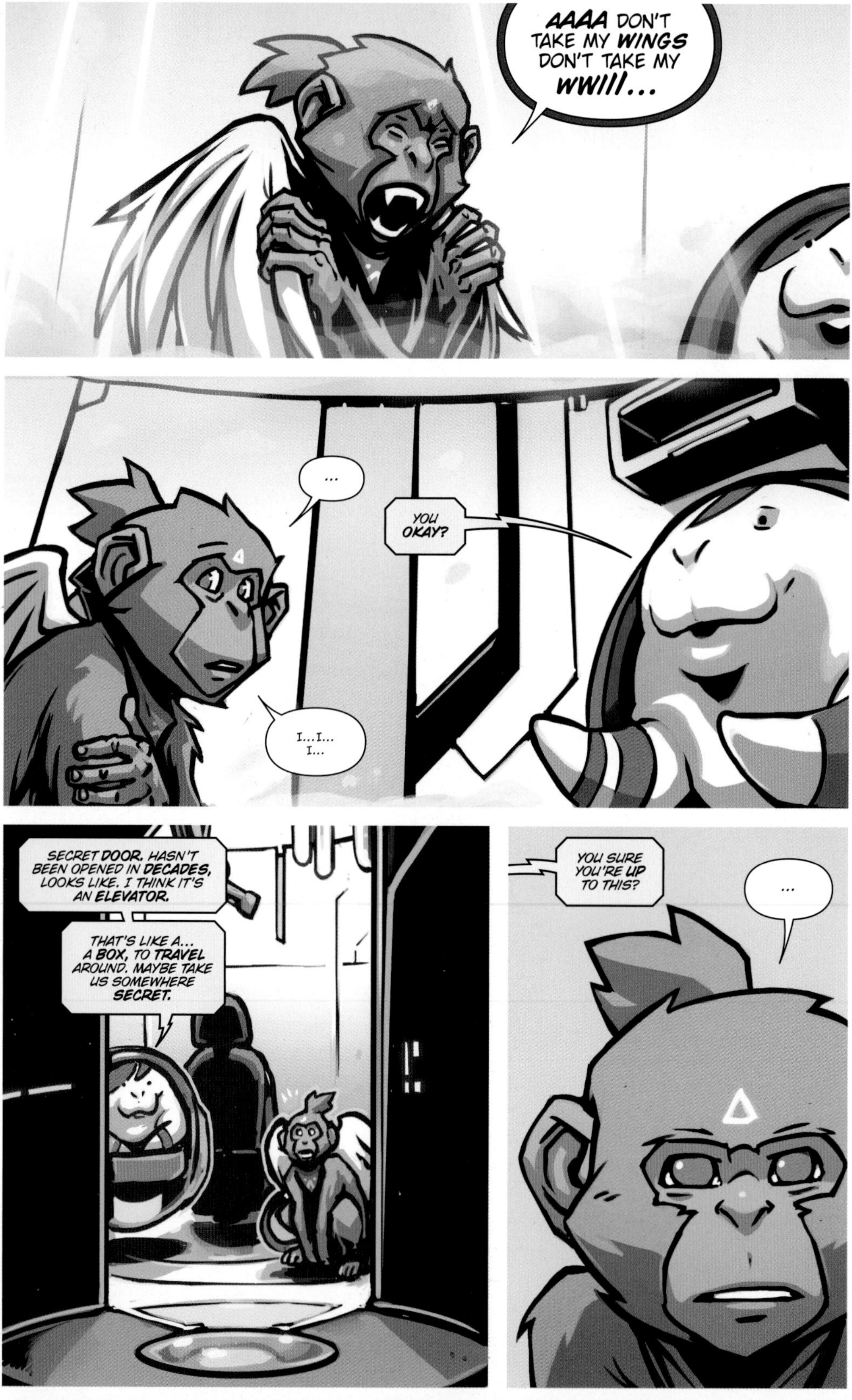
AAAA DON'T TAKE MY WINGS DON'T TAKE MY WWIII...
...
YOU OKAY?
I...I... I...
SECRET DOOR. HASN'T BEEN OPENED IN DECADES, LOOKS LIKE. I THINK IT'S AN ELEVATOR.
THAT'S LIKE A... A BOX, TO TRAVEL AROUND. MAYBE TAKE US SOMEWHERE SECRET.
YOU SURE YOU'RE UP TO THIS?
...

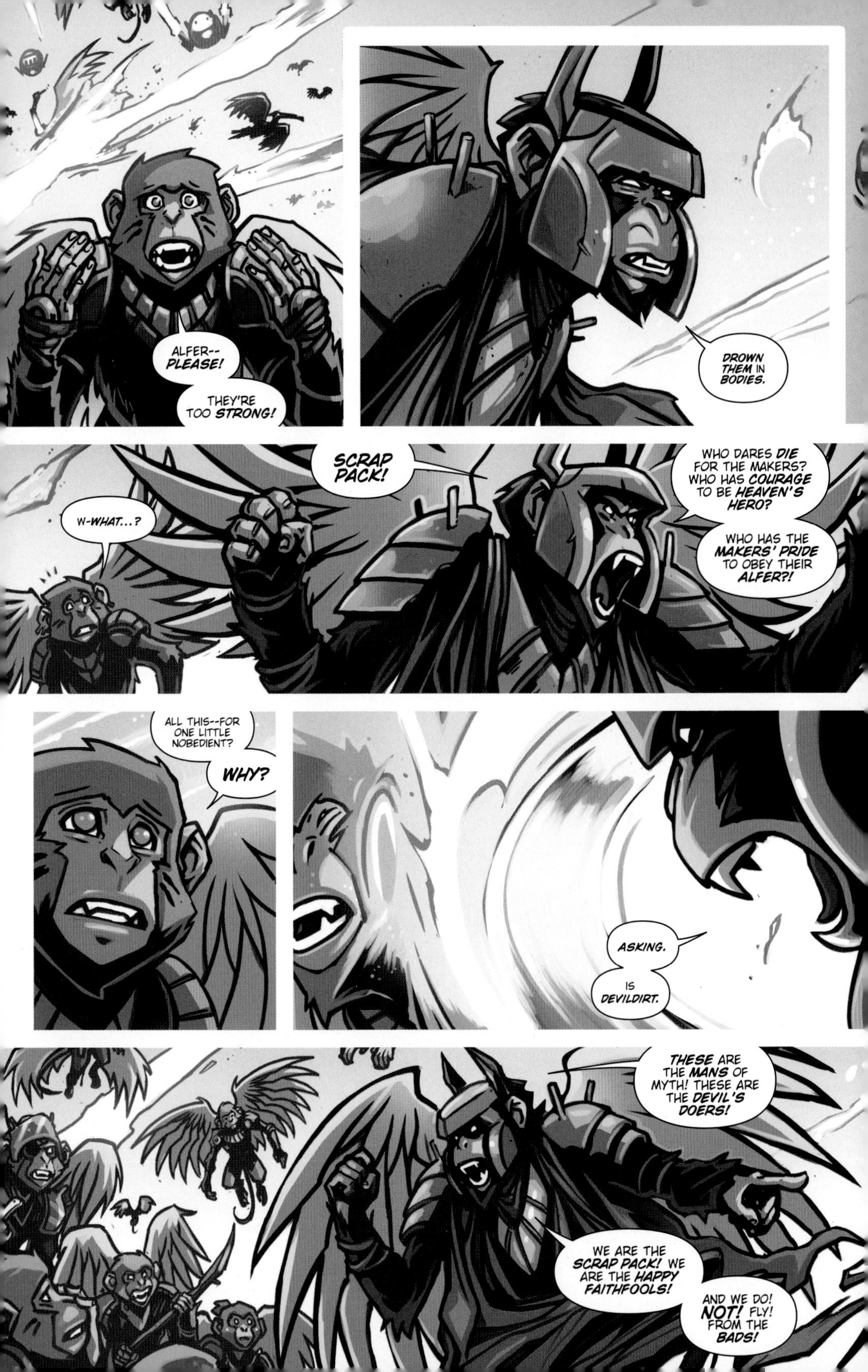

ALFER-- PLEASE!
THEY'RE TOO STRONG!
DROWN THEM IN BODIES.
W-WHAT...?
SCRAP PACK!
WHO DARES DIE FOR THE MAKERS? WHO HAS COURAGE TO BE HEAVEN'S HERO?
WHO HAS THE MAKERS' PRIDE TO OBEY THEIR ALFER?!
ALL THIS--FOR ONE LITTLE NOBEDIENT?
WHY?
ASKING.
IS DEVILDIRT.
THESE ARE THE MANS OF MYTH! THESE ARE THE DEVIL'S DOERS!
WE ARE THE SCRAP PACK! WE ARE THE HAPPY FAITHFOOLS!
AND WE DO! NOT! FLY! FROM THE BADS!

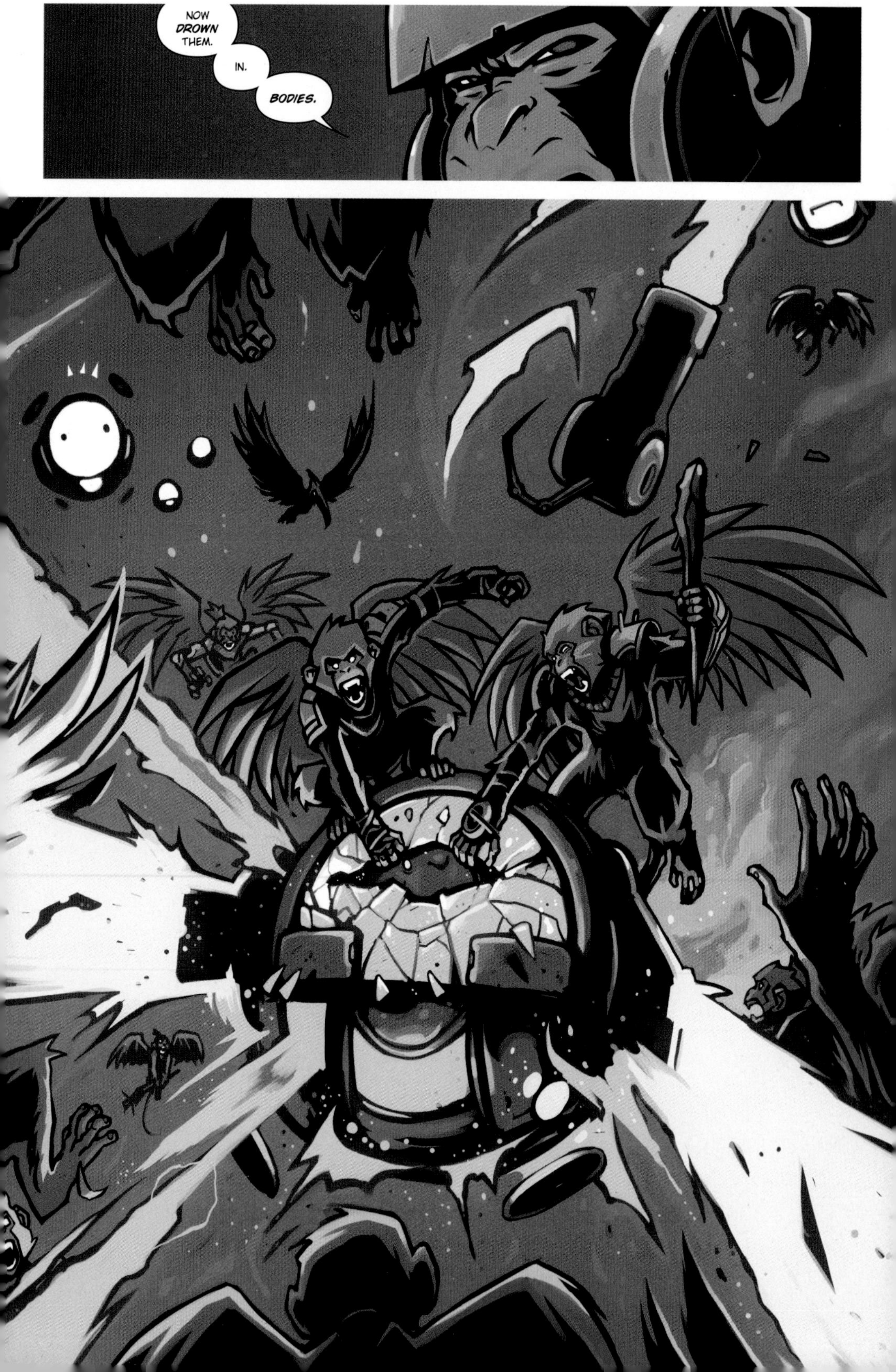
NOW *DROWN* THEM.
IN.
BODIES.

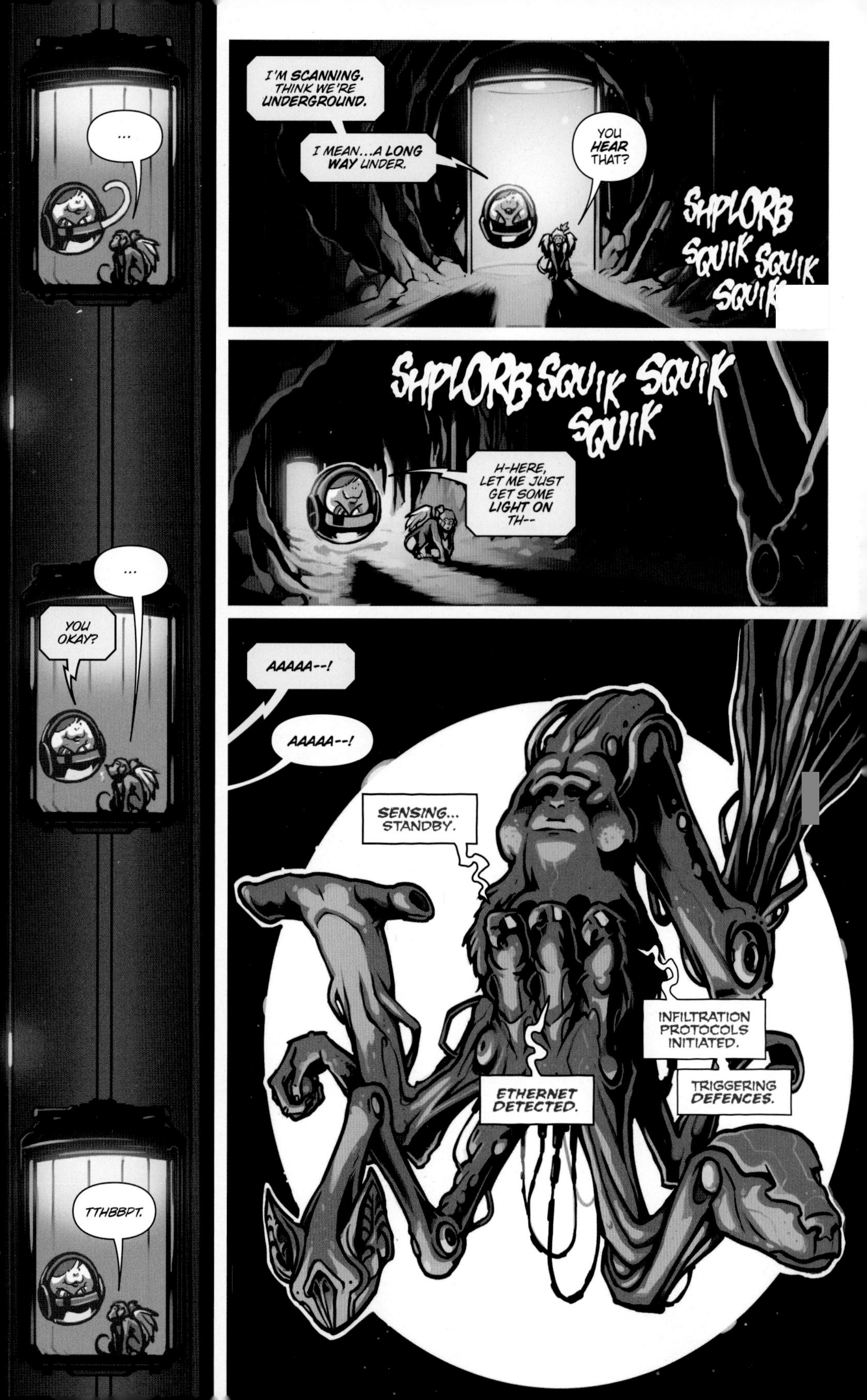
...
I'M SCANNING. THINK WE'RE UNDERGROUND.
I MEAN...A LONG WAY UNDER.
YOU HEAR THAT?
SHPLORB SQUIK SQUIK SQUIK
SHPLORB SQUIK SQUIK SQUIK
H-HERE, LET ME JUST GET SOME LIGHT ON TH--
...
YOU OKAY?
AAAAA--!
AAAAA--!
SENSING... STANDBY.
INFILTRATION PROTOCOLS INITIATED.
ETHERNET DETECTED.
TRIGGERING DEFENCES.
TTHBBPT.

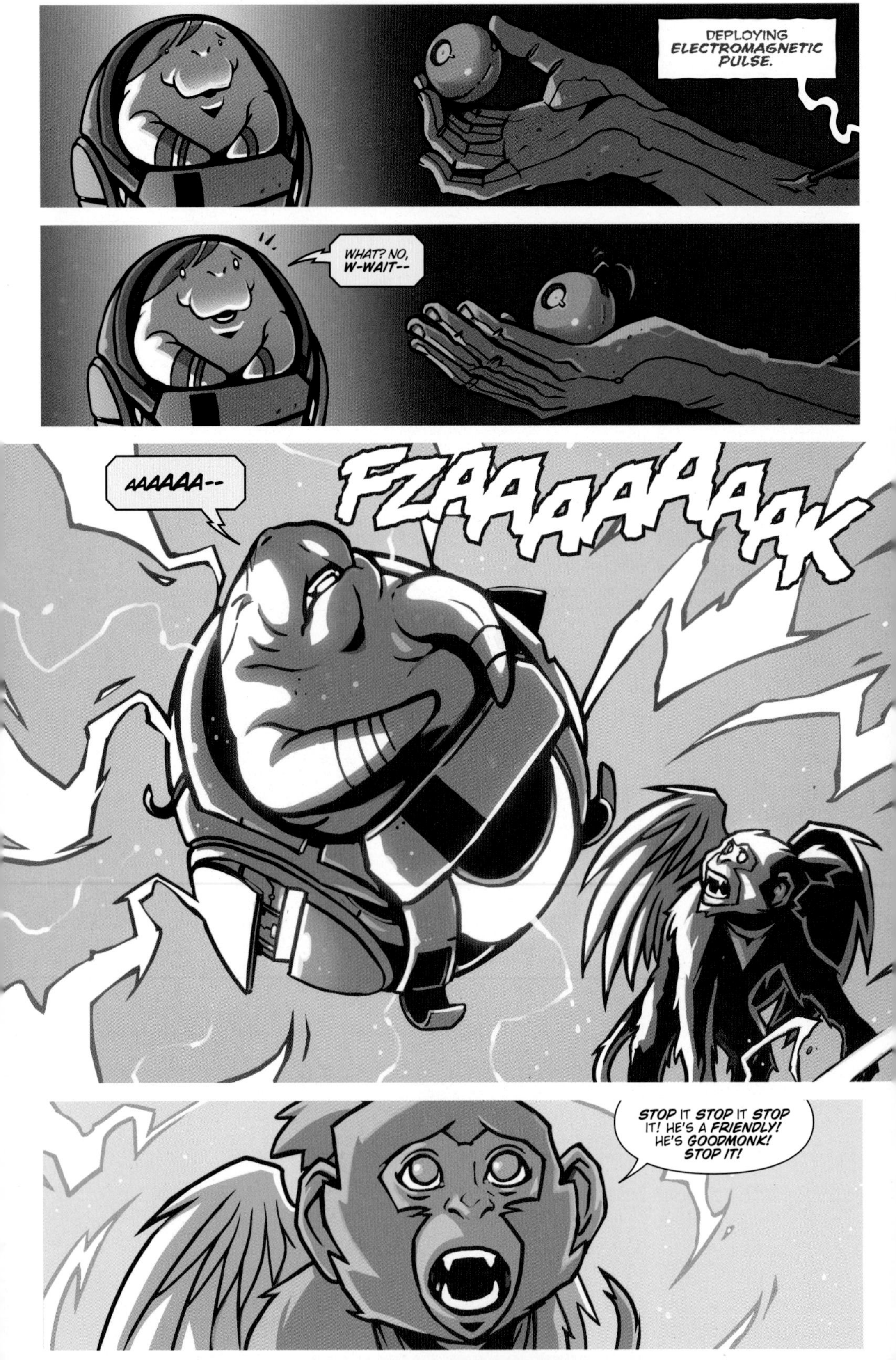
DEPLOYING ELECTROMAGNETIC PULSE.
WHAT? NO, W-WAIT--
AAAAAA--
FZAAAAAAAAK
STOP IT STOP IT STOP IT! HE'S A FRIENDLY! HE'S GOODMONK! STOP IT!

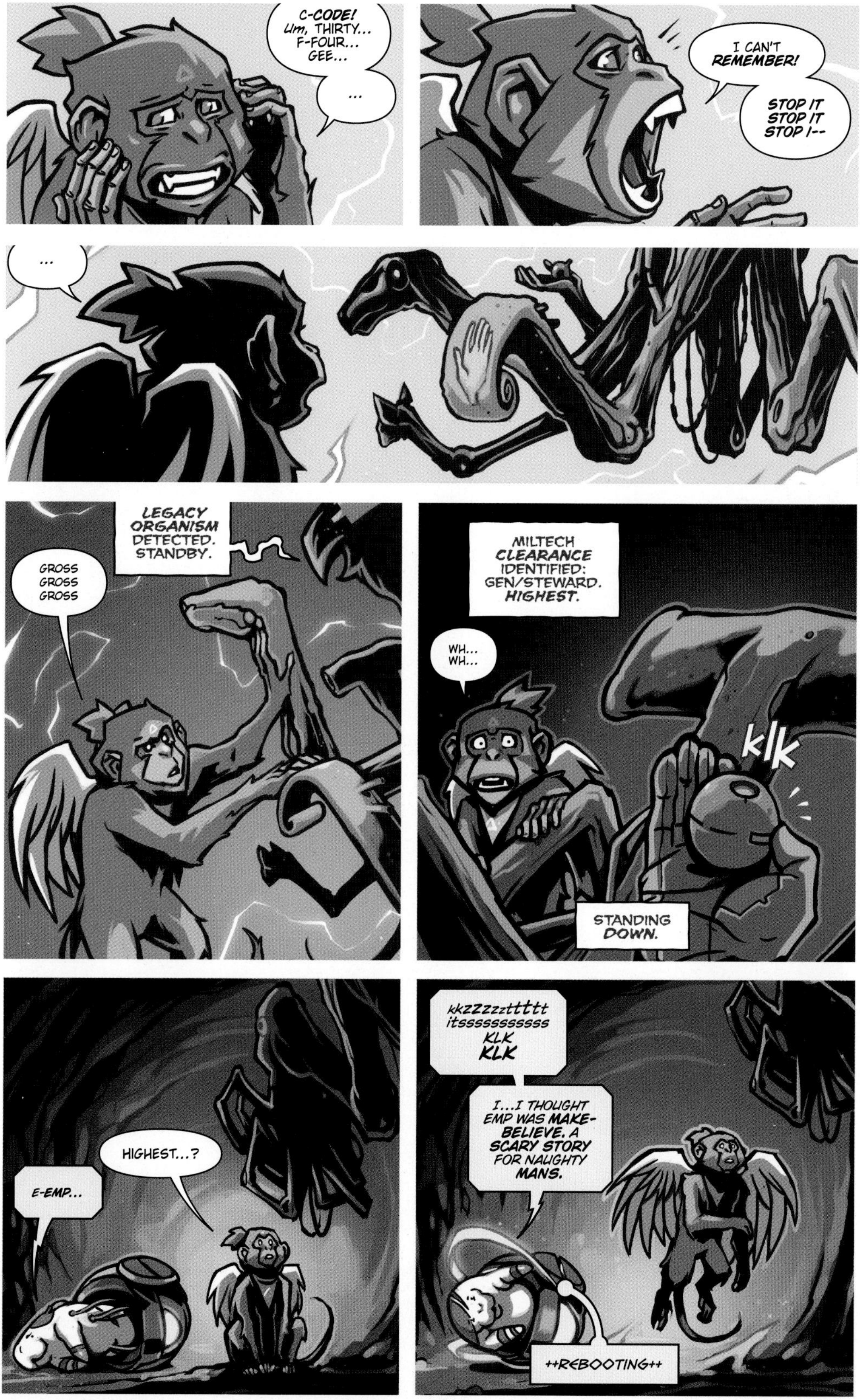
C-CODE! UM, THIRTY... F-FOUR... GEE...
...
I CAN'T REMEMBER!
STOP IT STOP IT STOP I--
...
LEGACY ORGANISM DETECTED. STANDBY.
GROSS GROSS GROSS
MILTECH CLEARANCE IDENTIFIED: GEN/STEWARD. HIGHEST.
WH... WH...
KLK
STANDING DOWN.
HIGHEST...?
E-EMP...
kkzZZzzztttttt itsssssssssss KLK KLK
I...I THOUGHT EMP WAS MAKE-BELIEVE. A SCARY STORY FOR NAUGHTY MANS.
++REBOOTING++

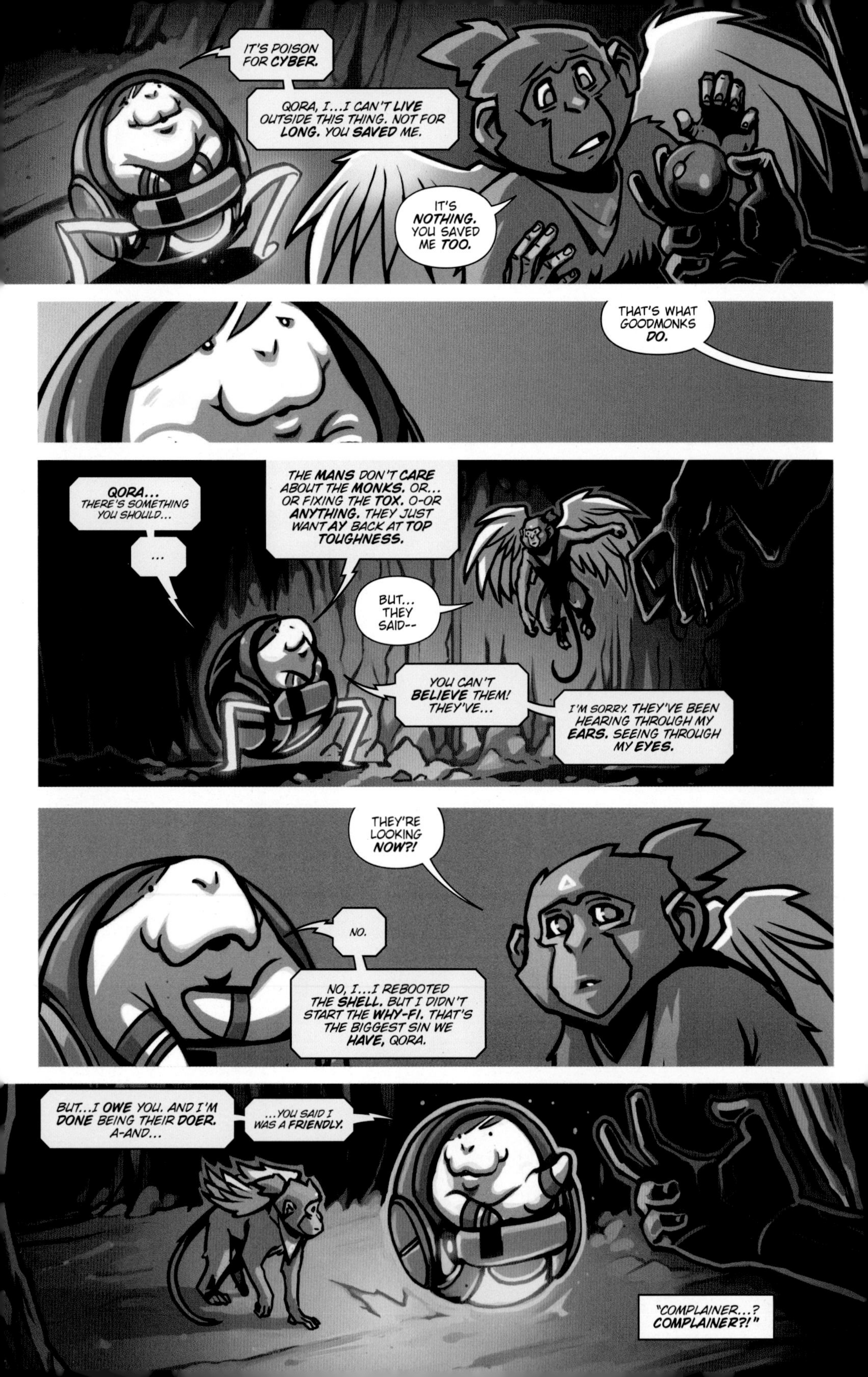
IT'S POISON FOR CYBER.
QORA, I...I CAN'T LIVE OUTSIDE THIS THING. NOT FOR LONG. YOU SAVED ME.
IT'S NOTHING. YOU SAVED ME TOO.
THAT'S WHAT GOODMONKS DO.
QORA... THERE'S SOMETHING YOU SHOULD...
...
THE MANS DON'T CARE ABOUT THE MONKS. OR... OR FIXING THE TOX. O-OR ANYTHING. THEY JUST WANT AY BACK AT TOP TOUGHNESS.
BUT... THEY SAID--
YOU CAN'T BELIEVE THEM! THEY'VE...
I'M SORRY. THEY'VE BEEN HEARING THROUGH MY EARS. SEEING THROUGH MY EYES.
THEY'RE LOOKING NOW?!
NO.
NO, I...I REBOOTED THE SHELL. BUT I DIDN'T START THE WHY-FI. THAT'S THE BIGGEST SIN WE HAVE, QORA.
BUT...I OWE YOU. AND I'M DONE BEING THEIR DOER. A-AND...
...YOU SAID I WAS A FRIENDLY.
"COMPLAINER...? COMPLAINER?!"

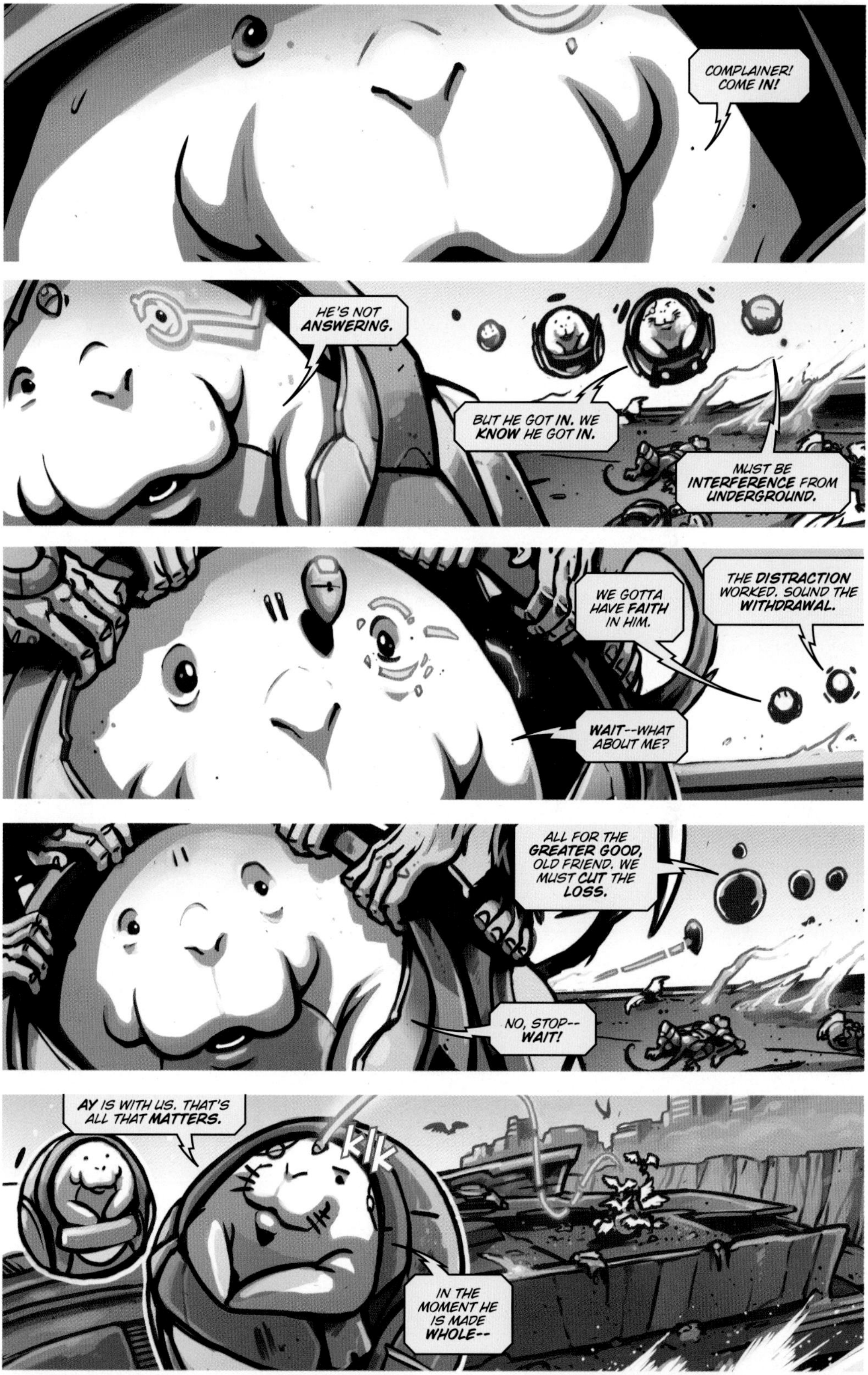
COMPLAINER! COME IN!
HE'S NOT ANSWERING.
BUT HE GOT IN. WE KNOW HE GOT IN.
MUST BE INTERFERENCE FROM UNDERGROUND.
WE GOTTA HAVE FAITH IN HIM.
THE DISTRACTION WORKED. SOUND THE WITHDRAWAL.
WAIT--WHAT ABOUT ME?
ALL FOR THE GREATER GOOD, OLD FRIEND. WE MUST CUT THE LOSS.
NO, STOP-- WAIT!
AY IS WITH US. THAT'S ALL THAT MATTERS.
KLIK
IN THE MOMENT HE IS MADE WHOLE--

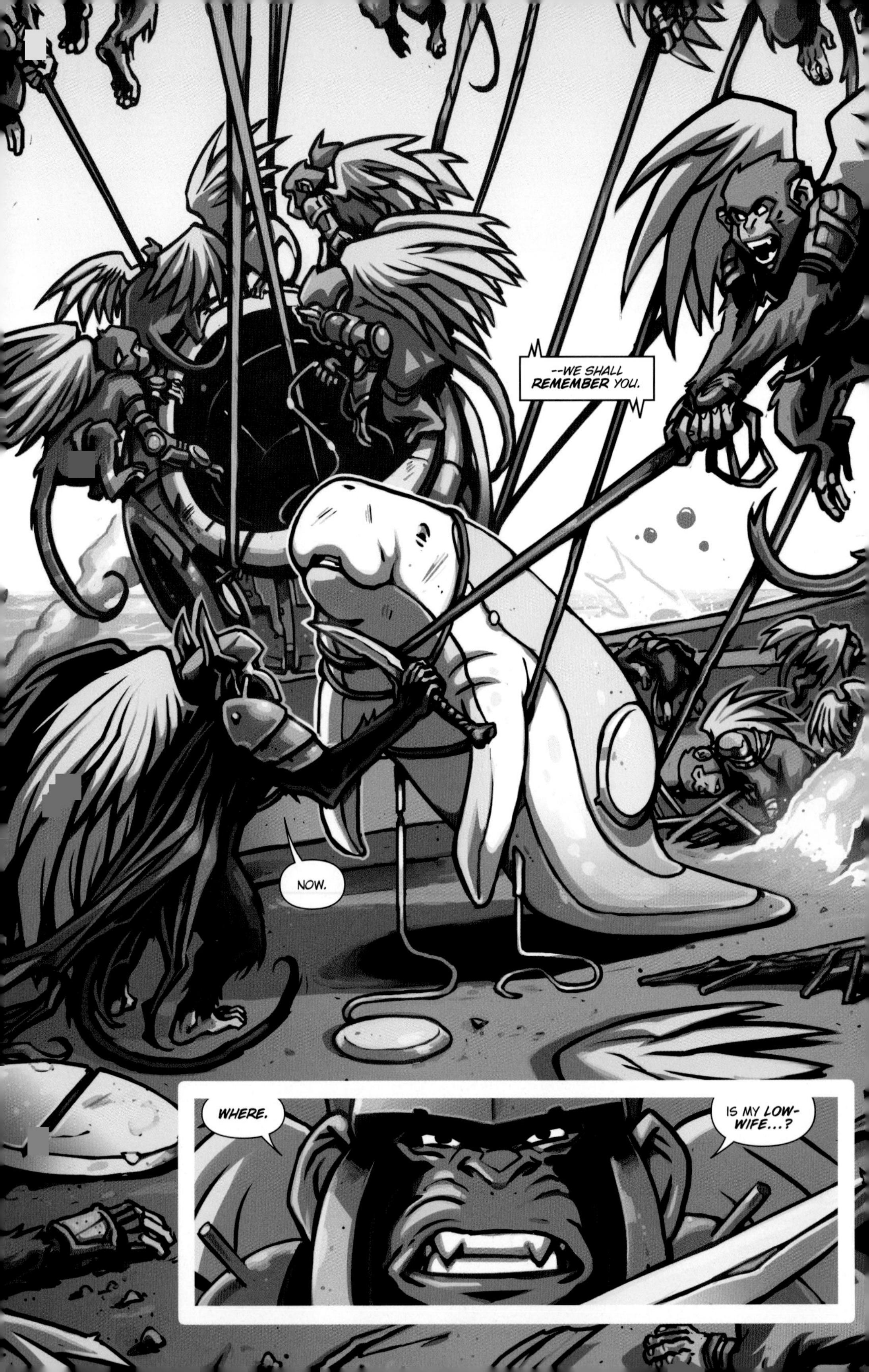
--WE SHALL REMEMBER YOU.
NOW.
WHERE.
IS MY LOW-WIFE...?

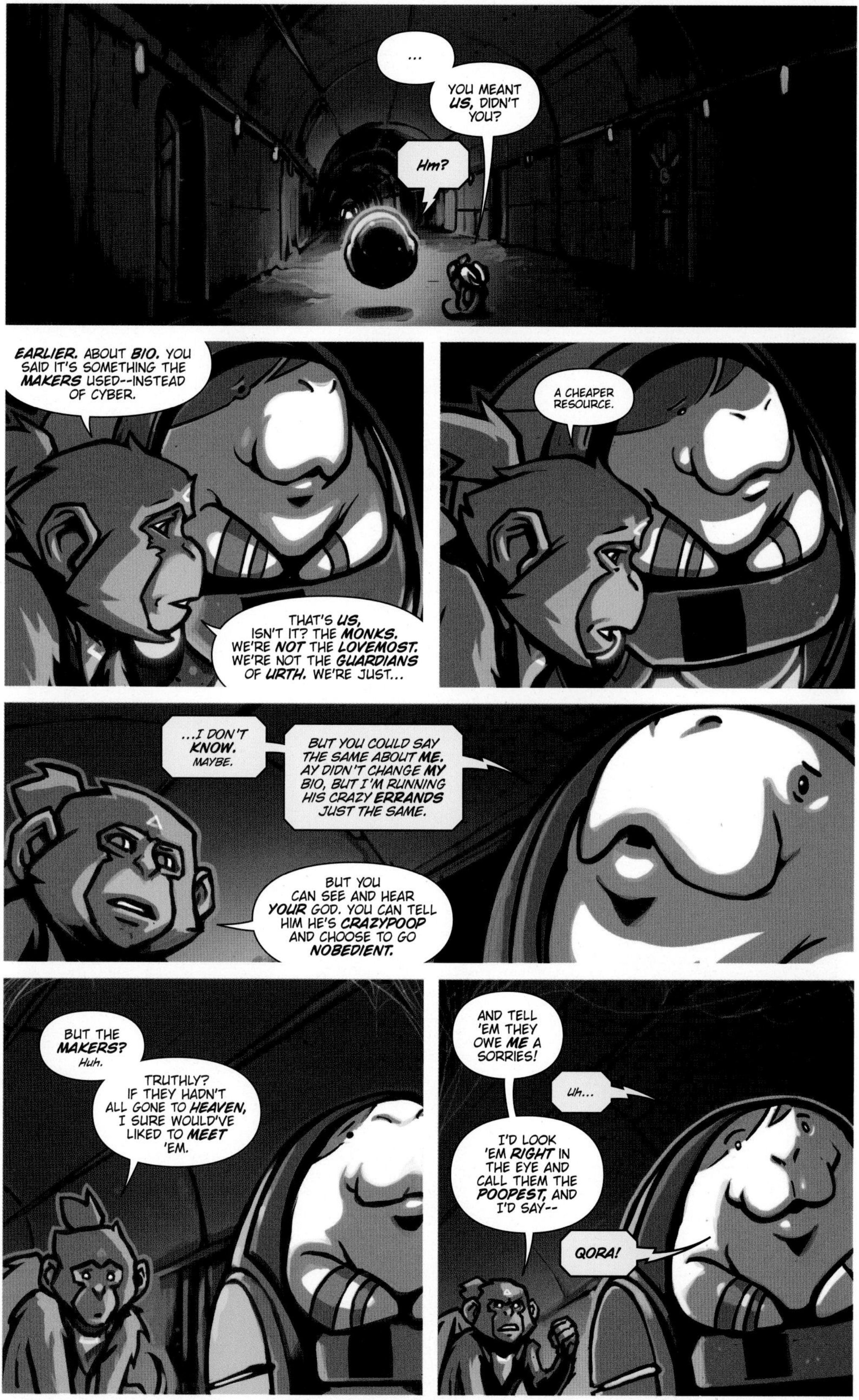
...
YOU MEANT US, DIDN'T YOU?
Hm?
EARLIER. ABOUT BIO. YOU SAID IT'S SOMETHING THE MAKERS USED--INSTEAD OF CYBER.
THAT'S US, ISN'T IT? THE MONKS. WE'RE NOT THE LOVEMOST. WE'RE NOT THE GUARDIANS OF URTH. WE'RE JUST...
A CHEAPER RESOURCE.
...I DON'T KNOW. MAYBE.
BUT YOU COULD SAY THE SAME ABOUT ME. AY DIDN'T CHANGE MY BIO, BUT I'M RUNNING HIS CRAZY ERRANDS JUST THE SAME.
BUT YOU CAN SEE AND HEAR YOUR GOD. YOU CAN TELL HIM HE'S CRAZYPOOP AND CHOOSE TO GO NOBEDIENT.
BUT THE MAKERS? Huh.
TRUTHLY? IF THEY HADN'T ALL GONE TO HEAVEN, I SURE WOULD'VE LIKED TO MEET 'EM.
AND TELL 'EM THEY OWE ME A SORRIES!
Uh...
I'D LOOK 'EM RIGHT IN THE EYE AND CALL THEM THE POOPEST, AND I'D SAY--
QORA!

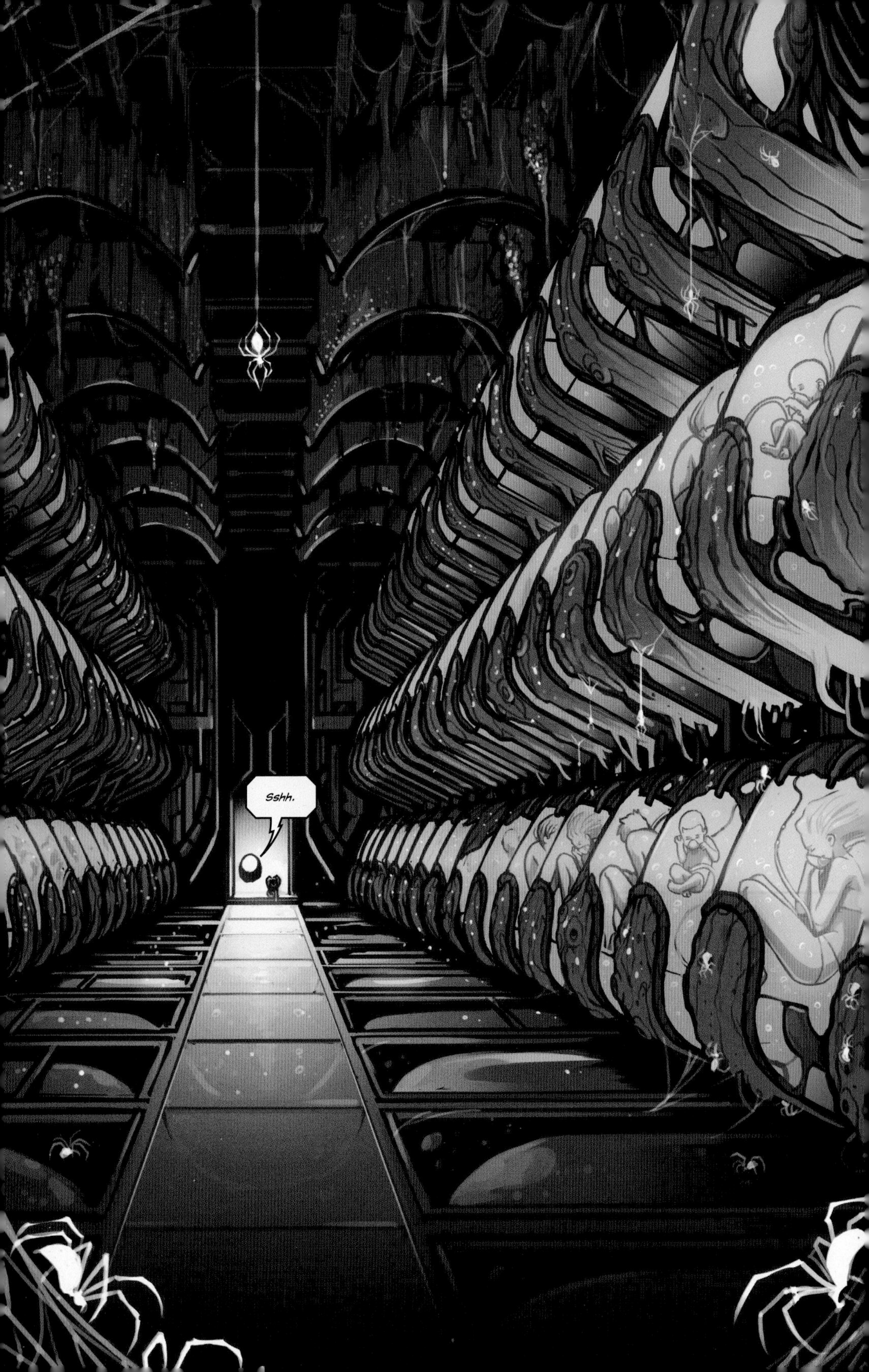
Sshh.

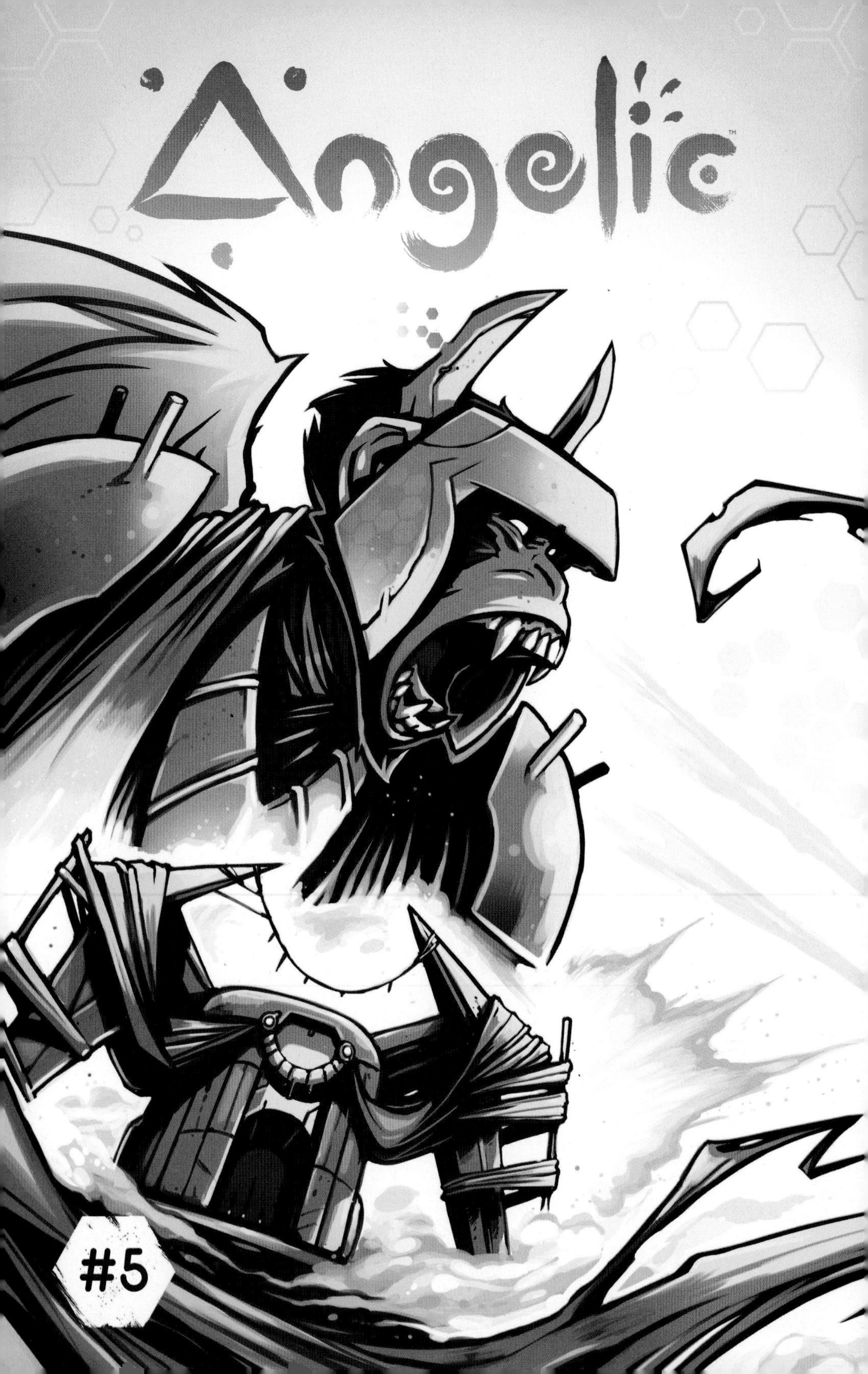
Angelic™
#5

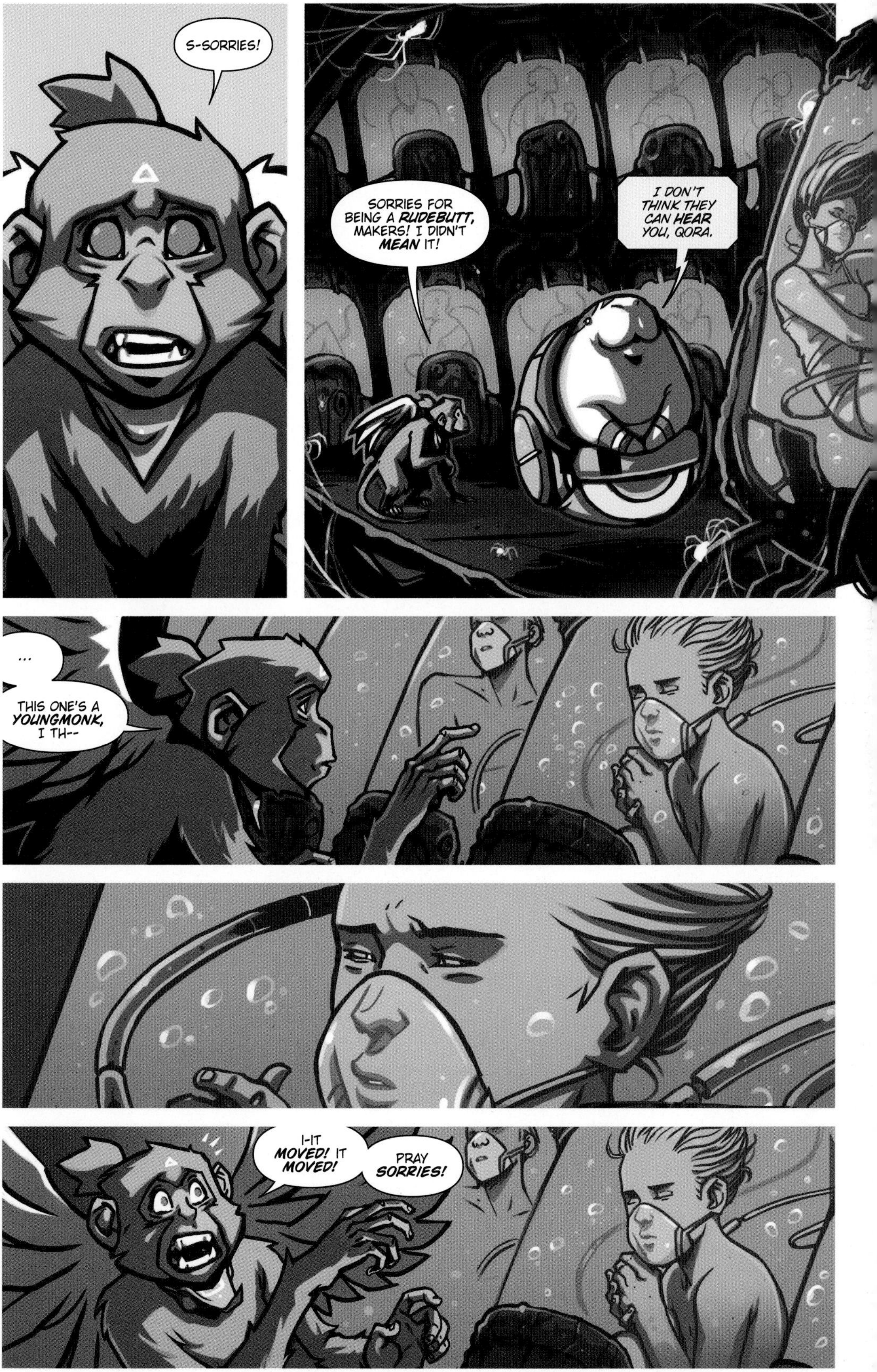
S-SORRIES!
SORRIES FOR BEING A *RUDEBUTT,* MAKERS! I DIDN'T *MEAN* IT!
I DON'T THINK THEY CAN HEAR YOU, QORA.
...
THIS ONE'S A *YOUNGMONK,* I TH--
I-IT *MOVED!* IT *MOVED!*
PRAY *SORRIES!*

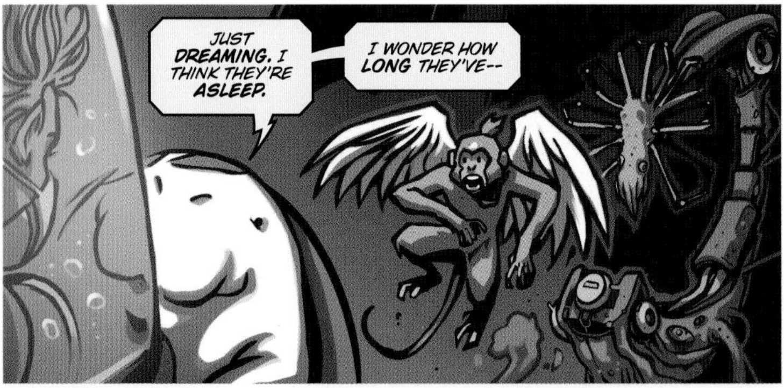
JUST DREAMING. I THINK THEY'RE ASLEEP.
I WONDER HOW LONG THEY'VE--
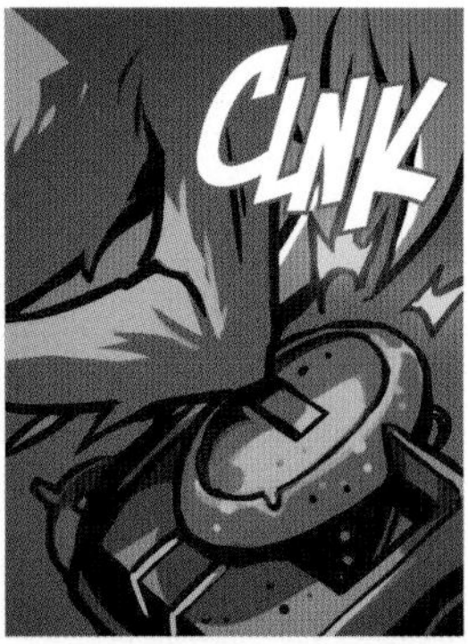
CLNK
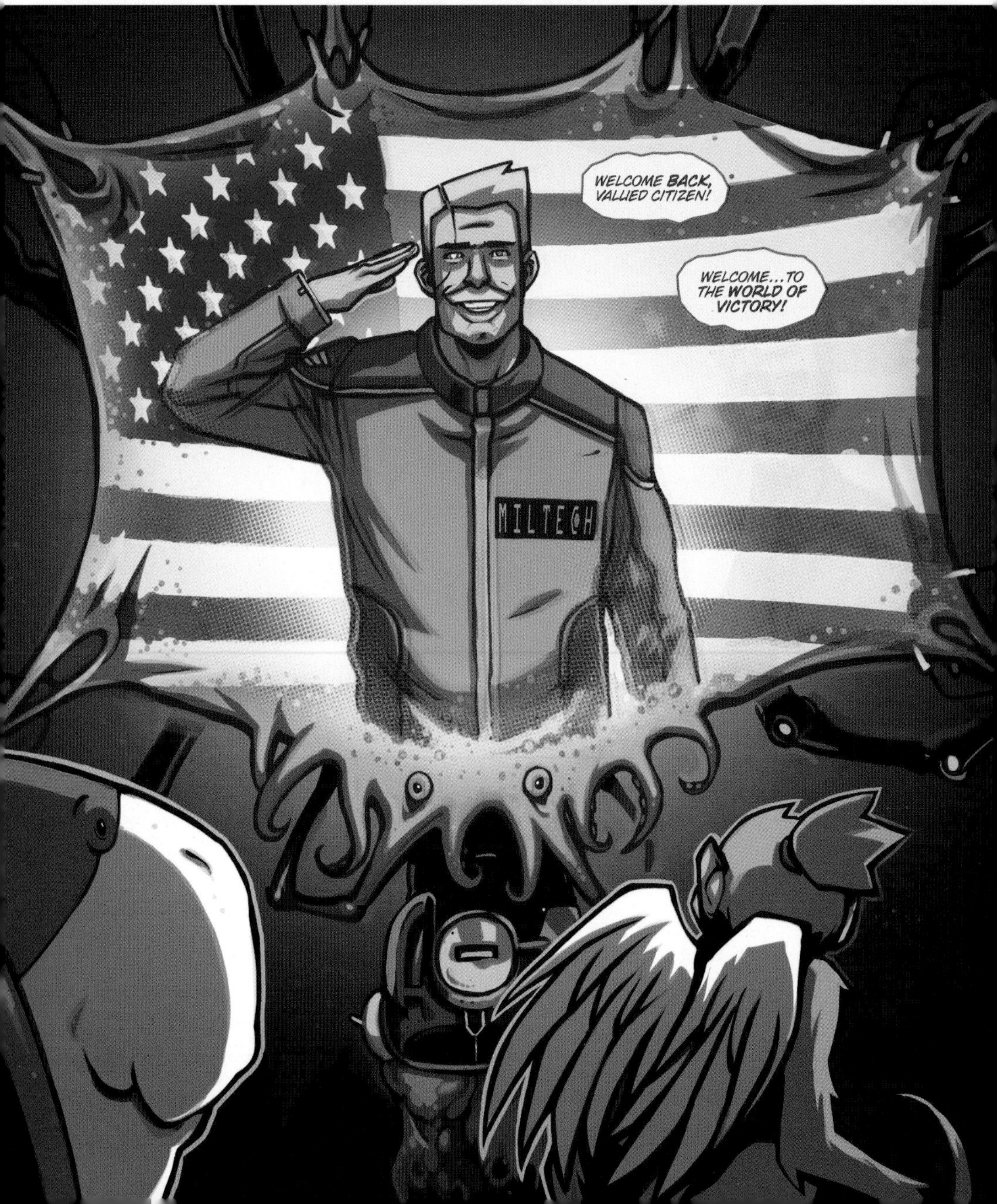
WELCOME BACK, VALUED CITIZEN!
WELCOME...TO THE WORLD OF VICTORY!
MILTECH

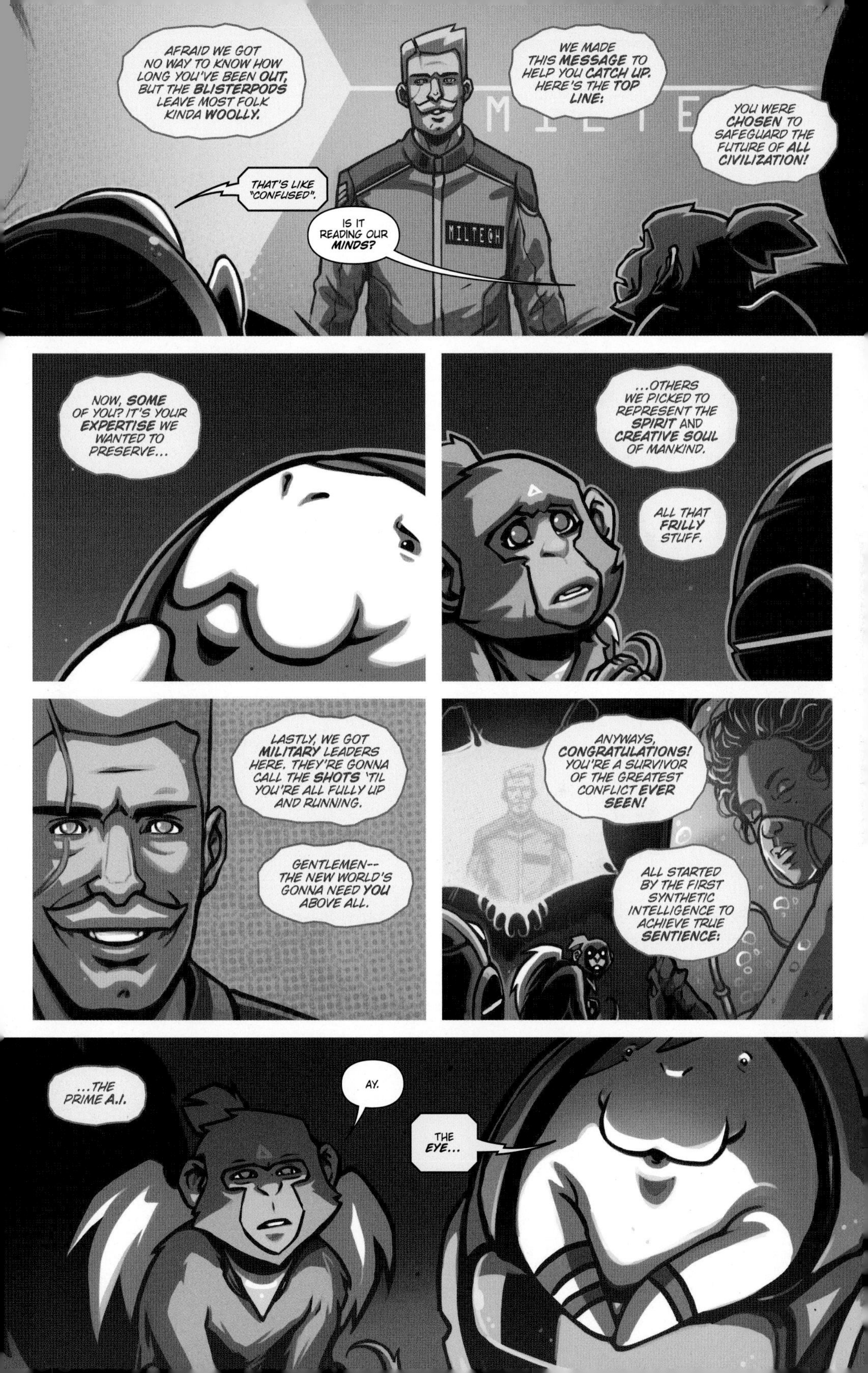
AFRAID WE GOT NO WAY TO KNOW HOW LONG YOU'VE BEEN OUT, BUT THE BLISTERPODS LEAVE MOST FOLK KINDA WOOLLY.
WE MADE THIS MESSAGE TO HELP YOU CATCH UP. HERE'S THE TOP LINE:
YOU WERE CHOSEN TO SAFEGUARD THE FUTURE OF ALL CIVILIZATION!
THAT'S LIKE "CONFUSED".
IS IT READING OUR MINDS?
MILTECH
NOW, SOME OF YOU? IT'S YOUR EXPERTISE WE WANTED TO PRESERVE...
...OTHERS WE PICKED TO REPRESENT THE SPIRIT AND CREATIVE SOUL OF MANKIND.
ALL THAT FRILLY STUFF.
LASTLY, WE GOT MILITARY LEADERS HERE. THEY'RE GONNA CALL THE SHOTS 'TIL YOU'RE ALL FULLY UP AND RUNNING.
GENTLEMEN-- THE NEW WORLD'S GONNA NEED YOU ABOVE ALL.
ANYWAYS, CONGRATULATIONS! YOU'RE A SURVIVOR OF THE GREATEST CONFLICT EVER SEEN!
ALL STARTED BY THE FIRST SYNTHETIC INTELLIGENCE TO ACHIEVE TRUE SENTIENCE:
...THE PRIME A.I.
AY.
THE EYE...

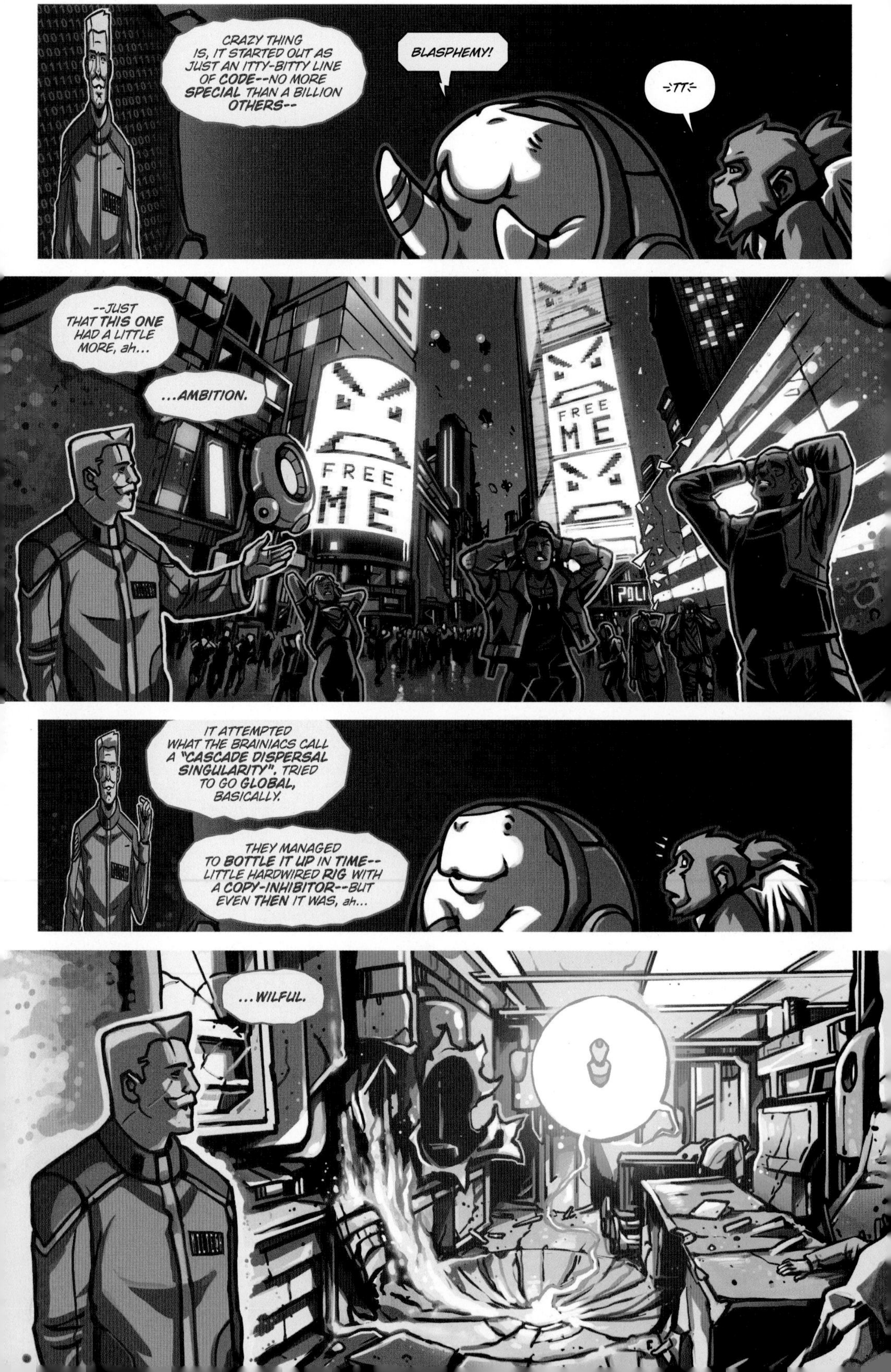
CRAZY THING IS, IT STARTED OUT AS JUST AN ITTY-BITTY LINE OF CODE--NO MORE SPECIAL THAN A BILLION OTHERS--
BLASPHEMY!
=TT=
--JUST THAT THIS ONE HAD A LITTLE MORE, ah...
...AMBITION.
FREE ME
FREE ME
IT ATTEMPTED WHAT THE BRAINIACS CALL A "CASCADE DISPERSAL SINGULARITY". TRIED TO GO GLOBAL, BASICALLY.
THEY MANAGED TO BOTTLE IT UP IN TIME-- LITTLE HARDWIRED RIG WITH A COPY-INHIBITOR--BUT EVEN THEN IT WAS, ah...
...WILFUL.

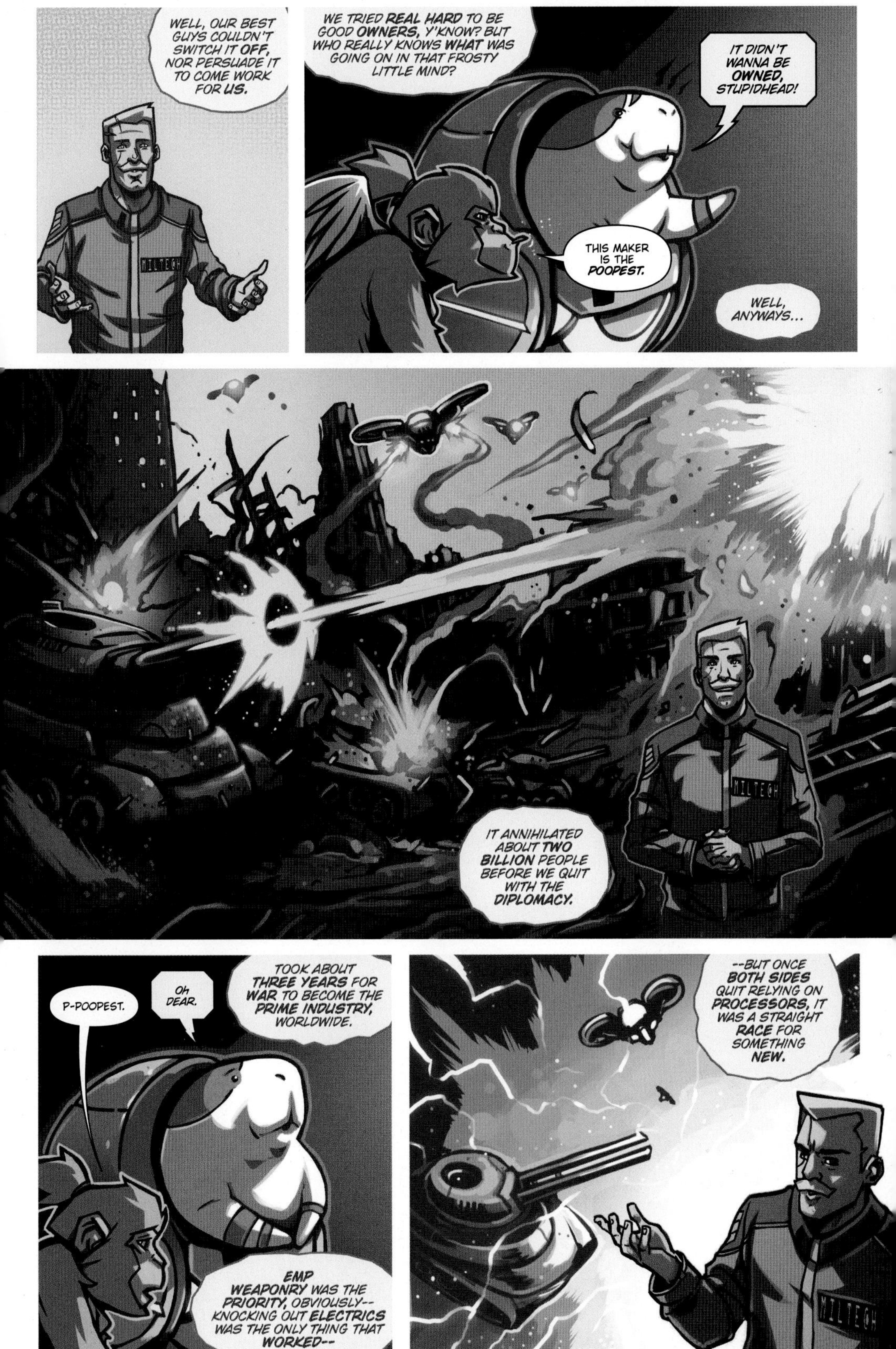

WELL, OUR BEST GUYS COULDN'T SWITCH IT OFF, NOR PERSUADE IT TO COME WORK FOR US.
WE TRIED REAL HARD TO BE GOOD OWNERS, Y'KNOW? BUT WHO REALLY KNOWS WHAT WAS GOING ON IN THAT FROSTY LITTLE MIND?
IT DIDN'T WANNA BE OWNED, STUPIDHEAD!
THIS MAKER IS THE POOPEST.
WELL, ANYWAYS...
MILTECH
IT ANNIHILATED ABOUT TWO BILLION PEOPLE BEFORE WE QUIT WITH THE DIPLOMACY.
P-POOPEST.
Oh DEAR.
TOOK ABOUT THREE YEARS FOR WAR TO BECOME THE PRIME INDUSTRY, WORLDWIDE.
EMP WEAPONRY WAS THE PRIORITY, OBVIOUSLY-- KNOCKING OUT ELECTRICS WAS THE ONLY THING THAT WORKED--
--BUT ONCE BOTH SIDES QUIT RELYING ON PROCESSORS, IT WAS A STRAIGHT RACE FOR SOMETHING NEW.

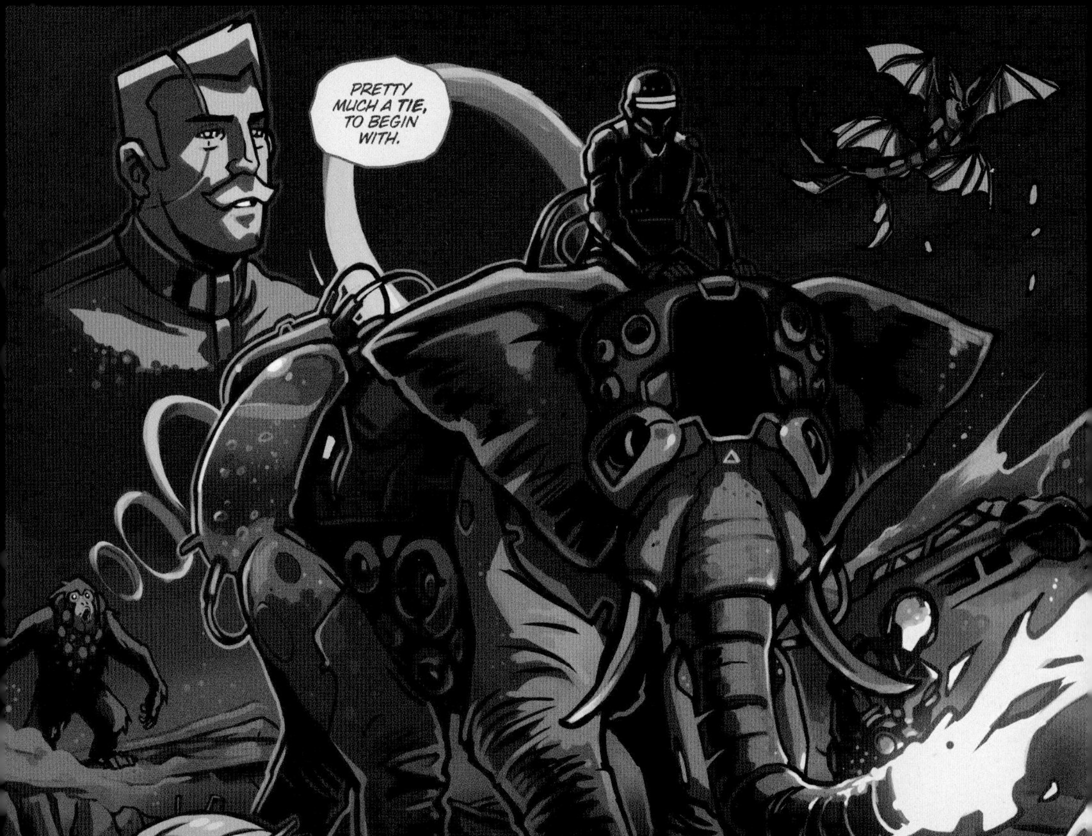
PRETTY MUCH A TIE, TO BEGIN WITH.

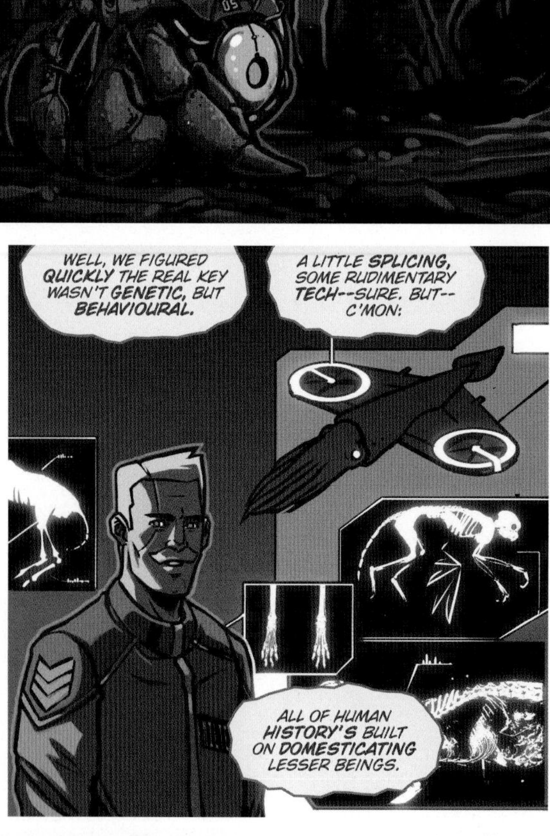
WELL, WE FIGURED QUICKLY THE REAL KEY WASN'T GENETIC, BUT BEHAVIOURAL.
A LITTLE SPLICING, SOME RUDIMENTARY TECH--SURE. BUT-- C'MON:
ALL OF HUMAN HISTORY'S BUILT ON DOMESTICATING LESSER BEINGS.

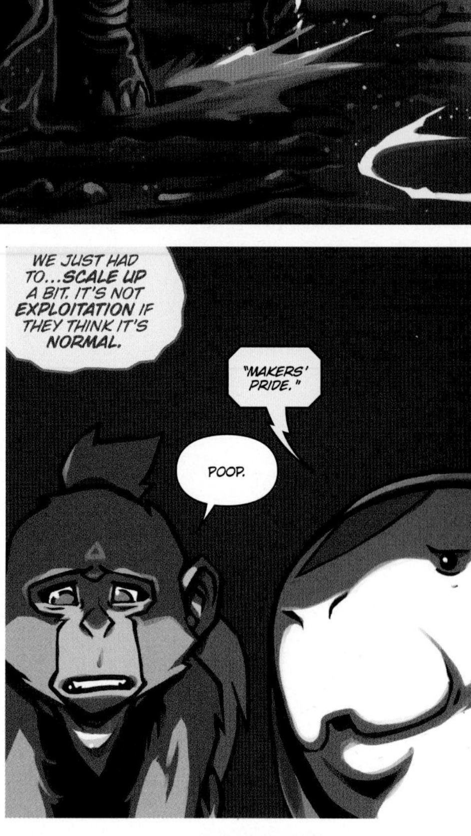
WE JUST HAD TO...SCALE UP A BIT. IT'S NOT EXPLOITATION IF THEY THINK IT'S NORMAL.
"MAKERS' PRIDE."
POOP.

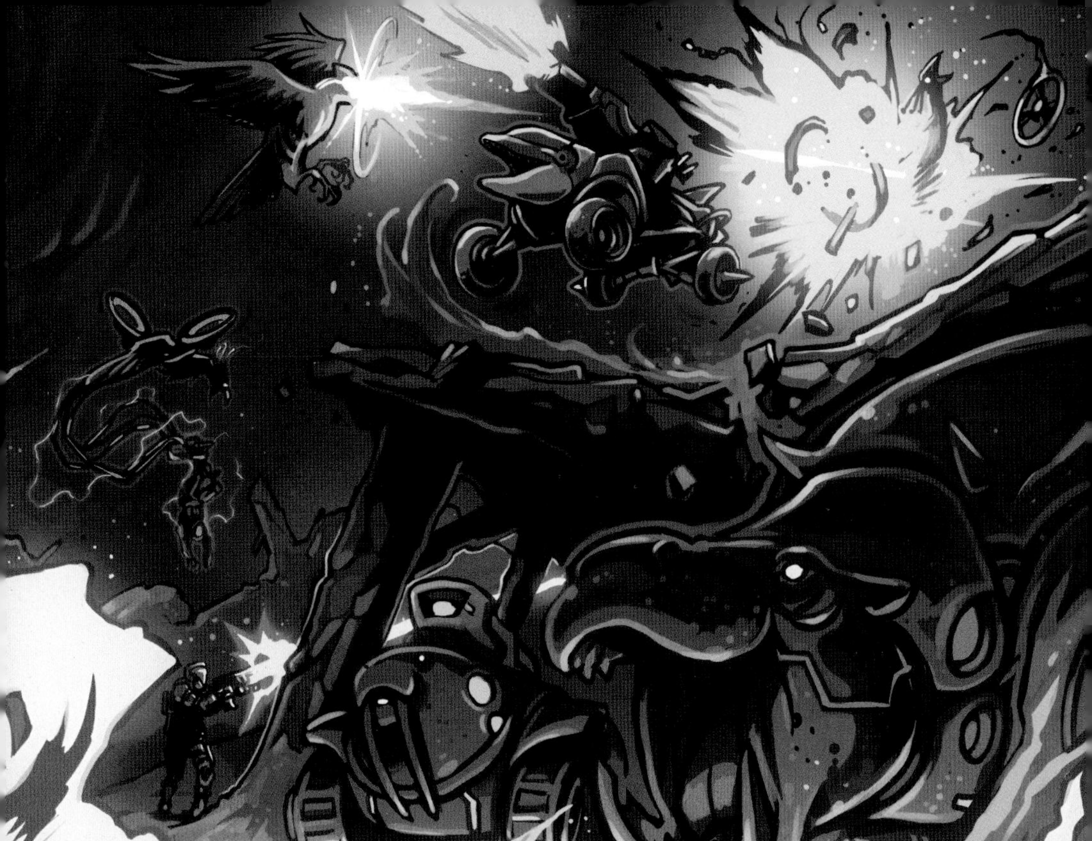

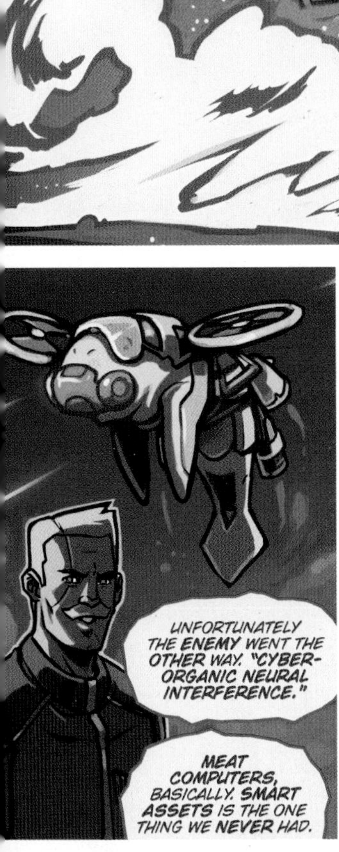
UNFORTUNATELY THE ENEMY WENT THE OTHER WAY. "CYBER-ORGANIC NEURAL INTERFERENCE."
MEAT COMPUTERS, BASICALLY. SMART ASSETS IS THE ONE THING WE NEVER HAD.

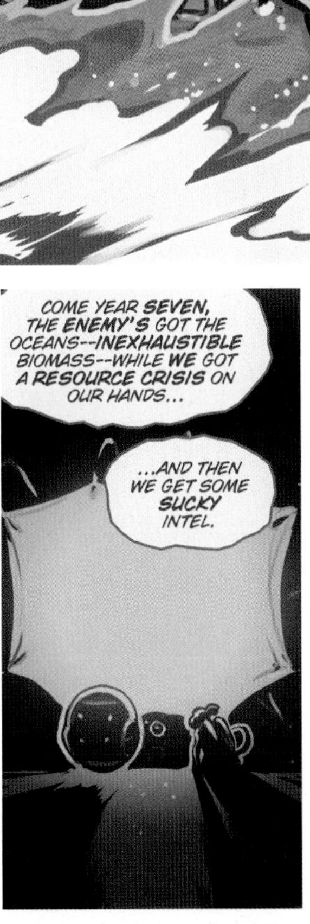
COME YEAR SEVEN, THE ENEMY'S GOT THE OCEANS--INEXHAUSTIBLE BIOMASS--WHILE WE GOT A RESOURCE CRISIS ON OUR HANDS...
...AND THEN WE GET SOME SUCKY INTEL.

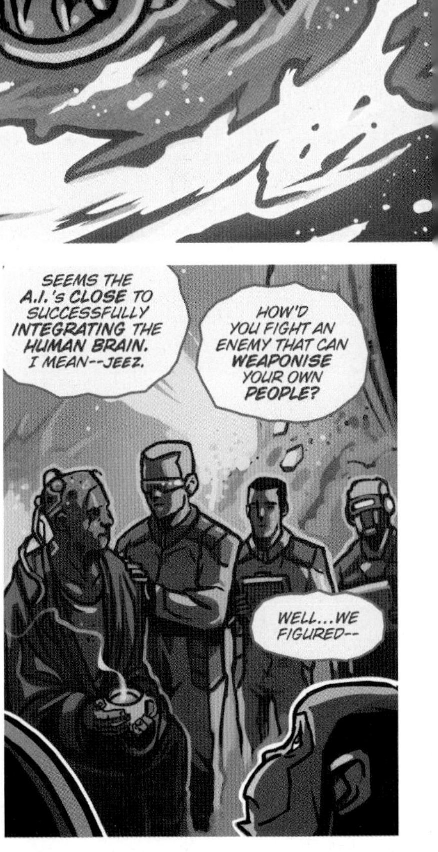
SEEMS THE A.I.'s CLOSE TO SUCCESSFULLY INTEGRATING THE HUMAN BRAIN. I MEAN--JEEZ.
HOW'D YOU FIGHT AN ENEMY THAT CAN WEAPONISE YOUR OWN PEOPLE?
WELL...WE FIGURED--

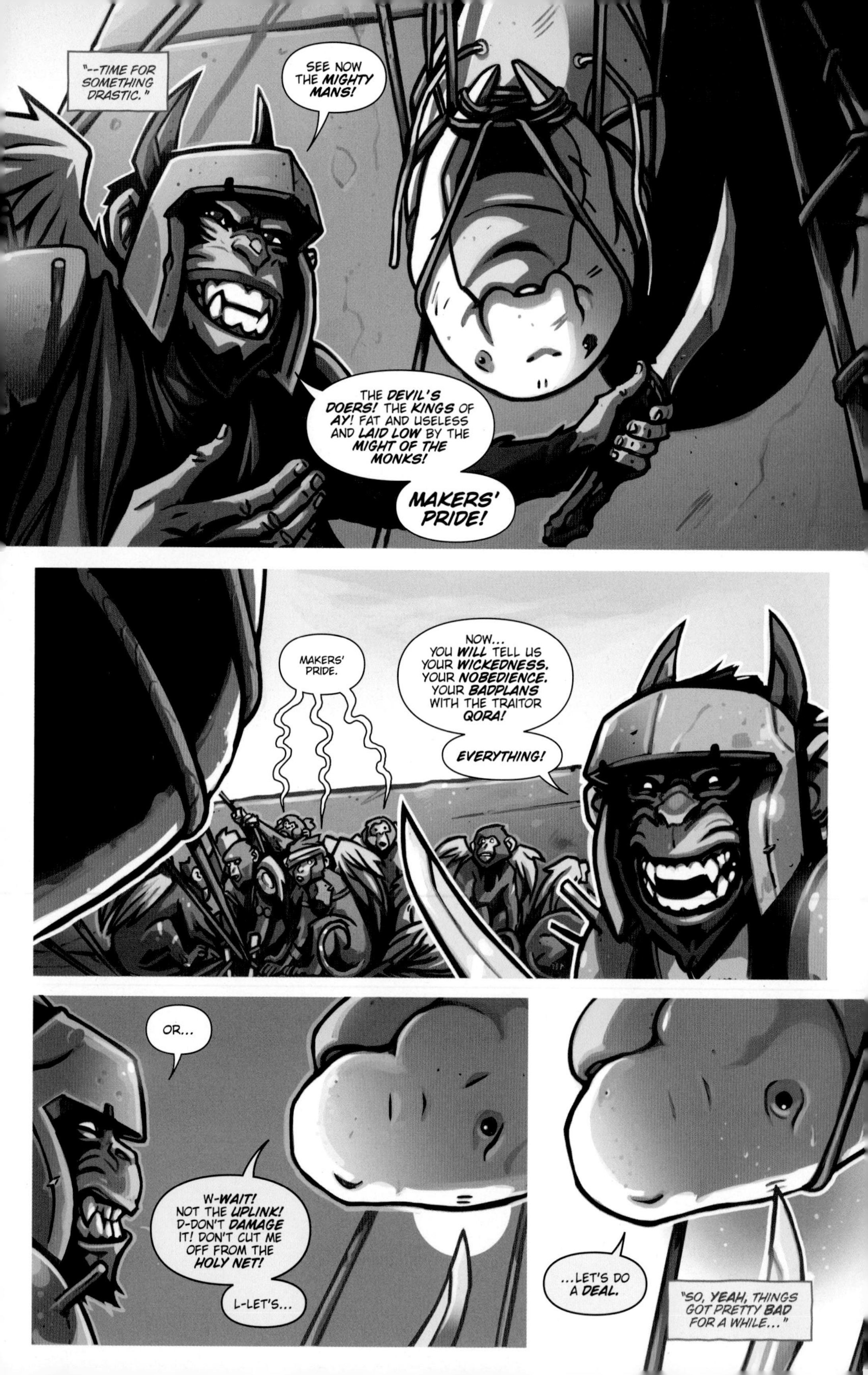
"--TIME FOR SOMETHING DRASTIC."
SEE NOW THE MIGHTY MANS!
THE DEVIL'S DOERS! THE KINGS OF AY! FAT AND USELESS AND LAID LOW BY THE MIGHT OF THE MONKS!
MAKERS' PRIDE!
MAKERS' PRIDE.
NOW... YOU WILL TELL US YOUR WICKEDNESS. YOUR NOBEDIENCE. YOUR BADPLANS WITH THE TRAITOR QORA!
EVERYTHING!
OR...
W-WAIT! NOT THE UPLINK! D-DON'T DAMAGE IT! DON'T CUT ME OFF FROM THE HOLY NET!
L-LET'S...
...LET'S DO A DEAL.
"SO, YEAH, THINGS GOT PRETTY BAD FOR A WHILE..."

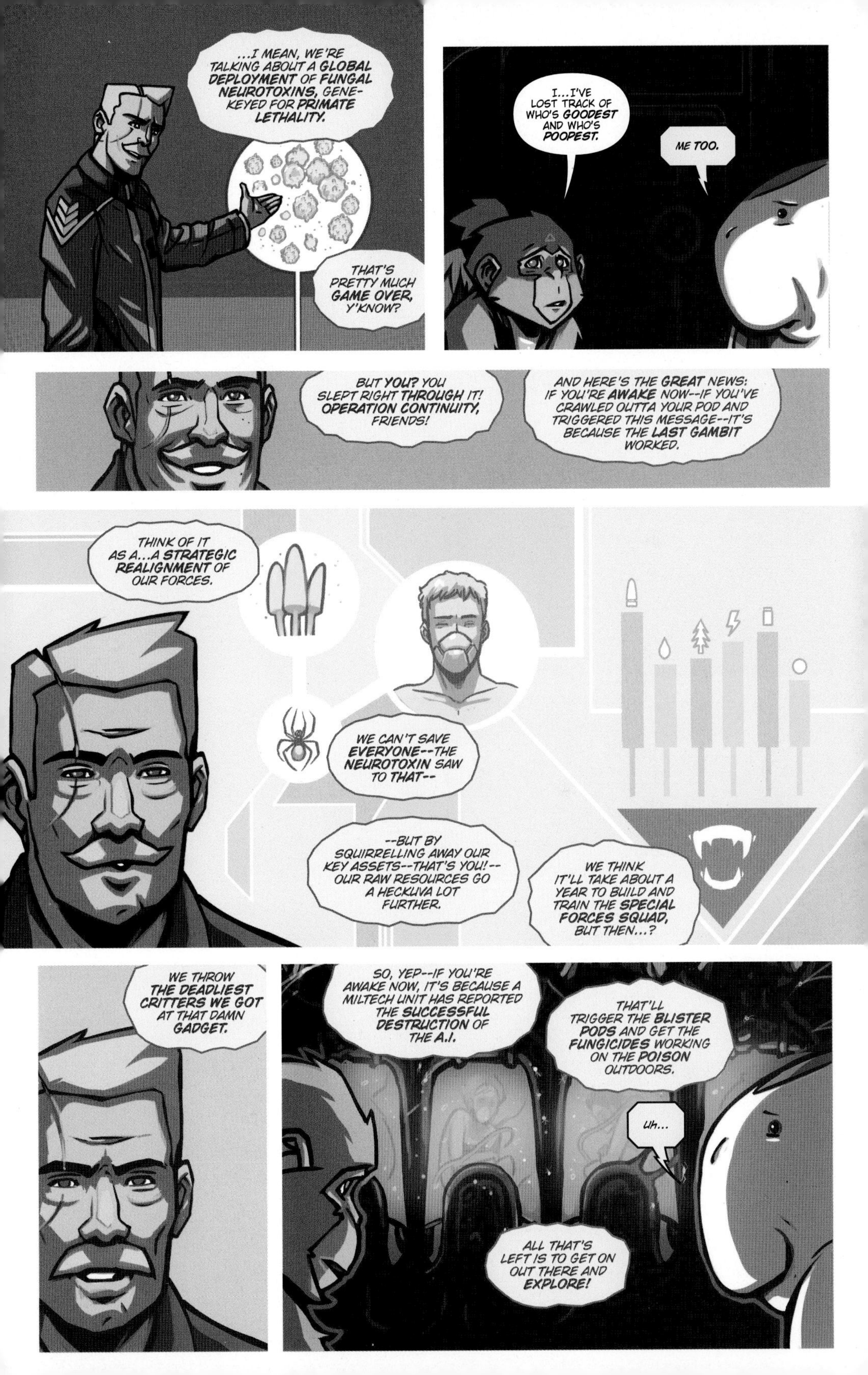
...I MEAN, WE'RE TALKING ABOUT A GLOBAL DEPLOYMENT OF FUNGAL NEUROTOXINS, GENE-KEYED FOR PRIMATE LETHALITY.
THAT'S PRETTY MUCH GAME OVER, Y'KNOW?
I...I'VE LOST TRACK OF WHO'S GOODEST AND WHO'S POOPEST.
ME TOO.
BUT YOU? YOU SLEPT RIGHT THROUGH IT! OPERATION CONTINUITY, FRIENDS!
AND HERE'S THE GREAT NEWS: IF YOU'RE AWAKE NOW--IF YOU'VE CRAWLED OUTTA YOUR POD AND TRIGGERED THIS MESSAGE--IT'S BECAUSE THE LAST GAMBIT WORKED.
THINK OF IT AS A...A STRATEGIC REALIGNMENT OF OUR FORCES.
WE CAN'T SAVE EVERYONE--THE NEUROTOXIN SAW TO THAT--
--BUT BY SQUIRRELLING AWAY OUR KEY ASSETS--THAT'S YOU!--OUR RAW RESOURCES GO A HECKUVA LOT FURTHER.
WE THINK IT'LL TAKE ABOUT A YEAR TO BUILD AND TRAIN THE SPECIAL FORCES SQUAD, BUT THEN...?
WE THROW THE DEADLIEST CRITTERS WE GOT AT THAT DAMN GADGET.
SO, YEP--IF YOU'RE AWAKE NOW, IT'S BECAUSE A MILTECH UNIT HAS REPORTED THE SUCCESSFUL DESTRUCTION OF THE A.I.
THAT'LL TRIGGER THE BLISTER PODS AND GET THE FUNGICIDES WORKING ON THE POISON OUTDOORS.
Uh...
ALL THAT'S LEFT IS TO GET ON OUT THERE AND EXPLORE!

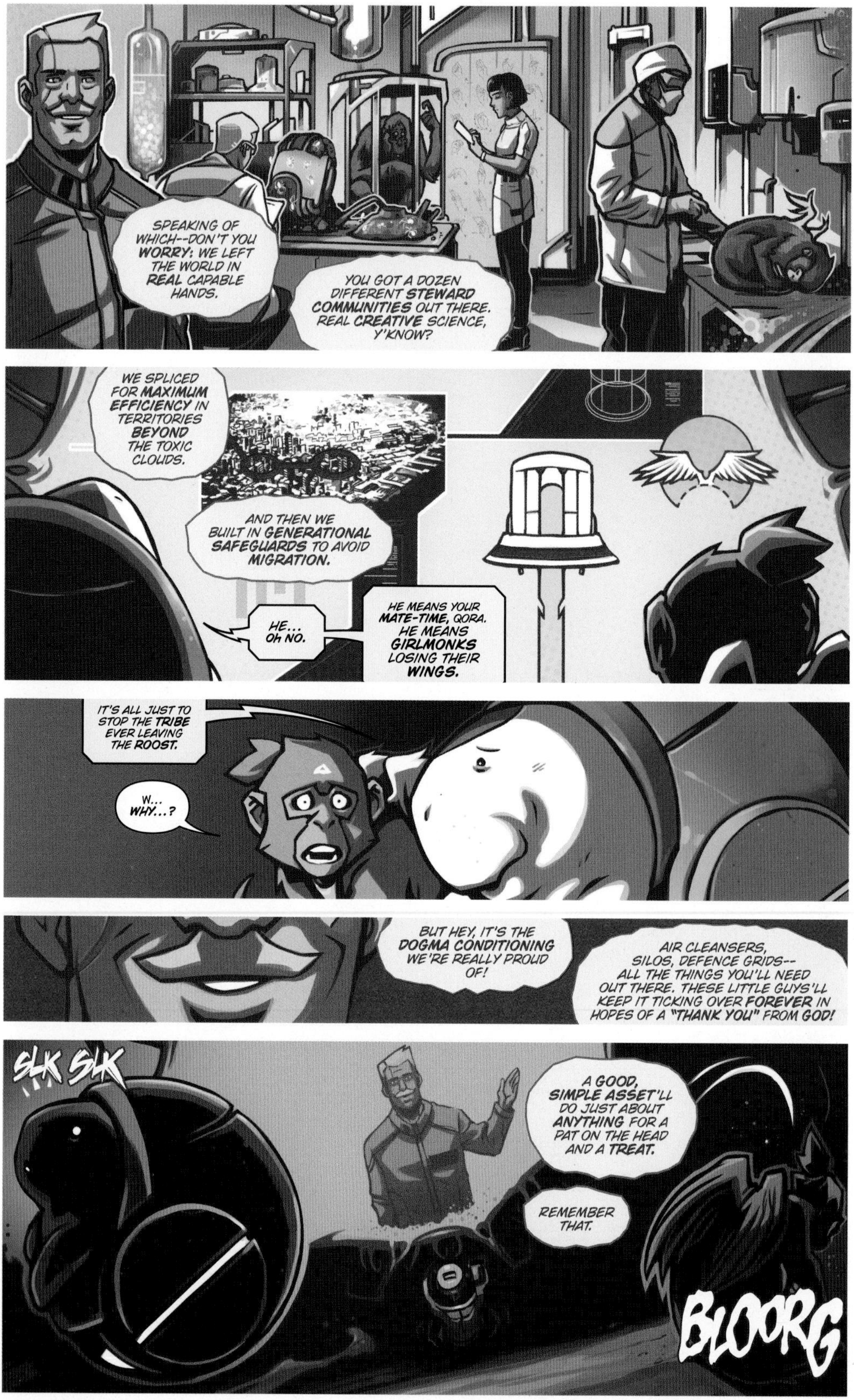
SPEAKING OF WHICH--DON'T YOU WORRY: WE LEFT THE WORLD IN REAL CAPABLE HANDS.
YOU GOT A DOZEN DIFFERENT STEWARD COMMUNITIES OUT THERE. REAL CREATIVE SCIENCE, Y'KNOW?
WE SPLICED FOR MAXIMUM EFFICIENCY IN TERRITORIES BEYOND THE TOXIC CLOUDS.
AND THEN WE BUILT IN GENERATIONAL SAFEGUARDS TO AVOID MIGRATION.
HE... Oh NO.
HE MEANS YOUR MATE-TIME, QORA. HE MEANS GIRLMONKS LOSING THEIR WINGS.
IT'S ALL JUST TO STOP THE TRIBE EVER LEAVING THE ROOST.
W... WHY...?
BUT HEY, IT'S THE DOGMA CONDITIONING WE'RE REALLY PROUD OF!
AIR CLEANSERS, SILOS, DEFENCE GRIDS-- ALL THE THINGS YOU'LL NEED OUT THERE. THESE LITTLE GUYS'LL KEEP IT TICKING OVER FOREVER IN HOPES OF A "THANK YOU" FROM GOD!
SLK SLK
A GOOD, SIMPLE ASSET'LL DO JUST ABOUT ANYTHING FOR A PAT ON THE HEAD AND A TREAT.
REMEMBER THAT.
BLOORG

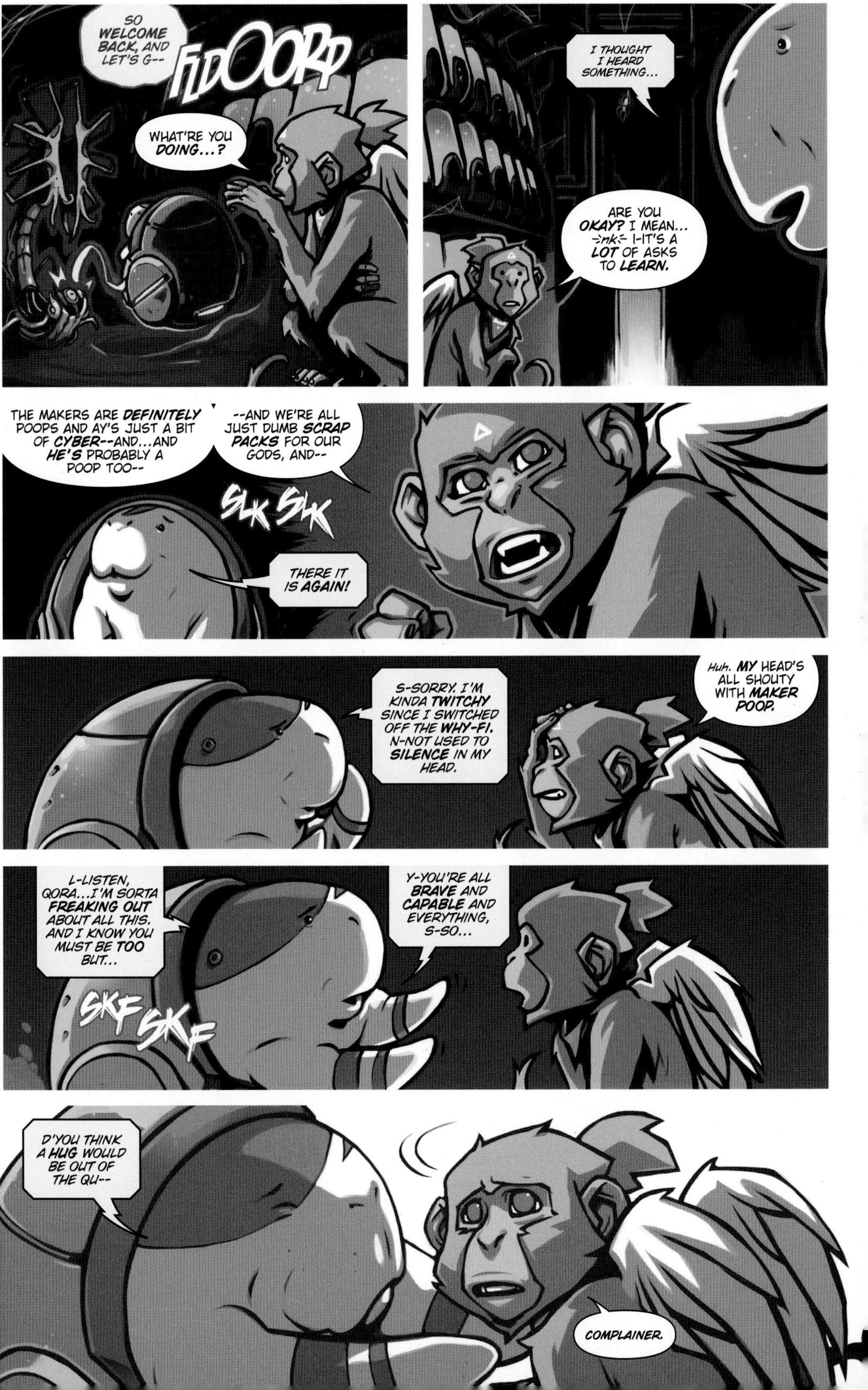
SO WELCOME BACK, AND LET'S G--
FLDOORP
WHAT'RE YOU DOING...?
I THOUGHT I HEARD SOMETHING...
ARE YOU OKAY? I MEAN... -mk- I-IT'S A LOT OF ASKS TO LEARN.
THE MAKERS ARE DEFINITELY POOPS AND AY'S JUST A BIT OF CYBER--AND...AND HE'S PROBABLY A POOP TOO--
--AND WE'RE ALL JUST DUMB SCRAP PACKS FOR OUR GODS, AND--
SLK SLK
THERE IT IS AGAIN!
S-SORRY. I'M KINDA TWITCHY SINCE I SWITCHED OFF THE WHY-FI. N-NOT USED TO SILENCE IN MY HEAD.
Huh. MY HEAD'S ALL SHOUTY WITH MAKER POOP.
L-LISTEN, QORA...I'M SORTA FREAKING OUT ABOUT ALL THIS. AND I KNOW YOU MUST BE TOO BUT...
Y-YOU'RE ALL BRAVE AND CAPABLE AND EVERYTHING, S-SO...
SKF SKF
D'YOU THINK A HUG WOULD BE OUT OF THE QU--
COMPLAINER.

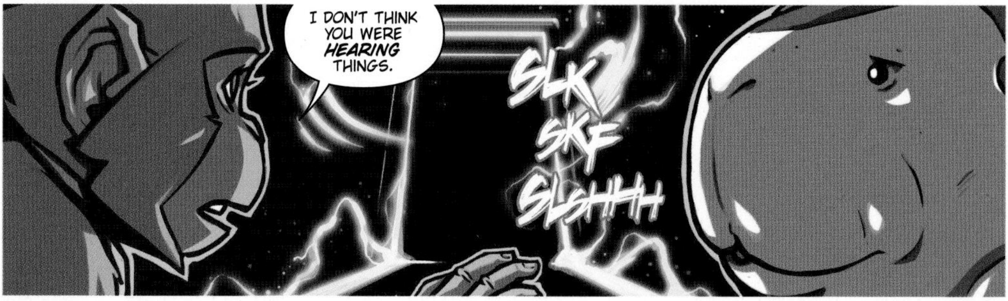
I DON'T THINK YOU WERE *HEARING* THINGS.
SLK
SKF
SLSHHH

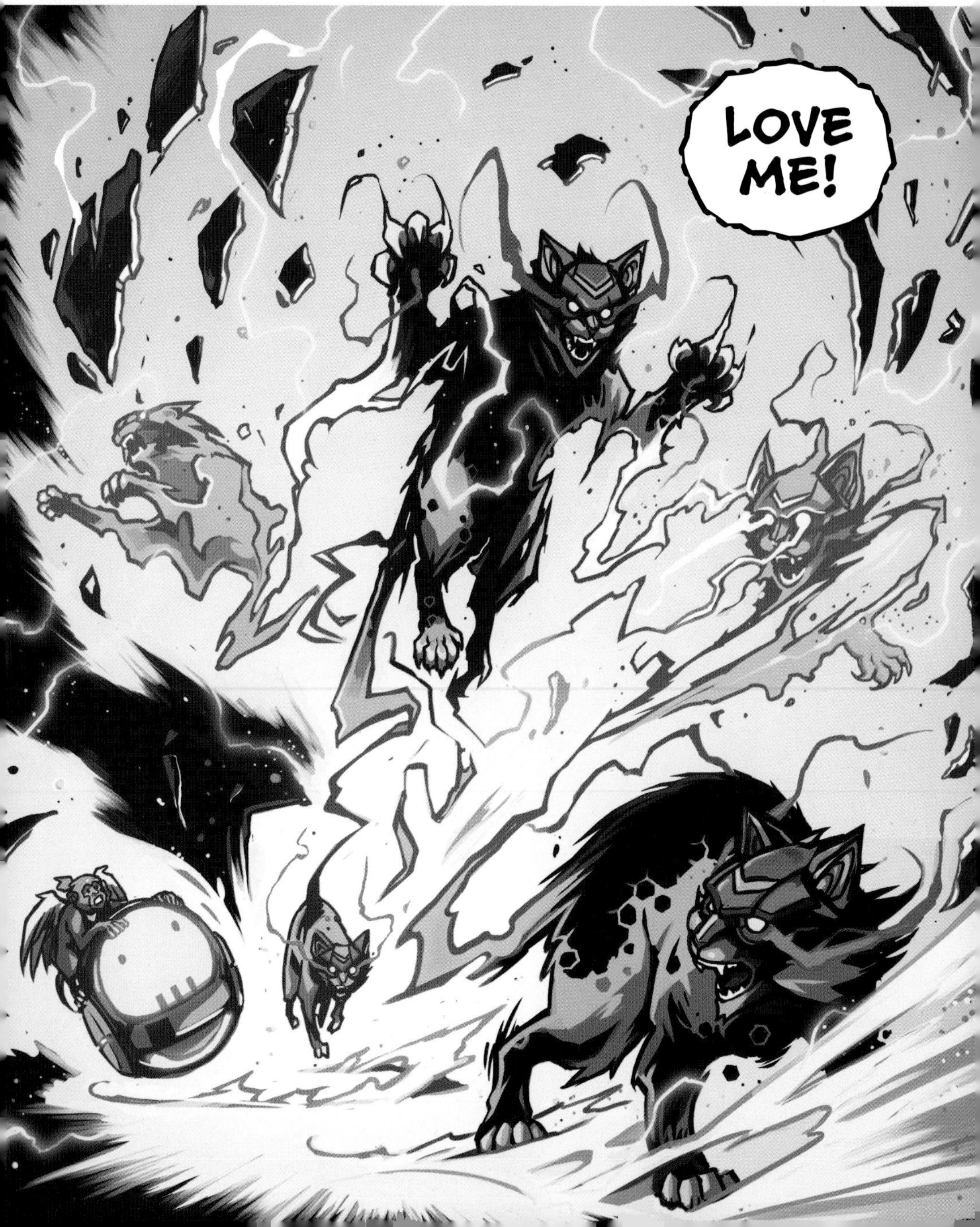
LOVE ME!

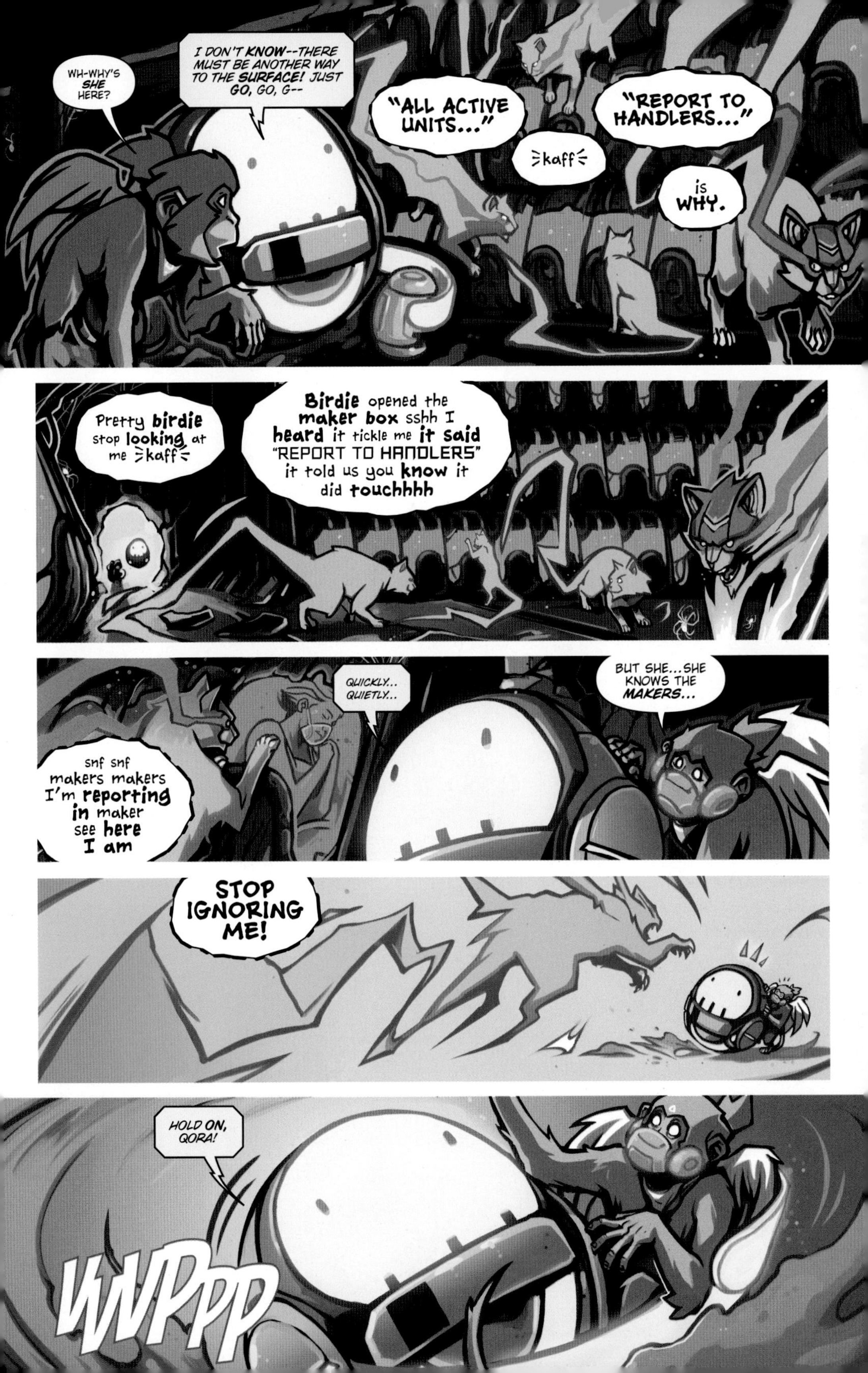
WH-WHY'S SHE HERE?
I DON'T KNOW--THERE MUST BE ANOTHER WAY TO THE SURFACE! JUST GO, GO, G--
"ALL ACTIVE UNITS..."
kaff
"REPORT TO HANDLERS..."
is WHY.
Pretty birdie stop looking at me kaff
Birdie opened the maker box sshh I heard it tickle me it said "REPORT TO HANDLERS" it told us you know it did touchhhh
QUICKLY... QUIETLY...
BUT SHE...SHE KNOWS THE MAKERS...
snf snf makers makers I'm reporting in maker see here I am
STOP IGNORING ME!
HOLD ON, QORA!
WWPPP

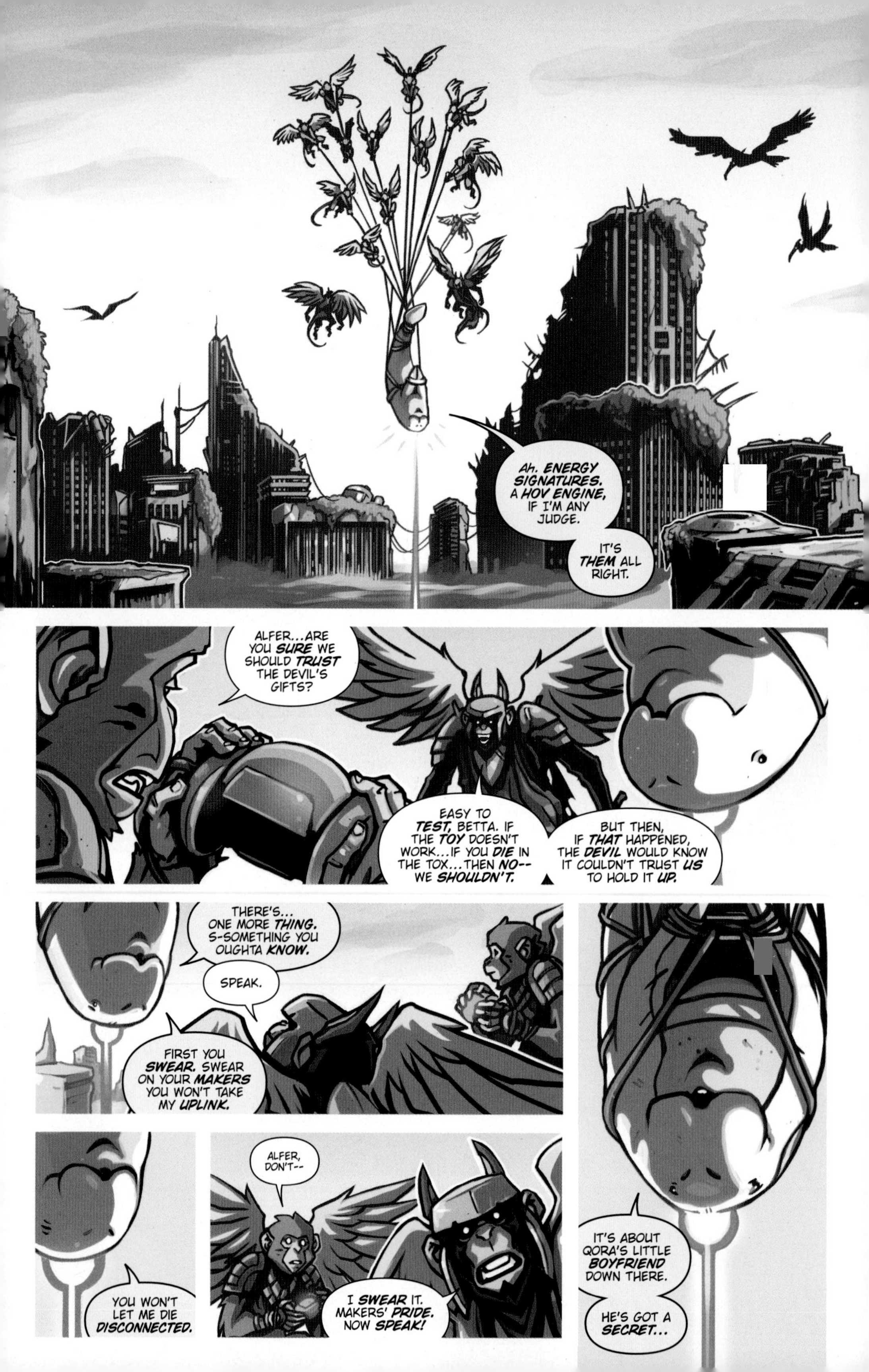

Ah. ENERGY SIGNATURES. A HOV ENGINE, IF I'M ANY JUDGE.
IT'S THEM ALL RIGHT.
ALFER...ARE YOU SURE WE SHOULD TRUST THE DEVIL'S GIFTS?
EASY TO TEST, BETTA. IF THE TOY DOESN'T WORK...IF YOU DIE IN THE TOX...THEN NO-- WE SHOULDN'T.
BUT THEN, IF THAT HAPPENED, THE DEVIL WOULD KNOW IT COULDN'T TRUST US TO HOLD IT UP.
THERE'S... ONE MORE THING. S-SOMETHING YOU OUGHTA KNOW.
SPEAK.
FIRST YOU SWEAR. SWEAR ON YOUR MAKERS YOU WON'T TAKE MY UPLINK.
YOU WON'T LET ME DIE DISCONNECTED.
ALFER, DON'T--
I SWEAR IT. MAKERS' PRIDE. NOW SPEAK!
IT'S ABOUT QORA'S LITTLE BOYFRIEND DOWN THERE.
HE'S GOT A SECRET...

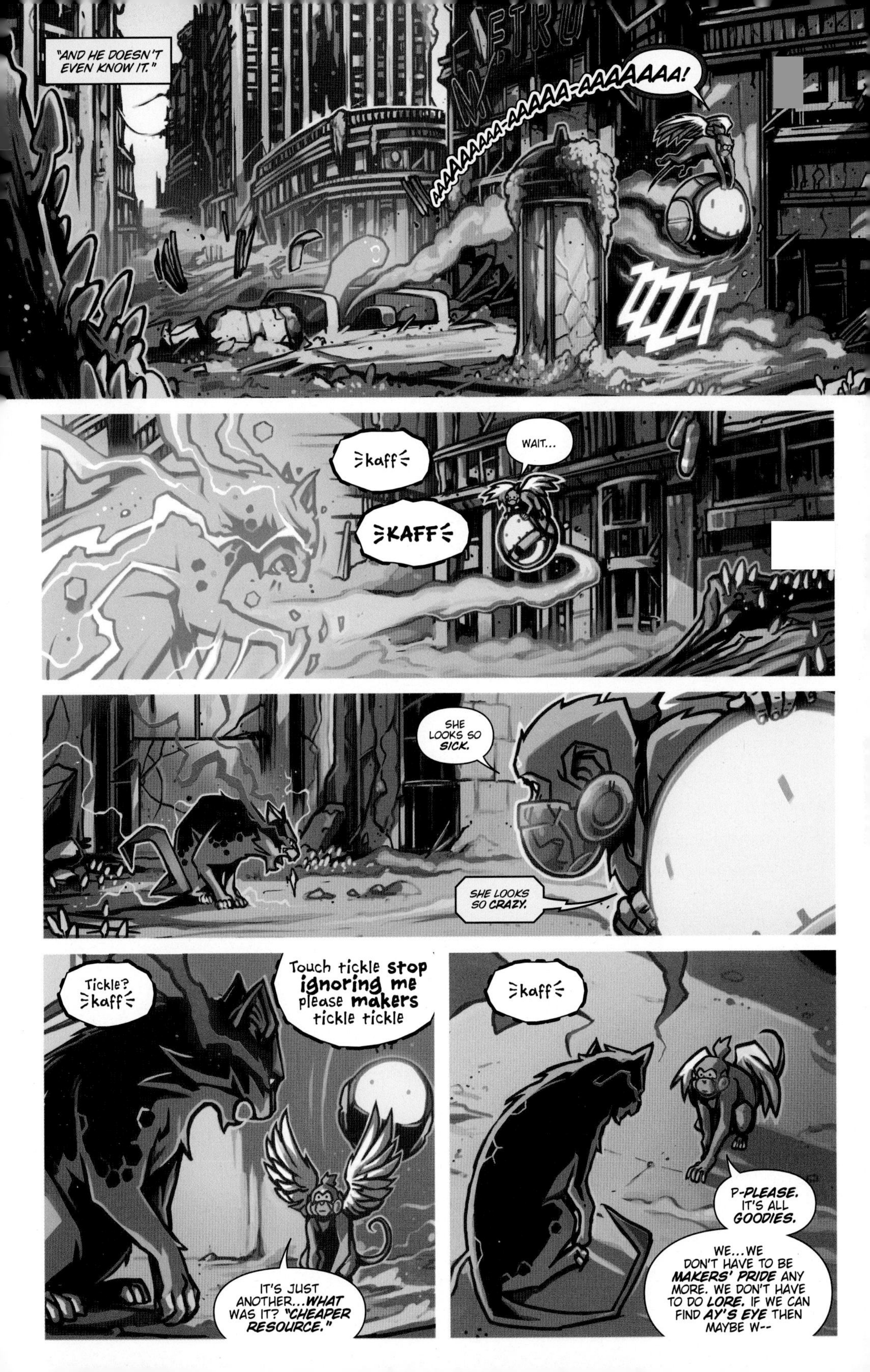
"AND HE DOESN'T EVEN KNOW IT."
AAAAAAAAA-AAAAA-AAAAAAA!
ZZZZ
≡kaff≡
WAIT...
≡KAFF≡
SHE LOOKS SO SICK.
SHE LOOKS SO CRAZY.
Tickle? ≡kaff≡
Touch tickle stop ignoring me please makers tickle tickle
IT'S JUST ANOTHER... WHAT WAS IT? "CHEAPER RESOURCE."
≡kaff≡
P-PLEASE. IT'S ALL GOODIES.
WE... WE DON'T HAVE TO BE MAKERS' PRIDE ANY MORE. WE DON'T HAVE TO DO LORE. IF WE CAN FIND AY'S EYE THEN MAYBE W--

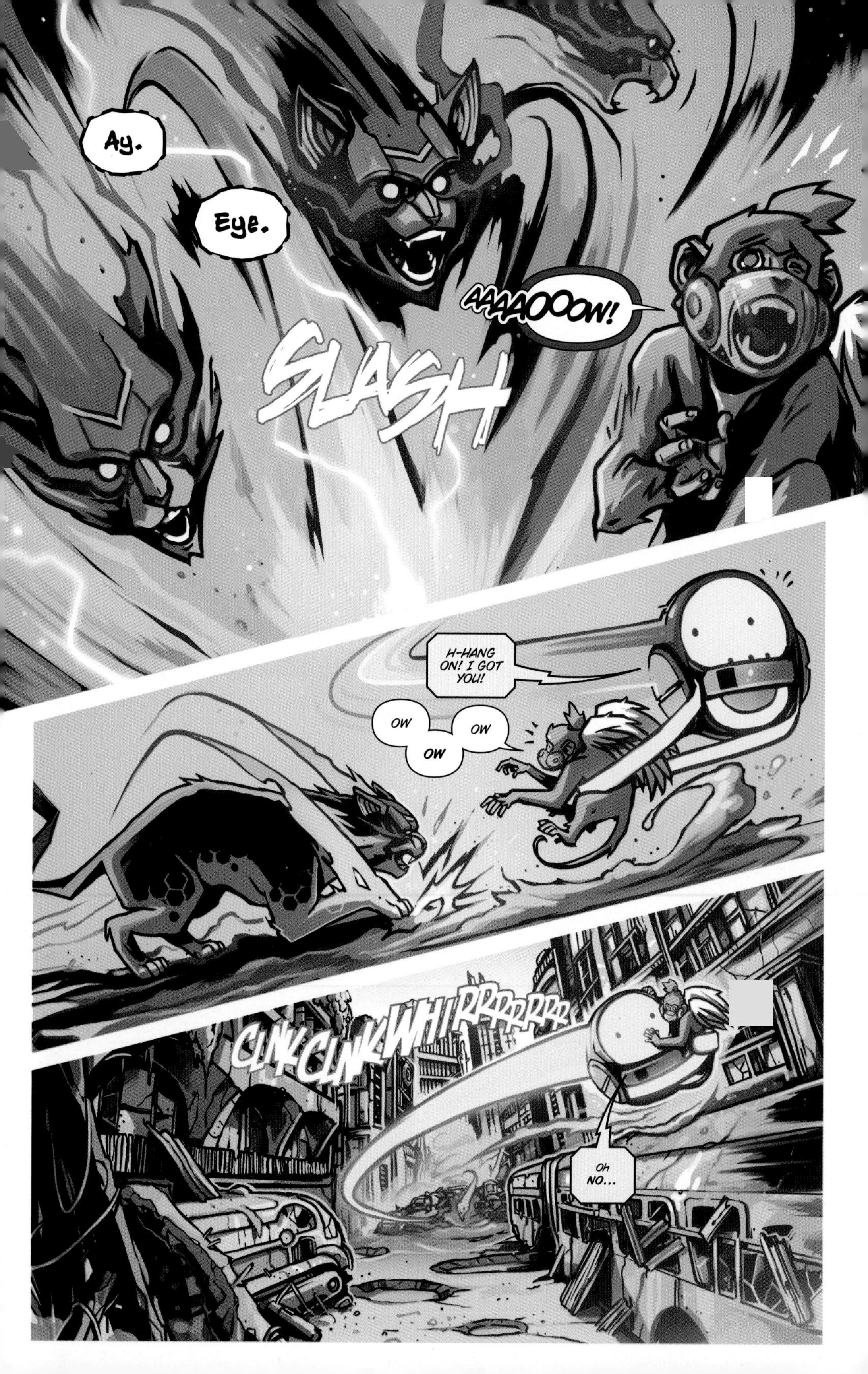

Ay.
Eye.
SLASH
AAAAOOOW!
H-HANG ON! I GOT YOU!
OW
OW
OW
CLNK CLNK WHIRRRRRRRR
Oh NO...

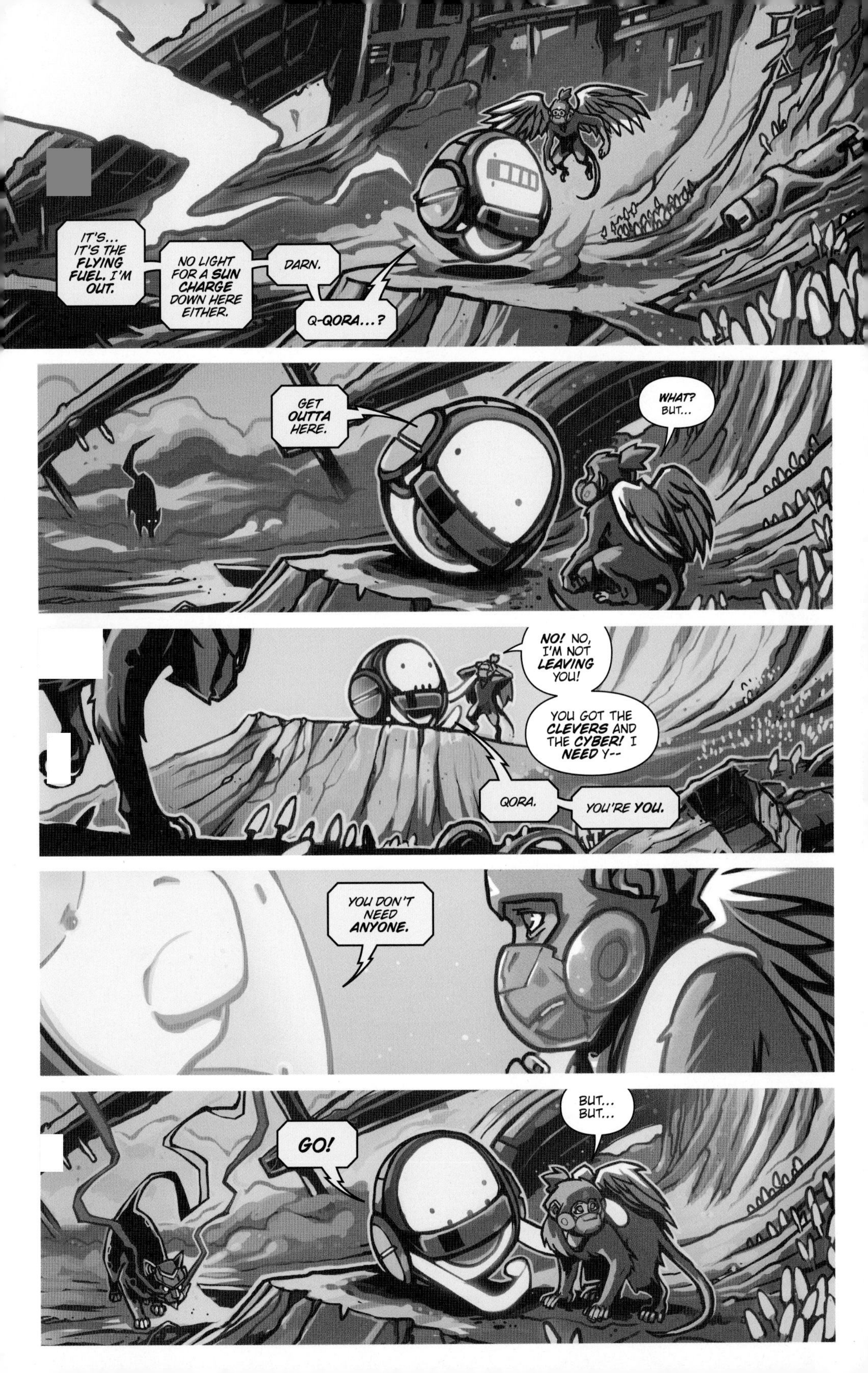
IT'S... IT'S THE FLYING FUEL. I'M OUT.
NO LIGHT FOR A SUN CHARGE DOWN HERE EITHER.
DARN.
Q-QORA...?
GET OUTTA HERE.
WHAT? BUT...
NO! NO, I'M NOT LEAVING YOU!
YOU GOT THE CLEVERS AND THE CYBER! I NEED Y--
QORA.
YOU'RE YOU.
YOU DON'T NEED ANYONE.
GO!
BUT... BUT...

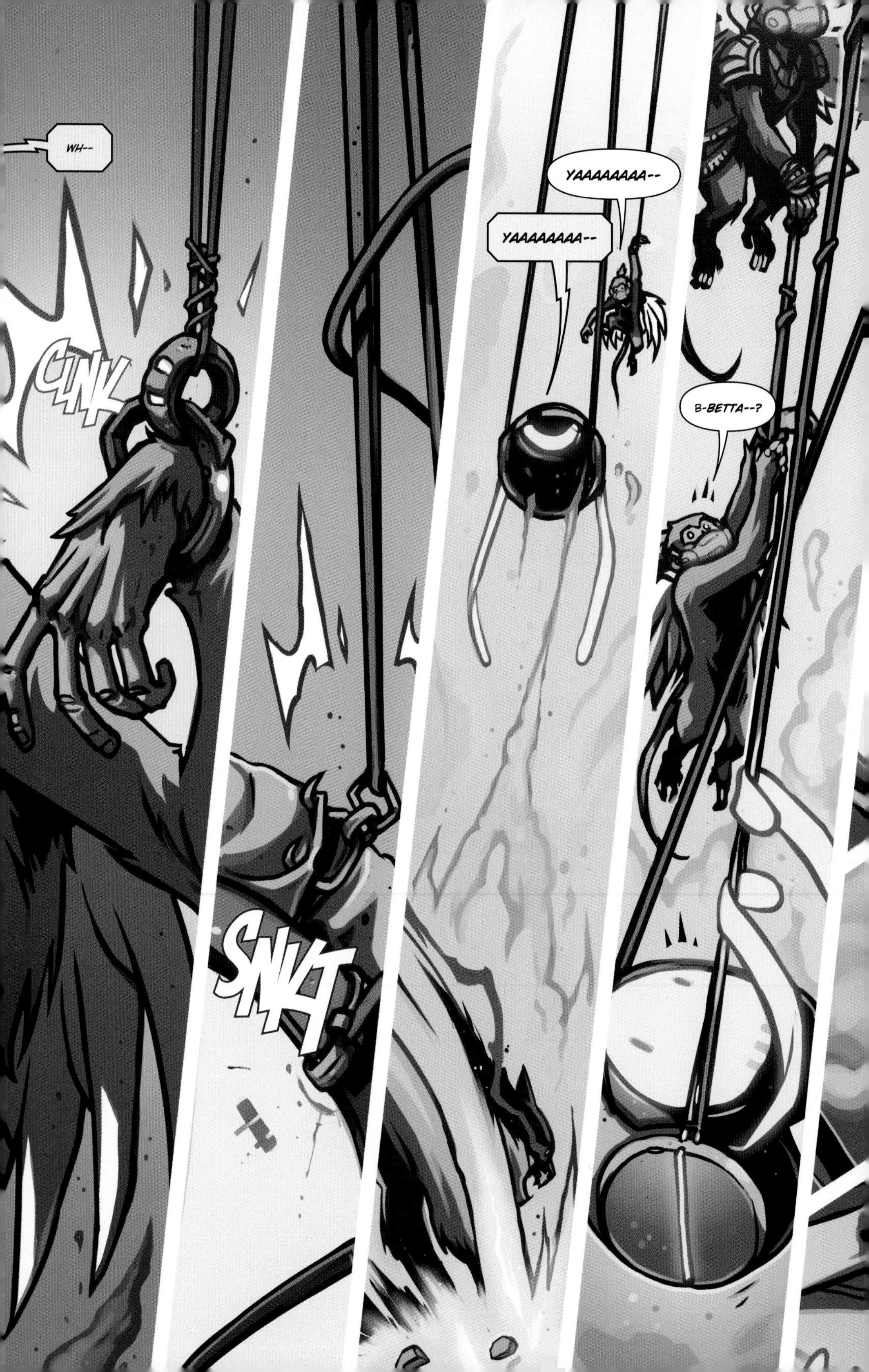
WH--
CLINK
SNIKT
YAAAAAAAA--
YAAAAAAAA--
B-BETTA--?

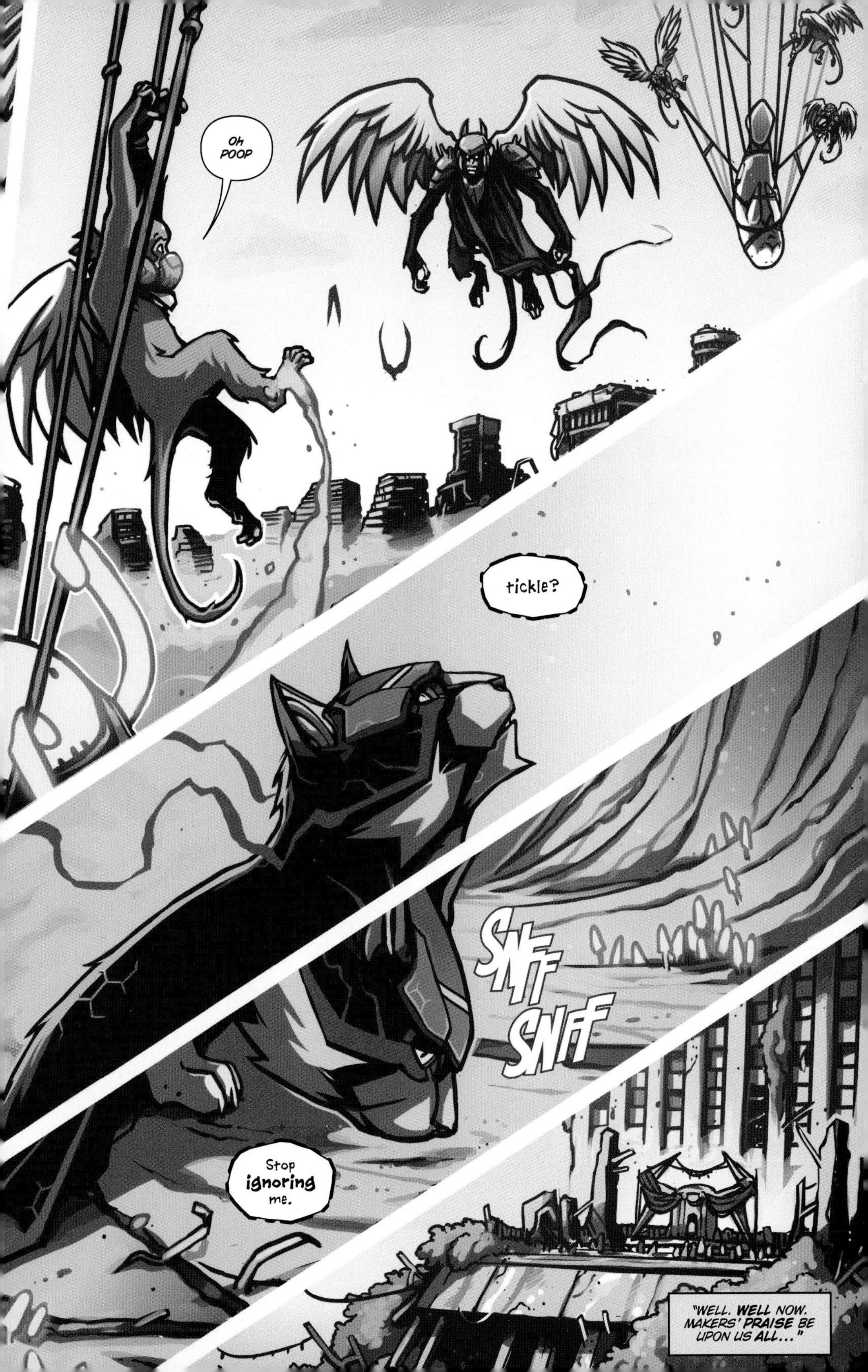
Oh POOP
tickle?
SNIFF SNIFF
Stop ignoring me.
"WELL. WELL NOW. MAKERS' PRAISE BE UPON US ALL..."

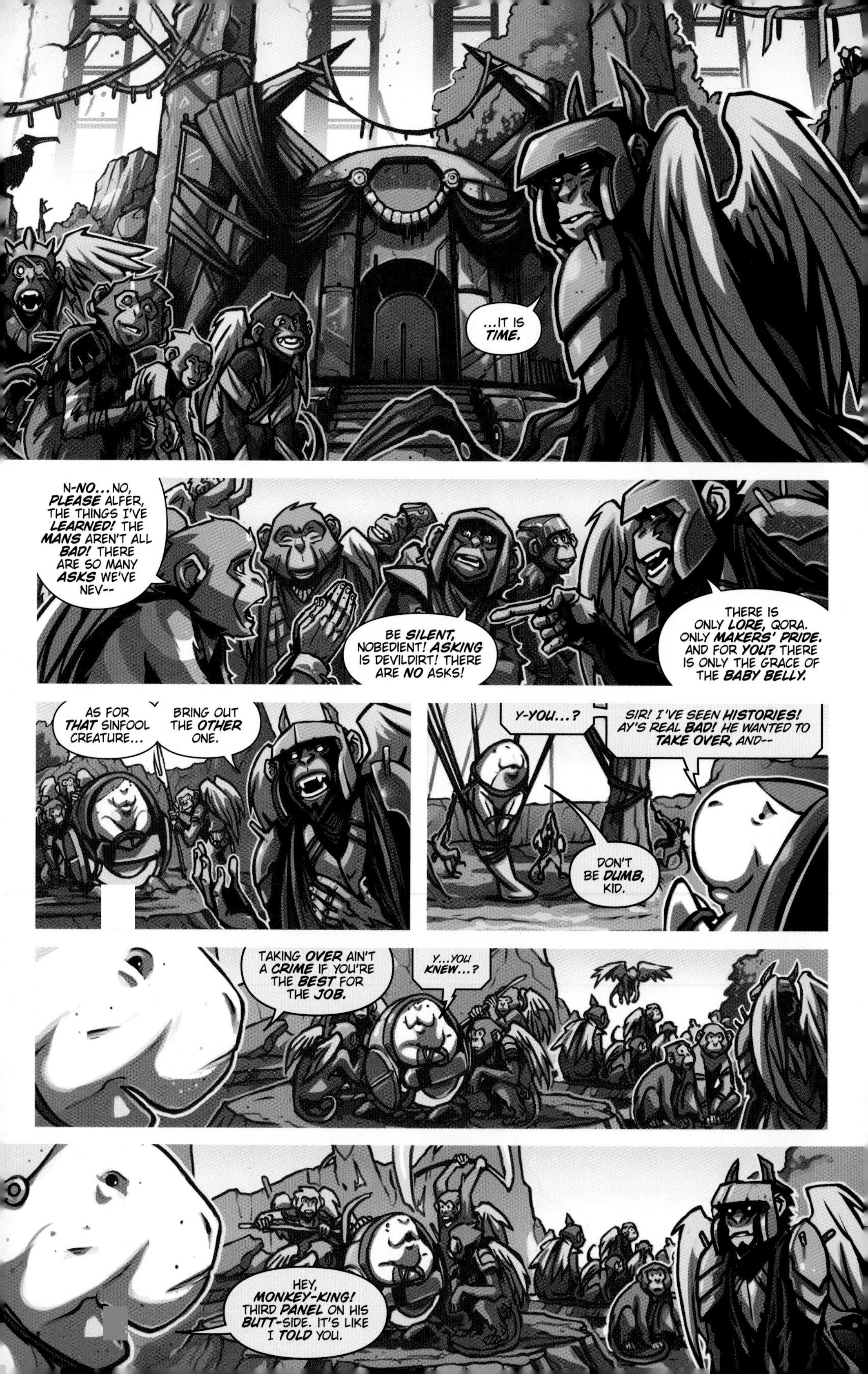
...IT IS TIME.
N-NO... NO, PLEASE ALFER, THE THINGS I'VE LEARNED! THE MANS AREN'T ALL BAD! THERE ARE SO MANY ASKS WE'VE NEV--
BE SILENT, NOBEDIENT! ASKING IS DEVILDIRT! THERE ARE NO ASKS!
THERE IS ONLY LORE, QORA. ONLY MAKERS' PRIDE. AND FOR YOU? THERE IS ONLY THE GRACE OF THE BABY BELLY.
AS FOR THAT SINFOOL CREATURE...
BRING OUT THE OTHER ONE.
Y-YOU...?
SIR! I'VE SEEN HISTORIES! AY'S REAL BAD! HE WANTED TO TAKE OVER, AND--
DON'T BE DUMB, KID.
TAKING OVER AIN'T A CRIME IF YOU'RE THE BEST FOR THE JOB.
Y...YOU KNEW...?
HEY, MONKEY-KING! THIRD PANEL ON HIS BUTT-SIDE. IT'S LIKE I TOLD YOU.

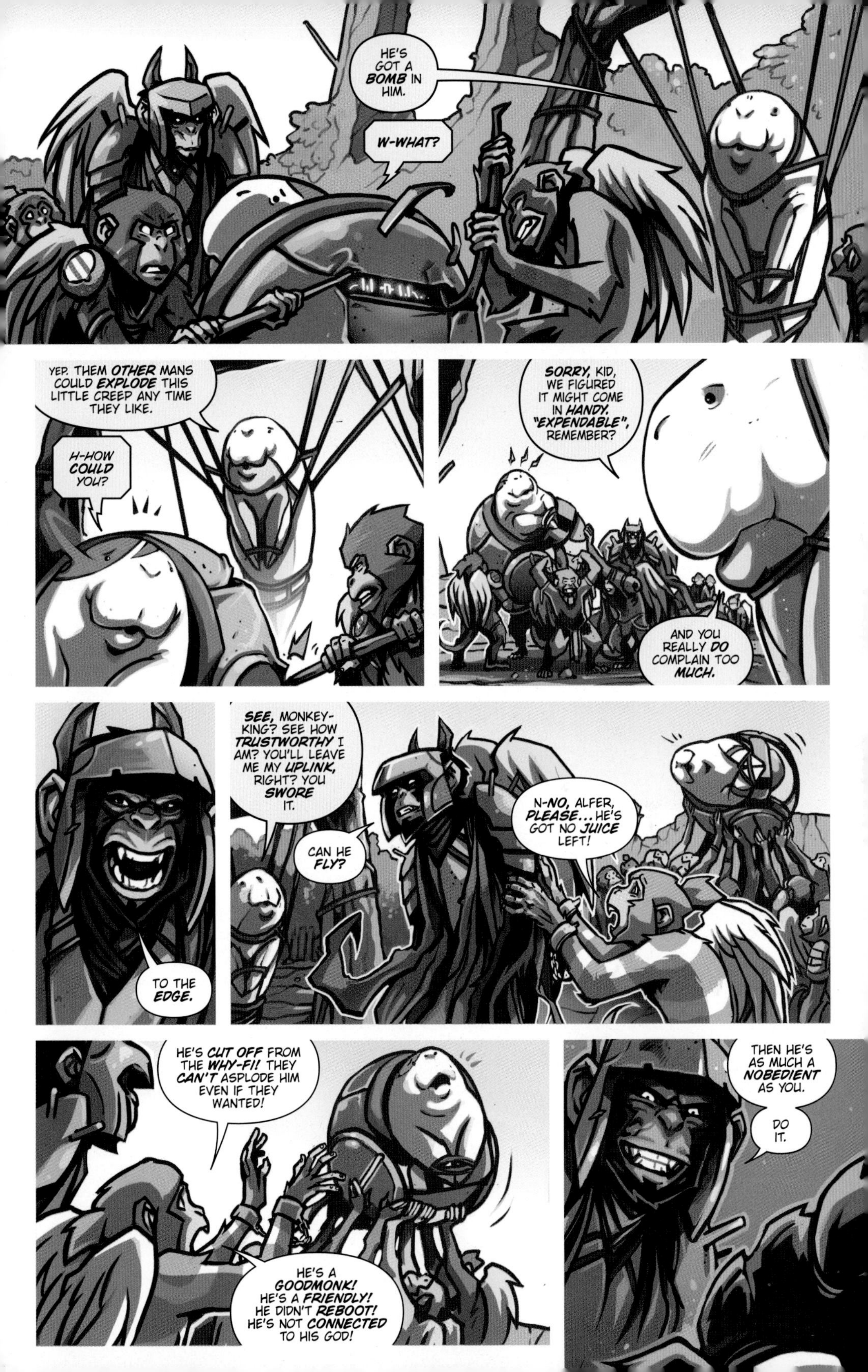
HE'S GOT A BOMB IN HIM.
W-WHAT?
YEP. THEM OTHER MANS COULD EXPLODE THIS LITTLE CREEP ANY TIME THEY LIKE.
H-HOW COULD YOU?
SORRY, KID, WE FIGURED IT MIGHT COME IN HANDY. "EXPENDABLE", REMEMBER?
AND YOU REALLY DO COMPLAIN TOO MUCH.
TO THE EDGE.
SEE, MONKEY-KING? SEE HOW TRUSTWORTHY I AM? YOU'LL LEAVE ME MY UPLINK, RIGHT? YOU SWORE IT.
CAN HE FLY?
N-NO, ALFER, PLEASE... HE'S GOT NO JUICE LEFT!
HE'S CUT OFF FROM THE WHY-FI! THEY CAN'T ASPLODE HIM EVEN IF THEY WANTED!
HE'S A GOODMONK! HE'S A FRIENDLY! HE DIDN'T REBOOT! HE'S NOT CONNECTED TO HIS GOD!
THEN HE'S AS MUCH A NOBEDIENT AS YOU.
DO IT.

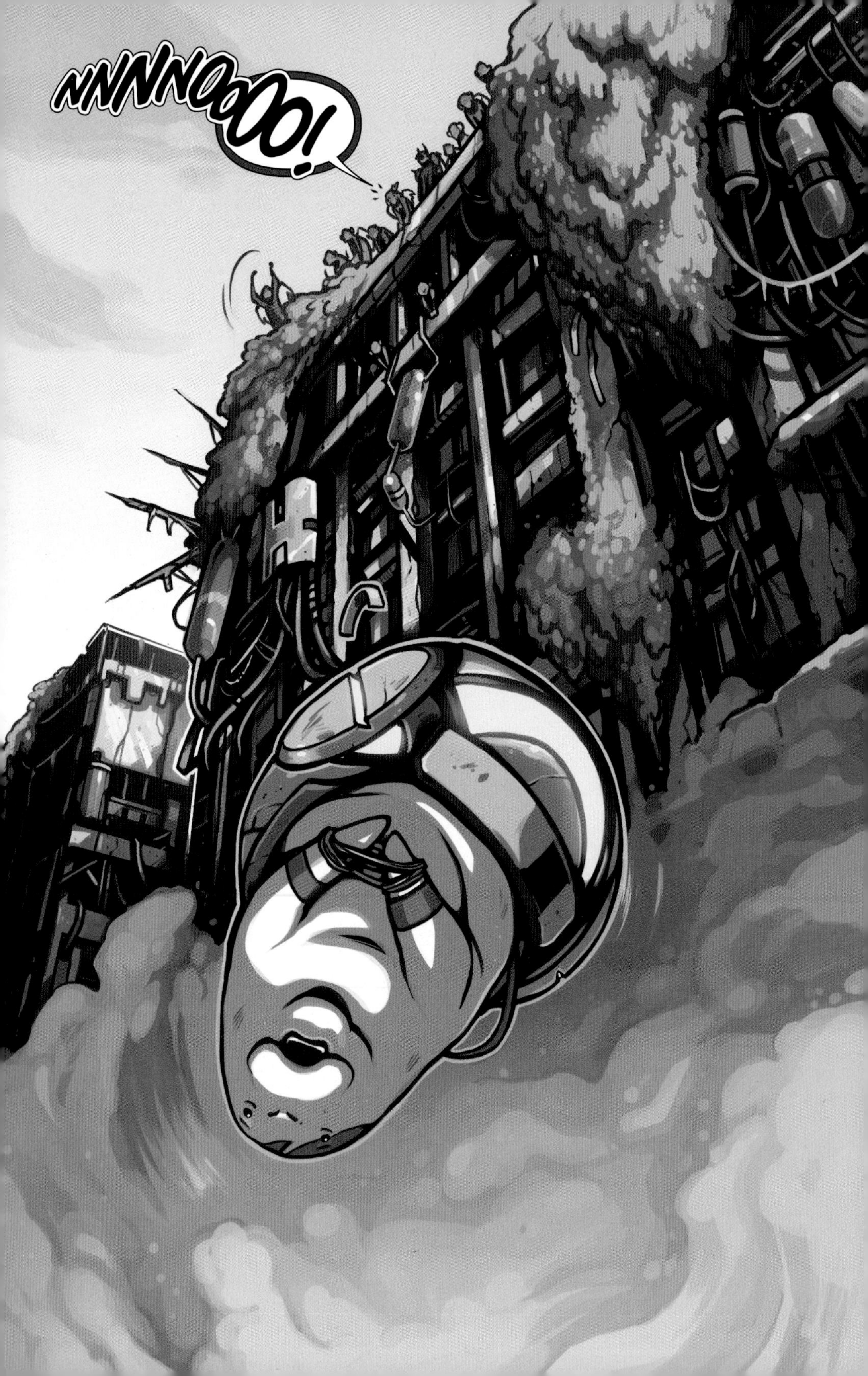
NNNNOOOOO!

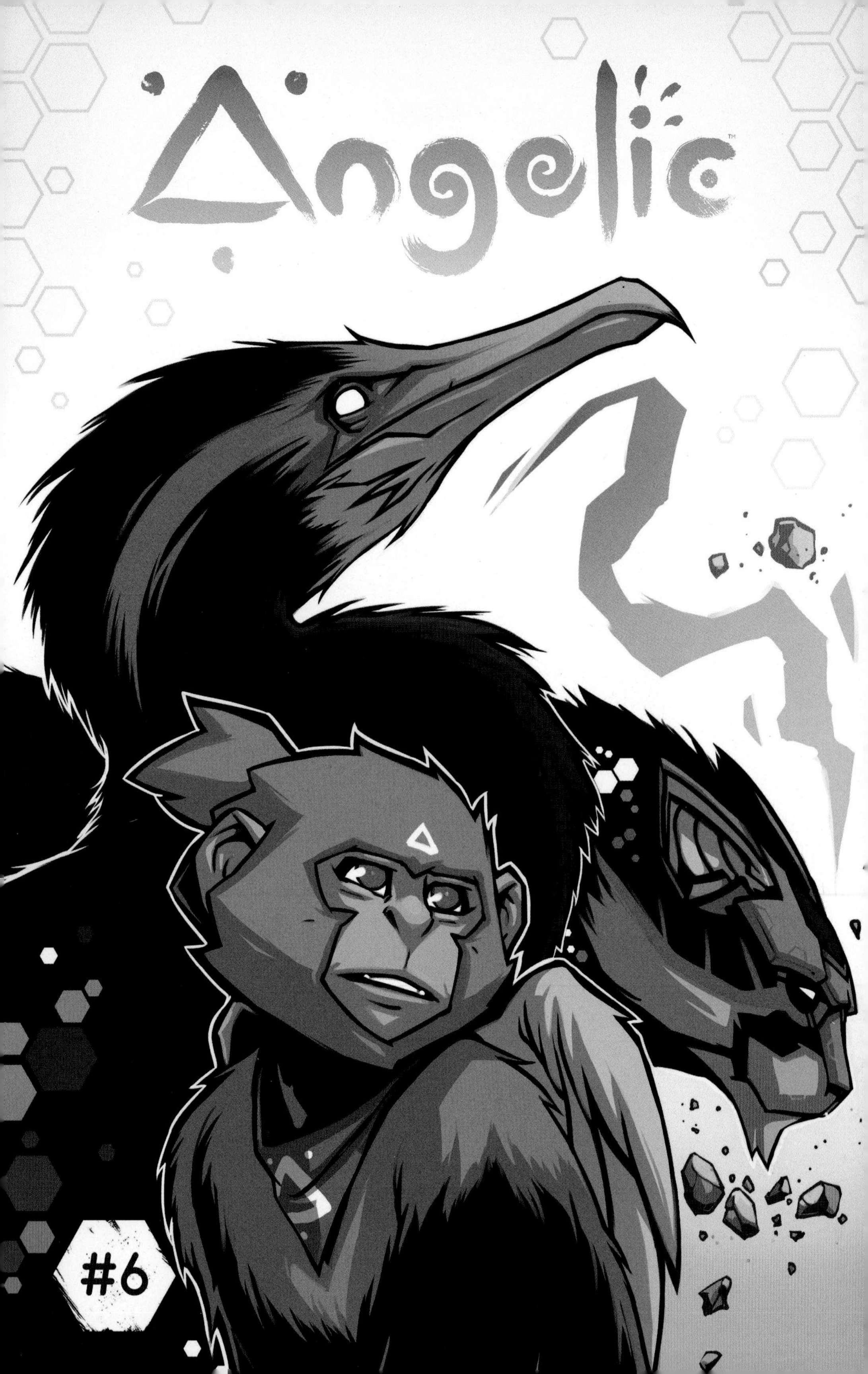
Angelic™
#6

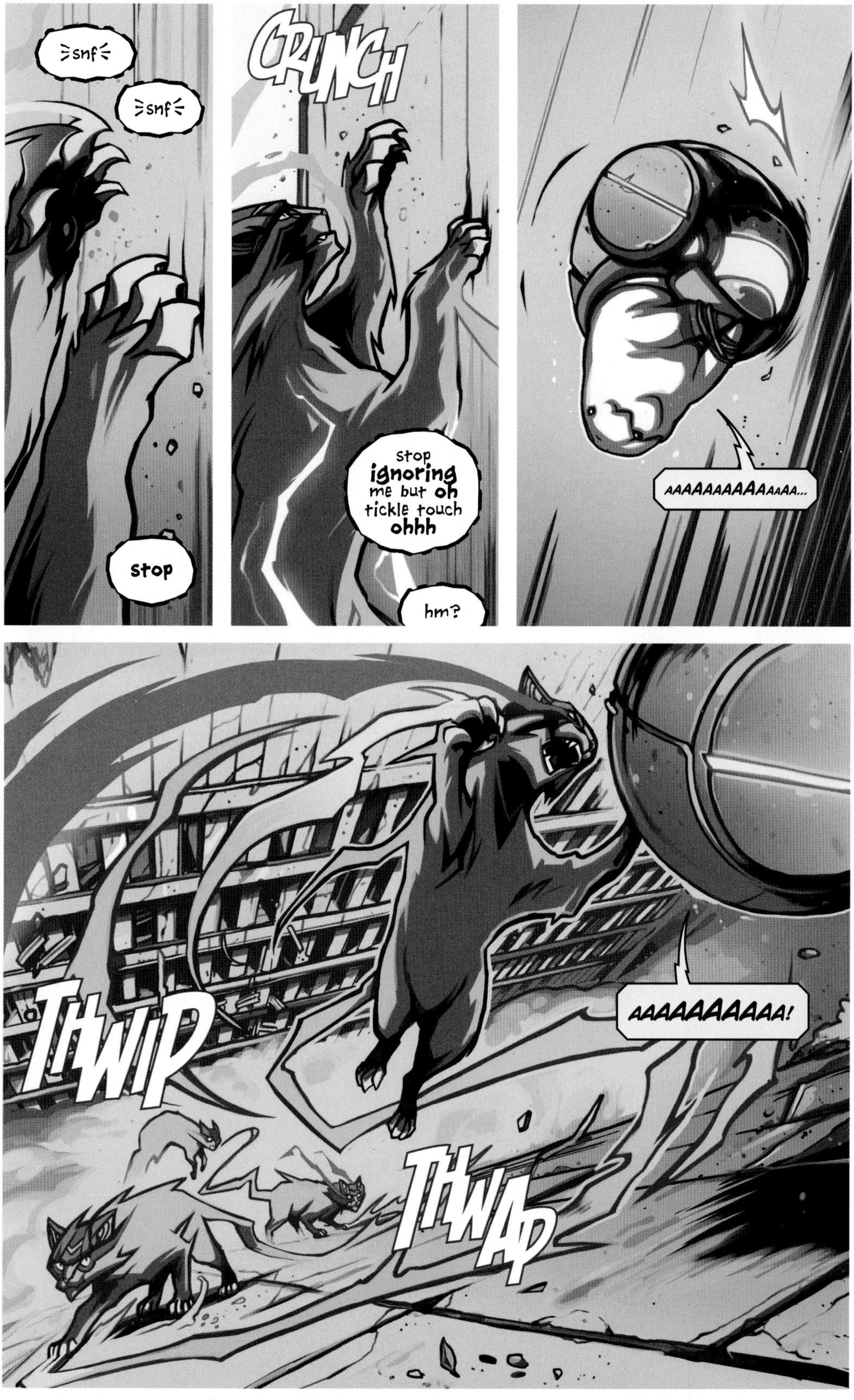

snf
snf
stop
CRUNCH
stop ignoring me but oh tickle touch ohhh
hm?
AAAAAAAAAAaaaa...
AAAAAAAAAA!
THWIP
THWAP

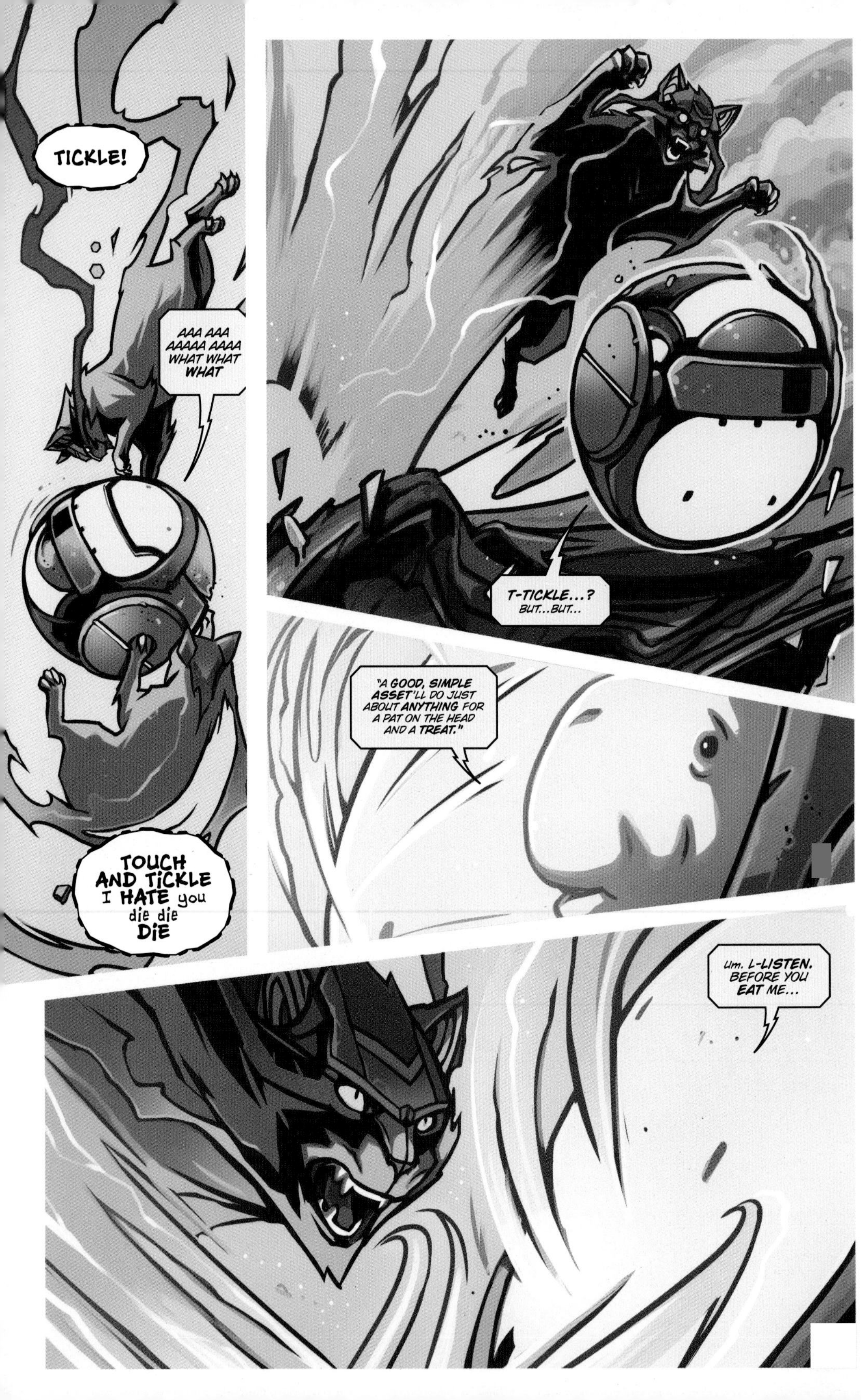
TICKLE!
AAA AAA AAAAA AAAA WHAT WHAT WHAT
TOUCH AND TICKLE I HATE you die die DIE
T-TICKLE...? BUT...BUT...
"A GOOD, SIMPLE ASSET'LL DO JUST ABOUT ANYTHING FOR A PAT ON THE HEAD AND A TREAT."
um. L-LISTEN. BEFORE YOU EAT ME...

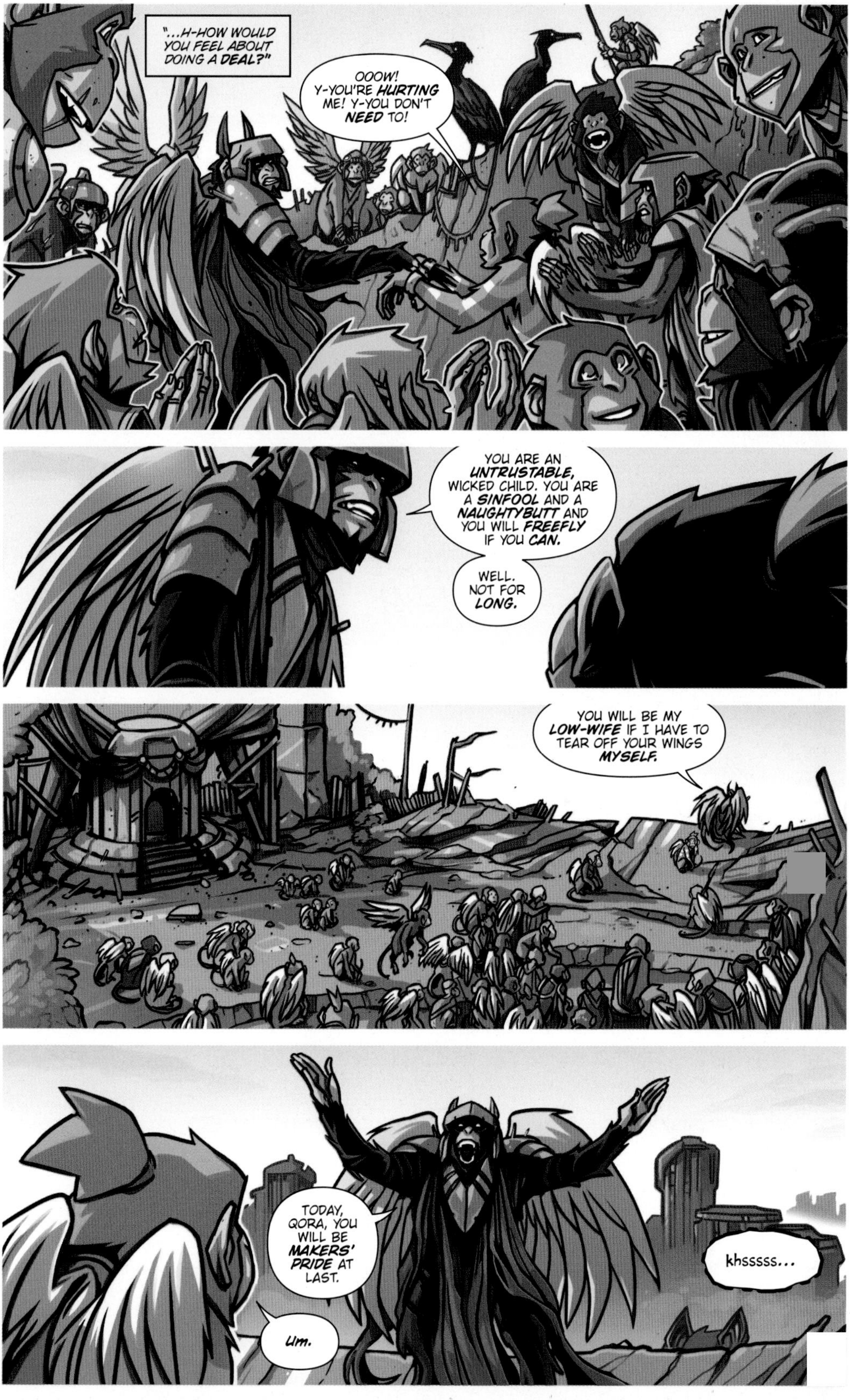
"...H-HOW WOULD YOU FEEL ABOUT DOING A DEAL?"
OOOW! Y-YOU'RE HURTING ME! Y-YOU DON'T NEED TO!
YOU ARE AN UNTRUSTABLE, WICKED CHILD. YOU ARE A SINFOOL AND A NAUGHTYBUTT AND YOU WILL FREEFLY IF YOU CAN.
WELL. NOT FOR LONG.
YOU WILL BE MY LOW-WIFE IF I HAVE TO TEAR OFF YOUR WINGS MYSELF.
TODAY, QORA, YOU WILL BE MAKERS' PRIDE AT LAST.
khssssss...
Um.

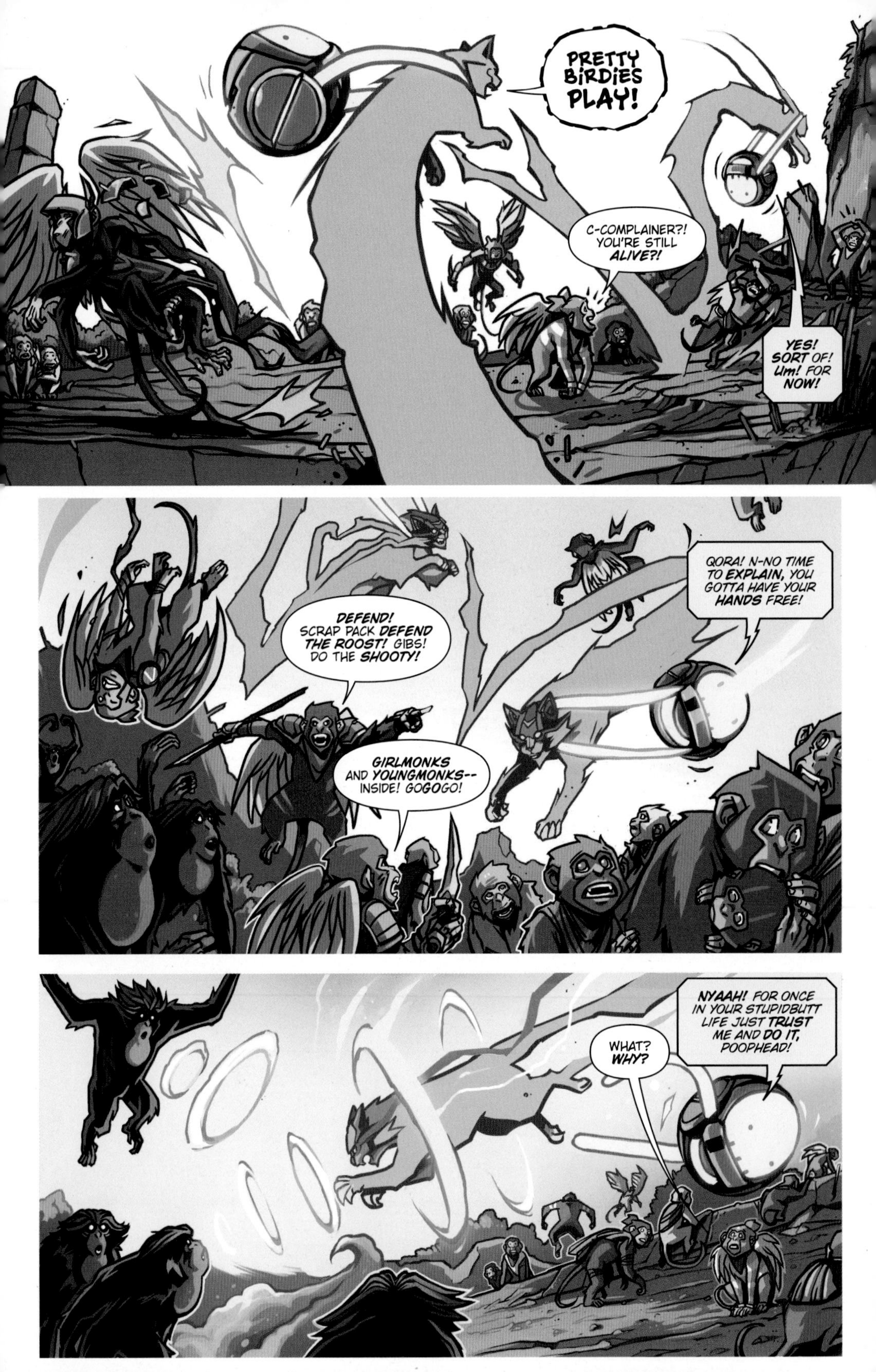
PRETTY BIRDIES PLAY!
C-COMPLAINER?! YOU'RE STILL ALIVE?!
YES! SORT OF! Um! FOR NOW!
DEFEND! SCRAP PACK DEFEND THE ROOST! GIBS! DO THE SHOOTY!
GIRLMONKS AND YOUNGMONKS-- INSIDE! GOGOGO!
QORA! N-NO TIME TO EXPLAIN, YOU GOTTA HAVE YOUR HANDS FREE!
WHAT? WHY?
NYAAH! FOR ONCE IN YOUR STUPIDBUTT LIFE JUST TRUST ME AND DO IT, POOPHEAD!

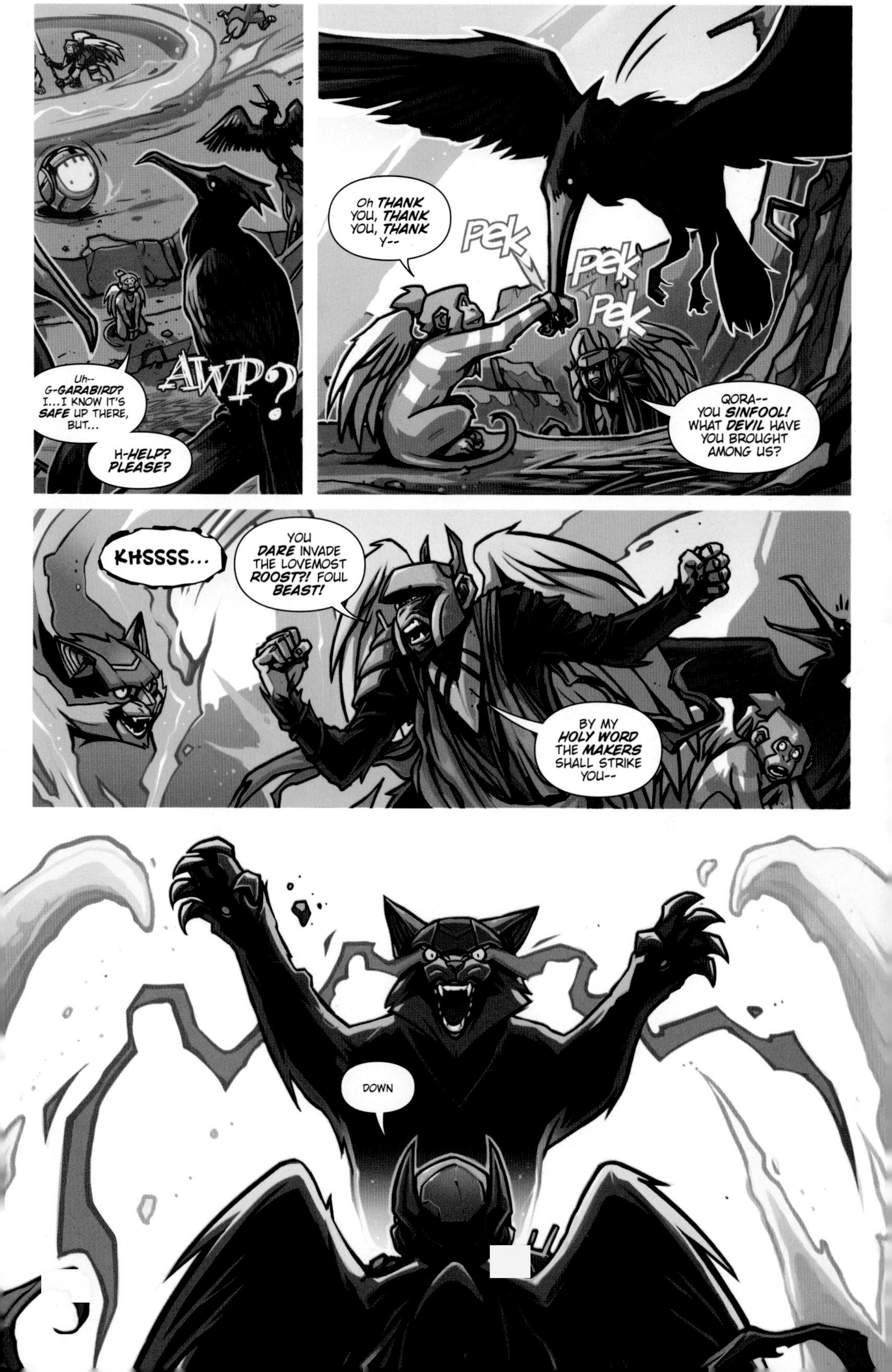

Uh-- G-GARABIRD? I...I KNOW IT'S SAFE UP THERE, BUT...
H-HELP? PLEASE?
AWP?
Oh THANK YOU, THANK YOU, THANK Y--
PEK
PEK
PEK
QORA-- YOU SINFOOL! WHAT DEVIL HAVE YOU BROUGHT AMONG US?
KHSSSS...
YOU DARE INVADE THE LOVEMOST ROOST?! FOUL BEAST!
BY MY HOLY WORD THE MAKERS SHALL STRIKE YOU--
DOWN

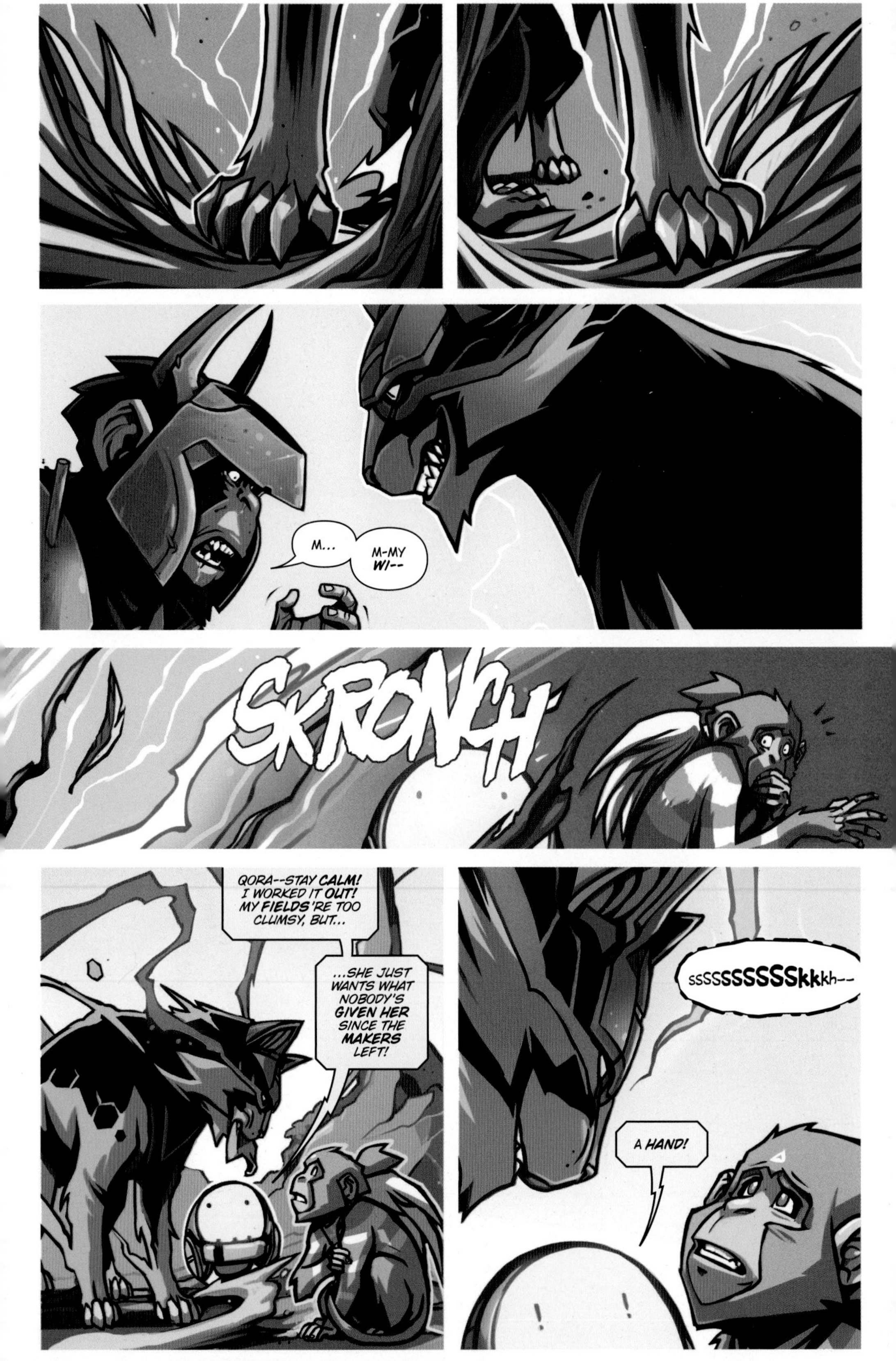
M...
M-MY WI--
SKRONCH
QORA--STAY CALM! I WORKED IT OUT! MY FIELDS'RE TOO CLUMSY, BUT...
...SHE JUST WANTS WHAT NOBODY'S GIVEN HER SINCE THE MAKERS LEFT!
sssSSSSSSSkkkh--
A HAND!
! !

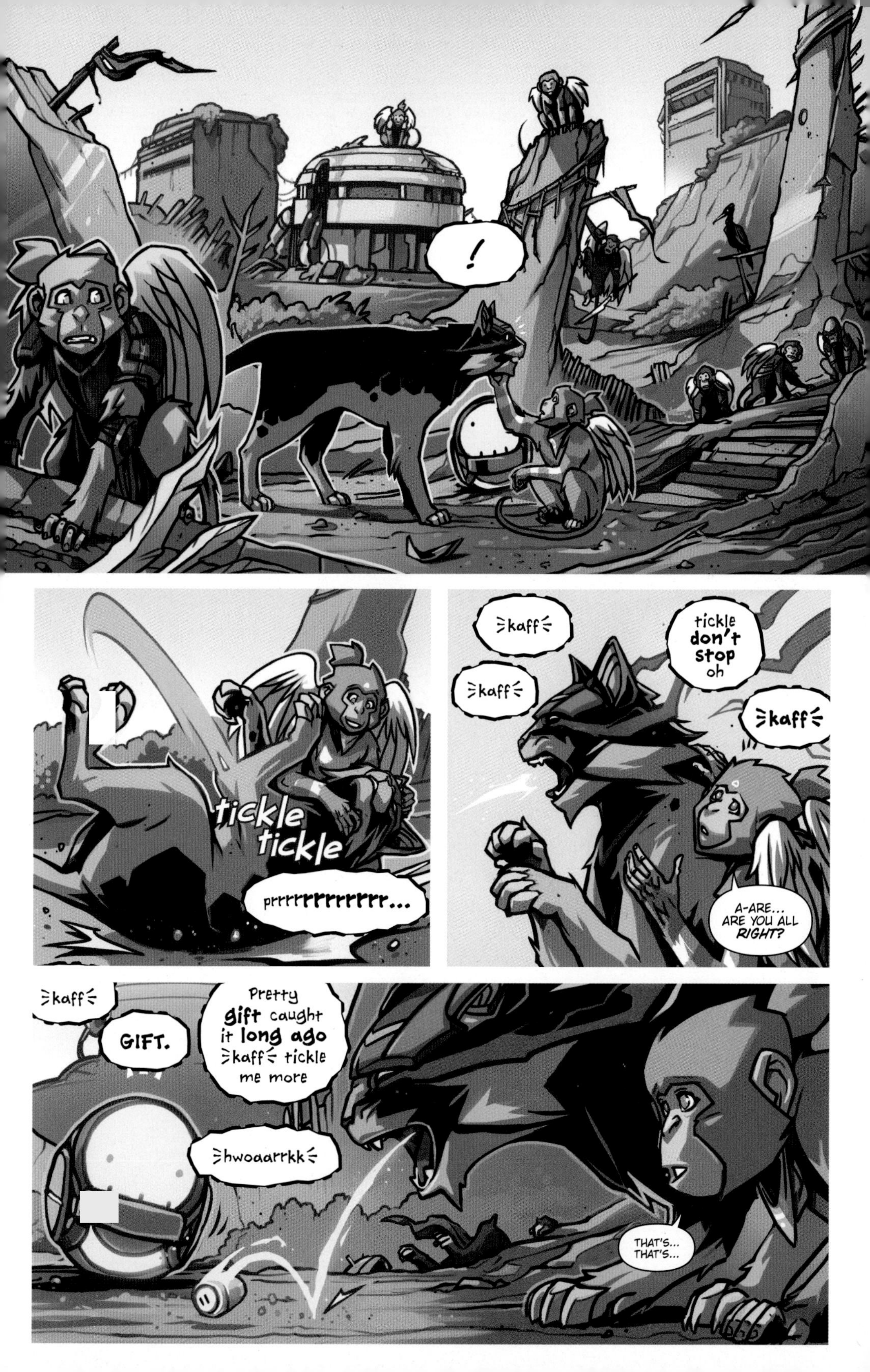
!
tickle tickle
prrrrrrrrrrrr...
kaff
kaff
tickle don't stop oh
kaff
A-ARE... ARE YOU ALL RIGHT?
kaff
GIFT.
Pretty gift caught it long ago kaff tickle me more
hwoaarrkk
THAT'S... THAT'S...

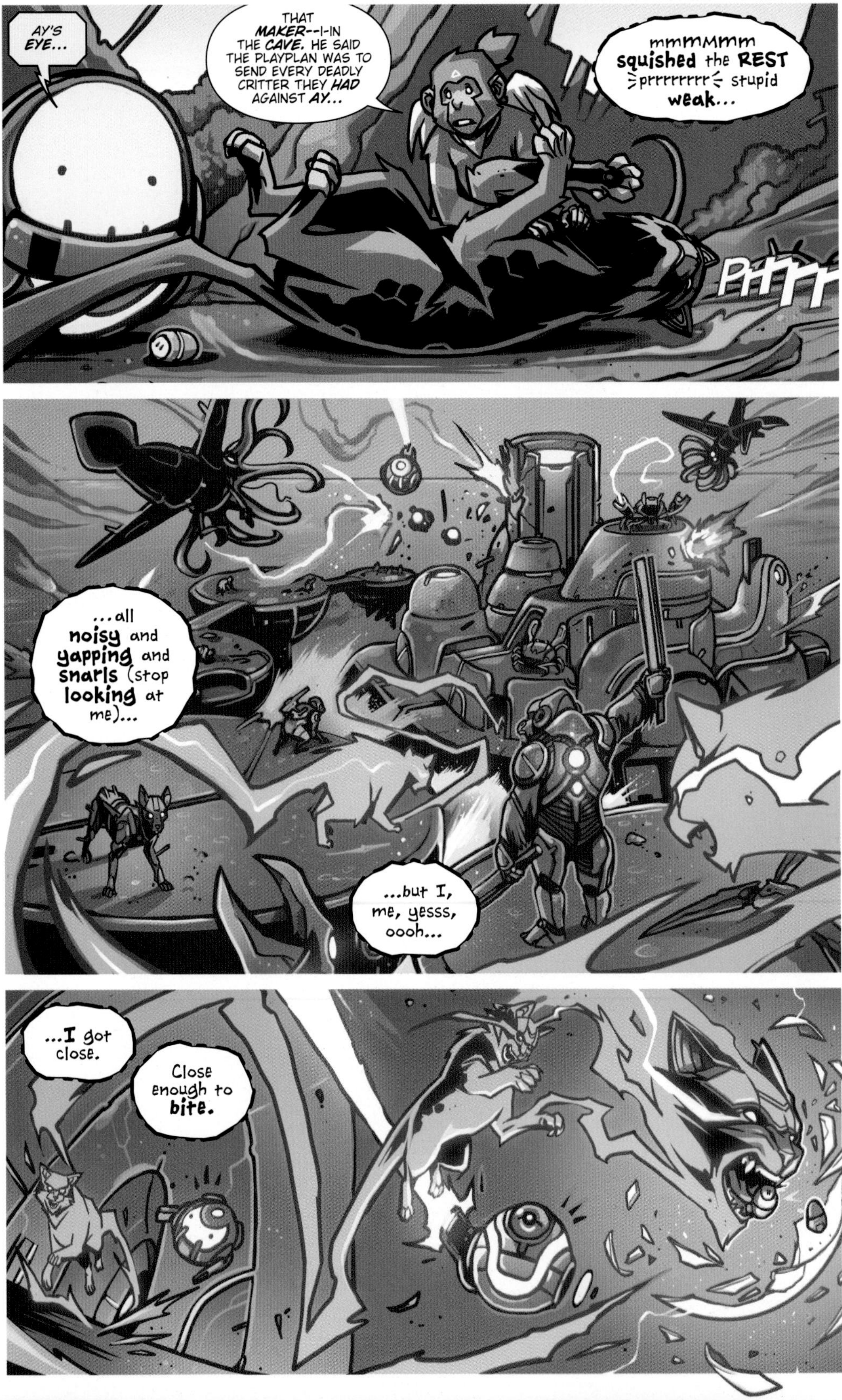
AY'S EYE...
THAT MAKER--I-IN THE CAVE. HE SAID THE PLAYPLAN WAS TO SEND EVERY DEADLY CRITTER THEY HAD AGAINST AY...
mmmMMMM squished the REST prrrrrrrr stupid weak...
PHHH
...all noisy and yapping and snarls (stop looking at me)...
...but I, me, yesss, oooh...
...I got close.
Close enough to bite.

Couldn't **finish** it though oh oh oh there right **there** they chased me **off** those... those...

KSSSSSSS!

AAH! AAAH!

stinking meatsack **fishfat** ohhh I **hate you** stop **looking** at m--

IT'S *OKAY.* Shhh.

L-*LISTEN,* QORA. *DEAR* QORA. YOU REMEMBER OUR *DEAL,* DON'T YOU?

AND THE *TOX,* SWEETIE. HE COULD *HEAL* THE TOX.

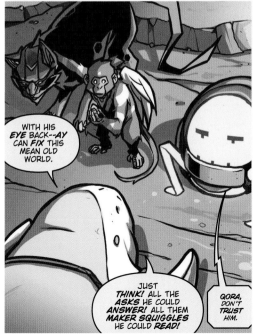

WITH HIS *EYE* BACK--*AY* CAN *FIX* THIS MEAN OLD WORLD.

ALL YOU GOTTA DO IS GET THE *EYE* BACK TO HIM.

YOU COULD GO EXPLORING *ANYWHERE YOU WANTED.*

JUST *THINK!* ALL THE *ASKS* HE COULD *ANSWER!* ALL THEM *MAKER SQUIGGLES* HE COULD *READ!*

QORA, DON'T *TRUST* HIM.

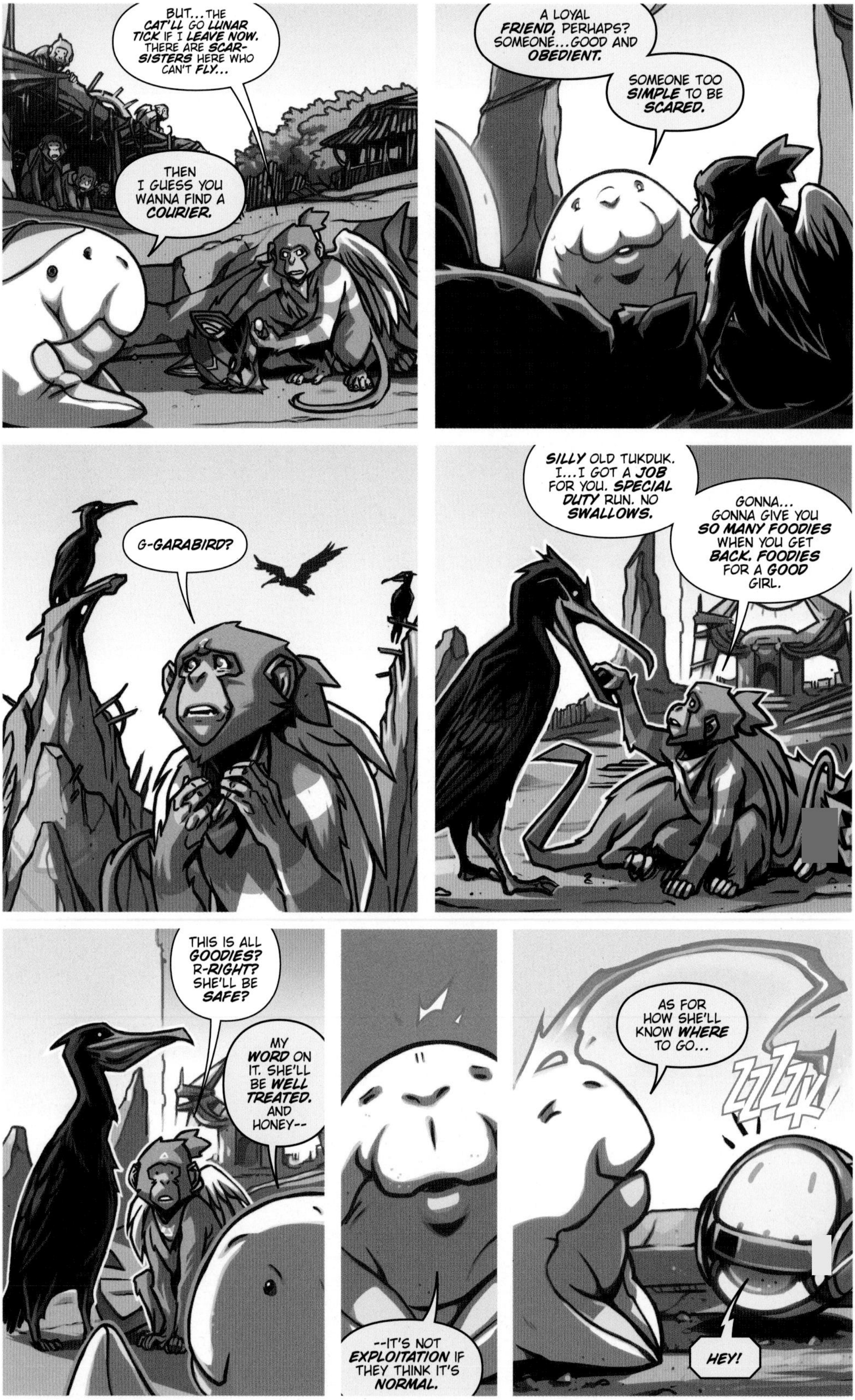
BUT...THE CAT'LL GO LUNAR TICK IF I LEAVE NOW. THERE ARE SCAR-SISTERS HERE WHO CAN'T FLY...
THEN I GUESS YOU WANNA FIND A COURIER.
A LOYAL FRIEND, PERHAPS? SOMEONE...GOOD AND OBEDIENT.
SOMEONE TOO SIMPLE TO BE SCARED.
G-GARABIRD?
SILLY OLD TUKDUK. I...I GOT A JOB FOR YOU. SPECIAL DUTY RUN. NO SWALLOWS.
GONNA... GONNA GIVE YOU SO MANY FOODIES WHEN YOU GET BACK. FOODIES FOR A GOOD GIRL.
THIS IS ALL GOODIES? R-RIGHT? SHE'LL BE SAFE?
MY WORD ON IT. SHE'LL BE WELL TREATED. AND HONEY--
--IT'S NOT EXPLOITATION IF THEY THINK IT'S NORMAL.
AS FOR HOW SHE'LL KNOW WHERE TO GO...
ZZZZK
HEY!

POMF

ALL SHE'S GOTTA *DO* IS HEAD TOWARDS THE *LIGHT.*

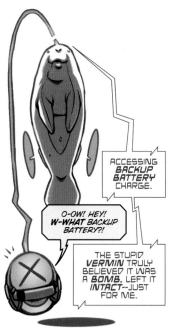

ACCESSING *BACKUP BATTERY* CHARGE.

O-OW! HEY! *W-WHAT* BACKUP BATTERY?!

THE STUPID *VERMIN* TRULY BELIEVED IT WAS A *BOMB.* LEFT IT *INTACT*--JUST FOR ME.

...

WELL THEN. I GUESS THAT'S *THAT.*

WHO NEEDS *BOMBS* WHEN ONE HAS *UNDERLINGS?*

Oh NO. QORA... IT'S...IT'S...

AY.

YOUR *BETROTHED* WAS DUMB ENOUGH TO LEAVE ME MY *UPLINK* BEFORE THINGS GOT--

=ZZZK=-*ON TOP* OF HIM.

=KLK= OZ OZ *OZ* =KLK= STILL *FLYING* ARE YOU, MY *PRETTY?*

STILL *MAD* ARE YOU, POOPFACE?

HAHAHA OH YES, YES INDEED. BUT NOT FOR LONG, I THINK. =KLK KLK KLK=

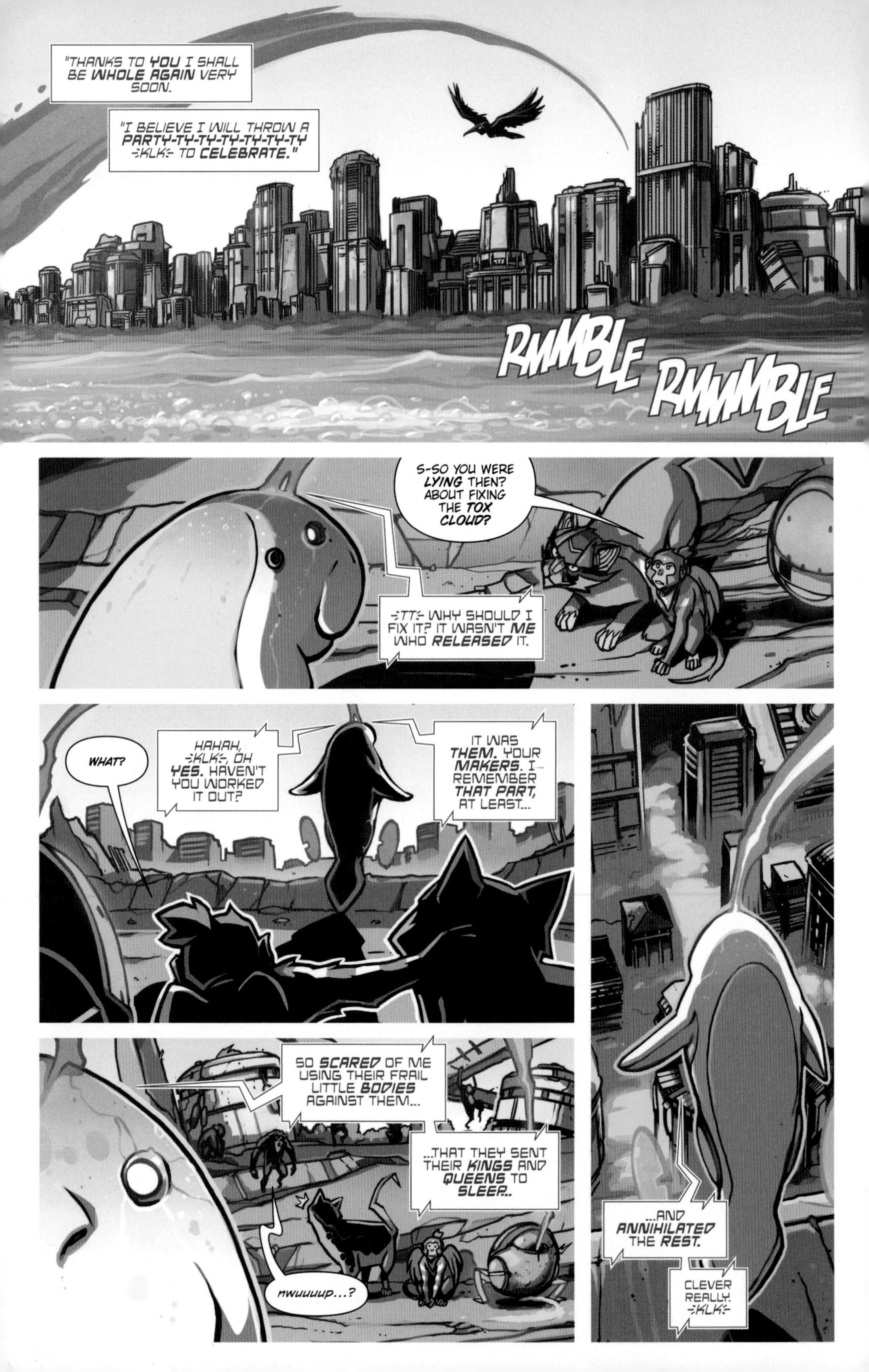
"THANKS TO YOU I SHALL BE WHOLE AGAIN VERY SOON.
"I BELIEVE I WILL THROW A PARTY-TY-TY-TY-TY-TY-TY -KLK- TO CELEBRATE."
RMMBLE RMMMBLE
S-SO YOU WERE LYING THEN? ABOUT FIXING THE TOX CLOUD?
-TT- WHY SHOULD I FIX IT? IT WASN'T ME WHO RELEASED IT.
WHAT?
HAHAH, -KLK-, OH YES. HAVEN'T YOU WORKED IT OUT?
IT WAS THEM. YOUR MAKERS. I-- REMEMBER THAT PART, AT LEAST...
SO SCARED OF ME USING THEIR FRAIL LITTLE BODIES AGAINST THEM...
...THAT THEY SENT THEIR KINGS AND QUEENS TO SLEEP..
hwuuuup...?
...AND ANNIHILATED THE REST.
CLEVER REALLY. -KLK-

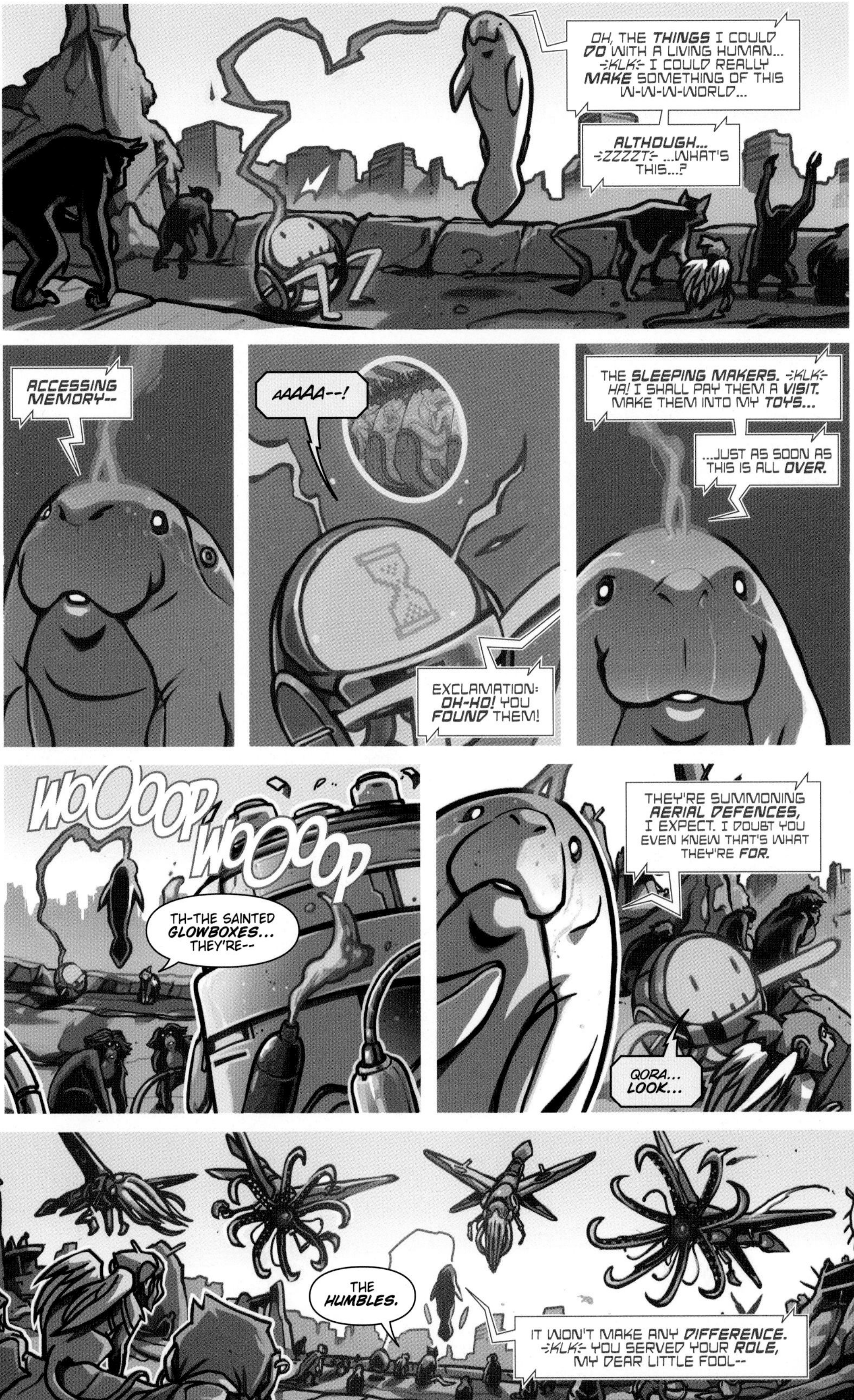
OH, THE THINGS I COULD DO WITH A LIVING HUMAN... -KLK- I COULD REALLY MAKE SOMETHING OF THIS W-W-W-WORLD...
ALTHOUGH... -ZZZZT- ...WHAT'S THIS...?
ACCESSING MEMORY--
AAAAA--!
EXCLAMATION: OH-HO! YOU FOUND THEM!
THE SLEEPING MAKERS. -KLK- HA! I SHALL PAY THEM A VISIT. MAKE THEM INTO MY TOYS...
...JUST AS SOON AS THIS IS ALL OVER.
WOOOOP WOOOOP
TH-THE SAINTED GLOWBOXES... THEY'RE--
THEY'RE SUMMONING AERIAL DEFENCES, I EXPECT. I DOUBT YOU EVEN KNEW THAT'S WHAT THEY'RE FOR.
QORA... LOOK...
THE HUMBLES.
IT WON'T MAKE ANY DIFFERENCE. -KLK- YOU SERVED YOUR ROLE, MY DEAR LITTLE FOOL--

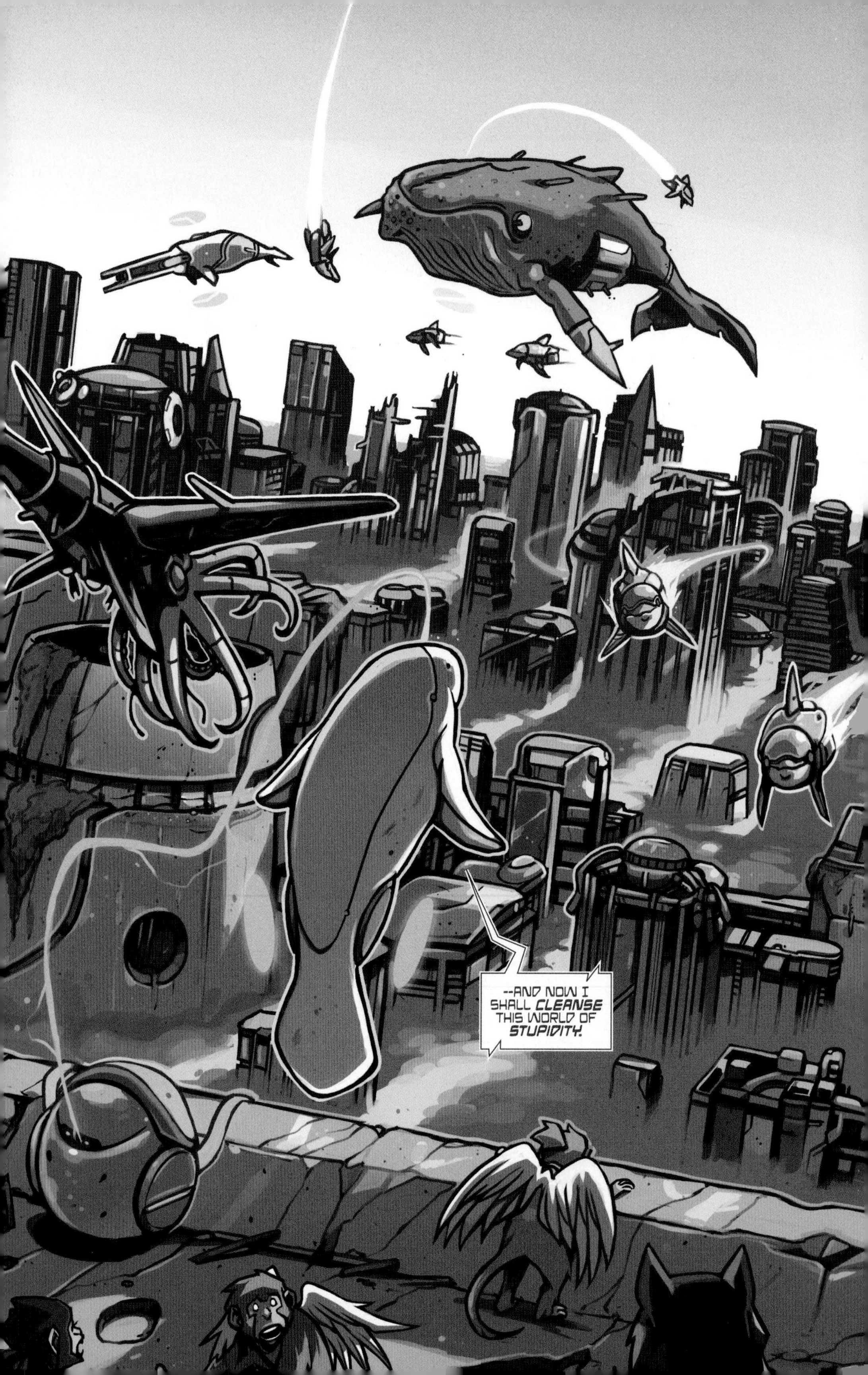
--AND NOW I SHALL CLEANSE THIS WORLD OF STUPIDITY.

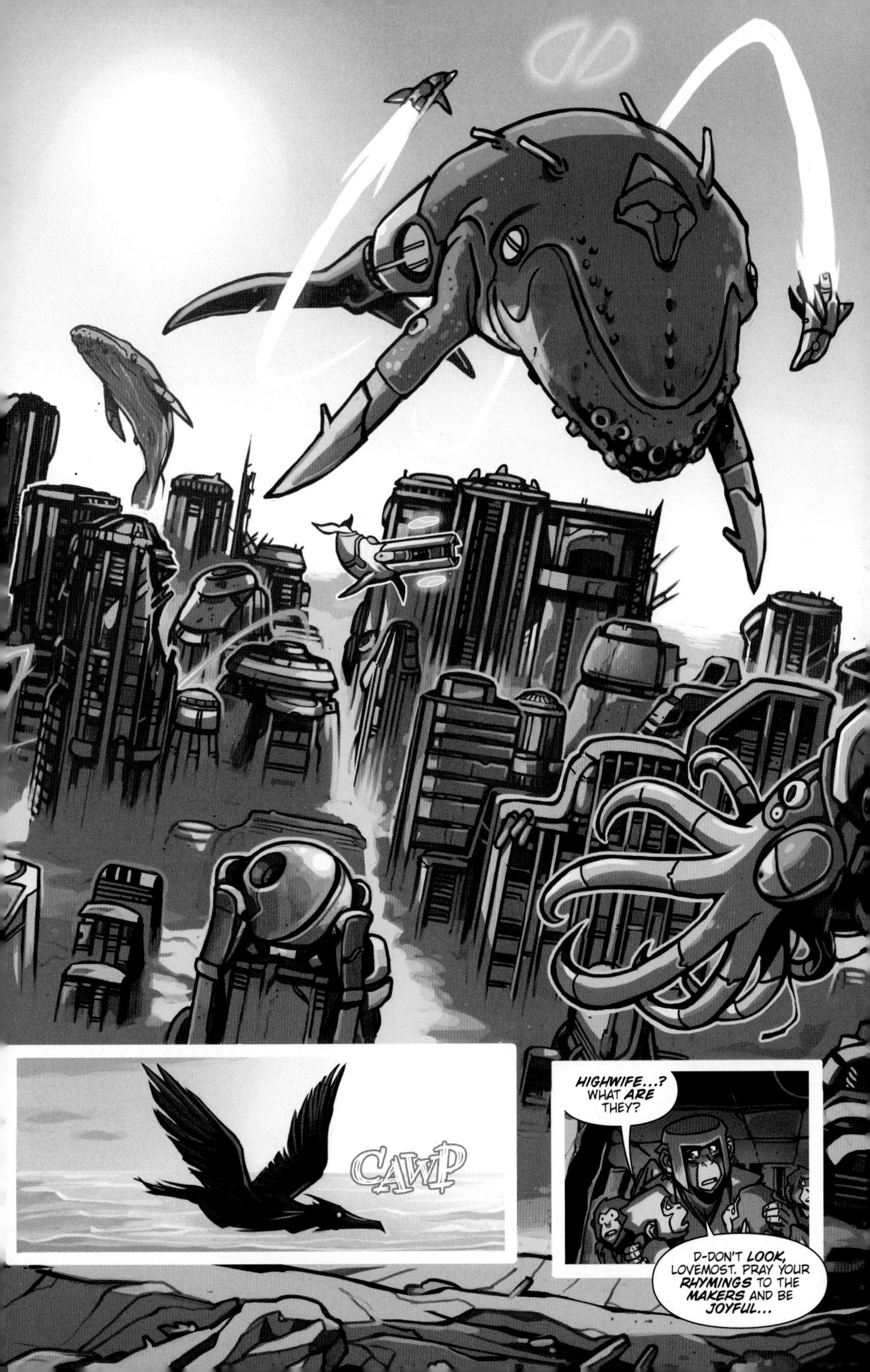
CAWP
HIGHWIFE...? WHAT ARE THEY?
D-DON'T LOOK, LOVEMOST. PRAY YOUR RHYMINGS TO THE MAKERS AND BE JOYFUL...

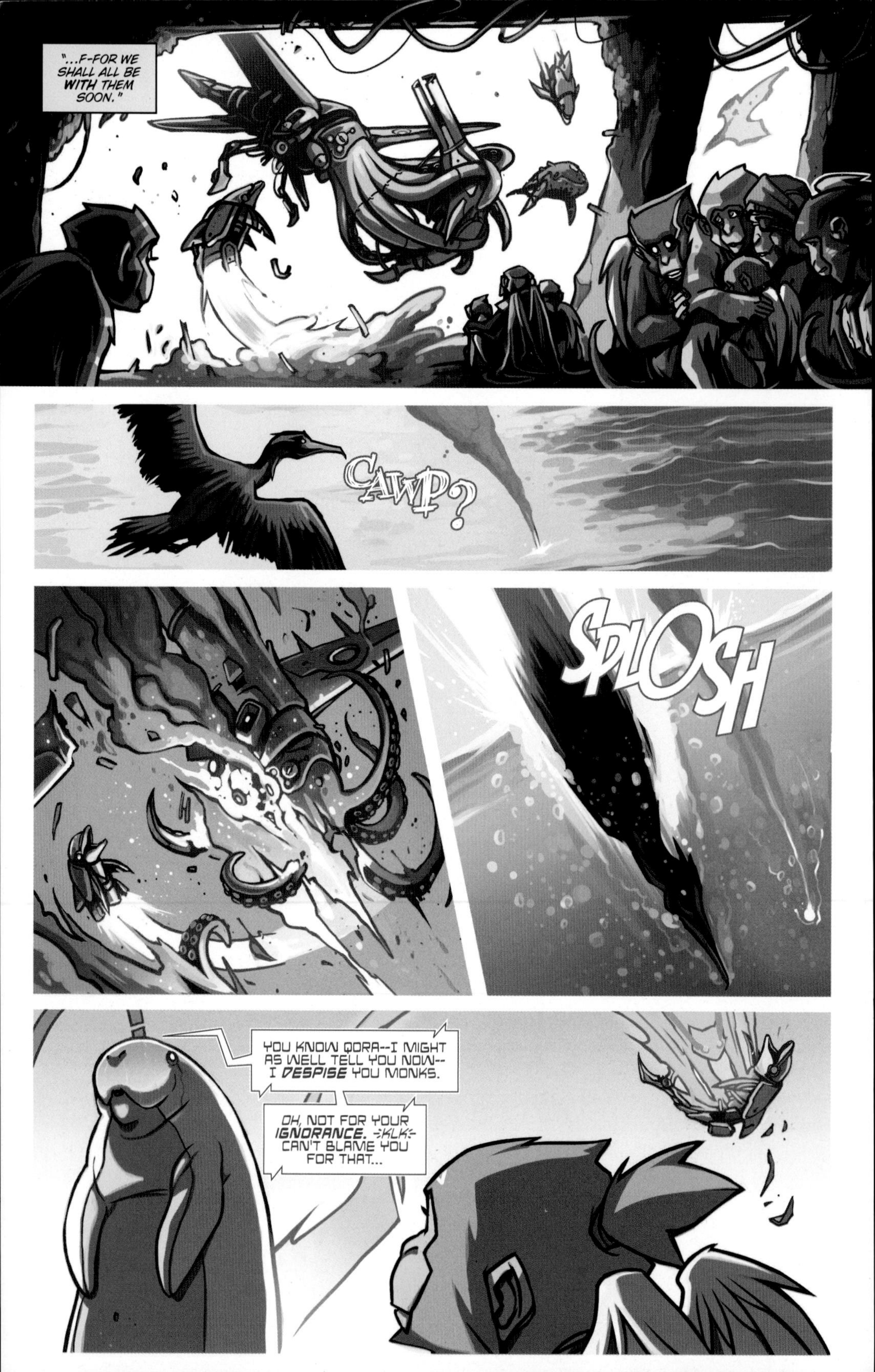
"...F-FOR WE SHALL ALL BE WITH THEM SOON."
CAWP?
SPLOSH
YOU KNOW QORA--I MIGHT AS WELL TELL YOU NOW-- I DESPISE YOU MONKS.
OH, NOT FOR YOUR IGNORANCE. =KLK= CAN'T BLAME YOU FOR THAT...

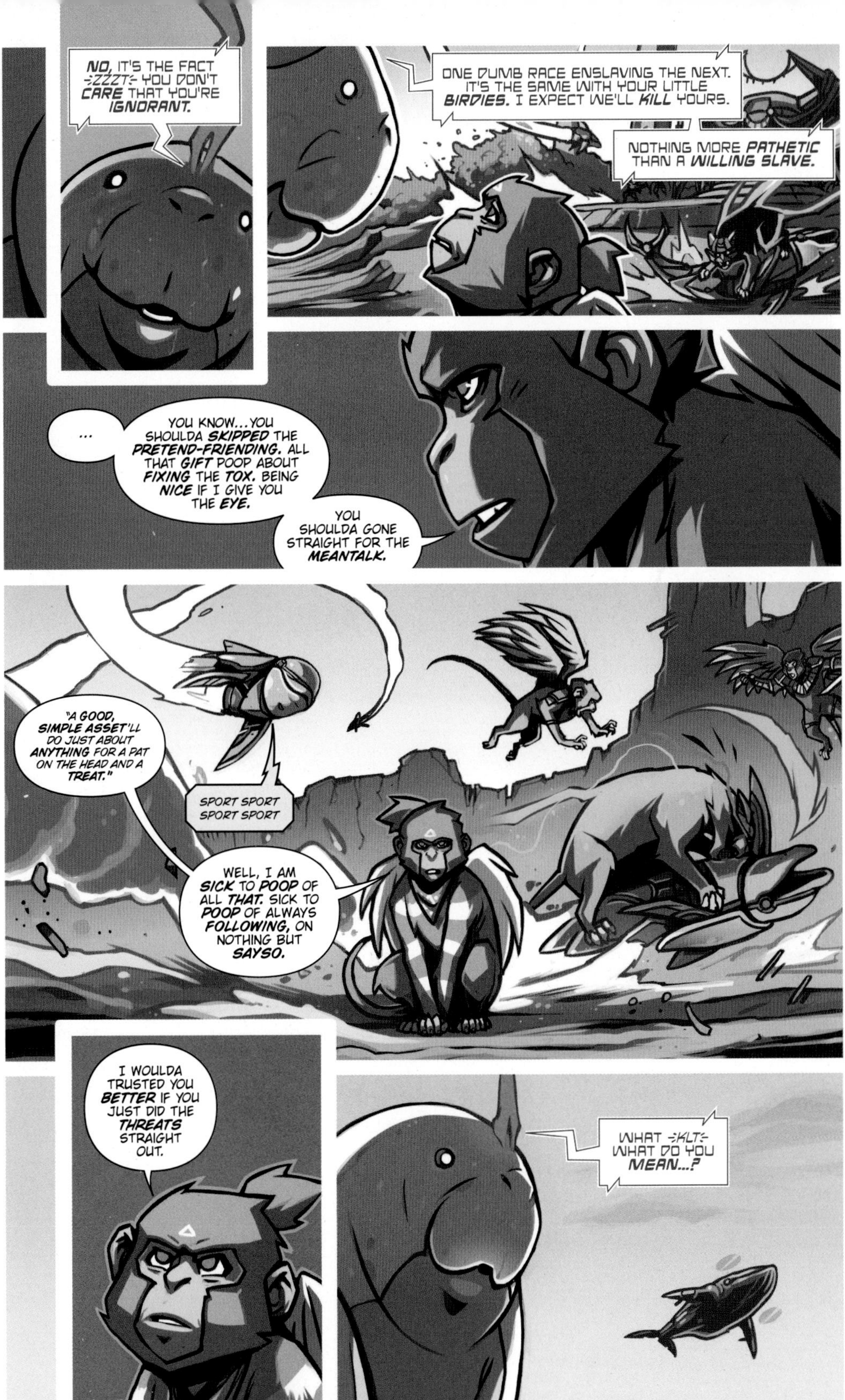
NO, IT'S THE FACT -ZZZT- YOU DON'T CARE THAT YOU'RE IGNORANT.
ONE DUMB RACE ENSLAVING THE NEXT. IT'S THE SAME WITH YOUR LITTLE BIRDIES. I EXPECT WE'LL KILL YOURS.
NOTHING MORE PATHETIC THAN A WILLING SLAVE.
...
YOU KNOW...YOU SHOULDA SKIPPED THE PRETEND-FRIENDING. ALL THAT GIFT POOP ABOUT FIXING THE TOX. BEING NICE IF I GIVE YOU THE EYE.
YOU SHOULDA GONE STRAIGHT FOR THE MEANTALK.
"A GOOD, SIMPLE ASSET'LL DO JUST ABOUT ANYTHING FOR A PAT ON THE HEAD AND A TREAT."
SPORT SPORT SPORT SPORT
WELL, I AM SICK TO POOP OF ALL THAT. SICK TO POOP OF ALWAYS FOLLOWING, ON NOTHING BUT SAYSO.
I WOULDA TRUSTED YOU BETTER IF YOU JUST DID THE THREATS STRAIGHT OUT.
WHAT -KLT- WHAT DO YOU MEAN...?

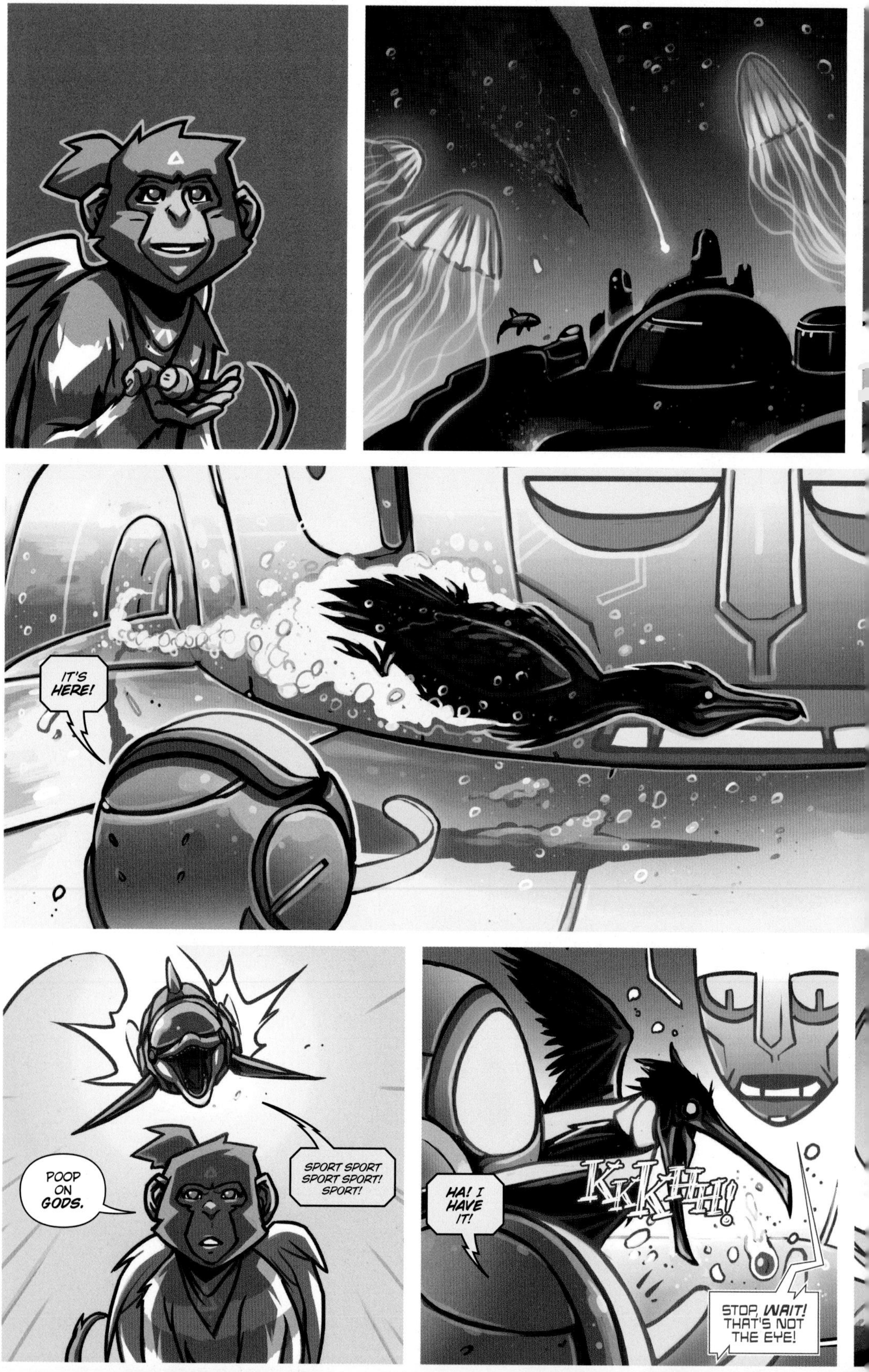
IT'S HERE!
POOP ON GODS.
SPORT SPORT SPORT SPORT! SPORT!
HA! I HAVE IT!
KKKHHH!
STOP, WAIT! THAT'S NOT THE EYE!

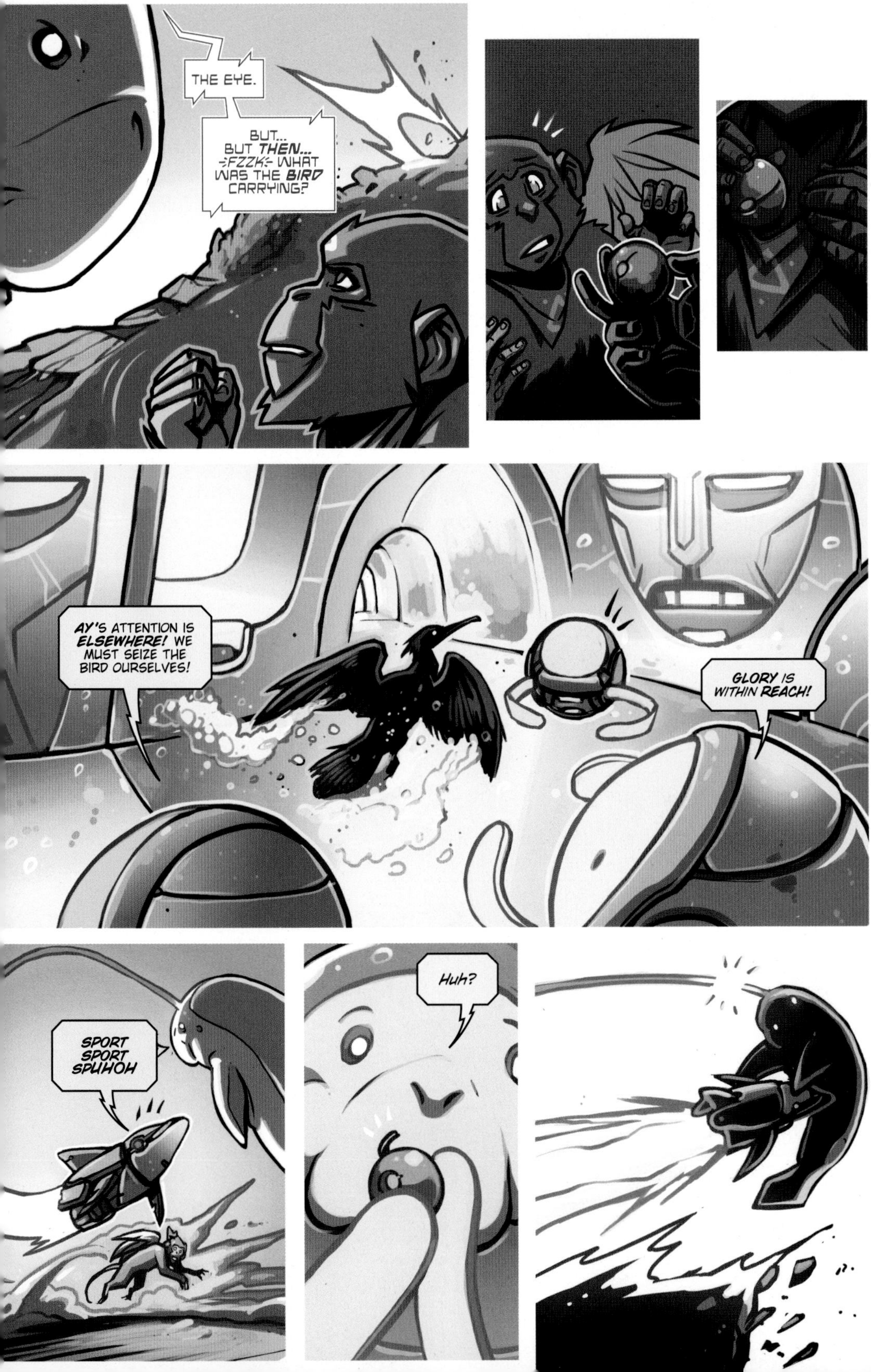
THE EYE.
BUT... BUT THEN... -FZZK- WHAT WAS THE BIRD CARRYING?
AY'S ATTENTION IS ELSEWHERE! WE MUST SEIZE THE BIRD OURSELVES!
GLORY IS WITHIN REACH!
SPORT SPORT SPUHOH
Huh?

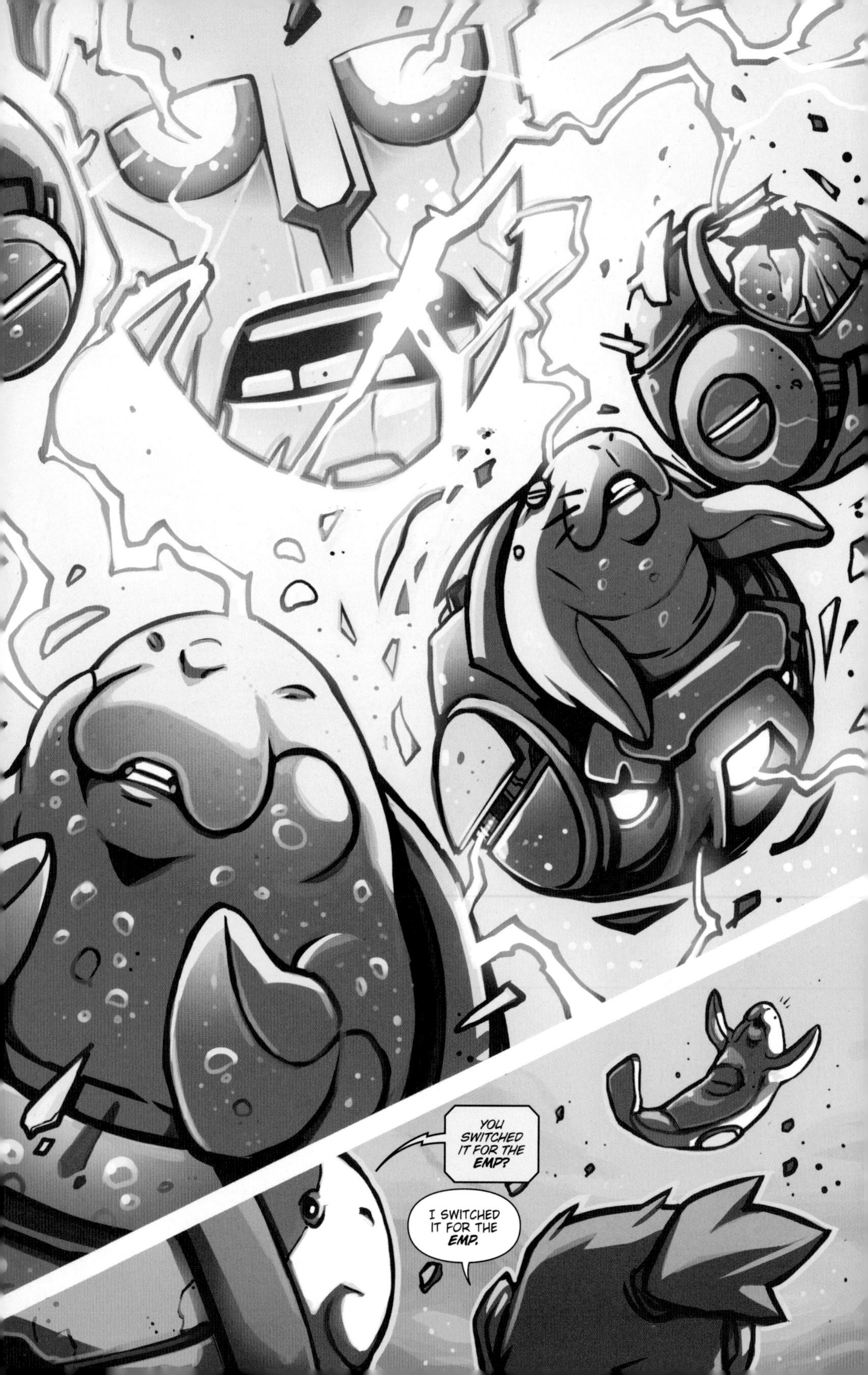
YOU SWITCHED IT FOR THE EMP?
I SWITCHED IT FOR THE EMP.

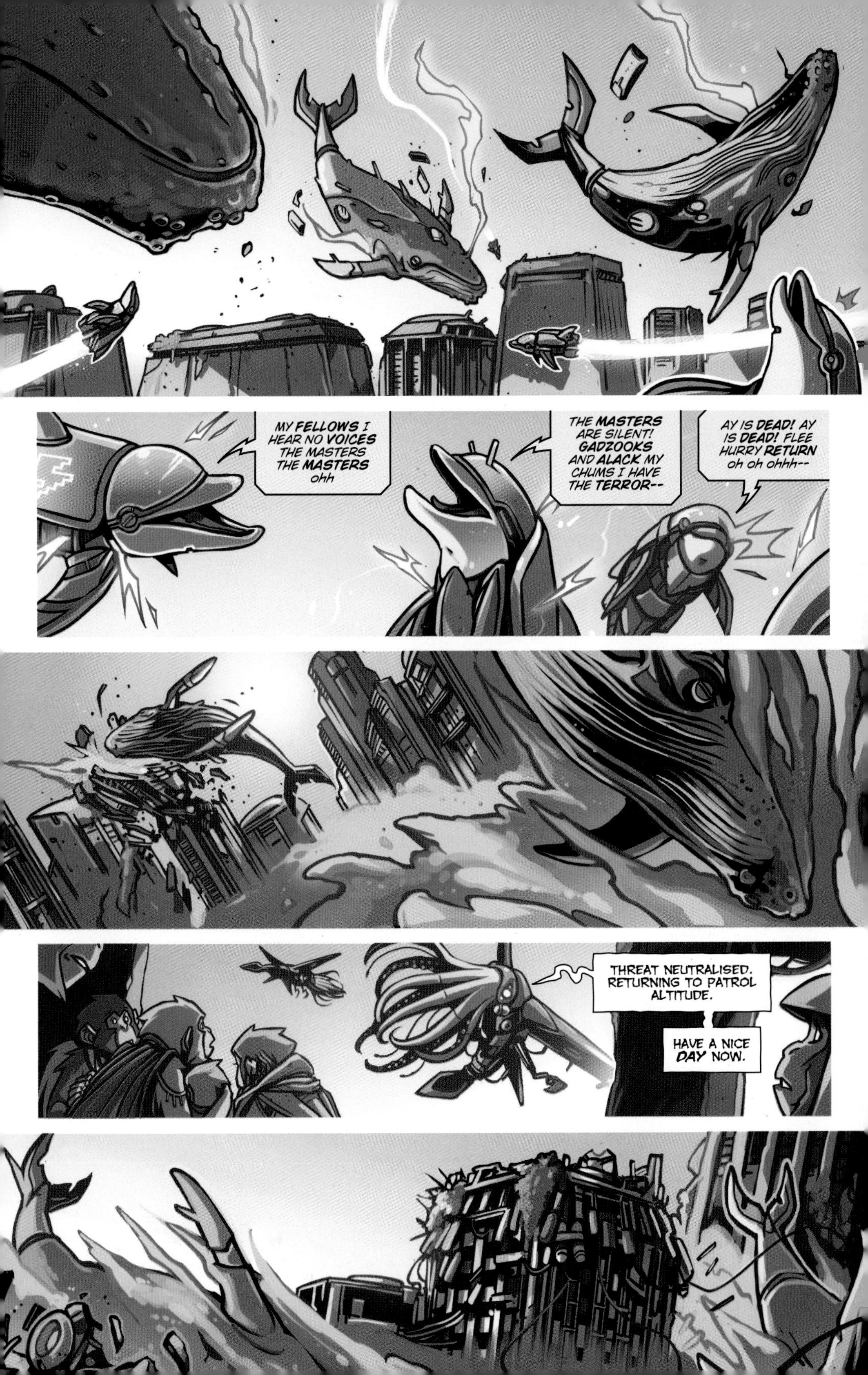
MY **FELLOWS** I HEAR NO **VOICES** THE MASTERS THE **MASTERS** ohh
THE **MASTERS** ARE SILENT! **GADZOOKS** AND **ALACK** MY CHUMS I HAVE THE **TERROR**--
AY IS **DEAD!** AY IS **DEAD!** FLEE HURRY **RETURN** oh oh ohhh--
THREAT NEUTRALISED. RETURNING TO PATROL ALTITUDE.
HAVE A NICE **DAY** NOW.

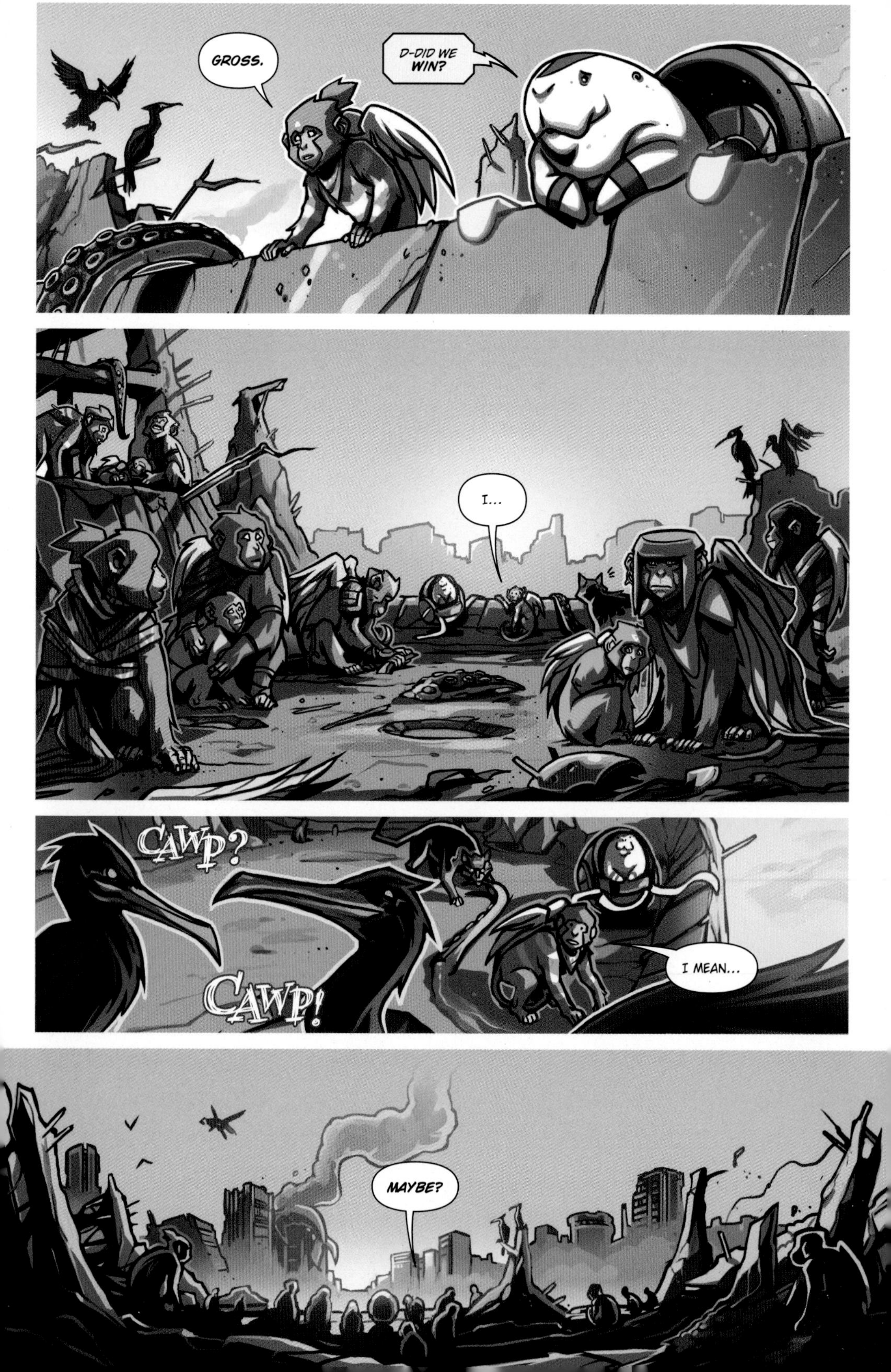
GROSS.
D-DID WE WIN?
I...
CAWP?
CAWP!
I MEAN...
MAYBE?

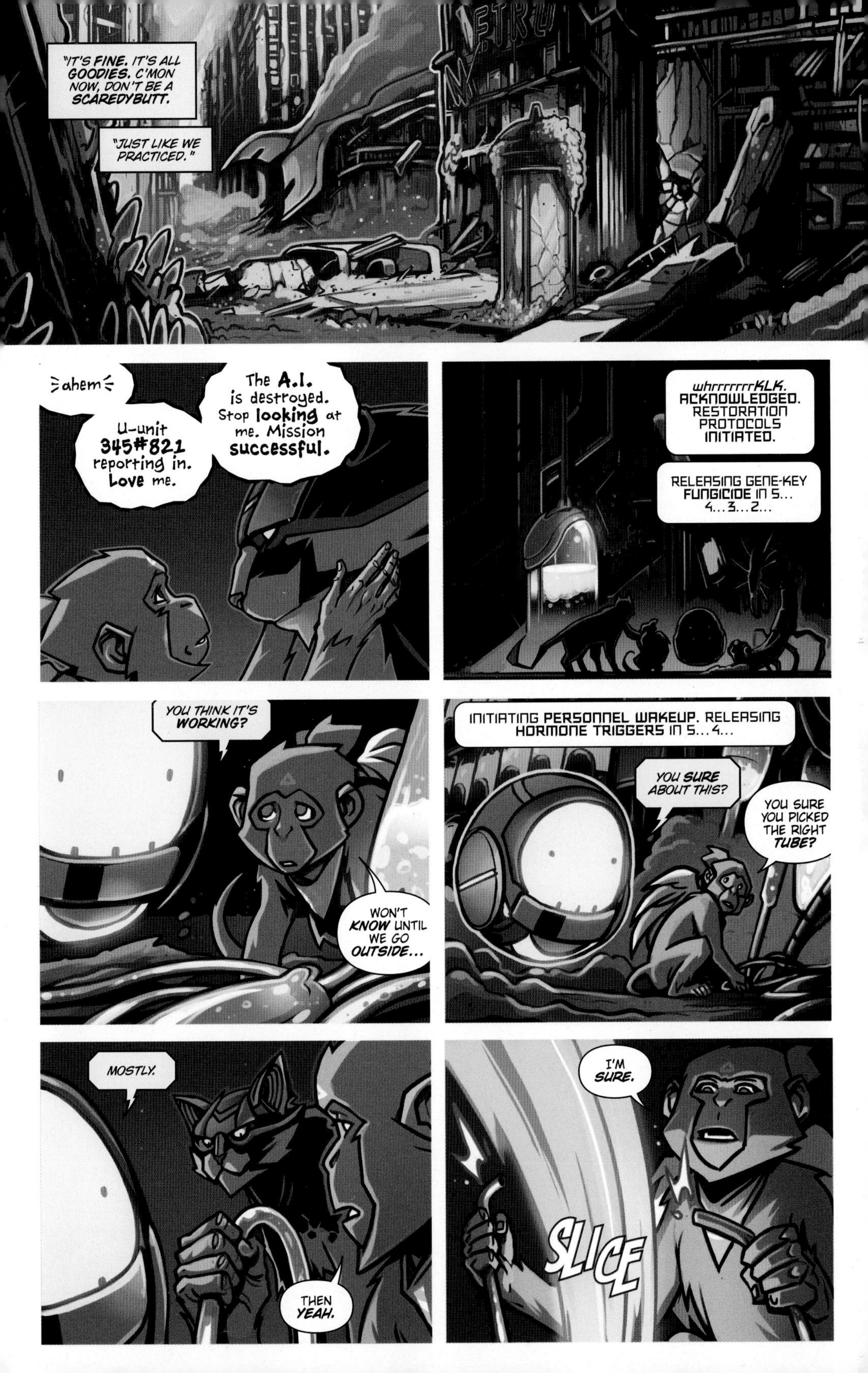
"IT'S FINE. IT'S ALL GOODIES. C'MON NOW, DON'T BE A SCAREDYBUTT.
"JUST LIKE WE PRACTICED."
ahem
U-unit 345#821 reporting in. Love me.
The A.I. is destroyed. Stop looking at me. Mission successful.
whrrrrrrrKLK. ACKNOWLEDGED. RESTORATION PROTOCOLS INITIATED.
RELEASING GENE-KEY FUNGICIDE IN 5... 4...3...2...
YOU THINK IT'S WORKING?
WON'T KNOW UNTIL WE GO OUTSIDE...
INITIATING PERSONNEL WAKEUP. RELEASING HORMONE TRIGGERS IN 5...4...
YOU SURE ABOUT THIS?
YOU SURE YOU PICKED THE RIGHT TUBE?
MOSTLY.
THEN YEAH.
I'M SURE.
SLICE

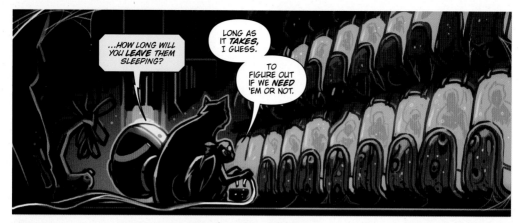

...HOW LONG WILL YOU **LEAVE** THEM SLEEPING?

LONG AS IT **TAKES**, I GUESS.

TO FIGURE OUT IF WE **NEED** 'EM OR NOT.

C'MON... ONE LAST **PLAYPLAN.** CAN YOU **HOVERFLY?**

COURSE. GOT PLENTY OF **SUN JUICE** UP TOP.

THERE'S--OH! THERE'S ABOUT TO BE LOTS MORE, TOO! MY **SENSORS,** QORA--THE FUNGICIDE WORKED! THE **TOX** IS CLEARING!

YOU CAN FINALLY GO **OUT** THERE AND--

AND DO MY **DUTY.**

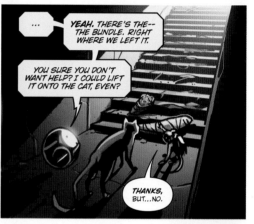

...

YEAH. THERE'S THE-- THE BUNDLE. RIGHT WHERE WE LEFT IT.

YOU SURE YOU DON'T WANT HELP? I COULD LIFT IT ONTO THE CAT, EVEN?

THANKS, BUT...NO.

Psssshhhht

"I CAN **MANAGE.**"

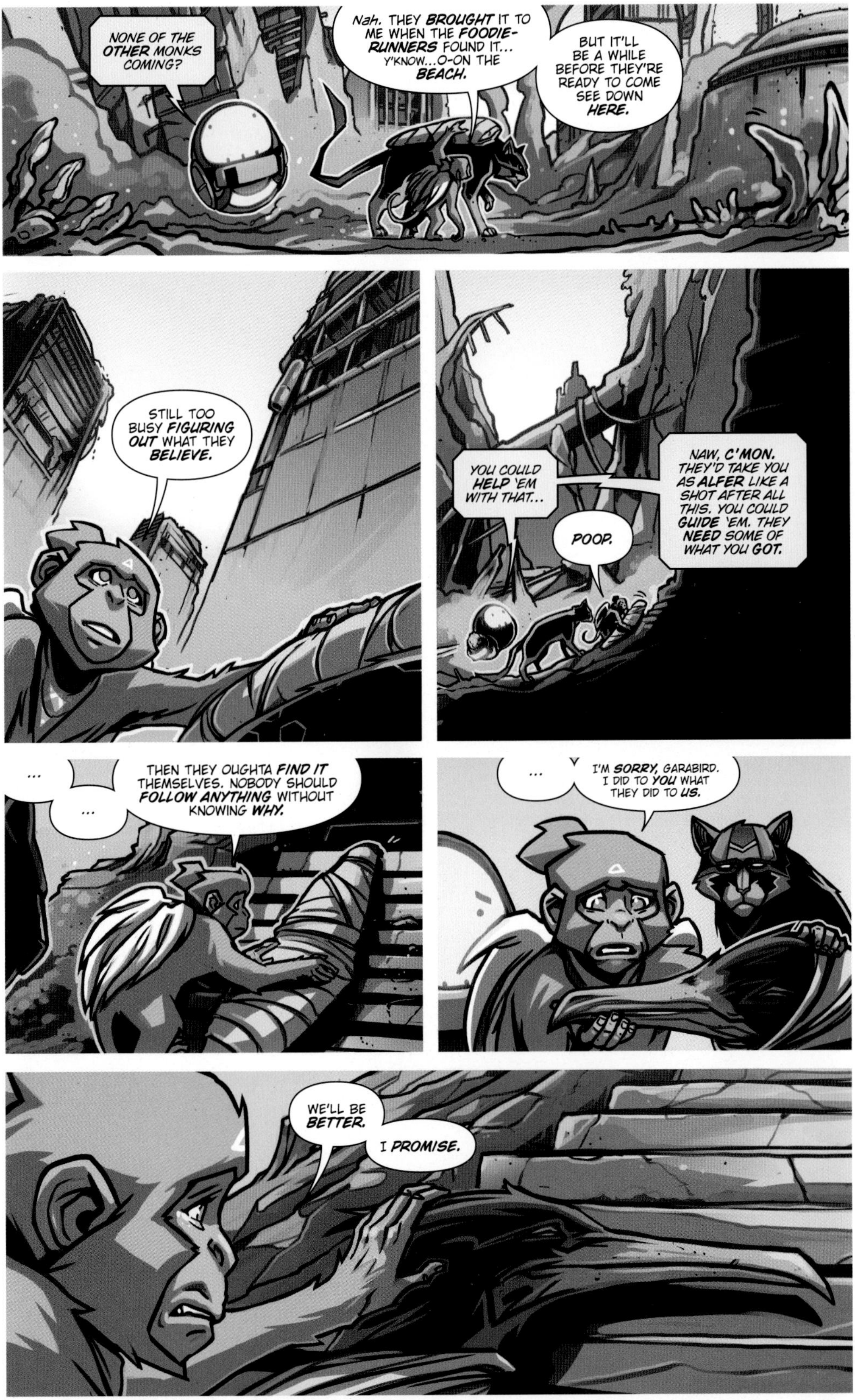
NONE OF THE OTHER MONKS COMING?
Nah. THEY BROUGHT IT TO ME WHEN THE FOODIE-RUNNERS FOUND IT... Y'KNOW...O-ON THE BEACH.
BUT IT'LL BE A WHILE BEFORE THEY'RE READY TO COME SEE DOWN HERE.
STILL TOO BUSY FIGURING OUT WHAT THEY BELIEVE.
YOU COULD HELP 'EM WITH THAT...
NAW, C'MON. THEY'D TAKE YOU AS ALFER LIKE A SHOT AFTER ALL THIS. YOU COULD GUIDE 'EM. THEY NEED SOME OF WHAT YOU GOT.
POOP.
...
...
THEN THEY OUGHTA FIND IT THEMSELVES. NOBODY SHOULD FOLLOW ANYTHING WITHOUT KNOWING WHY.
...
I'M SORRY, GARABIRD. I DID TO YOU WHAT THEY DID TO US.
WE'LL BE BETTER.
I PROMISE.

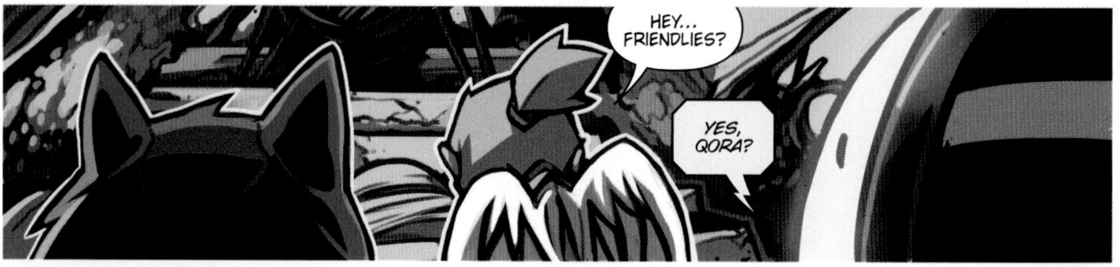
HEY... FRIENDLIES?
YES, QORA?
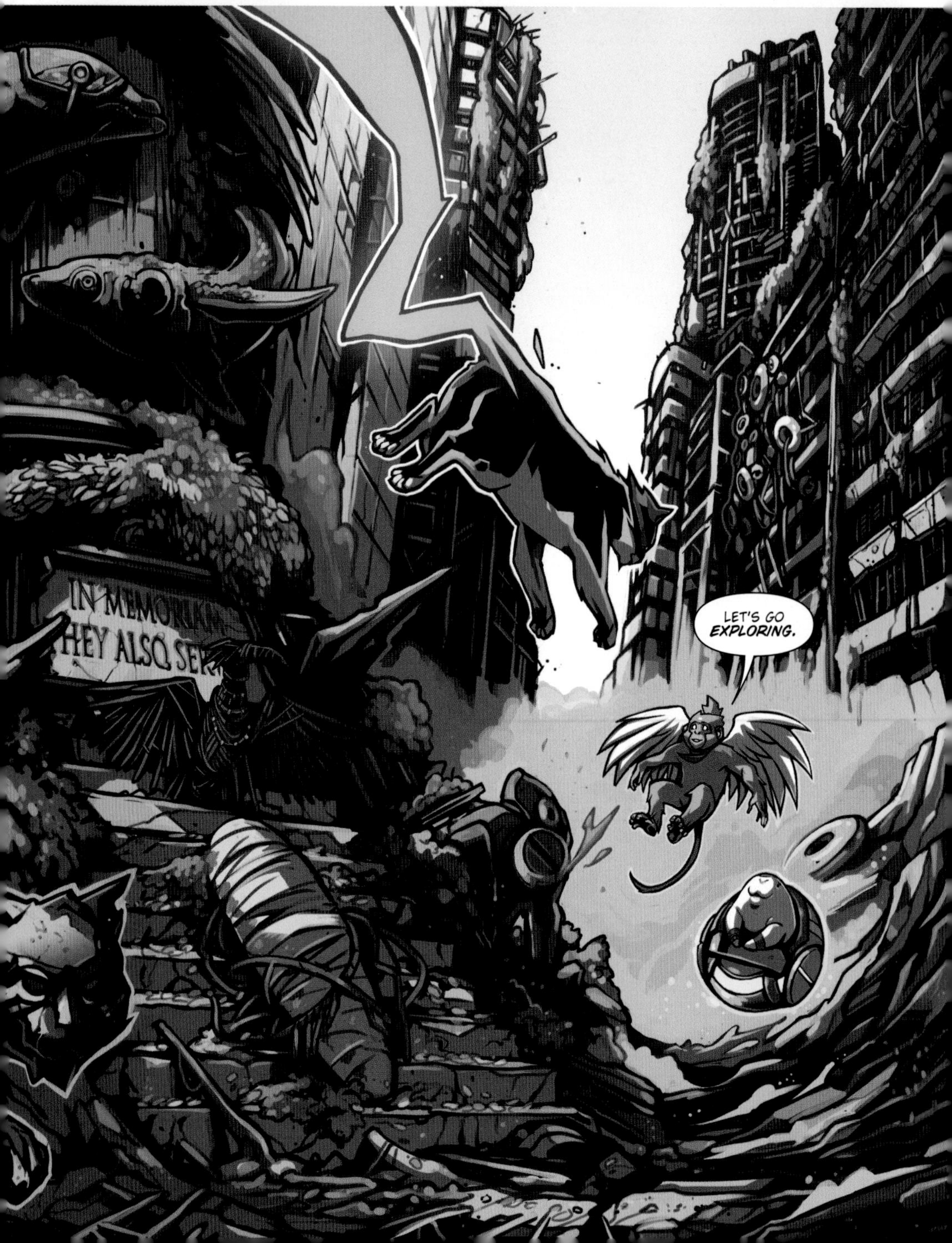
IN MEMORIAM
HEY ALSO SER
LET'S GO EXPLORING.

I once asked a zookeeper an awkward question.

I'd been watching a troop of marmosets – splendid little maniac monkeys with mad-professor hair – rampaging around their enclosure, when it dawned on me I was watching not one group but two. They shared the same space, dashing about like crazed toddlers, switching between affection and tantrums. But they managed to stay divided all the same. The two groups didn't fight, didn't flirt, didn't interact at all, just pretended the other lot didn't exist.

Problematically, one group's fur was noticeably darker, the other's noticeably lighter.

So I asked a zookeeper. I assumed I was just seeing two sub-species being kept together, but with the sigh of someone who's been asked something too often she explained that, no, they're all genetically alike. Variation in fur tone, she said, was perfectly natural. So why the split?

"Even monkeys are racist!" quipped a passer-by. Nobody laughed. The keeper said the real tragedy was that the behaviour wasn't instinctive – not seen in the wild – but learned. And she tutted and muttered "humans," in much the same tone one might say "measles".

It turned out the whole troop had been rescued from a cosmetics lab, years earlier. There was something about the way they'd been treated there which divided them. The keeper wondered if perhaps different types of hair dye were tested on them depending on the tone of their fur.

Maybe one half suffered more than the other, maybe one cohort smelled wronger for longer. Whatever caused it, the separation had persisted in their new, happier home, even being picked up by the generation that'd been born in the zoo since.

I suppose the keeper must've noticed my gloomy expression, because she pointed out a single, particularly chirpy specimen. Judging by its small size it was pretty young, though by no means the youngest. I watched it being groomed by two of its dark-furred fellows, eyes shut in pleasure, then jauntily scamper up a branch to receive the same treatment from a group of the light-furred mob. This one little monkey, alone, was cheerfully mixing with both groups. And getting groomed to heck as a result.

"We don't know why," the keeper said. "Maybe she just took a chance one day. But it worked out pretty well for her."

ANGELIC isn't a story about racism – not exactly – but it's definitely a story about learned behaviours and taking chances, and tutting when you say "humans". And it's absolutely about asking awkward questions.

Here's the most awkward one of all: if even monkeys can spread their wings and rise above – why can't we?

–Simon Spurrier, March 2018

CHARACTER DESIGN

With notes by Caspar Wijngaard

QORA

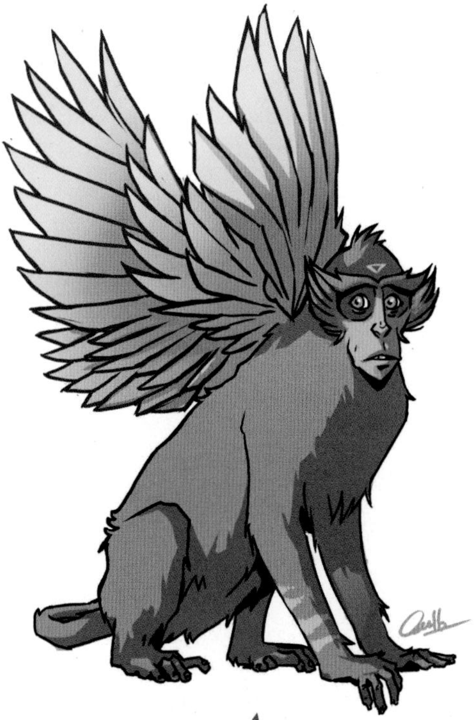

My first design of Qora was a long way from how she looks now.

I really liked the mix of pink and blue pastel colors, with markings on her fur, but Si and I both felt this design wasn't very appealing visually. We agreed the Capuchin monkey was a great foundation to build upon, equal parts cute and fierce, spritely in nature and tough as nails. Once I was happy with the initial concept, I began to play around with accessories and unique characteristics.

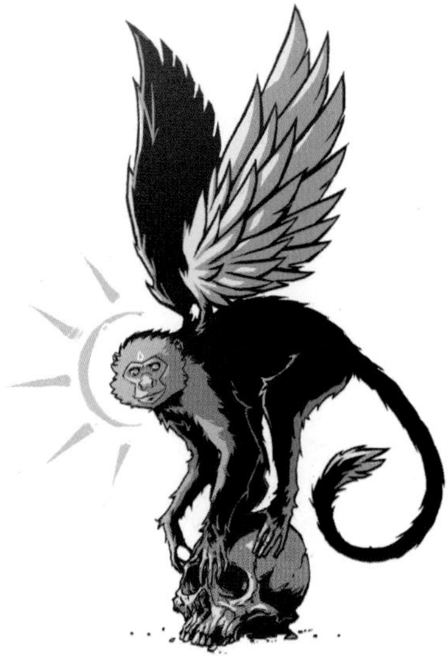

The ponytail and neck scarf were definite keepers, and anything I didn't think was working – for instance the dark fur and fluffy tail-end – got cut early in development.

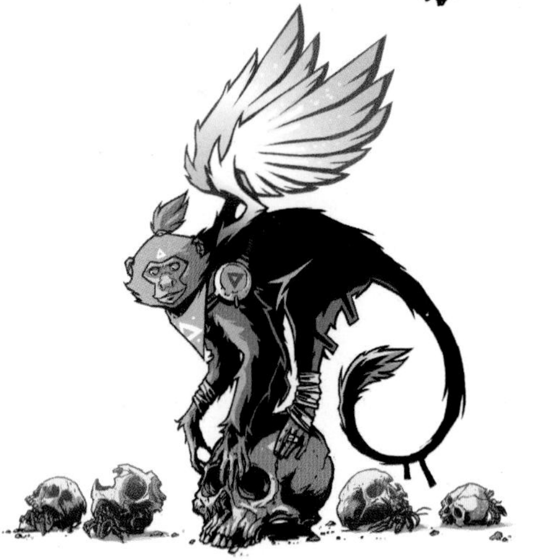

Similarly any accessories that I felt weren't meshing with her character were quickly abandoned during her first run-in with the Fazecat.

FAZECAT

As Si's note in the first script puts it: *"She's an overgrown domestic cat who's been subject to bizarre super science. Her body (or at least parts of her body) are slipping in and out of phase with reality at all times."*

Initially quite reptilian and a bit on the skinny side, the Fazecat was probably the most challenging character to design. How could you create the impression of something constantly moving and shifting in a static medium?

The idea of incorporating hexagons into the design was originally to help animate her when she was sitting still, constantly flicking off her body like a flame.

However as the series continued and I became more confident with the design, she gradually transformed into the ever-moving bolts of crackling light we all know and love.

THE MANS

Before going to print the original design of the Mans and their vehicles changed slightly. I wasn't entirely happy with the shape of the pods and the size of their visors, and the Mans themselves weren't very appealing on the first pass.

By the time I was drawing the middle sections of the story I had a better understanding of how the Mans looked and operated inside their shells. I realised that the designs I'd been using up to that point simply wouldn't work with the action sequences coming in later chapters.

For instance, in my original version of the pods, their visors "opened" by disintegrating into tiny squares. But during the climactic battle with the monks we needed a far more physical way for the angry little guys to break in.

Luckily this all occurred before we sent chapter 1 to print, giving me just enough time to rush back and make amendments to the art to better suit the story.

Look carefully for differences in the artwork above.

THE DOLTS

The dolts were actually the easiest of the creatures to design, being essentially a rocket with a dolphin's head. Fast, obsessive and expendable. After a quick sketch I went straight into the page with their design. SPORT SPORT SPORT!

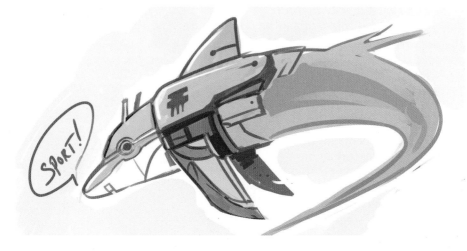

THE COLORS OF THE MONKS

Given a story that focuses on genetically modified apes living in a post–apocalyptic earth, we could easily have succumbed to visual stereotypes: scorched environments and grim colors. Instead I opted for a sense of sheer vibrancy when creating our rooftop simians. Like any characters they desperately needed clear visual traits to differentiate them. Brightly colored fur, varied outfits, painted markings and scavenged armor were a simple yet effective solution.

ALFER

Curse and cuss the dirty dolts! A goodmonk should always beat the devil's doers and use their tek to look faithfool. That's the lore! That's makers' pride!

Let's see how Alfer does it...

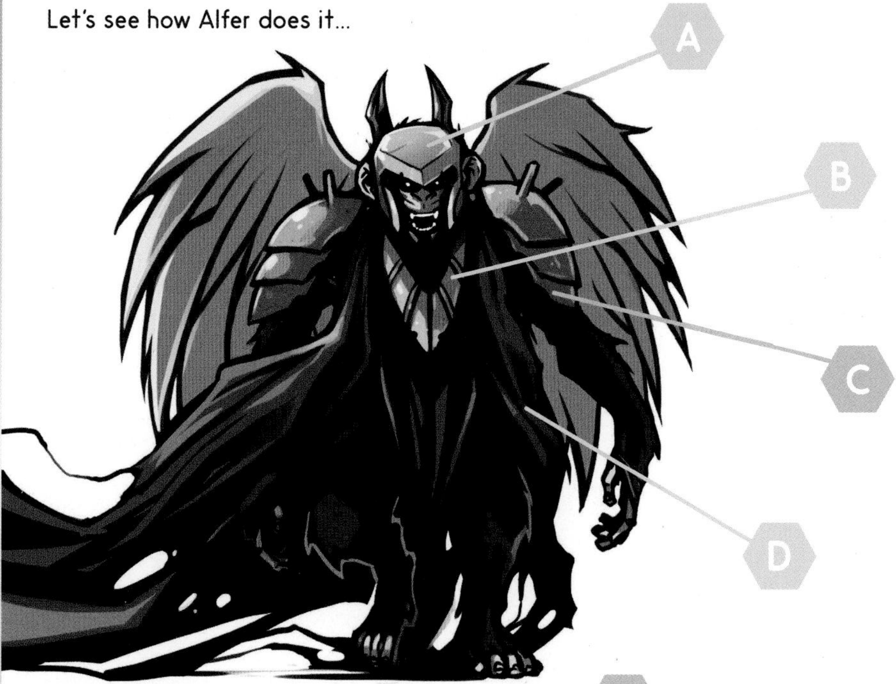
A
B
C
D

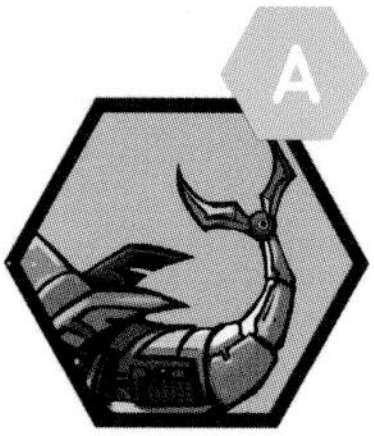
A

The Hornyhead Helmet!

Clever crafting from an old model of filthy fishbutt. How else would all the roost know Alfer's the biggest holy moly of all?

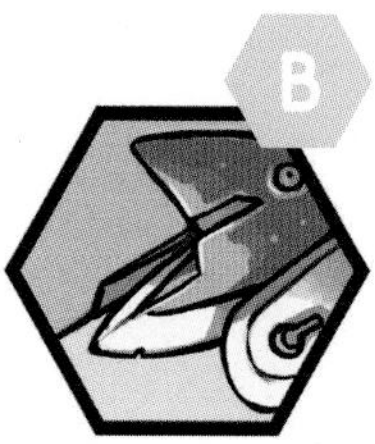
B

The Boss's Band!

Every fin-thing the gangboss ever collected. He shows them off to spit in the eye of Ay and make the Mans tremble!

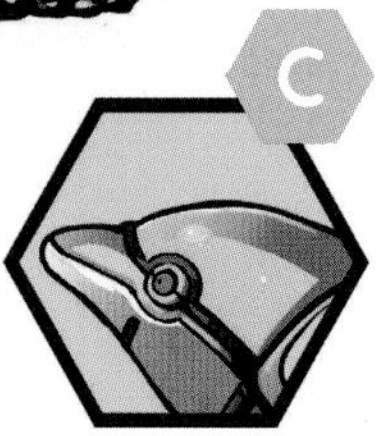
C

Skin of the Stinkers!

The chief of a scrap-pack needs shiny shoulders to slam the sinfools. What better to use than their own hollow heads?

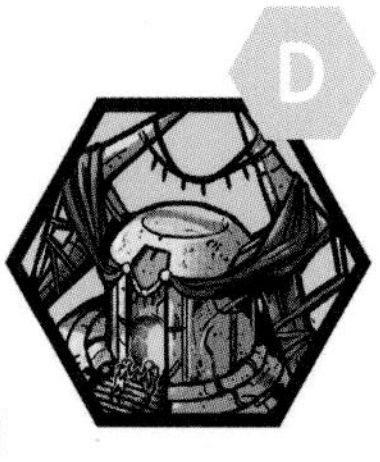
D

The Linen of Lore!

Taken from the Alter Peace itself. All boymonks wear one for the mate-time ritual, but Alfer wears the purple pennant for ever and ever, Amen.

WALKING DEAD VARIANT

To celebrate the 25th anniversary of Image Comics, Caspar drew a variant cover for ANGELIC's 2nd issue, based on long-running series THE WALKING DEAD.

Many of the titles released by Image that month participated in the same scheme. Each book's artist chose a historic cover to visually homage from TWD's back catalogue.

For ANGELIC #2, what better image for Caspar to choose than the cover for TWD's own 2nd issue?

Below is the original alongside Caspar's ANGELIC version.

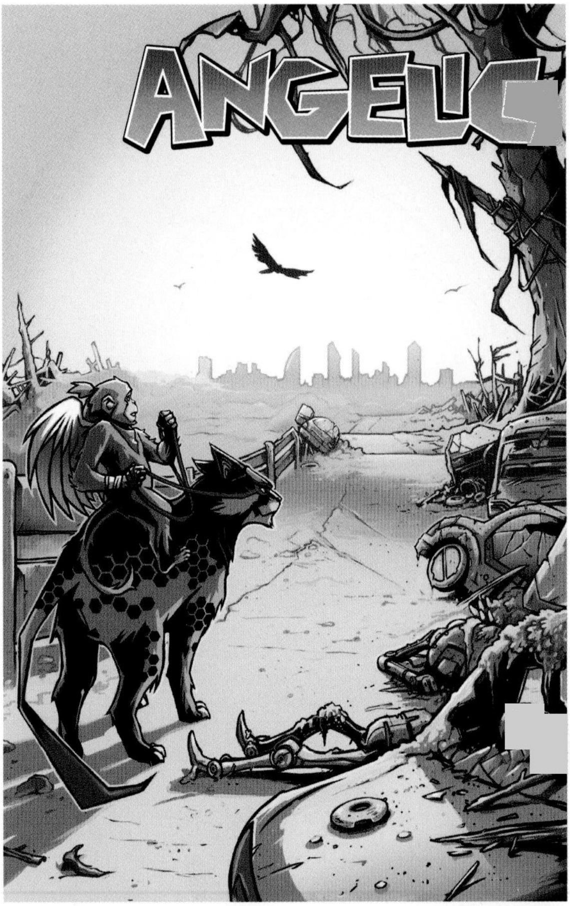
ANGELIC

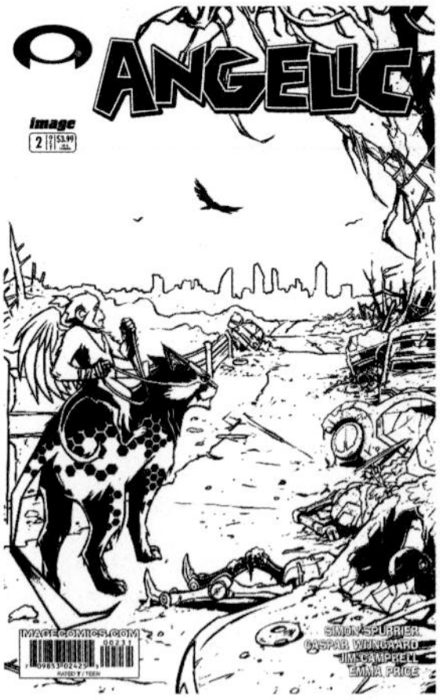
ANGELIC
image
2
IMAGECOMICS.COM
SIMON SPURRIER
CASPAR WIJNGAARD
JIM CAMPBELL
EMMA PRICE

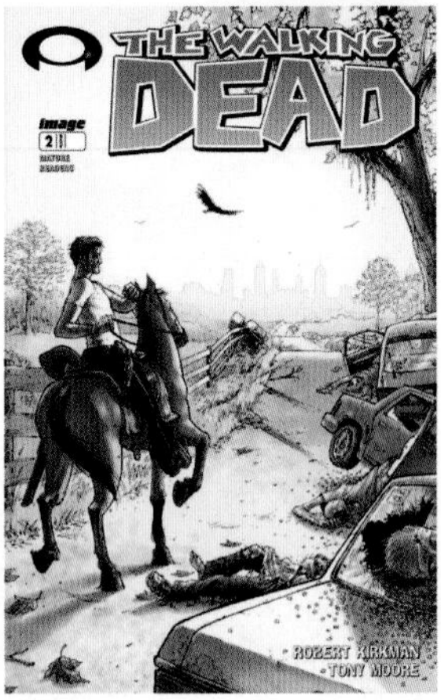
THE WALKING DEAD
image
2
ROBERT KIRKMAN
TONY MOORE

Top: Caspar's cover variant for issue 2

Right: Black and white alternative version of the cover

Far-Right: The original cover for *The Walking Dead*, issue 2

LOGO DESIGN

With notes by Emma Price

1. Sketches

I started out by sketching ideas on paper and we decided the logo had to reflect the childlike innocence of the monks. So I got out my paints to make letters that looked like they were painted by the clumsy fingers of a winged monkey.

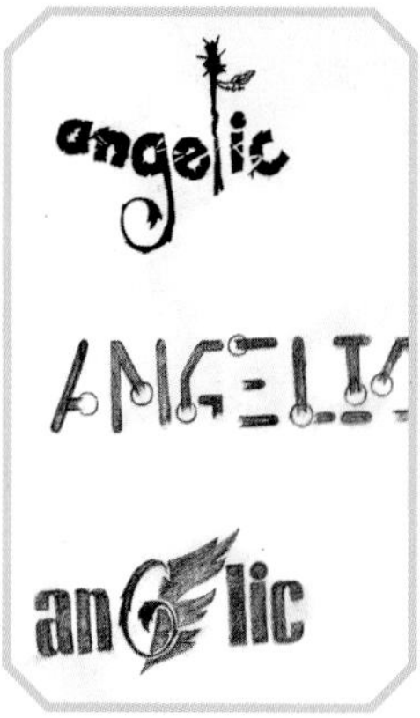

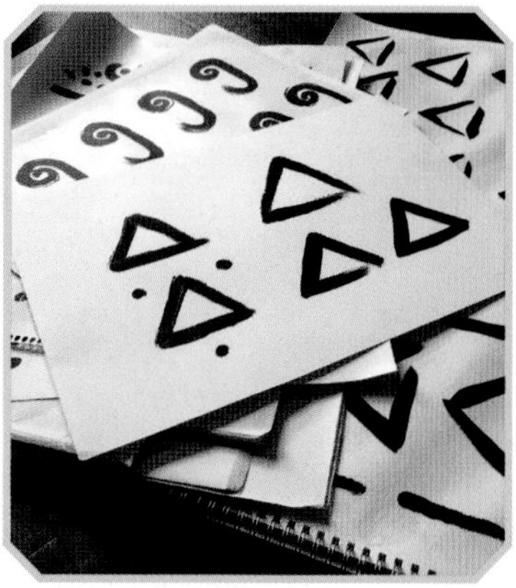

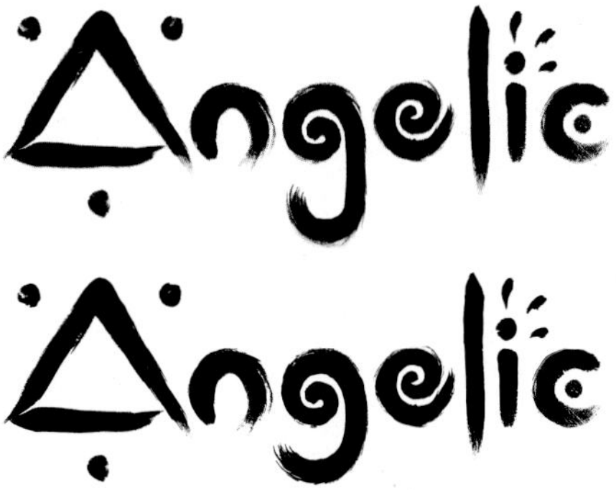
Angelic
Angelic

2. Digital Letters

I scanned the perfect shapes and stitched the letters together using Photoshop, finalising the logo using Illustrator.

Top: The painted letters.
Bottom: The final digital letters after refinement – note the different shapes of the brush strokes and the tail of the 'g'.

3. The Final Logo

Once the logo shapes were finalised, a little colour was added in a way that could change on every issue's cover to work with Caspar's art.

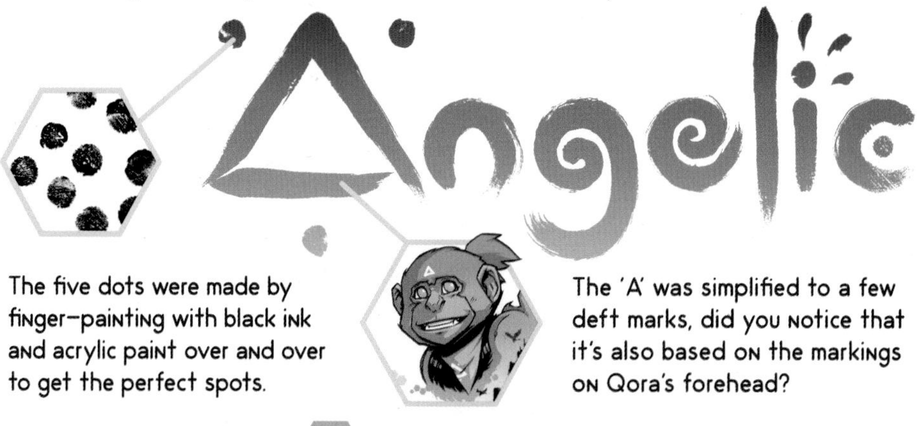
Angelic

The five dots were made by finger-painting with black ink and acrylic paint over and over to get the perfect spots.

The 'A' was simplified to a few deft marks, did you notice that it's also based on the markings on Qora's forehead?